A GOOD MAN

PJ MCILVAINE

BLOODHOUND
— BOOKS —

For my beloved brother Michael Peter Jonneaux, who forever will be mon petit prince.

"A Native American elder once described his own inner struggles in this manner: Inside of me, there are two dogs. One of the dogs is mean and evil. The other dog is good. The mean dog fights the good dog all the time. When asked which dog wins, he reflected for a moment and replied, The one I feed the most."

— *George Bernard Shaw*

It's funny/not funny the things you remember about the worst day of your life.

It was a hot, humid, hazy, August afternoon.

We had hot dogs and baked beans for dinner. Later, I had a cosmic orchestra of gas and flatulence. Mom thought it was hilarious. Palmer accused me of being a show-off. He wasn't entirely wrong.

Afterward, as we did every Sunday night, we watched The Ed Sullivan Show.

I drifted off to sleep as rain pelted the roof. The sky blinked off and on like a flashlight. The roar of thunder filled all the empty spaces.

My brother Palmer—forever thirteen—shook me awake, his hands red and sticky. I thought it was from a cherry ice pop—but I know now it was blood. Our mother's blood.

"Hide, Brooks." Palmer took in a huge gulp of air. "You know where. And don't come back, whatever you do. The monster. He's in the house."

I ran up to the dunes at Ditch Plains Beach as fast as my stubby legs could carry me, soaked and chilled to the bone.

A week later, I woke up in a hospital bed. A nurse jabbed me with something.

My father gripped my hand. "You're all right, son," he whispered. "It's over."

But of course, it wasn't. And I was far from all right. I didn't know it then, but I do now. You have no idea how deep the rot goes until you bite into the apple and see a wriggling worm.

CHAPTER ONE

Sheldon Adler, my agent at Crown-Hawkins and my brother from another mother, is late as usual. No fucking surprise there. When you're meeting Sheldon, you have to tack on an hour at least. I'm at our usual table at La Bonne Grenouille, the best little French bistro in Manhattan that no one has ever heard of, sipping a glass of ice-cold watermelon seltzer. Sheldon has been my literary agent—no, make that literary savior—since he read my first published short story that didn't involve erect penises in *The New Yorker*. He contacted me out of the blue and suggested Hey, why don't you write a book and I'll sell it? I wrote *Fallen Angels* in twenty-four days in a drug haze. When it was finally published, it sold less than two hundred copies, but Sheldon was so fucking proud you would've thought it sold two million. I resigned myself to being a failure. Months later, the book was plucked out of obscurity by the senior literary critic of *The New York Times* and nominated for a Pulitzer. A tabloid dubbed me "The Heroin Hemingway." The name stuck, even though I've been sober and drug-free for more than twenty-five years.

Sheldon got me my first million-dollar advance. He's the wolf that other wolves hire, and his reputation is well-earned. My biggest supporter, he stayed with me through the lean, mean years when I wrote truly terrible books. Despite my abysmal marital track record, I'm extremely loyal. I wouldn't dream of leaving Sheldon and believe me, other agents have tried to poach me. And unless I did or said something unacceptable that blew up on social media—which is why I don't have any social media accounts—Sheldon wouldn't kick me to the curb or toss me under the bus. All my skeletons are out there. Well, most of them.

A portly man with a vague resemblance to the great Mafia chronicler Mario Puzo, Sheldon huffs his way to our table. I can't say it to his face, but Sheldon needs to lose forty—make that fifty —pounds, if not for himself, then for his young children. I'm sixty-five and I can still fit into the jeans I wore when I was nineteen. It takes discipline and willpower, of which I have plenty to spare.

After we order and exchange our typical innocuous pleasantries about the weather, politics, and soccer, for we're both rabid fans, Sheldon downs a gin and tonic. It's his first of the day and not his last. "Brooks, how is the book coming along?" he booms in a guttural Brooklyn accent that has other diners turning their heads.

"Great," I reply cheerfully. "It couldn't be going any better. Gold, pure gold."

He tilts his head. "Cassie says you haven't been sleeping well."

Cassie's my third and—if I have anything to say about it—last wife. She interviewed me for a puff piece and months later, when the pregnancy test was positive, I knew I'd met my Waterloo, no thanks to Abba. An abortion was out of the question. Now we have two children under six, our lives are a merry-go-round of sweet chaos. Last fall, I had a vasectomy so there will be no more miniature Andersons polluting the planet.

I finish my seltzer and signal for another. "You know I never

sleep well when I'm writing. I do my best work after midnight."
In the old days, that didn't necessarily apply to writing.

The waitress delivers our meals: me, a grilled chicken Caesar
salad with extra feta, and Sheldon a porterhouse with crispy
julienne potatoes and parmesan creamed spinach. I eye his steak
with unconcealed envy, but Cassie's always after me to eat
healthier. I sigh and add more dressing to my salad. Cassie would
be pleased.

"Yeah, I know. You have the constitution of fucking
Secretariat. You did drugs with Keith Richards and Lou Reed."
Sheldon cut into his steak; it's not just blue, it's bloody raw. Just
looking at it makes me queasy. "But this is different. You're
writing about your goddamn family."

"I can be objective."

Sheldon puts his fork down. "Not about this, Brooks. Come
on. The cold-blooded executions of your mother and brother—"

I suddenly lose my appetite. Sheldon means well. Cassie does,
too. But this quasi-intervention is the last thing I need. "Sheldon,
you know as well as Cassie that I had no choice. I wasn't going to
let that fucking guttersnipe drag my mother through the mud."
The fucking guttersnipe in question is Marshall Reagan (no
relation to the former president), a douchebag posing as a
journalist. His brand is writing scandalous, unauthorized
biographies of the rich and famous because he knows he can get
away with it. No dirt, no sleaze, is beneath him. And when he
can't find anything salacious, he makes shit up and pulls it out of
his ass like saltwater taffy.

"You don't know that."

"Oh, but I do know. I know exactly the angle he'd take. That
my mother was having an affair with Julian." Julian Broadhurst,
born in Lancaster, England, in 1942. An artist who was
supposedly the protégé of Peter Max. Julian had long blond hair
and drove a robin's-egg-blue Aston Martin. Palmer and I loathed
him. "And when Mom wanted to end it, he killed her. But that

wasn't enough, fuck no. When my brother tried to protect her, Julian killed him, too." I shake my head, the bile percolating like a fresh pot of coffee. "My mother was brilliant. Graduated from Mount Holyoke with honors. And she was utterly devoted to my father. To us. The idea that she'd have a summer fling with that bohemian scumbag—" I choke on the words (or is it a sliver of chicken that went down the wrong pipe?). "And you know damn well that when that cocksucker Reagan's done tarring and feathering her, he'll start in on my father, who has been nothing less than a fucking saint. Saint Bernard." I rap my fist on the table. "It's fucking ludicrous."

Sheldon nods, sympathy oozing from every pore. "All I'm saying is that you have a lot on your plate. The book. The next book. Your father's gala. You're writing a speech for that, right? Jesus fucking Christ, Brooks. You're not Superman. It's bound to take a toll on you."

"So, what are you suggesting? I can't return the advance. It's already spent." Six million gone in a heartbeat. Lawyers. Trust funds. The new house in Water Mill. And I was finally able to get my ex-wives off my back with a tidy lump sum. For the first time in years, no alimony to shill out every goddamn month. All thanks to Sheldon, who hadn't budged an inch during the multi-house book auction. He earned his commission ten times over.

"No one's suggesting that. That's crazy." Sheldon's halfway through his steak. "But we can ask to push the deadline back by a couple of months."

"No." I'm a stubborn son of a bitch. If there's one thing I'm known for, it's living up to my contractual obligations. I've never missed a deadline. I could be fucking pushing up daisies and I'd still deliver.

Sheldon sighs. "Why are you being so goddamn obstinate?"

"I'm well into the book now, it's just a matter of research."

"Really?" He gives me a side-eye. "Cassie says you've barely written the first chapter."

I'm annoyed. Mostly because Cassie's right. "It's all in my head, Sheldon. Don't worry."

"Well, I do. Worry, I mean." Sheldon furrows his bushy eyebrows; he looks like a caterpillar on meth. "I know how good you can be, Brooks. But you push yourself way too hard."

I make a half-hearted stab at my chicken. He could've added—but tactfully didn't—that he also knows how bad I can be. My books still sold phenomenally well, even that fucking godawful picture book *Rocco the Stinky Raccoon*, nominated for a Caldecott. I was ecstatic when it didn't win.

By the time we say our goodbyes, it's three o'clock. If I hurry, I can see the kids for a minute before they're trundled off to gymnastics or karate or whatever activity Cassie has planned. Mark loves *Star Wars* and *Hulk*. Audra's obsessed with unicorns. I buy them far too many toys. I love my children desperately, but I don't pretend to understand them. That's Cassie's deal. She's the hardass. I'm the marshmallow man.

We live in the Dakota on the UWS (upper west side) close to Central Park. Our apartment has a bird's-eye view of the park. The Dakota's where John Lennon was shot. We still have tourists who make pilgrimages. I wasn't there the night it happened, but I'd like to think I'd have stopped Mark Chapman in his tracks. I'd bought into the Dakota with the advance I'd gotten for *Fallen Angels*. I never would've been able to afford it otherwise. That book's the gift that keeps on giving. It's been optioned by movie production companies at least a dozen times but it'll never get made. I've reconciled myself to that.

"Daddy's home!" I shout as I enter the foyer.

The kids always run to see what I've bought. Today I have a Baby Yoda electronic gizmo for Mark and a big unicorn doll for Audra. But no excited squeals greet me. Instead, there are two packed suitcases by the door. I walk into the living room and marvel once again at our panoramic views of Central Park.

Cassie, her eyes red, sits on the sofa.

"Bad day with the kids, baby?" I bend down to kiss her.

She turns her head. This isn't a good sign.

"Where are the munchkins?" I toss my suit jacket on a chair.

"With my sister in Providence." Her voice is flat.

I'm surprised. Tammy's coming down on the weekend. Why would she have come early and taken the kids?

Cassie stares at me. If her eyes were bullets, I'd be a corpse. "Dr. Schultz's office called. They said you missed your six-month check-up."

Dr. Schultz. Shit. I try to act casual but my heart thumps like a boom box. I can talk myself out of this one. I've done it before. "Damn, I guess I forgot to give them my new cell number. I'll call in the morning, they're probably closed now."

"Kind of like how you forgot to tell me about your vasectomy?" Her voice rises an octave.

I cringe. I'm in for it now. And I fucking deserve it.

"I'm not stupid, Brooks."

No. That's one thing Cassie isn't. She's brilliant in every respect, far more than I could ever hope or aspire to be. I'm painfully aware that I'm the reason she hasn't gotten the jobs and accolades. I'm the anchor that weighs her down. "We talked about it, Cassie."

"No. *You* talked about it. Not me. Not ever." Cassie's so mad her body trembles. "Who else knows?"

"Dad."

"Of course. I bet he was thrilled." My father wasn't in favor of this marriage. It was nothing against Cassie. He'd been against all my marriages. When I told him Cassie was pregnant, he was apoplectic. You can't be serious, he said. You're too old to be a father. And too fucked-up, he could've added. But he eventually came around.

"Who else?"

"Nobody. I mean, nobody important," I stumble. "Look, I'm sorry."

"Sorry that you had it done or sorry that I found out?"

The truth was both, but I'd done enough damage for one evening. "Baby, I admit, it was a stupid thing to do. I wasn't thinking clearly. But you know, maybe not going to the check-up was a good thing. Maybe it didn't take. And if it did, I can get it reversed. If they can reattach a penis, they can fix this, right?" I nervously chuckle. That's my default posture. When in a difficult situation, I make a feeble attempt at humor. Usually, it worked. Not this time.

"I'm going to stay at Tammy's. I don't know for how long."

I try not to make a face and fail. Tammy hates me. Well, maybe hate is too mild: detests, loathes, abhors. Tammy would revel in this. "Please, honey. Don't do that. We can work this out."

Cassie holds up her hand. "Since you began this book"—the book she and Dad were vehemently against from the start, probably the only thing in the universe they agree on— "you haven't been the same."

"That's not true," I protest.

"It is true even if you don't want to admit it. You got the book advance and then a vasectomy. And you don't see that's a huge problem? What about last night?"

I give her a look. "What about it?"

"I found you in Audra's room at two in the morning. Over her bed holding a baseball bat."

What? I shiver as if I've fallen through a river of ice. Water fills my lungs, and I can barely breathe. "That's preposterous!" I gasp.

"Muttering about monsters. And it wasn't the first time." She shot me a look I knew all too well from my boarding school days. I hated it then and I hate it even more now. "You almost had me convinced that writing about what happened to you would be a catharsis. Exorcizing old ghosts and demons. But the opposite is happening, and it scares the shit out of me. It kills me to say this, but I have to protect the kids and I'm not sure they're safe around you right now."

Cassie's words hang in the air. *Jesus fucking Christ.* Talk about a gut punch. The kids aren't safe around me? I adore Mark and Audra. I'd die for them in the blink of an eye, with no hesitation. I cut Mark's umbilical cord. I spent weeks in the neonatal unit with Audra. I changed diapers, I rocked them to sleep, they lacked for nothing materially. "You don't mean that," I retort. "You're upset and angry about the vasectomy."

"That's a separate issue. But fuck yeah, I'm angry. I'm fucking livid."

No one says "fuck" quite the way Cassie does. To my shame, I feel myself getting hard. Embarrassed, I cover myself with a sofa pillow and hope she doesn't notice.

She does and averts her eyes. "This is a problem, it's a huge fucking problem. This is beyond my field of expertise, Brooks. I'm a freelance editor, not a therapist."

"Therapists," I jeer. I'd had my fill of them. Never again. They're the modern-day equivalent of leeches. "I sleepwalk. You knew that from day one. I never hid it."

"This is more than sleepwalking. I want to help you, but I can't if you won't admit it's a problem."

"And your way of helping is talking to Sheldon?"

"Not just Sheldon. I spoke to Bernard, too. He's worried about you. He's noticed the change in you, we all have. Your father and I, we're never going to be best friends, but I'm telling you, we're united on this."

My throat tightens as if someone's wrapped a cord around my neck. I'm that eight-year-old kid shivering in the dunes, peeing on myself. "It's been a rough winter. When I'm writing I can be an ogre. Maybe this vacation is what you and the kids need. The kids—" I stop myself. "I'll call them in the morning. Better yet, why don't I drive you there and I can tell them goodbye in person."

Cassie picks up her handbag, the one I gave her last Christmas. A trendy, expensive designer label. To me they all look alike, so I asked the saleslady to give me the most popular one. I take that to mean Cassie isn't entirely through with me yet. My marriage hung on this fucking bag. That's how desperate I am. "I can drive myself." Of course she can. We got his and hers matching Priuses with the book advance.

Cassie walks to the front door.

I follow and sniff her perfume like a love-sick puppy. "It's getting late. Why don't we order a very expensive meal, chill out with an old Bogie movie, and you can leave first thing." I smile, in full Errol Flynn rogue mode.

Determined, she shakes her head. "You can't fuck your way out of this one, Brooks." She slams the door behind her so forcefully that my framed certificate from Caldecott falls off the fucking wall.

Immediately, my cell phone buzzes. I ignore Dad's call. I'm not in the mood for another St. Bernard lecture on what a fucking mess I've made of my life. It's suddenly very hot in the apartment. Or is it me? I tell Alexa to lower the temperature by five degrees, her calm demeanor a stark reminder of how quiet the apartment is without the kids screaming in the background. *He pulled my hair! She grabbed my crayon!*

I go upstairs into my writing lair. I must compartmentalize what just happened, otherwise, my head will detonate into a thousand pieces. Cassie and I have weathered worse. She'll come back. She has to. I'll call Dr. Schultz and fix this mess. For now, I must work on Dad's speech. I pull out the desk chair and find it's already occupied by one of Audra's unicorn dolls.

Dad's receiving a prestigious humanitarian award from the United Nations. Now pushing eighty-two or eighty-six depending on how many martinis he's drunk, he's evolved into an elder statesman on retainer as a crisis handler/negotiator. He advised LBJ on Vietnam. Nixon, too, although Dad couldn't stand the prick. Dad begged Ford not to pardon Nixon because the voters and history would judge Ford harshly. Dad was right. Clinton made him a Special Envoy to Sarajevo. GW Bush called on him to head the 9/11 Commission, but Dad declined due to other "commitments". Obama had him on speed dial. Dad has brokered peace agreements between nations and factions that were considered impossible. No one deserves this award more. I've been allotted roughly fifteen minutes to tell the world how I feel about him. I'd need fifteen years.

I touch a computer key. In Google Drive, the opening lines to my father's speech flash on. *"My beloved father, Bernard Stewart Anderson, is a generous, kind, honorable, decent man who embodies everything fine and good in this world. A man who has earned the respect of world leaders no matter their political persuasion. A man who goes out of his way to help the weak and oppressed. And he's also a man who bore the ultimate tragedy with dignity and grace. No one knows Bernard Anderson better than I, his surviving son."*

CHAPTER TWO

1966 was a fucking horrible year. No doubt about it.

Officially, our summer home was within the confines of Montauk. Unofficially, everyone knew our neighborhood as Ditch Plains, a stone's throw away from what many call—me included—one of the finest beaches on Long Island, if not in New York and the world.

My mother's family vacationed in Montauk in the 1920s. Eventually, they bought land overlooking the bluffs and built summer cottages on the same block. Shacks, really—no insulation, only good to use from June to September. But by the time we started going there, the shacks were houses with heating and indoor plumbing. When it got too hot, Palmer and I slept on cots on the screened porch. To a city boy, it was like camping out in the woods. We loved it.

But that summer—1966—things were different. Usually, our cousins joined us, but Aunt Flo, Mom's younger sister, had just given birth to twins. I was bummed, as I had a minor—okay, major—crush on Cousin Sophie, Aunt Flo's eldest. Sophie had laughing eyes and strawberry curls. Everyone called her Berry. We were best friends. I never minded being Ken to her Barbie. As things turned out, I never saw Berry again. She was on vacation in Martha's Vineyard when a car driven by a drunk, off-duty corrections officer ran a red light and slammed into her as she crossed the street. He claimed the brakes malfunctioned and got off with a suspended sentence. She was only seventeen.

Palmer was equally displeased, as he'd planned on doing all sorts of nefarious things with Cousin Brad—Uncle Philip's only child—but Uncle Philip was a career diplomat with the State Department and had just been assigned to Japan. If things weren't gloomy enough, our maternal grandfather, William, an executive at IBM, was still in mourning over losing Grandma Emily to pancreatic cancer the year before.

As we packed for the trip and Mom made sure we brought enough clean underwear, she reminded us that we'd still have other kids our age to play with besides the locals. The other houses that Grandpa William owned had been rented out to families whose husbands were college professors like Dad. And Dad would join us when he could as he was teaching summer courses at New York University. That was a given.

At that time, we were living in what we had nicknamed the "Big House" in Flushing, an easy commute for Dad to NYU for his political science courses. He was preoccupied with summer school and writing papers that were published in journals no one had ever heard of. We had a live-in housekeeper—Mathilde, a sweet French girl on a student visa—who made the best crepes that I've ever tasted, delicate and light with a touch of butter and sugar. I've been to France many times in a futile attempt to replicate those marvelous crepes. As fate would have it, Mathilde wouldn't be coming to Montauk. Her sister was getting married in Nice and Mathilde was the maid of honor. Mathilde had left in early June as soon as her term was finished. She wasn't expected back until just before Labor Day when Palmer and I would be returning to school. Of course, that didn't happen either.

I've often wondered how different our lives would've been if only Aunt Flo hadn't given birth when she did. Or if only Uncle Philip hadn't moved to Tokyo. If Grandma Emily had still been alive to greet us at the summer house with a plate of warm pecan and raisin oatmeal cookies. If Mathilde had been there to keep us kids in line. Would *everything have happened just the way it did? Because it's a fact that after that summer, our families disintegrated. I'm not sure why. Grief? Embarrassment? Shame? Anger? And then Grandpa William died of a massive heart attack the day after Mom's funeral. It's a conundrum that has kept me up many nights through the years and was—let's not kid ourselves, boys and girls—a major reason for my addictions.*

Knowing what I know now, I should've told Mom I didn't want to go to Montauk that summer. That I wanted to stay close to Grandpa William and Berry. That we could have a great summer right where we were.

If only.
If only.

CHAPTER THREE

"I've gotten the reports from the FBI. I put it all in the autopsy box, along with the others, Mr. Brooks." Miss Drake's crisp British accent snaps my wandering attention back like a rubber band. Along with Sheldon, Miss Drake's an indispensable cog in the well-oiled Anderson machine. I'd put out a call for an administrative assistant fifteen or so years ago. Miss Drake had been the first and only applicant the agency sent over. Apparently, my reputation for being a ballbuster scared everyone off. I was dubious that this mature British lesbian in a stiff gray suit was up to snuff, but politely agreed to a two-week trial thinking she'd quit in a day. Now almost seventy-five, Miss Drake lives uptown with a parakeet since the death of her partner. Despite my entreaties that she should cut her hours since her hip replacement, she insists on coming in four days a week to do all the thankless, cumbersome tasks best-selling authors hire other people to do. Miss Drake's my right hand. I still don't know her first name. She calls me Mr. Brooks and I call her Miss Drake. I suspect it will stay that way.

The autopsy box is exactly what Miss Drake calls it: a medium-sized cardboard box filled with every police report regarding Mom and Palmer's case that I'd been able to beg, bribe, buy, or steal. For months the box has been sitting behind my desk on a filing cabinet, a grim and constant reminder that I'm alive and they're not. I'd been putting off looking through the box even though I knew it had to be done. I was the only one who could do it. I can't palm this task off onto poor Miss Drake.

"And Mr. Bernard called. He expects you at noon for lunch."

I glance up from the computer. *Fuck.* Was it Wednesday already? Cassie and the kids have been gone for three days. It feels like three years. The apartment is too quiet and empty. The days weren't too bad. I keep myself reasonably busy. There's always an email to answer or a call to make. But the nights are torture. I can't remember the last time I slept through the night.

Dad and I always have lunch on Wednesdays: grilled salmon, asparagus, rice pilaf, and for dessert, fruit compote. Most weeks I enjoy it. Dad always has some juicy morsel of gossip that hasn't made Page Six or TMZ, but today I'm on edge and wired.

"Not sleeping well, Mr. Brooks?" Miss Drake's too polite to mention that when she let herself in, she found me sprawled out on the living-room sofa under a *Mandalorian* throw blanket.

"I never sleep well when Cassie and the kids are away." This was true because technically they'd never been away for this long a period. But last night, I checked the baby-cam tucked inside a hideous oversized unicorn that stands guard by Audra's bed. The camera didn't lie. It captured me, a black-and-white ghostly figure holding a baseball bat signed by Lou Gehrig (from my sports memorabilia collection, an expensive hobby but I can afford it) muttering about monsters. I was fucking horrified. After seeing that, I honestly couldn't blame Cassie for fleeing with the kids.

Miss Drake adores Cassie. I can tell. Miss Drake doesn't get emotional—she's the embodiment of the British stiff upper lip— but she's different around Cassie. Softer, not so brittle. I suspect

Cassie's the daughter Miss Drake never had. "Would you like to have flowers sent to Mrs. Cassie?"

Thank God for Miss Drake. "Yes, by all means. Peonies. At least four dozen. No, make it six." Peonies are Cassie's favorite flower bar none. When the real estate agent first took us to the property in Water Mill—which was well over our price range—I knew we had to buy it the second Cassie saw the peony garden.

"If you're going to meet Mr. Bernard for lunch, you should get going. Traffic is horrendous this time of day," Miss Drake reminds me as she hands me an umbrella.

Mr. Bernard—I mean, Dad—is the picture of punctuality. It was a source of endless amusement for Mom, who loved to tarry and make a grand entrance. She'd joke that Dad would be early for his funeral.

Dad lives in a tony three-story brownstone on the East Side. Henry Kissinger—Dr. K. as Dad calls him—used to live on the block back in the day. His Secret Service detail annoyed the hell out of everyone. Now the neighborhood's a mix of day traders and social media celebrities. After we ate grilled salmon in the solarium—Dad's private chef was a disciple of the late and greatly missed Anthony Bourdain, who intimidated even me—we pad into the library. Dad has his cigar and brandy in hand. I'm armed with a watermelon spritzer.

"Are you done with the speech for the gala yet?" Dad tries to sound nonchalant. It's like asking a cat not to meow.

I'd surmised this was coming, so I'm prepared. "It's almost done. A few more tweaks here and there. I'm sure you'll be happy with it. Would you like to—"

Dad laughs the request off. "No, no. I trust you, son. You can knock that kind of thing off blindfolded." He pauses, his long, thin fingers curling around his glass. He's the only man I know who has his manicurist on stand-by. "But if you'd like a second opinion, I'd be willing to look at it and offer suggestions. A memorable speech is like a fine wine that one savors long after the bottle is empty." And he should know. I've heard the whispers about him ghostwriting Reagan's Berlin Wall speech.

I took a long sip of my drink, but inside I boiled. I don't want or need his suggestions. I'm a best-selling novelist. I've sold millions of books. I was nominated for a fucking Pulitzer. And an Oscar. I won a Emmy. I can string a speech together. But I have only myself to blame. Why the fuck did I give him an opening?

"Are you going out to the new house this weekend?" Dad puffs on his Cuban cigar. I never developed a taste for nicotine. One of the few—exceedingly few—vices I've never been tempted to use regularly. Palmer would sneak a smoke behind the dunes, but I think it was more to impress girls than anything else.

"That's the plan, but it depends. We'll see." I hired a contractor to do renovations on the house: open walls, gut the kitchen, and install a whole house generator, among other improvements. Hell, you'd think for the price I paid it would be move-in ready. But who the fuck was I kidding? I wasn't buying a house. I was buying memories. Memories to make with Cassie and the kids. *If* she came back. The few phone calls we'd had since she left hadn't been promising.

"You look haggard, son. Are you sleepwalking again?"

My throat tightens. I never stopped, thank you for asking.

"What about the night terrors?"

I nod, terse. The night terrors had begun shortly after I'd been released from the hospital. We never returned to the Big House, instead living in an apartment close to Dad's job. I understood why, but I still hated it. The apartment wasn't home, it was just four walls. Anyway, at night I'd wake up in a cold sweat, screaming gibberish. The psychiatrist said that was common in kids who'd survived trauma. Today, we call it post-traumatic stress disorder.

Dad refills his glass. He drinks too much in my opinion, but he doesn't ask, and I've learned not to volunteer. "Now for your new book, do you plan on going back to the scene of the crime, as it were? For research?"

I shrug. "I don't see the point." After Grandpa William's death, the summer houses were sold. If the family had held on to them, the land alone would now be worth many millions.

Dad leans forward. "Look, if you've changed your mind about writing the book, that's fine. I can write a check for the advance right now, no questions. It's your money, really. And it's going to be all yours when I'm fucking maggot food."

I wince. I've written some excruciatingly brutal, graphic scenes. I'm no wallflower. But Dad can be exceptionally crude. It's not the kind of thing you expect from a distinguished, refined statesman. For a second, I wonder how Dad has amassed such a fortune that he's able to write a check for six million without flinching. Not that I hadn't asked, but his answer is always the same: if people wanted to pick his brain, he'd charge them an arm and a leg. "Dad, it's not about the money. Well, maybe at first, but not now. I need to do this."

"To do what?" He sounds bemused. "Set the record straight? Has your memory of that night returned?"

"No," I reluctantly admit. I remember that night up to a point. After that, it's just a vast, bottomless black tar pit.

"Then what is the point? I don't understand. No one cares. We know who did it. Really, Brooks. You need to let it go. It's ancient history."

I stare at him, incredulous. *No one cares? Let it go? Ancient history?* "Maybe you don't care, but I do. I won't have trash written about Mom by that scumbag Marshall Reagan."

Dad airily waves his hand. "They wrote trash then. The things they dreamed up. It was hideous. That it was a cult sacrifice. Wife swapping gone wrong. Or a child sex-trafficking ring among the elite. As if we were elite." He shook his head, disgusted.

What? This is a new one, and I'd heard plenty. I choke down a wave of acid.

Dad's face contorts in anger. "As if your mother and I would engage in such—" His grimace reflects his disdain. "Reporters hounded me for months. And it wasn't just me. Other families were besieged by those fucking press piranhas. They didn't deserve to be harassed."

The other families? Then I realized he meant the families who'd rented Grandpa William's other houses.

"Son, listen to me. It doesn't matter what you write. Someone will find a way to twist it. And my opinion, for what it's worth, is that your time and talent would be better spent on more promising projects. You don't lack ideas, do you?"

I laugh. I'm not as prolific as Stephen King, but close. I had hundreds of ideas. I'd never live long enough to write all of them. "Dad, I'm fine. Really."

"Well, if you change your mind, the offer still stands."

I'm surprised that he hasn't asked about Cassie and the kids. I assume that Cassie told him, but maybe not. They had a prickly relationship, that was for damn sure.

"I do have something else I need to discuss with you, Brooks." Dad's now in professorial mode: clinical, methodical, and unemotional. I know that mode all too well. "I've updated my will on how to handle my personal papers."

I raise an eyebrow. "Well, aren't they going to Yale?" Yale is Dad's alma mater. Dad came from modest means, so going to such a distinguished university was a huge accomplishment. My paternal grandparents had died before I was born. Dad liked to recount how in 1867 our great-great-grandfather Olaf Andreson came to America with nothing in his pocket but a needle and thread. A tailor by trade, he was successful in the new world and opened a dry goods store. At some point, tired of people mispronouncing his last name, he had it legally changed to Anderson.

"Not all of them. It's all in the new will. There are a hundred or so boxes in a storage facility in Queens. Those go to Yale with the stipulation that they're not to be opened until seventy-five years after my death."

I want to say isn't that a bit excessive, but I don't.

"And then there's also a safety deposit box." Dad pinches his fingers and pauses dramatically. "You're to burn those documents, Brooks. I mean it. Throw them in a bonfire, a firepit, douse them with kerosene—the method is up to you. Be as creative as you want. But I want them destroyed. This is non-negotiable." He chomps down on his cigar like W. C. Fields.

Burn them? Is he out of his fucking mind? "Dad, are you sure? Those papers are historic. I know you. You documented everything. Why in hell would you want to burn them?"

"Because I don't want to end up like Robert Fucking McNamara, that's why," he snaps, his words slurring. "A wonderful, honorable, decent man who was put through a meat grinder. They fucking broke him." Dad has told this story countless times. After Mom and Palmer died, McNamara called Dad to express his condolences. As it turned out, he'd read Dad's articles in those obscure journals. They soon became fast friends and colleagues. When McNamara passed away, Dad was one of his pallbearers. "Do you have any idea of the havoc my papers would create if they were publicly released? They'd put the fucking Pentagon Papers to shame. Let me put it this way, son. If one day I jump off a parking garage in the Bronx—" He gives me a knowing leer and chuckles. I don't think he's ever set one toe in the Bronx. Is Dad serious or joking? I vote for the latter.

"I'm telling you about this now because I wanted you to hear it from me. From my lips. I insist you follow my instructions down to the letter. Promise me." He gives me a defiant glare.

I don't understand, but I realize this is important to him. "Of course, yes. You have my word."

The issue settled, Dad slapped his knee. "Oh, you're never going to believe who's going to announce they're running for President next year."

"Jeff Fucking Bezos?" I quip.

Dad dismisses me after an hour or so. Something has come up, an urgent conference call with an African president who is fighting off a military coup.

Since no one is waiting for me at home, I take my time. I linger at a bookstore and gently chide the manager because the only title of mine prominently featured in their window display is the horrific *Rocco the Stinky Raccoon*. The manager thinks I'm hilarious. I'm dead serious.

When I finally get home, it's just about dusk. Miss Drake is long gone. The apartment is quieter than a mausoleum. For dinner, I peck on a wilted salad kit that's a week past its expiration date.

Afterward, I FaceTime with the kids, who seem to be blissfully unaware that anything's amiss. Mark is proud that he's mastered the art of armpit farting. Audra babbles about a new Barbie Princess, her second favorite toy in the world. Cassie's polite but perfunctory. She's careful not to look at me.

"I made an appointment with Dr. Schultz," I say in the hopes it will break the ice.

No reaction from Cassie.

"Are you coming home this weekend?" I ask.

She's noncommittal and makes small talk about the weather. Before I can get in another word, she mumbles good-bye and clicks off as the kids holler off-screen.

I'm fucking miserable. I miss the screams. I miss the fights. I miss stepping on Legos. I miss burps in my ear. The silence is killing me.

I make myself a fresh glass of lemon-lime seltzer and settle down in my lair for the night. Fuck it, I'd put off the autopsy report long enough. Oh, I'd read plenty of coroner's reports, seen crime-scene photos that made even the most hardboiled detective weep. I remain detached and objective, free of emotion. I learned this from Dad or maybe in another life, I was a cop.

This is different. This is my family, not strangers. I rustle through the autopsy box as John Hiatt howls at the moon in the background. I love music despite the fact I can't sing a lick or play a note. But I can recognize greatness in others. In my music journalist days, I was an early champion of Bruce Springsteen.

The efficient Miss Drake has done me the kind favor of breaking down the reports: one from the local authorities, namely Sheriff Thad Cooper, who'd been the first cop on the scene. There was also a case file from the state police and a score of voluminous documents from the FBI. Why this case garnered the attention of the FBI is a mystery to me. Lastly, there's the coroner's report.

I know all the gory details from the newspaper accounts: Mom suffered over thirty-five puncture wounds, many defensive. She put up a hell of a fight. None of those wounds would've been fatal. No, she died from her head being smashed to bits like a piñata at a kiddie birthday party. The weapon had never been found. It could've been a hammer, a shovel, a fireplace poker, a cudgel of some kind—take your pick.

Palmer died from suffocation. His throat gutted, he choked on his blood. The wound had been deep; any deeper and he would've been decapitated. He died quickly, as if that was any solace. Since Mom's blood was on his hands and clothing, the working theory was that he'd tried to help her during the attack or immediately after.

Julian Broadhurst almost made it to his beloved Aston Martin. His body was found a hundred or so yards from it, Mom's kitchen shears embedded in his heart. Her fingerprints were on them. As perverse as it sounds, it gives me a great deal of pleasure to imagine that she'd plunged the shears into him with her last breath. Does that make me a fucking psychopath? I hope not.

I open Sheriff Cooper's file and switch to clinical, observant mode. The initial crime-scene black-and-white photos are horrendous and stark. The pictures don't seem real. They look staged. Mom and Palmer are grotesque thespians trapped in an awful Off-Broadway play. Another set of photos, this time in color, are far worse. So much fucking blood everywhere; on the walls, the ceilings, the floor. The fury that gripped Julian didn't seem human. It was a primitive, primordial rage. The photos told the story more than my words ever could. And it was only thanks to Palmer's entreaties that I'd been spared. As much of a pest as I was, he'd protected me. He sacrificed himself for me. I owed him my life. I took a long gulp of my seltzer.

I set the gory photos aside. I doubt I'll ever return to them, the images forever seared in my mind like steaks on a hot grill. I pick up the autopsy report and skip over Julian's. Palmer's autopsy is a clinical two pages and revealed nothing I hadn't known before. I went to Mom's report: *Shirley Anne Tobias Anderson, Caucasian female, age 35. Cause of death: catastrophic head injury, skull fracture, and significant subdural hemorrhage.* Even if Mom had survived, she would've been a fucking rutabaga.

I continue reading. Buried in a paragraph, almost as an afterthought, I stumble upon this phrase: *"The victim, at the time of death, was roughly twelve weeks pregnant."* Confused, I read the paragraph again. This must be wrong. I scour through the remaining page. There's no other mention of it except for that one sentence. If Mom had been pregnant—and I wasn't yet ready to accept that she was—why was this the first I'd heard about it? This alleged pregnancy hadn't been reported in the papers. Had Mom known she was pregnant? And Dad? Guilt washes over me. *I should've been there. I could've done something. Anything.*

The shrill ring of the landline pierces my heavy breathing. I know landlines may soon be obsolete, but I still had one out of habit or maybe sheer laziness. It was in Cassie's maiden name: Cassandra Ramona Whitman. Not many people had the landline number: Dad, Sheldon, Miss Drake, and companies selling an extended car warranty. I'm somewhat comforted by the fact that

Dad still had a landline, so I wasn't the only neanderthal in the world. I grabbed the phone. "Hello?"

"The son of a bitch got what was coming to him," Dad crows.

I'm still in shock over Mom's autopsy report. "Who are you talking about?"

"Check your goddamn email!" Dad thunders before he hangs up. This is from the man who asked Mark how to put a movie on his Netflix watchlist.

I immediately click on my email. It's a link to the *New York Post* so everyone knows it must be true: "Muckraker Journalist Marshall Reagan Found Dead in Montauk." A particularly unflattering photo of Reagan runs with the story.

Elated, I pound my desk. *Hell, yeah! One less cocksucker.* I smile for the first time in days. If I was still drinking, I'd have drunk an entire bottle of Jack Daniel's. Fuck it, make it two.

"Cassie, you'll never believe—" I yell, then stop.

CHAPTER FOUR

"The detectives are here, Mr. Brooks. They're in the library." Miss Drake sounds as if she's dragged a mangy cat in from the rain. "I took the liberty of reminding them that your time is limited."

"Thank you, Miss Drake." Detectives. I'm mildly surprised about that. Two cops for a routine interview? I'm not at all surprised that the police had asked to speak with me about Marshall Reagan. It's standard operating procedure. Our bad blood, feud, vendetta—whatever it was called—is well-publicized. Since news of the death broke, I've been inundated with calls for comment. I had Miss Drake release a two-word statement: "Good riddance."

I stroll into the library which is now a playroom for the kids. An easel filled with Audra's attempts at drawing. Mark's Lego table.

The detectives—a white man and a black female, how politically correct—sit on the cheap faux leather sofa we'd bought online. I'd wanted something a bit more elegant, but Cassie said with kids it didn't make sense. She was right. She's always right. Not having her here is a physical ache like a phantom limb.

"Thank you for seeing us on such short notice, Mr. Anderson. I'm Detective Jonah Dodge and this is my partner, Detective Linda Clemente." A heavy-set man who resembles the actor Paul Giamatti, he flashes a badge as he stands.

I smile as we all shake hands. "Have you come to tell me to get the hell out of Dodge?" I crack.

The detective sighs.

I sit down opposite them in an overstuffed chair. One of Audra's crayons peeks through the cushion. I fight the impulse to stick it back in.

"My wife Rosemary is a huge fan of yours. I mean, huge. That HBO series—" Detective Giamatti, I mean, Dodge, gushes. "The one with Nicole Kidman and Mark Ruffalo. And the guy from *Jaws*."

I nod in proud acknowledgment. "Richard Dreyfuss. *Three Rivers*." A drama-thriller set in Holyoke, it had been a tremendous success. I wrote the series bible and ten episodes in a white-hot fever after Audra's birth, when it had been touch-and-go. It wasn't even finished when Sheldon sold the rights to it on the back of a paper napkin with the caveat that not a single word of what I wrote would be changed. That show is the reason why I got such a huge advance on the new book. HBO—now rebranded as Max for some ungodly reason—is hounding me for a second season. Everyone's onboard except me. As I keep telling the corporate suits, some stories aren't meant to have a sequel. Besides, everyone died. The end.

"Mr. Anderson, I'm sure you know why we're here." Detective Clemente is all business in a blue skirt, but her designer high heels look uncomfortable. I do like the cornrows piled on her head. It's the right touch of defiance and authenticity.

"Marshall Reagan," I say.

"You didn't care for the deceased, did you, Mr. Anderson?" Detective Dodge sounds apologetic.

I don't know why. I hated Reagan's guts and I'm not afraid to say it. "Detective, if you've done your research, you know that no one cared for the deceased, including me. The man was universally despised."

"You told a reporter that you wanted him dead." Detective Clemente didn't beat around the bush. Oh, was this a bad-cop, good-cop scene from a Dick Wolf procedural?

"No, that's not what I said. I told *Vanity Fair* that Marshall Reagan was a festering boil on the anus of humanity and if he didn't stop his harassment, I'd turn his balls into castanets."

"Yes, well—you had a restraining order against him," Detective Dodge kindly points out, his face pulpy red.

I sure as hell did. "He showed up here one day out of the blue. He was going to write a book about the Ditch Plains murders and wanted my cooperation, a sixty-forty split." Just the idea of it made me sick. "As if I'd ever work with that creep. He wouldn't take no for an answer. He showed up at all hours, bombarded me with texts and emails. The last straw was when he took photographs of my kids playing in Central Park. So yes, I got a restraining order."

"You were angry," Detective Clemente observes.

"Damn straight. I was livid. But not enough to kill the bastard if that's what you're inferring." Reagan was found beaten to a bloody pulp at an Airbnb he'd rented. From the state of decomposition, he'd been there a while. Based on what I know, the working theory is that it was a hook-up that went bad. I'm not surprised. To sum it up, the dude was a sick fuck into real kinky shit. The police are doing their job, I get it. But they're wasting my time and theirs.

"That's not what we're inferring, Mr. Anderson. Not at all." Detective Dodge glances at his partner. "But we know that he was still working on his book. Or at least he was until quite recently. What do you know about that?"

"It's news to me." Reagan went ballistic when my book was sold at auction. I still had his profane and revolting messages on my voicemail. I'd undercut him with my book so there was no financial incentive for him to keep at it. I figured he'd cut his losses and sink his fangs into another corpse.

"Not according to Priscilla Garrett, Julian Broadhurst's daughter," Detective Dodge continues.

"*Alleged* daughter," I hoot. Julian wasn't even listed on her birth certificate. I'd done my homework. And when the murders happened, she was barely four years old. What the hell did she know? In a word, nothing.

Detective Dodge picks at a stain on his tie. "Apparently, the deceased spoke to her not too long ago. He intimated that he'd discovered something about the murders that he claimed was incendiary."

"Incendiary?" I stare at them, bewildered.

"It seems Marshall Reagan had another version of the events. One that didn't have Julian Broadhurst as the killer of your mother and brother. What do you have to say about that?" Detective Dodge bellows, Judge Judy on steroids.

I shoot out of my chair. "Excuse me, but I've heard enough of this fucking garbage."

"Mr. Anderson, please," Detective Clemente says.

"Please, what? Marshall Reagan was a scumbag. He'd write anything for a buck. No one took him seriously. He didn't have a book deal; he had a one-page proposal that was so salacious no reputable agent or publisher in town would touch it because they knew I'd sue the fucking daylights out of it. Now may I suggest that instead of wasting your time and mine asking me about restraining orders, you should be investigating what escort services he used."

"And we are looking into that, Mr. Anderson. Your father told us the same thing but in much stronger and more colorful language. We just came from seeing him." Detective Dodge shakes his head. "He's a character, your old man."

"Well, he did tell Vladimir Putin and Kim Jong Un to go fuck themselves." One of the many anecdotes Dad loves to recount. At his age, he doesn't mince words and doesn't suffer fools and dictators gladly. But I'm confused. Why didn't Dad tell me he was being interviewed?

"Just a few more questions, Mr. Anderson. May we speak with your wife?" Now it was Detective Clemente's turn. I felt as if I was watching a quarter-final match at the U.S. Open. And I fucking hate tennis.

"I'm sorry, but my wife is away for a few days in Providence."

"Italy?" Detective Dodge writes something down in a spiral notebook.

I grit my teeth. "Providence, Rhode Island."

"So, you've been here at your apartment all by yourself? You haven't gone anywhere?"

"I haven't been to Montauk if that's what you mean. I've gone to lunch with my agent and my father. You can check the building security cameras. And my secretary, Miss Drake, can attest that I've been here as well." I give them a look. "Now I have to get going. I should've been on the road a half-hour ago. My aunt is in Mt. Vernon." Aunt Flo's my best hope of finding out if Mom had really been pregnant when she died. There's no one else. Uncle Philip's in an assisted-living facility in Baltimore and believes that Dwight Eisenhower's still the president. As for Dad, that was a dead end. He shuts down like a bank vault when it comes to that awful night.

"So, you don't think it's strange?" Back to Detective Clemente. If I was a referee, I would've called a foul. "That Marshall Reagan is investigating an infamous case where the victims were brutally beaten to death and the same thing happens to him in the town of the original murders." Was she a fan of gritty noir Swedish crime shows like Dad? Because it sure sounds like the plot of one.

"I wouldn't say it's strange. I'd say it's poetic justice. And you can quote me." I follow the detectives to the front door.

"Well, if you plan on taking any trips out of state in the near future—" Detective Dodge begins.

"I don't take trips while I'm working. That's how I'm able to write shows for premium cable networks. Good afternoon." I slam the door behind them, irate. What a complete fucking waste of time. Rattled, I find Miss Drake and tell her I'll be out for a couple of hours.

"Don't forget your umbrella, it might rain," she says. Again, with the goddamn umbrella. It could be ninety fucking degrees with a clear sky. Still, I acquiesce, and like a trained puppy, I grab an umbrella and my car keys.

On the drive, I play Steve Earle and John Fogerty; you know, the good stuff. Usually, their music mellows me out, but there's traffic due to a nasty accident and I'm constantly hitting the brakes.

I pull into Aunt Flo's driveway well past lunchtime. Cousin Althea greets me with a frosty smile. "You're late," she hisses as she avoids my hug. I've never laid eyes on her before this day, but she has Grandma Emily's chin.

The house and grounds look much the same as the last time I'd been there: Thanksgiving 1964, save for the *"For Sale"* under the magnolia tree in the front yard. That November, Grandma Emily was still with us, her cancer diagnosis months away. The entire family had assembled for turkey, ham, and pumpkin pie. Afterward, we played touch football in the backyard. It was chilly and I kept losing my cap. Mom cheered us on from the patio with a cup of hot chocolate. Even though Aunt Flo and her late husband Charlie—a big, goofy guy like John Candy whose heart gave out too soon—had lived in the house for decades, to me it would always be Grandpa William's.

Aunt Flo's in the sunroom. A petite woman who barely reaches my shoulders, she totters as she walks towards me. She looks and sounds marvelous, her short gray pixie haircut showing off her high cheekbones. "I was afraid you weren't coming," she whispers as she kisses me. "It's been such a long time. But you're here now, that's all that matters." She was the glue who gamely tried to hold the family together after the funerals, to no avail. The pain was too deep. But she always sends cards on birthdays, anniversaries, and presents for Christmas. I respond with extravagant flower deliveries on her and Mom's birthday—as if flowers could fill the void in our souls.

She gesticulates at me to sit in a wicker chair next to her. She carefully eases herself down in a lounge chair decorated with "Spring Chicken Crossing" pillows. The backyard, which was always lush and green, looks unkempt with brown spots and soggy leaves.

"I'm glad you were well enough to see me. Althea tells me you've been a bit under the weather." Althea had moved back home after her divorce.

"I'm fine. Althea worries if I sniffle." She thumps her heart. "I don't drink, I don't smoke, and I haven't been with a man in years. Heaven knows why I stick around, it's so goddamn boring." She squeezes my hand. "Oh, my darling Brooks. I'm so proud of you. How you turned your life around. Your mother would be proud too. You were the apple of her eye. Oh, she loved Palmer to the moon and back, don't get me wrong," she quickly adds. "But you were special."

I don't know if this is true. A part of me wants to think so, and badly. I chuckle with a heavy heart. "Mom had a way of making everyone feel special."

Aunt Flo nods. "She did, didn't she? She was a colt, wild and free. No one could tame her, not even Bernard. Oh, the memories. How we'd cut school to smoke and drink beer in the woods above the football field. The way we'd dance to Elvis Presley after dinner. It was indecent. The looks Dad gave us." She laughs heartily. "That poor, dear man. He earned his gray hairs." She stops and smiles. "Listen to me. There I go again. I tell you

31

not to dwell on the past, and I do the same thing. How are Cassie and the children?"

"They're great. The writing is going well. We just bought a new house. It's great," I repeat on autopilot, not feeling great in the slightest. "Althea isn't happy I came to see you."

She lets out a deep sigh. "Althea isn't happy, period. The divorce hit her hard. If Gil had left her for a woman, that would've been one thing. But another man—" her voice trails. "I don't know why she married him in the first place, to be honest. Maybe if they'd had children, they'd still be together. But maybe it's better that they didn't." She brightens. "But Eric's doing well." Eric is Althea's twin. He lives in California and writes screenplays. He'd sent me a sample of his work and asked me to read it with an eye to referring him to Sheldon. I didn't get past ten pages; it was rubbish. When I gently told him it wasn't the kind of material my agent would be interested in, Eric retorted with a grandiose missive about how he was going to be bigger than Aaron Sorkin. That was the last I'd heard from him.

I cough nervously. It was time to deal with the elephant in the room. "I'm so sorry, Aunt Flo. About Berry's funeral. I wanted to go but Dad overruled me." We were living in Virginia then, an easy commute for Dad who'd taken a position at a think tank in Washington, D.C. I was in a bad place mentally and emotionally, numbing myself with increasing amounts of drugs and alcohol. Dad thought Berry's funeral would reopen old wounds—as if those wounds had ever healed.

Her eyes flood with tears. "You have nothing to apologize for, sweetheart. I know how much you loved Berry. And how she adored you, my word. When you went missing that dreadful night, Berry was hysterical. She wanted to drive out to join the search because she insisted she was the only one who could find you. And then when we were at the hospital and we had no idea —" She chokes up, unable to continue.

"You came to the hospital?" I'm stunned. This is the first time

I've heard of this. Dad never mentioned it—but he buried important things like a squirrel socked away acorns.

"Not just us. Your grandfather—even your Uncle Philip. As soon as he heard, he got a special leave. We wanted to be with you, but you were in such a deep shock I don't think you would've been aware." She hesitates. "We never blamed Bernard. Not once, not ever. I told him that repeatedly, but I don't think he believed me. He was furious when we broached the idea of you coming to live with us once you were better."

My stomach drops like an anvil. All this time, I've believed that the family blamed me. I tear up. If I had lived with Aunt Flo and Uncle Charlie, would I have gone down that dark, lonely path? I can't deal with it, so I do what I do best. I shut it down.

"Your father was so busy with his work he didn't have time for you. I don't say that in a bad way, of course. It's just that Charlie and I thought it might help your recovery if you were with your cousins." She makes a stewed prune face. "I didn't like what the doctors were doing to you, and I made no secret of it. Pumping you up with drugs. You were a little boy. A scared, defenseless, little boy. That was no way to deal with it. And if your grandfather had still been alive, he wouldn't have tolerated it."

"Dad believed he was doing the right thing," I meekly offer in his defense.

"I'm sure he did. But you needed love and support—not sleeping pills." She falls back, spent. "I had a bad feeling that entire summer. Terrible nightmares, too, until I gave birth to the twins."

This was my opening. I may not get another chance. "Aunt Flo, I found out something about Mom during my research. It bothered me and I was hoping you could—I have her autopsy report. It says she was pregnant, early days. Did you know? Could the report be wrong?"

After a moment, she curtly nods. "It's not wrong."

An atom bomb detonates in my head.

"Shirley didn't say it in so many words, but when she came to visit me after I'd had the twins, she asked me if I had any prenatal vitamins. I thought it was odd, considering that Bernard didn't want any more children. You know she had a miscarriage after you were born."

That I did know. I couldn't have been more than four. I remember Mom sitting me and Palmer down and telling us she was going to have a baby. She lifted her sweater and showed us her tummy. It looked like an avocado pit.

"Your mother was so excited. She wanted a girl more than anything." Aunt Flo turns somber. "But there were problems right from the start. Then, at six months, she went into premature labor. Even if she had carried the baby to full term, it wouldn't have lived. Her organs were inside out. The doctors refused to let her see the baby. Shirley was inconsolable."

I ache for Mom and the sister I lost. When Cassie was pregnant with Mark, some of the prenatal testing had come back indicating an anomaly. Thankfully, the tests had been wrong. Even though Cassie had put on a brave face, I knew she'd been worried. I was too. But Mark was—is—perfectly healthy in every way. The first thing he did after he was born was pee on the obstetrician. We knew that worked.

"I went to the hospital to see her," Aunt Flo continues. "The door was closed, but I could hear your parents shouting. Then Bernard stormed out. I think he was embarrassed that I'd heard them."

"Do you know what they were arguing about?"

"No. When I went in, Shirley asked if she could come to our house to convalesce. She was emotional and agitated and she didn't want you and Palmer to see her like that. I agreed, naturally. She could stay as long as she liked. But when I came to pick her up, she was already discharged, and Bernard had taken her home."

I remembered that too. I wasn't sure what had happened, but I knew it was terrible. Mom stayed in bed and cried for days. We ate Swanson frozen dinners until we got sick. Even now, I can't look at a frozen dinner without puking. And Dad got rid of all the baby girl stuff Mom had begun accumulating in the spare bedroom.

"Marriage was a tremendous adjustment for your mother, but she was determined to make it work. She was so young, and Palmer came right away. She had to grow up in a hurry." She gives me this melancholy smile. "But that's all I know, Brooks."

I thank Aunt Flo for being so welcoming and open. She insists on walking me to my car and holds on to my arm for support. "You wouldn't happen to be interested in buying the house, would you? I'd give you a family discount."

"We just bought a house," I gently remind her.

She goes on, oblivious. "You have money, you can afford it. It's a huge property, over three acres. Too much maintenance for this old bird. We haven't opened the pool in years. It needs a family, rambunctious kids, and a dog. It would be perfect for you, Brooks. You could convert your grandfather's old workshop into your office."

"We'll think about it," I demur.

"I just thought I'd bring it up. Eric has no interest in it. It would be nice to keep it in the family since Philip—" She sighs. "The truth is, I'm selling it for him."

"If that's what you're worried about, I can help," I blurt.

"I've always felt guilty about what happened. It should've been Philip's house. But he was in Japan, so we bought him out. When he eventually came back to the States, he got involved with that hideous Maddox man and lost his shirt."

I flinch. Bernie Maddox? *Fuck no.* I'd met Bernie back in the nineties at a cocktail party. As high as I was, I wasn't impressed. He'd tried inveigling me and Dad into investing in his company,

35

but we smelled his bullshittery a mile away. "You didn't invest with that asshole, did you?"

"No, no. Charlie wouldn't go for it. But I guess what happened is that Philip got too much money out of it, at least initially. The court did—oh, what do they call it—"

"A clawback?"

Her face lights up in recognition. "Yes. By that time, Philip had no idea of what was going on. He could barely remember his name. Now he's in that veteran's facility and every time I talk to him he sounds worse. I considered bringing him here, but Althea won't have it. With the money I'd get from selling, I can put Philip in a better facility near here for whatever time he has left. He was never the same after Brad died." Yes, poor Brad had been in a Special Forces unit in Iraq and was killed in a tragic case of "friendly fire." I can still see him and Palmer digging foxholes on the front lawn of the Big House for their miniature toy soldiers.

Aunt Flo grips my arm tight. I'm taken aback by how strong she is. "For better or worse, family is all we have."

"We'll work something out, I promise." And I mean it. "But whatever you need, just ask."

She kisses me on the cheek. I'm sure it's left a stain. "Now that the door is open, Brooks, don't be a stranger."

I thought of that as I drove away listening to Marc Cohn going to Memphis. It also reminded me of a line I'd written in *Fallen Angels*: *Family. We don't get to choose which family we're born into. It's a big fat cosmic roll of genetic dice. Sometimes, we get lucky, and other times, it's craps.*

CHAPTER FIVE

My mother came screaming into the world and left the same way. She was born a month early in the back of a Studebaker during a late August thunderstorm. She was doted upon by my grandparents. Mom was the epitome of a tomboy and excelled at everything she did: swimming, track, gymnastics, horseback riding. But she loved reading most of all and had decided, at the precocious age of seven, that she was going to write a book about mermaids taking over the world because, well, why not?

To me, Mom was the most beautiful woman in the world. She had Elizabeth Taylor eyes and a temper to match. Five-foot-three in her stockinged feet with porcelain skin, she usually tied her long, curly black hair back in a chic bow. Her horse laugh was infectious. She was obsessed with bad puns and knock-knock jokes that only she found amusing. A natural-born flirt, Mom loved to wear tight sweaters and skirts. As young as I was, I noticed the reaction she elicited from men when she'd walk us to school. It was a cacophony of wolf whistles and rude remarks. Mom didn't let it bother her. She simply hiked her skirt up higher and walked a bit faster. At the beach, she wore skimpy cut-out bikinis that left little to the imagination. She certainly had the figure for it. But Palmer hated it. He hated the way men looked at her, hated the catcalls. He was protective of her—some would say, overly possessive.

I'm not sure how Mom and Dad first met. She said it was in a bookstore. He said a bar. Dad was a pale-faced ice blond, tall, and thin —that's the Nordic side, with some British mixed in. I could easily see Dad falling in love with Mom. I mean, who wouldn't?

However, they were polar opposites. Dad loved classic literature. Mom devoured trashy romance novels. Dad enjoyed fine cuisine. Mom lived on hamburgers and pizza. Dad was a wine fanatic. Mom thrived on Tab. Dad listened to opera. Mom was a rock-and-roll girl down to her blue suede shoes. Dad was deliberate in everything he said and did. Mom was impulsive, a free spirit. But somehow it worked. As a kid, I thought they were madly—embarrassingly so—in love. Like the books Mom read.

The morning we left the Big House, Dad saw us off. We usually left the last weekend in June and didn't return until right before Labor Day, when school started up again. In the back seat, Palmer looked glum. He'd already decided that the summer was going to be a waste.

"Chin up, Palmer," Dad said as he leaned into the window. "You never know what's going to happen."

I wish I could say as we pulled away from the house that I had—like Aunt Flo—a bad feeling about going to Montauk. But I didn't. I was happy to get away. Thrilled, in fact. I loved going to the beach. I loved making sandcastles and looking for crabs. I was a true water baby and utterly fearless. Even though Berry and Brad weren't going to be around, I just knew it was going to be a great summer. The best one ever, maybe.

If only.

CHAPTER SIX

The meteorologists say the weekend is going to be a washout. The remnants of tropical storm Hugo, currently battering the Carolinas, are on a direct path for the East End according to the computer models. I hope they're wrong, but they're not. The drive out to Water Mill late Friday clocks in at a miserable five hours due to the pouring rain and numerous fender benders. I pick up an order of Thai and settle in for a Hulu night. But at least I have my umbrella.

Cassie elects to stay in Providence since the weather is so lousy. I'm sure that's not the only reason. While the divide between me and Cassie still seems wide, the last several times we've spoken she doesn't seem so distant and cold. Maybe the peonies are bridging the gap. Cassie perks up when I admit that I've made an appointment with Dr. Chris Richter; he's on the list of therapists Cassie's sent me. I assure her repeatedly that I take her concerns seriously. *Fuck, yes.*

"It's a start," she says.

I back off, satisfied.

As I eat my dinner, I think about the call I got while I was driving. "James" is close to retiring from the New York City

Police Department—high ranking—and I promised him long ago that I'd never compromise his identity or his pension. When we first ran into each other, he was a flatfoot on the bunco squad. I was in my *annus horribilis*—one of many—selling cheap neckties and knock-off designer bags on city street corners by day. At night, I wrote mediocre short stories on an old typewriter with a bum "A" key. James would hand me a ticket for peddling without a license. I'd throw the ticket away, high-tail it to another street and get another ticket. Like a dunce, I gave him Dad's address. Eventually, Dad ended up getting hundreds of tickets. I don't know if they were ever paid. Nan—my then girlfriend who became my first wife—wanted to be a model for *Vogue* but at five foot two, the only jobs she got were posing in lingerie for the Sears catalog. We lived in a walk-up over a restaurant run by the mob that never had any customers.

"Brooks, don't make the mistake of underestimating Dodge's good-old-boy demeanor," James warns. "He's a certified bloodhound. And for some reason, you're on his radar. He used to be in homicide—a real pain in the ass—until he wrangled a transfer out east thanks to his pops being a big union honcho. Everyone was glad to get rid of the bastard. Don't antagonize him. He'll make your life fucking miserable."

"What about Clemente?" I ask.

"She's a peach. Nice family. I hear she makes a mean curry goat."

I don't sleep any better at Water Mill. The Thai was too spicy. After tossing and turning with heartburn, I give up at dawn. The contractor's coming by at ten, so I go out early and buy coffee and donuts. From what I've seen thus far, the renovations are going well. The kitchen is nearly done. Cassie will be pleased they were able to fit in the outrageously expensive eight-burner commercial stove she pined for.

We'd gone into contract just a few months before Covid broke. The seller went down a little and we went up a little. Now the realtor says we could easily list the house for triple what we paid even without the renovations. That we might have a bidding war—four pristine acres in a prime South Fork location is a rarity and supply is scarce. I'm not interested. I can envision Cassie and me growing old in this house—that is, if there's still a Cassie and me.

The meeting with the contractor goes as I expect. For what I'm paying him, he should've bought breakfast. He assures me yet again that the house and pool will be ready by Memorial Day—it's early April, still plenty of time, he insists. I intend to hold him to our deadline. I've spent a mint on the house upgrades, but the fixes for the pool and outdoor patio have sent the budget into the stratosphere. Naturally, we must have a new pool heater, a cutting-edge saltwater system, water slides for the kiddies, a jacuzzi, plus a gourmet outdoor kitchen with a wood-burning pizza oven imported from Italy for the grown-ups. Oh, and three firepits for cold winter nights. Cassie doesn't know about all this; it's really a love letter to her, this house.

Later, the landscaper joins us. An old-timer, he's worked for Martha Stewart and Steven Spielberg. We survey the grounds. He says we need more sprinkler zones and retaining walls. I have a couple of ideas of my own: a gazebo in the extended peony garden and a pirate ship playhouse for the kids. I toss out some numbers, they throw some back, and we happily meet in the middle.

It's a little past one when they leave. Thankfully, the storm's over and the sun starts to peep through a bank of stray clouds. There's even a rainbow. Before I decide on lunch, I call Cassie. They're having a picnic. I hear Mark and Audra yell in the background. I tell her to take lots of pictures and videos. I miss them so much. How the fuck did I get to be such a goddamn softy in my old age? Heroin Hemingway, my ass.

I'm just about to call in an order for a salad when my cell

phone rings. It's a number I don't recognize, but I pick it up anyway, just in case.

"Hey, Mr. B," Marilyn, my second wife, purrs. The "B" is for bastard or big depending on her mood.

I grimace. How the hell did she get my number? I can't get rid of Marilyn. She's like a bad case of the crabs. We met at Elton John's Oscar party. I was thirty-five and the new Thomas Wolfe —I've been the new something every other decade or so. She was twenty-four with fake boobs, an aspiring ingenue. The next Camilla Sparv or Britt Ekland. Forty-eight hours later we got married at a Las Vegas wedding chapel. Elvis—disguised as a doorman—was a witness. I barely remember it. I've no explanation for the marriage other than it felt like a good idea at the time. We fucked like rabbits but never lived under the same roof. Two years into this fiasco, she announced she was pregnant. I could've been the father or any number of John Does. She didn't want a child, any child. I gave her five thousand dollars. The procedure was legal then. I expected her to go to a reputable doctor. But Marilyn, being a fucking cheapskate, elected a do-it-yourself method that ended up with her losing her uterus and ovaries. After the divorce, we were addict/fuck buddies off and on, but that lunacy had been over long before Cassie. "What the hell do you want?" I bark.

"Come on, Brooks, don't be such an ass. It wasn't all bad," Marilyn coos.

"It was, and I have the therapy bills to prove it. Don't tell me you've burned through our settlement. You're not getting another dime from me."

She laughs this irritating baby doll laugh and thinks it's a turn-on. It's not. "I heard you were out east all by your lonesome and I thought you could use some company." We still travel in the same social circles, so it wouldn't have been difficult for her to get my new number and address.

"Sorry, that's a hell to the fuck no," I say emphatically.

"You sure? I could be there in a half-hour."

"If you do, I'll call the police."

"And here I thought you'd be broken up about Marshall Reagan." She pauses to catch her breath. "You know, the toad hit me up about you."

I'm not surprised. I've heard as much through the grapevine. "What did you tell him?"

"Nothing. Because you never talked to me about it."

This is true.

"It's your last chance, Brooks." She lowers her voice. Why do I get the feeling that someone else is listening? "I still get wet remembering how you loved to fuck me hard from behind. I felt your dick all the way in my throat. And when you'd come and make me lick—"

I hung up, disgusted with myself that I hadn't done it sooner. I make a mental note to ask Miss Drake to get me a new number.

The phone rings again. I hesitate for a second until I realize it's Cassie. "Baby, you're never going to believe who just called me—"

"Brooks." Cassie's voice sounds off-kilter.

She doesn't say another word. She doesn't have to. I know something terrible has happened. "Cassie, what's wrong?" I hear screams in the background.

"It's Audra." She bursts into sobs. "She was fucking attacked!"

For a moment, I think I've misunderstood Cassie. Audra attacked? The back of my head pounds and my throat goes dry.

"It mauled her! The fucking animal! Her legs!" she screeches, barely sounding human.

Mauled. It's a horrible word—even more horrible images flash. This can't be happening, and certainly not to my beautiful Audra. Mauled by what? A bear? A coyote? A raccoon? A wolf? There are no fucking wolves in Providence. I try to stay calm, but my mind is like a tornado. "Where the fuck are you?"

"We're going to the hospital. They just put her—I don't know where we're going. Brooks, I don't know where," she spits out, on the verge of hysterics.

"I'll find out, don't worry. Hang on, baby. Tell Audra that Daddy's on his way." I think of Mark. Dear God in sweet fucking Heaven, not him too. My *Star Wars* warrior. How could our kids be mauled in broad daylight? "Mark. Was he attacked too?"

Cassie cries too hard to reply. The line goes dead.

Useless fucking cell phone. Frustrated, I bang it against the counter. "Fuck, fuck, fuck!" I scream.

CHAPTER SEVEN

Once I call Sheldon and things are set in motion, it feels like a blur and that it's all happening to someone else. He and his wife Phoebe are stunned speechless. I'd casually and briefly dated Phoebe, a brainy staff writer for *Saturday Night Live* (think Tina Fey with thicker glasses), before she dumped me for some random dude she met at a book signing. We'd done nothing improper or even mildly inappropriate, but I was still miffed. My ego was bigger than the Goodyear blimp. What woman in their right mind would dump me? When I learned that the random dude was Sheldon, I was delighted. I still am. They're perfect for each other. I was the best man at their wedding. We vacation together. They are Audra's godparents.

Sheldon says not to worry, he'll take care of everything. He'll get my car back to Manhattan. Within minutes, a helicopter lands on the acre I'd cleared for the peony garden and the pirate playhouse. I don't know what strings he's pulled, but I owe him. We are in mid-air when Sheldon calls. I can hardly hear him through the whir of the blades. "Brooks, they're at Rhode Island Hospital, it's affiliated with Brown. It's the best goddamn trauma center in the region. Audra couldn't be in better hands. You'll be met by a police escort." He hesitates. "It's already on the fucking internet."

"What's already on the fucking internet?" I ask, perplexed. I can't imagine what it can be.

"The attack. Probably off a neighborhood Ring or security camera. I bet they saw a big payday, the motherfucking parasites." He begs me not to watch it, and I promise.

The fucking animal story. Cassie and I giggled about it. We'd be in bed watching the eleven o'clock news and wonder what animal story would run. We were rarely disappointed. Mama Bear protectively helps her cubs across a busy highway. The cat whose head got stuck in a bottle. A flock of wild turkeys gamboling across a lawn. And my all-time personal favorite, the bull that broke out of a slaughterhouse; that story had been an endless source of hilarity for weeks. Now, my own animal story was probably the lead. *Fucking A.*

Of course, I watch the goddamn video. The quality isn't bad as these things go. Tammy and her husband Rob—a state trooper assigned to the Governor's detail—have a large, fenced-in backyard, big but not too big. Cassie and Tammy go in and out of the house and put food on the patio table. Audra kicks a ball around. Mark is by the fence with his *Star Wars* lightsaber. And inexplicably, there is Dad in his ratty, rumpled, brown corduroy jacket, a relic from his university days, sitting in a lawn chair not far from Audra. I'm bewildered. What the fuck is Dad doing there? I've no time to ponder that because out of the corner of the screen a big beige ball tears across the yard and ferociously clamps down on Audra.

The screams. There's no word to describe them. If I'd been in a car, I would've pulled over and puked my guts out. But I'm in a helicopter. We can't make a pit-stop. I gag and choke the vomit down.

The next thing I see is Dad flying toward Audra. He's armed with the lawn chair and whomps the beast with it. Dad's physically active for a man of his advanced age—he plays squash three times a week, he does daily laps in a pool—but I had no clue that he could move so fast or that he was so strong. After a couple of good whacks, the dog finally releases Audra, but instead of running away, the animal turns on Dad and chomps down on his arm. Dad doesn't flinch or yowl; he's a tough old nut.

Me, I'm in such a rage that I could tear the dog's fucking head off with my bare teeth.

Cassie's now in the fray. She throws a bowl at the dog—it looks like it was filled with potato salad—and then takes off her sneakers and thwacks the dog over and over. It's going to take more than Nikes to stop this beast. Tammy holds a screaming Mark back. Finally, Rob, in a white undershirt, smiley face boxers, and moccasins, rushes up with a gun. He pushes Cassie aside and with his free hand manages to get the dog off Dad. Rob hurls the psycho dog like a javelin and then aims and shoots it. It's almost like a ballet maneuver. You'd think the dog would give up, that it'd had enough. Hell, no. *Cujo Two* keeps charging, its fur matted with blood. Rob gets off two more shots right into the dog's head. It's gruesome. The dog twitches, then stops moving. Thankfully the video ends, one minute and forty-three seconds of mayhem. My first thought: the video shows that Audra didn't do anything to provoke the animal. My second: Jesus, all the animal activists will be up in arms. My third: boo fucking hoo.

As Sheldon promised, there's a police escort to the trauma center. Reporters circle like vultures and shout questions as I rush past them, head down. I'm sorely tempted to tell them to fuck off, but I resist and ignore them.

Cassie is in a private waiting room right off the Emergency Room. I see her before she sees me. Her hands and clothes are smeared with blood. She bursts into tears and collapses into my arms.

"Where is she? Where's Dad and Mark?" I ask.

It takes a few moments for Cassie to speak. I've never seen her so upset. Ever. I want to kill the dog all over again, but I push my fury aside and focus on Cassie.

"Mark's with Rob and Tammy at their house," she finally says. "They took your father in another ambulance. He didn't want to go, but Rob insisted."

I don't like Rob much—he's a bit too much of a gung-ho macho man for my taste and I suspect he voted for Trump—but what he did today cancels that.

Cassie clings to me. "Bernard. Thank God for him. He fucking saved Audra."

Which led me to my next question. "Why was he there? How did he know you were at your sister's?"

"He called me last night. He said he missed the kids and that you told him we were at Tammy's. He was in the area visiting friends for the weekend, but he didn't think he'd have time to come by. Then he called later this morning and asked if he could spend the afternoon with us because his plans had changed. Honestly, I almost said no."

Mystery solved. Dad has friends near and far: ex-pats, diplomatic pals, and retired (and not so retired) politicos. He's a frequent house guest and always brings a bottle of expensive wine. He can't drive anymore—his cataract surgery notwithstanding—but he still has a car and a chauffeur and makes good use of both. Frankly, the only thing that surprised me was Dad confessing he missed the kids. Dad isn't an absent grandfather, let me be clear. He comes to the birthday parties and goes dutifully overboard at Christmas. But Dad isn't a doting grandparent. It's on his terms and when he's available. He's around and then he's not. But this time, Dad's exactly where he needed to be. Audra is alive because of him. I shudder to think what would've happened otherwise.

Cassie stares at me. "Shit. I just remembered."

"Remembered what, baby?"

"Dad said the dog nipped him." She nods, her face chalky. "I was in the kitchen with Tammy. Dad came in and said the dog had lunged and nipped him for no apparent reason. He asked if the dog was safe to be around the kids. Tammy assured him that Rover was a cuddle buddy, a loveable golden puffball. They researched the breed, and it was considered one of the best among young kids. A goldendoodle." Tammy and Rob don't have kids yet and don't seem to be in a rush, if you ask me. "Tammy said that Rover was just being playful, and Dad took it the wrong way." Cassie's chest heaves with fresh sobs. "This is my fault. If we had gone with you to Water Mill like you wanted—"

I cradle and kiss her. "No, baby, you can't think like that. There was no way for you to know that the cuddle buddy was *Jaws* in disguise. None. It was a fucking accident." I say this for Cassie's sake, but I want to throttle Tammy, a smug know-it-all with bleached unibrows who grows her own organic heirloom tomatoes and buys fancy free-range eggs.

"Her leg, Brooks. There was so much blood. You weren't there, you didn't see."

It's not the time or place to tell Cassie about the horrific video.

"What if she loses her leg? Or she can't walk? What if she's maimed for life? What if—" She puts her hand over her mouth, her eyes feral.

"She's going to be fine," I assure her.

"You don't know that for sure," she exclaims.

And she's right, of course. I don't know a goddamn thing.

The door swings open. It's a middle-aged man in hospital scrubs: Dr. Mowbray according to his name tag. Dark brown hair, a manicured goatee, Indian descent. "Mr. and Mrs. Anderson?" he asks in a clipped accent.

I take a step. "Our daughter. How is she?" I don't recognize my voice; it's strangled and foreign. I'm back in the hospital when Audra was born far too early at twenty-four weeks due to Cassie's placenta previa. Audra was just a little over a pound, a wrinkled raisin obscenely hooked up to a maze of tubes and machines. The doctors told us to hope for the best but prepare for the worst. Cassie, a lapsed Catholic, insisted that the baby had to be baptized immediately. Dad, who is agnostic, roused a cardinal from St. Patrick's at four in the morning. Audra Beatrice was baptized before the sun rose. It was a crisis every hour, but she defied the odds at every turn. As I sat by Audra's incubator, I begged Mom to watch over her and made all kinds of promises to God—any god, I didn't care who or what. Later that day, I found a penny on the floor and took it as a sign that someone up there heard my pleas, despite my many transgressions. I had the lucky penny encased in plastic; it never leaves my wallet.

When Audra was six months old, we were finally able to bring her home. That long first night, Cassie and I stayed by her crib and watched her breathe. The doctors were cheerfully pessimistic; yes, Audra had come this far but she might be developmentally delayed or prone to infection and illness. Once again, Audra proved them wrong, meeting and sometimes exceeding her milestones. Now a healthy spitfire, you'd never know that she'd been at death's door. She jabbers like a blue jay and bosses Mark like a Mafia don. I can't imagine a world without my sweet Audra in it.

When Cassie's obstetrician reassured us that she could have another baby, that the placenta issue was rare and unlikely to occur again, I smiled and nodded and thought no fucking way. Cassie had almost died giving birth to Audra. I wasn't about to risk her life or the life of our unborn child. I've never been a fan of condoms, but after that ordeal, I used them religiously. I mean, I used them until my vasectomy. It's funny, Cassie never asked why I stopped. I don't think she liked them much either.

Dr. Mowbray smiles. "The surgery went well."

Surgery. My knees buckle. It's only because Cassie's holding on to me that I manage to stay upright.

"Twenty-five stitches on her forearm. It was fortunate she was wearing a thick sweater. Excellent insulation. And no wounds to her face. Not even a scratch." He takes a breath.

I've been around enough doctors to know this isn't good. I brace myself.

"But we are concerned about her leg injuries. In particular, the right leg."

Cassie buries her head in my chest.

"The canine bites were significant, leading to substantial blood loss. We anticipate some permanent or residual damage to soft tissue, nerves, muscles, and tendons. Of course, we won't know the extent for some time." Dr. Mowbray stops when he sees my look of sheer terror. "But we must think positive. In the best-case scenario, your daughter may only require minimal plastic surgery and rehabilitation."

"And the worst?" I ask.

"We don't deal with hypotheticals, Mr. Anderson. Now, we're giving her a round of antibiotics to ward off infection. We will be watching her closely for the next forty-eight hours."

"Is she going to lose her leg?" Cassie whimpers. She has my arm in a death grip.

"No, no." Dr. Mowbray seems genuinely startled, the first real sign of emotion beneath his placid professional demeanor. "Your little girl should recover in due time. Children that age are strong and resilient. There's no reason to expect any other outcome. But that brings me to my next concern. The video."

"What video?" Cassie tugs my sleeve.

"I'll explain later," I murmur.

"Since the attack was unprovoked and the animal's history is uncertain or unreliable, we've begun vaccine treatments."

I go blank. "Vaccine? For what?"

"Rabies, Mr. Anderson."

Cassie stifles a scream.

Fucking *Cujo*. I hate that goddamn movie. I'm sorry, Stephen King.

"The standard course of treatment is four injections over fourteen days. We will do the same with the elderly gentleman as a precaution. He is—" He looks at me.

"My father," I proudly say.

Dr. Mowbray turns to Cassie. "And you, Mrs. Anderson. No bites? No punctures or scratches?"

"No, I'm fine. Our son, too, he wasn't—" Cassie grabs my hand. Her wedding ring digs into my palm. It feels good. "When can we see her? When can she come home?"

"I take it you don't live in Providence?"

"Our primary residence is Manhattan," I answer.

"The next few days are critical. But when she improves, we can consider transferring her. Dr. Shannon at New York-Presbyterian is one of the top pediatric plastic surgeons in the country. I know him personally. I will call him on your behalf and brief him on the case."

"Thank you, Dr. Mowbray, for taking care of our little girl." The doctor's no Dr. Marcus Welby, but I sense he genuinely cares about Audra.

"Please may I see her now?" Cassie sounds like Oliver asking for another bowl of gruel.

"Very well, but only one parent at a time."

I patted Cassie on the back. "You go first. I'll find out how Dad's doing."

Cassie shoots me a look of quiet gratitude. "*Love you*," she silently mouths.

"Love you more," I whisper. And I did. I'd been an asshole for so many fucking years. A part of me still couldn't believe that a fine woman like Cassie—warm, engaging, brilliant—was with a sad, pathetic, imperfect lug like me. Yet here we are.

As I wait for news about Dad, I check my phone. There's an avalanche of texts and voicemails from friends, the press, you name it. In the copter, I texted Miss Drake and instructed her to issue a boilerplate statement asking for privacy during this difficult time—good luck with that. Miss Drake was distraught when I told her what had happened; she loves Mark and Audra to bits and is their honorary grandma.

I scroll down; there are messages from the governor, senators, and even the president. To be honest, the only other time I'd gotten so many messages was when I'd been nominated for an Academy Award for Best Original Screenplay. The movie was garbage—the producers were cokehead fuckwads—but at least the check cleared, and I accrued enough credits to join the Writer's Guild. I didn't win that year, but my consolation prize was a hand-job under the table from the wife of a famous actor. Oh, those were the days.

Impatient, I go into the hallway and spot Dad in a wheelchair. He's being pushed by an orderly who sports a thatch of scraggly Chia Pet hair.

"Brooks, will you kindly tell this young man that I'm capable of ferrying myself around," Dad grumbles.

I sigh, relieved. Dad's okay, ornery, and cantankerous as ever.

"Sir, as I've explained, as long as you're in the hospital—" the Chia Pet orderly starts.

"That's okay. I'll take it from here. I'm his son." I fish in my back pocket, take out my wallet, and hand the orderly a hundred-dollar bill. "Treat the family to a nice dinner tonight."

The Chia Pet orderly mumbles thanks and shambles off.

I push Dad over to a bank of windows. "How are you feeling?"

"Why does everyone keep asking me that? I'm fine. Just a scratch." He shoves the sleeve of his jacket up a few inches. A bandage covers his arm. "Sixteen stitches."

"That's not a scratch, Dad," I say, my tongue thick. I cuff the old badger's neck. "We owe you big time, Dad. When I think of what could've happened. If you hadn't been there, if you hadn't—"

"Son, please. I did what you or anyone else with an ounce of courage would've done. And don't forget, Cassie was no slouch either. I was looking forward to that potato salad. It had bacon in it. The goddamn doctor says I can't have bacon that often." He sounds wistful. "What about Audra?"

"The doctor says she should be okay. Potentially, she might need plastic surgery and rehab." It hurts just to say it.

Dad shakes his head and grimaces. "At least she had that sweater and pants on. I had a bad feeling about that mutt from the get-go. The beast damn near tore my hand off. I told your sister-in-law, but she thought I was exaggerating. As if I'm some kind of doddering fool." He sounds properly offended.

Dad doesn't like public outbursts of affection, but I embrace him anyway. "What the hell were you doing in Providence? Visiting friends?"

"Mmm. Milton and Whitney Abrams. Milton was an undersecretary at the State Department. Whitney makes a darn good paella. They were stationed in Spain for several years. There was an estate sale and Milton thought we'd pick up some good buys." Dad's a huge coin collector. As a kid, I watched him as he inspected old coins with a magnifying glass. "I got the dates mixed up, it's next weekend. Anyway, since I'd checked into my hotel and I'd already spoken to Cassie, I wanted to see my grandchildren. It's been far too long. Mark's growing like a weed. And that little Audra, what a personality." He stares at me, anguished. "She's going to be okay, isn't she? You're not hiding something from me?"

Dad's concern touches me deeply. "No, no. The doctor was extremely optimistic." I take a breath. "They started the rabies shots."

"With me as well. It's a nuisance to be sure, but I certainly don't want my brain to turn to yogurt." Dad leans back in his chair, exhausted. He looks his age and more. "They wanted me to stay overnight for observation. I told them it was out of the question. Save the room for someone who really needs it."

"Dad, maybe you should—"

He waves me off. "How long are they going to keep Audra?"

"I'm not sure. They're already looking into transferring her to a hospital in Manhattan when she's—" I nearly say out of danger. "Better."

"That's good." He smiles. "A good sign."

"A really good sign."

A perky woman with a blonde bob in a polished blue Hillary Clinton pantsuit walks up. Her name tag boasts: *H. Holliday, Sr. Concierge Manager*. "Mr. Anderson?"

"Yes?" Dad and I chirp.

"Good afternoon. It's a pleasure to meet you. I'm Hayley Holliday. I'll be your personal liaison for your stay. Anything you need, I'm delighted to assist you." She sounds as if we're VIP guests in a luxury five-star resort on the French Riviera instead of a trauma hospital because my kid has been viciously mauled and possibly maimed for life by a golden puffball. "We have a gorgeous suite entirely at your disposal if you'd like to get some rest. A mini-kitchen and bar, sleeping accommodations for four, a private bath and shower, hot tub, and complimentary wifi."

I'm tempted to ask if it includes travel bottles of body wash and shampoo. "Thank you. I'm fine for the time being. Do you need my insurance information? I don't think anyone's asked for that."

"It's all been taken care of, Mr. Anderson. The suite as well. You just focus on your daughter's well-being."

Sheldon's one efficient son of a bitch.

"That's good to know. I think my father's tired, although he won't admit it."

"Don't worry about me," Dad growls. "I have a suite at the Admiralty. And it's paid for through Tuesday. I'm not going to let that view go to waste."

"The Admiralty is only a short drive. The hospital has a complimentary car, you can use it as long as necessary. Would you like that, Mr. Anderson?"

"I would indeed." Dad grabs my hand. "Call me as soon as you get any news. Or text. Whichever. I'm going to order a porterhouse, medium rare. It's a pity I can't drink anything because of these goddamn meds. I had a very expensive bottle of wine on ice." Ms, Miss, or Mrs. Holliday whisks Dad down the corridor.

I check my cell again. There are a couple of voicemails from Detective Dodge. The fucking nerve to bother me at this time. I delete his messages without listening to them. Now I'm getting antsy. What's taking Cassie so long? Has Audra taken a turn for the worse? Dr. Mowbray's words about the next several days being critical play like a loop in my head.

"Hey, brother."

I look up. It's Sheldon in a rumpled sweat-suit and sneakers. He looks as bad as I feel. We hug ferociously. "You didn't have to come. I know Bella has a cold." Bella's his youngest, eighteen months old. What a charmer. Cheeks like Red Delicious apples. She could be a Gerber baby.

"You couldn't keep me away. What kind of a godparent would I be? And Phoebe, she's a goddamn wreck, she hasn't stopped crying over that fucking video. You know it's gone viral? CNN, Fox, *Daily Mail*, the *NY Post*. The animal do-gooders have their pitchforks ready. PETA is calling for an investigation."

I'm incredulous and livid. "An investigation of what?"

"Into how the dog was treated. Was he abused? Is that why he went psycho? Was the video doctored? Why did he have to shoot the dog? Why didn't he use a Taser?"

I throw my hands up in disgust. I've more important things to deal with. "My daughter could be damaged and scarred for life. Pardon me if I don't give a goddamn Tootsie Roll about the fucking dog."

"I'm with you, buddy. We're all praying for Audra. She'll pull through, I know it. And your dad?"

"You know him, he's as tough as they come. Brass balls. It's going to take a hell of a lot more than a rabid dog to get him down."

Sheldon clears his throat. "That's great. Look, I hate to bring this up now, but we have to take care of some business."

I groan.

"I know, I know. I hate to lay it on you, but—Max is breaking my chops. They want a second season. Everyone does. Nicole Kidman, Mark Ruffalo, even Richard Dreyfuss."

I laugh. "What is wrong with these dumb fucks? There is no second season. Everyone's dead." Nicole was strangled, Mark "accidentally" fell into a woodchipper, and Richard—well, parts of him—are scattered over the Eastern seaboard.

"They don't care. And they're willing to pay through the nose. What do you want me to tell them?"

I'm not in the mood to deal with these morons. "Tell them I'll think about it, okay?"

"Fine, that's better than a flat no. But get a load of this." He pauses dramatically. "Amazon is in negotiations to pick up the rights to *Fallen Angels*."

I snort. This project is like Lazarus, it keeps rising from the dead. "Do they know how much it's going to cost them to pick up the rights? The last time I totaled it, it was close to six million."

"It's Jeff Fucking Bezos, it's a drop in the bucket to him. He wants it, he says it's a prestige project. And he's probably the only one aside from Netflix who could afford it. But he has one condition: he wants you to rewrite the last draft and make it more, you know, uh, family friendly."

I give Sheldon a side-eye. More family friendly? Is he out of his fucking mind? Has Jeff Fucking Bezos even read the damn book? "Sure, sure," I mutter, not meaning it. Over the years, I'd written a dozen different adaptations of the fucking book, and most of them were for free. I'm done with it. "Anything else?"

"Yeah. One more thing. I'm sorry to have to tell you this, Brooks." He coughs. "It's Nan."

I shrug. "Nan who?"

"You know—your first wife. She passed away last night."

What the hell? I haven't spoken to Nan in decades. Our marriage was fueled by our two shared passions: drugs and sex. When the drugs petered out, so did the sex. After six tumultuous years, we got an acrimonious divorce. At the time, I was feeding off the trough of a small stipend that Grandpa William had left me. The only asset I had was a draft of *Fallen Angels*. Sheldon was a junior agent then and had submitted the manuscript to every publishing house in the city. It was soundly rejected. I still have the letter that Sheldon got from the senior Random House editor: *"Dear Mr. Adler, you couldn't pay us to publish this drivel. I took ten hot showers after reading it and I still feel dirty."*

But Sheldon pressed on, undeterred. Eventually, he talked a small but reputable press up the Hudson into acquiring it. No advance, royalty only. I was thrilled. A year later, the book is published and sinks like a stone in the ocean. No critic worth his or her salt bothered to review it. I'm crushed.

Now I'm working part-time in a bookstore in Brooklyn. I'm convinced my writing career is as dead as the enormous turkey hanging in the butcher's window in *A Christmas Carol*. I write oddball pornographic short stories for men's magazines under the pen name "Ernst Hempway"—clever, eh? I'm barely able to buy the drugs I need to keep my addiction in check. I'm to the point where I almost want to inject bleach into my veins and be done with it all. I hadn't yet hit rock bottom, but I was pretty damn near close.

And then—drum roll—yes, the fucking tooth story, which I've related gleefully to Stephen Colbert and Jimmy Fallon. It almost sounds like a joke: a man with an abscessed tooth on vacation with his family in the Catskills goes to the dentist on a hot July morning. In the waiting room, the dentist had a box filled with discarded books. The books are basically fireplace fodder. The man with the bum tooth spotted my book in that pile and began reading it while he waited. As it turned out, that patient was the senior book critic for *The New York Times*. When he returned from his vacation, he wrote a glowing, front-page review of it in the Sunday edition, the kind of review one can only dream about if you're high on crack. Because of this critic's rotten tooth, my life changed in an instant. I'm suddenly hailed as a new literary sensation and I wasn't poor—well, not *as* poor—anymore.

And how does this tie into Nan, my first ex-wife? Because in our divorce, since the book was my only asset, Nan's astute divorce lawyer stipulated that she was to get fifteen percent of any future royalties I might receive from *Fallen Angels* in perpetuity or until either one of us died. Since at the time I didn't think I was going to last two more years, I signed the damn papers without a second thought or getting another opinion, which I couldn't afford. It was one of the most epic mistakes of my life. I promised myself that if I ever got enough money in hand, I'd pay off both Nan and Marilyn for good. And that's exactly what I did. Marilyn had been a tough negotiator, fighting over pennies, but Nan had promptly accepted my lawyer's lowball offer. And now Sheldon says she's dead? Right after she cashed my goddamn check?

"Are you sure?" I ask.

"I read about it on TMZ on the way here. She was in a bad way, she lost her parents and brother last year. It looks like an overdose."

"Jesus," I mutter, contrite. I had no idea. Nan's only two years younger than I am.

"As Sinatra said, that's life. You should have Miss Drake write up a statement."

Sheldon's right. Although Nan cost me dearly with that stupid stipulation, I never wished her ill or harm. "You're right. Something to the effect that I hope Nan finds the peace in the next life that eluded her in this one." Cheesy, but effective. Miss Drake can clean it up.

Sheldon shot me a look. "Not *her*. The damn dog."

I snort. Sheldon must be joking. He's not. "What do you mean, the dog?"

"Well, you know—that it all happened so quickly and there was no other way."

I stood, infuriated. I don't get angry at Sheldon that often. The last time, hell, I can't even remember what it was. It couldn't have been of any consequence. "Oh, maybe I should also apologize for Audra getting in the way of the dog's teeth while he chomped on her leg."

Sheldon's face turns beet red. "That's not what I meant, Brooks. You know that. But your brother-in-law is getting death threats. And it's not just from the animal nutjobs. It's from some of your fans."

Death threats? This is insane.

Sheldon takes out his cell and shows me a Facebook Live stream: protesters camped out at Tammy's place chanting and holding signs: *"Dog Abuser," "Animal Killer," "Dogs Have Rights Too,"* and similar tripe.

I clench my teeth. What the hell is this screwy world coming to when a dog's life is more valuable than a child's? What if it had been their kid? "Rob's a fucking hero. They should give him the keys to the city. Hell, I would've ripped the dog's throat out with my bare hands."

My phone pings. Finally, a text from Cassie; she's taken a photo of Audra. My stomach drops at the sight of our baby so helpless in a hospital bed. I show the picture to Sheldon. "I don't want to hear another word about that goddamn dog."

"How's Mark doing?" Sheldon asks, now mollified. "Is he still at your sister-in-law's?"

I nod. Poor Mark. I need to call him and make sure he's okay.

"That's the main reason I'm here. Why don't I take him to my house? You guys have enough on your hands. I'm working from home this week; we'll have a blast. And you know Levi would love it." Levi is Sheldon's oldest son, born six months after Mark. The two boys are inseparable.

"Are you sure?" I hate to impose, but I don't relish the idea of Mark staying with Tammy and Rob, especially if their house is under siege.

"Phoebe's already got the spare bedroom ready." Sheldon lives in Park Slope in a vintage brownstone, a real showplace, that he'd inherited from a great-uncle.

"Thank you, Shel. You're the best." And he is.

"Nothing to thank me for. You keep the Max suits dangling so I can juice the price up," Sheldon says with a sly grin and wink-wink.

I check my phone again. Another text from Cassie: *Baby is waking up.*

"Audra's starting to rouse. I have to go. I'll let Tammy know you're coming to get Mark." I sprint down the corridor then stop. I don't even know what floor they're on. I begin to text Cassie when I get a call from Aunt Flo.

"Brooks, Althea just told me what happened." Aunt Flo's voice trembles. "Please tell me the baby will be okay."

"I think so, but we have to keep an eye on her. I'm just on my way to see her. As soon as I know more, I'll call back."

Her relief is palpable. "Thank God. I was so worried. Please give Cassie my best and kiss Audra for me." She stops for a second. "Brooks, after your visit, I remembered something."

I'm impatient to hang up, and I'm not really paying attention. All I can think about is Audra. I'll move heaven and hell to make her better. If Dr. Shannon won't take her case, I vow to find someone who will. "Aunt Flo, I don't mean to be rude but—"

"It's about the Jurgen family. The father, I believe his name was Bjorn or Benny or something like that. He was a colleague of your father's. They rented one of your grandfather's cottages that summer."

I remember the Jurgen kids; how could I not? Sigrid, a slight, sad girl with long blonde pigtails, was two years older than me. We played Doctor in the dunes. When Sigrid described to me in graphic detail how babies were made, I was horrified and insisted it was anatomically impossible. She had an older brother—Tor, fifteen or so, a mean, cruel son of a bitch who liked to bash the small garden frogs we'd find with rocks. Palmer called him a rotten egg. When we told Mom about Tor, she sternly forbade us from playing with the Jurgen kids. I was mildly disappointed. I wanted to hear more about this baby thing.

"Your grandfather would have never rented the cottage to them if he had known. About Bjorn or Benny. He was a fugitive from Sweden—a pedophile." She lowers her voice. "He bolted on the eve of his trial and came to the States under an assumed identity. It was in all the papers. Barely a month after your mother and Palmer passed, the Jurgen family died in a head-on collision on Dune Road."

Aunt Flo has my attention now.

CHAPTER EIGHT

I'm not exactly sure when Julian Broadhurst and his Aston Martin came into our lives. The days were long and lazy in Ditch Plains. Palmer and I had a routine that we'd perfected. We'd get up early, watch cartoons (my favorite was Road Runner, his was Mr. Magoo) and wolf down cereal. While Mom took a shower, we'd head out for the day. We'd ride our bikes, hang out at the beach, or play games in someone's basement or backyard. Some days Mom would tell us to come home for lunch and afterward, we'd find another place to go for the afternoon. Back then, people didn't worry about what their kids were doing when they were out of sight. We'd return home around five or so. Mom would fix us dinner, we'd take showers, and then watch TV (if the reception and weather permitted). By nine we'd be in bed. As we dozed off, Mom listened to the radio and enjoyed a glass of wine as she read through her slush pile. She adored the Rolling Stones and that summer their songs seemed to be on constant rotation: "Under My Thumb," "Paint It Black," and "19th Nervous Breakdown."

Just because Mom was on "vacation" didn't mean that she didn't work. She started out in an entry-level position in public relations at Random House and worked her way into the children's department as an editor. In those days, being an editor of children's books was pretty much the career graveyard for anyone with intelligence and ambition, and Mom had plenty of both. But she truly loved it. I later learned that she'd been a champion of Theodor Seuss Geisel—otherwise known as Dr. Seuss—who hadn't been a real doctor at all. I know poor Dr. Seuss has fallen into disrepute, but he gave us the Grinch, for fuck's sake.

I remember the stacks of manuscripts that Mom toted home to read. The manuscripts—all bound hard copies, since PDFs or doc files hadn't yet been invented—were piled against our living-room wall, the only place Mom could work and still keep a reasonable eye on us kids. Often, she'd read pages to us. If we fell asleep, she passed without going on. If we stayed awake, she'd put it aside for further review. I attribute my love of books and writing solely to her.

I gather that her job as a children's book editor had been a source of friction between my parents. Dad thought it was beneath her. I guess he eventually wore her down because in early January of 1964 she got a job at Simon & Schuster as an executive editor in their art department. She had her own office, a fancy business card, and was invited to all the gallery shows for new, up-and-coming artists. I believe that's where she first met Julian Broadhurst.

Palmer and I came home one day and the Aston Martin was parked in front of our house. Mom sat on the front porch. Next to her, holding a beer, was the long-haired man who, weeks later, bashed her head with a blunt object so hard that her coffin had to be closed at her funeral. Mom and the man seemed chummy. "Hey, Palmer, Brooks," Mom called. "This is Julian, he's a friend from work."

"Hello," I boomed. It pains me now to realize how innocent and trusting I was.

Palmer regarded this interloper with unconcealed suspicion. In Dad's absence, Palmer took his role as the de facto head of the household seriously.

Julian reached into his pocket and threw a couple of quarters at us. They landed on the small patch of sand and grass that was our front yard. "For ice cream," he said in a thick accent. I knew it was British— not suave, James Bond British, but close.

I picked the coins up. "Thank you," I chirped.

Palmer glowered. "When is Dad coming up?"

"Maybe this weekend," Mom answered.

"That's what you said last weekend," he shot back.

"Well, you can ask him yourself the next time he calls," Mom replied. "You probably talk to him more than I do."

I didn't know what to make of that remark. Dad usually called a couple of times a week to see how we were doing. Note I said "usually." He was always busy in the summer months. This summer, he seemed to be extra busy. To be honest, I couldn't remember the last time Dad had called.

That night, Mom invited Julian to stay for dinner: meat loaf, noodles, peas, and mushroom gravy. This was a Sunday meal, not a Wednesday one. Mom seemed very—what's the word?—hyper. Palmer kept his head down and pushed his peas around on his plate.

Later, after we were snug in bed, Palmer whispered to me. "I don't think Dad's coming at all."

"Of course he is," I whispered back. "Why wouldn't he?"

I heard Mom and Julian laughing in the living room. It sounded like they were having fun, and it seemed wrong to me. Mom shouldn't be having a good time when Dad wasn't around, I thought.

That is when Palmer hatched the idea of the monster.

CHAPTER NINE

I t's been ten days or so since the dog attack. We're back in the city. Audra's now under the care of Dr. Shannon, who is everything Dr. Mowbray said he would be and more. Although Audra's still in the hospital, she's healing nicely from her injuries. It looks like she may need plastic surgery—maybe not as much as the doctors initially thought—but Dr. Shannon says it's too early in her recovery to tell. But barring complications, we can probably take Audra home soon. She takes her rabies shots like a champ, not even a whimper. Lollipops and unicorn toys help.

Dad's doing remarkably well. He hasn't missed one session of squash. A private nurse administers his rabies shots, and he acquiesces with a fair amount of groans and grumbles. He's able to drink again, which helps his mood considerably. I know there are women fluttering around.

The media frenzy has died down since the police investigation officially cleared Rob. No less than the governor commends him for his selfless heroics. Meanwhile, PETA continues to rake in thousands of donations based on the video. I quip to the press that Rob should get a cut. I'm half-serious.

Naturally, the tabloids have nothing better to do than dig up my sordid history. I hung up on a reporter from the *Daily Mail*.

Miss Drake's able to confirm Aunt Flo's story about the Jurgen family. The father—his real name was Waldo Borgstrom—was an elementary schoolteacher accused of molestation. His subsequent escape from Sweden while under heavy police guard had been such a scandal that it nearly toppled the government. Once in the United States, a tipster alerted the FBI to his whereabouts. With the authorities closing in, he went on the run with his family and hit a deer. The car was totaled and burst into flames. The deer was never found.

We settle into a new routine. During the day, I take care of Mark while Cassie stays with Audra. It's the reverse at night. I watch Audra fall asleep as she hugs a unicorn toy that's twice her size. I bring my laptop and I'm able to get a shitload of work done on the new book. Well, up to page forty—but it's something. First drafts are garbage anyway.

Max is still nipping at my heels, and as Sheldon foretold, the price goes up the longer I hold out. Since I've no intention of writing a sequel, it's become a game so my "asks" are increasingly outlandish. I'm like a rock band that demands only brown M&M's backstage.

Jeff Fucking Bezos is still sniffing around *Fallen Angels*, but a new player is giving him agita: Elon Musk—of all people—who's now decided that he wants to make movies in addition to building cars and rocket ships. To each his own. As Sheldon says, this is getting ratfucking interesting.

Today, I exit the down elevator at the Dakota and see Detectives Dodge and Clemente in the foyer. *Shit.* I'd left Mark in the more than capable hands of Miss Drake while I went to my first therapy appointment with Dr. Richter, an extremely expensive analyst. To my credit, even with everything going on, I hadn't canceled or postponed. I'm determined to prove to Cassie that I deserve a second chance.

I haven't pressed her for anything. Cassie's cordial to a fault but there's a gap between us as wide as the Grand Canyon. I desperately want my wife back. I miss watching goofy movies with her at midnight with our toes touching or how she sneaks up on me when I'm in my lair and plants herself in my lap. The silence between us is deafening. I'd rather she yells at me and gets it all out. The truth—and I'm not ashamed to admit it—is that I need Cassie far more than she needs me. She can easily replace me with a better, younger, richer, and more handsome version. Cassie is in my blood, in every sinew of my being. I don't want anyone else. The idea of having sex with another woman repulses me. Me, the King of one-night stands.

With all this rattling in my head, the last thing I want is to deal with these two boneheads from Suffolk County. I manage a weak smile. "Nice to see you," I bleat. It's a lie and we all know it, pleasantries aside.

Detective Dodge shoots me a stern, schoolmarm look. If he thinks this is supposed to scare me, he's sadly mistaken. "I'm disappointed. You haven't returned my calls, Mr. Anderson."

"Well, Detective, I have been kind of preoccupied, if you read the papers."

"Is your daughter doing better?" Detective Clemente asks.

"She is, thank you. She's gotten so many unicorn toys we could open a store." It had gotten out that Audra loved unicorns and now we were overrun with critters. We let Audra pick out a few that she liked and donated the rest. Audra didn't need ten talking unicorns on a leash. "If you don't mind, can this wait? I'm on my way to an appointment."

"This won't take long." Detective Dodge's manner makes it clear that no isn't an acceptable answer.

I sigh and follow them to a couch in the lobby. We all sit down.

"Mr. Anderson, do you remember what you told us the last

time we spoke? About not leaving your apartment at all the night Marshall Reagan was killed?" Detective Dodge snaps.

"Yes, of course," I reply.

"And you're sure about that?"

Is he being deliberately obtuse? I give him my best dumb-as-rocks look. "Yes. I was home. I'm sure of it."

Detective Dodge whips out his cell phone. "Then how do you explain this?" He clicks on a link. It's a grainy security video of me in a T-shirt and boxers pacing in the corridor directly outside our apartment. "This was taken at three-fifteen in the morning—the morning that Marshall Reagan was killed. That is you, isn't it? That's not your body double?" He sounds and looks smug, as if he's caught me doing something monumental, like masturbating on a subway train during rush hour.

I stare at him, then at her. "Detective Dodge, I'm sleepwalking. I've done it since I was a kid. I've written about it in my books. I've been to sleep clinics. Hell, everyone in the goddamn building knows I sleepwalk."

"But that's not what you said, Mr. Anderson," he continues. "You said you never left your apartment."

Detective Clemente has the good sense to look embarrassed.

I'm not amused. "This is ridiculous. I had no idea until you showed me this. What do you want me to say? Look, have you checked the security cameras at the place where Reagan was murdered?"

Detective Dodge looks uncomfortable. "Yes. Unfortunately, the cameras were turned off."

"Oh, so you mean Reagan turned them off. So, whoever he was entertaining, he didn't want anyone to see. And I bet you checked the cameras of his neighbors. Or were they switched off as well?" I rise, tired of this bullshit. "Call me when you have an irrefutable video showing me sleepwalking out of this building, getting into my Prius, and then sleep-driving to Montauk. Until then, I've nothing more to say. Excuse me." I walked away.

And then Detective Dodge mutters under his breath: "I know you, Anderson."

I return to him like a boomerang. "What did you just say?"

"Just that it's quite a coincidence that people you hate are dropping like flies. First, Marshall Reagan, and now your ex-wife, and all the money from your settlement is still in her bank account. I mean, talk about bad luck. What did she have on you? Let's be real."

"Have on me?" I'm incredulous. I stare at Detective Clemente, who at least has the decency to avert her eyes. "Let me get real with you, Detective Dipshit. You don't know a goddamn thing about me. And I've no clue why you've got such a fucking hard-on about me either." I'm vaguely aware of shocked gasps and whispers around me, but I'm too angry to give a fuck. "But I do know this. You've got some goddamn nerve showing up here unannounced and badgering me when my daughter's still in the hospital. I'm the last person you should be messing with. Now take your dog-and-pony show somewhere else."

Detective Dickwad takes a step toward me, fists clenched. His partner grabs him by his coat sleeve.

"I'm not telling you again, you supercilious sack of shit. Stay away from me and my family or I'll have your fucking badge for breakfast." I jerk my thumb at Detective Clemente. "I'd watch your back if I were you. Your partner's a sick mofo. He's going to get you killed if you're not careful."

Detective Dodge lunges at me and clips me in the jaw. I stumbled back and fall into a potted plant. Detective Clemente gets Dodge in a shoulder hold. "Enough!" she bellows.

I pick myself up, no worse for wear. *What a fucking idiot.* As I storm out, there's a thunderous roar of laughter, applause, and whistles. The Dakota's affable long-time doorman, Fernando, waits outside. Fernando and I go way back. "Cops," I gripe.

In return, Fernando gives me a thumbs-up sign and hails a cab.

I get to Dr. Richter's office late. He's in a glass high-rise where the rent's the equivalent of a small fortune, but for what he charges an hour—no insurance accepted—he can afford it. The waiting room is decorated in what I call therapeutic psycho pap. Bleached walls. Framed photos of lush, verdant, faraway landscapes. A tabletop burbling waterfall with soothing stones. The obligatory hewn coffee table with magazines of the month is artfully arranged. It was as dull and uninspiring as a Taco Bell menu.

The receptionist—I can't tell you what she looks like, she blends into the drab interior so well—ushers me into the doctor's inner sanctum. The doctor sits behind an oversized desk that's so big it must have its own heating element. But it's not Chris Richter who greets me. No, this is a faux Nicole Kidman in a monochrome and shapeless outfit that the real Nicole Kidman wouldn't be caught dead in. Nicole—I mean, Dr. Richter—stands and extends her hand. "I'm Dr. Richter. I'm pleased to meet you —" She glances down at her appointment schedule. "Mr. Anderson."

After I shake her hand, we sit down. I guess she notices my dismay over her gender. "Sorry to disappoint you, Mr. Anderson. I get that a lot, I'm afraid." There's a slight edge to her voice. "Is my lack of a penis going to be a problem for you?"

I gamely smile. "No, not at all. I've had plenty of analysts, both male and female." It's tempting to add that if any of those eggheads had helped me, I most likely wouldn't be here now. But I'm already in a lousy mood, so why compound it?

"I'm sorry to hear that." Dr. Richter consults her notes. "So, you're married with children."

"Yes." I pause, unsure. "You mean to tell me that you don't know who I am? You don't Google your patients?"

Her smile is tight as she tugs on her bra strap. Cassie always complains that her bras don't fit right or that the underwire digs into her breast. I read somewhere that it's a statistical fact that most women don't wear the correct bra size. Where's Howard Hughes when you need him?

"No, Mr. Anderson. All I know is what you told my secretary when you called to make the appointment."

I didn't completely buy this, but okay. Maybe the doctor isn't computer savvy, although I notice her Mac desktop is top-of-the-line. I doubt it's just for show.

"What do you find so amusing, Mr. Anderson."

"I'm sorry. It's just that you could be Nicole Kidman's doppelganger. I'm sure you get that a lot too. I worked with Nicole on my TV series. Nice lady. Beautiful kids. And her husband plays a mean guitar."

Dr. Richter doesn't crack a smile. She reminds me of a hard-boiled egg whose shell won't peel off easily. "Well, Mr. Anderson, if you ask me, you resemble Richard Gere in *Autumn in New York*. Do you think you look like Richard Gere?"

"Hell, no," I snort. But when I was in my full beard phase, people did say that I looked like Leonardo DiCaprio in *The Revenant*. At the time, I thought it was a compliment. Now I'm not so sure.

"Then I don't think I resemble Nicole Kidman in the slightest." Dr. Richter brushes aside a tangle of long, blonde curly hair. "But I did like her in *The Undoing*. That hair. Those clothes. And the house. Hugh Grant, not so much. Can you picture him as a murderer? I mean, really." She scoffs at the notion. "Donald Sutherland was robbed."

I agree with her. Donald Sutherland *was* robbed.

She removes her tortoiseshell glasses. "Now that we've established that we look like movie stars, Mr. Anderson, what seems to be the issue that those other therapists couldn't cure?" Her tone is a mix of curiosity and bemusement.

The moment of truth. I shift my feet, my leather shoes suddenly too small. "I screwed up, Dr. Richter. I didn't mean to, but I did. But first, let me say this. I deeply love Cassie, my wife. I love my kids. We have a nice life. But—I had a vasectomy, and I didn't tell Cassie." I wince. It sounds cold and callous and awful, even though I'm not cold and callous and awful. Old rake Brooks, yes, but not the new, improved Brooks. I'm not a saint but neither am I a sinner. "You see, Cassie had a difficult pregnancy, our daughter was born premature and—"

"Mr. Anderson." Dr. Richter sounds like my fourth-grade chorus teacher when we forgot the words to "*Moon River*." "That's an excuse, and not a particularly good one. How would you feel if your wife had her tubes tied without telling you?"

Fuck. She had me there. "You're right. I'd feel terrible. And mad and betrayed. I agree with you. It was me. It was all me. I wasn't thinking clearly. It was an impulsive decision. But it's just not about the vasectomy." I'm waiting for the sperm test results from Dr. Schultz who managed to squeeze me in—squeeze being the operative word. According to the doctor, the odds that the vasectomy hadn't taken weren't good. He prided himself—as he put it with a leer—on capping the pump.

"So, what do you believe your problem is, Mr. Anderson?"

"Among many? Intimacy. Letting my guard down. Really letting go. Trust issues. Anger management. Guilt. Lots of guilt. I'm like an onion."

"An onion?"

I nod. "I've been told that by more than one therapist. That I only peel so far. And then I stop. I shut down. I say what people want to hear. I do what they expect. I smile. I joke. Take drugs, drink. The whole gamut. To mask the pain, guilt, and shame. And the more pain, guilt, and shame I felt, the more I'd take. I've been sober and drug-free for many years. I'm proud of that. The addictions I have now are my wife, my kids, and my writing. And soccer. I'm a big soccer fan." The words spill out of my mouth like dominos. "Let me make it easy for you. I've been variously diagnosed as bipolar with schizophrenic tendencies, depression, anxiety, mood disorder, seasonal disorder, attention deficit disorder, and several other choice acronyms." But probably one word sums it up best: *asshole.*

Dr. Richter jots something down. Her hands are perfectly manicured; a pink ombré with diamond tips. It's the only touch of color in the room. "So, you're a writer? What kind?"

"The usual. Novels, screenplays, articles, short stories, grocery lists—"

"Successful?"

I chuckle as I think of Sheldon. "My agent would say so."

"In other words, you have it all, Mr. Anderson. A loving wife and family. Money is no object. Has it occurred to you that having this procedure was an attempt to sabotage your wonderful life?"

No, I hadn't thought of that. To me, it's black and white: Cassie wants another baby. I don't. It has nothing to do with our wonderful life. "Possibly. But as I mentioned previously, it's deeper than that. When I said I felt tremendous guilt—it's because my mother and brother were violently murdered when I was only eight years old."

Dr. Richter shoots me a blank stare. "Well, it's not uncommon to kill your family members, is it? Authors kill their parents and siblings all the time." She suddenly notices my aghast look. "Oh, my God. So, you're not referring to—"

"No," I say flatly. "It happened. It's not something I made up."

She furiously scribbles. "Oh, I'm so sorry, Mr. Anderson. I had no—and you were eight?"

I nod, the pain as sharp as a knife buried in my chest. "It happened in Montauk. We were there for the summer."

"A random attack?"

"No. It was a man my mother knew, not that a stranger would make it any easier to deal with. I was there. I mean, *I was there.* My brother protected me. He told me to hide. That much I remember. The rest—I just don't know. I'm told that I hid in the dunes for hours. The police found me. Days later, I woke up in the hospital. And that's when I knew they were dead, and I was alive. I don't remember anything else."

"You can't remember what happened or won't?" Dr. Richter looks at me, pensive.

I'm silent. I don't know the answer. Just then my cell phone pings. "I have to check this, forgive me." It's a text from Cassie: *Audra can come home tomorrow* punctuated with exclamation points, hearts, rainbows, and unicorn emojis.

I'm elated. "It's my wife about our daughter, Audra's been in the hospital and now it looks like—"

"Mr. Anderson." The chorus teacher is back, and it sounds like detention. "I must insist that you turn that off. No cell phones during sessions. I thought my secretary made that clear."

"She did. I'm sorry, I forgot." I turned the phone to mute and put it away. I exhale and focus. "I'm currently writing a book about that night. About the murders. I want to remember. I need to remember. It's crushing me. I want to get this weight off me once and for all, Dr. Richter. That's the truth of it."

"To sell books, Mr. Anderson?" she deadpans. Oh, she was fucking good. Not as good as Nicole Kidman, clearly—but good.

"No," I answer, annoyed. "For my own peace of mind. This black hole in my memory—it's overshadowed my entire life. I'm sick and tired of it. I tried numbing it and filling it with other things. That didn't work out too well. And at my age with two young kids, I don't want to feel incomplete—or broken—anymore." That was the theme of my second novel, *Broken Bridges*. It hadn't sold as well as my first book after all the hoopla —second novels rarely do—but the advance had been enough to buy the apartment above me in the Dakota and make it one huge sweeping suite. "Isn't there a way now to recover lost or buried memories? Repressed or regression memory therapy, isn't that a thing?"

"Not here," Dr. Richter sniffs. "I must be clear, Mr. Anderson. I'm a psychologist and a damn good one. I'm not a carnival hypnotist or a Houdini. If that's what you want—some mystical mumbo-jumbo new-wave therapy—you need to find another doctor. Second, I don't believe in repressed memories. I prefer the term dissociative amnesia. You have a memory disorder from your childhood trauma. I liken it to being in prison, say solitary confinement. We need to find the key to unlock those memories. I don't believe in medications or truth serums. There's no magic bullet. Those buried or locked memories could return on their own—or not at all."

"I don't believe in drugs either, so we agree there." About the only things I haven't tried are meth and ayahuasca. Now I won't even look at a Tylenol bottle at the supermarket.

"If you're not ready to peel that onion, Mr. Anderson, then you're just wasting my time and yours."

"No, I am. I mean, I want to try. One part of me is afraid. My father thinks this is an exercise in futility, that it's dredging up things best left in the past." Dad's quite loquacious on the subject.

"And he may be right. Are you prepared for that possibility?"

I blithely nod. "Living with this uncertainty, this fear—look, knowing the truth can't be worse than that." I really believe that.

She jots down a few more notes. "And your father, how did he—"

"He was a fucking rock—excuse me. A rock of Gibraltar. He was extremely protective of me, maybe overly so but understandable given what happened. Dad put up with a lot— and I mean, a lot. There were times when he didn't know if I was dead or alive. When he was afraid that the next phone call would be to announce that I'd overdosed. But he never quit on me. He's a true statesman, he's negotiated peace agreements and brokered truces, he's saved lives—really saved lives. He's a great man and I know I've been a disappointment to him, despite my, uh, literary success." I wipe my eyes. Palmer should be here living his best life. There's not an hour that goes by that I don't miss him.

Dr. Richter looks at her calendar. "I can see you every

Tuesday at this time. Does that work for you? Very well." She closes her notebook. "I've got an assignment for you, Mr. Anderson. I want you to go back to the summer of 1966—scratch that, the entire year. Make a playlist of popular songs. TV shows you watched. Books you read. At some point, you may have to return to the dunes, not just mentally and emotionally, but physically. Do you understand?"

I grit my teeth. I can't stomach listening to the Beatles or the Rolling Stones. If their songs come up on the radio, I change stations. I can't even watch *The Twilight Zone*, one of Palmer's favorite shows. And going back to Montauk? Unfathomable. Just thinking about it makes me break out in a cold sweat.

"Mr. Anderson, there's still so much we don't know about the mind. It's a wonderfully strange, delicate thing. Anything and everything can trigger a memory. We have to be open to all possibilities, no matter how remote. Can you do that? If not, you're just throwing your hard-earned money down the drain."

Can I? One part of me wants to say, sorry, I've made a terrible mistake, let's call the whole thing off. To run away and hide like that scared, out-of-his-fucking-mind eight-year-old with rain and lightning crashing down around him. But I'm sixty-five fucking years old, and I'm tired of this shit. I take a leap and nod.

"Good. Until our next session, Mr. Anderson." She stands. "Oh, one more thing. I'm curious. How did you find me? I don't generally advertise, it's more of a word-of-mouth thing. Referrals from satisfied clients or another doctor."

"Actually, it was my wife. She sent me a list of names and you —" I blush, sheepish.

"You thought I was the only man on the list." Dr. Kidman—I mean, Dr. Richter—laughs. At least she hasn't taken offense.

I'm in a taxi when Sheldon calls. "Well, for someone who hates social media, you certainly are on social media a fucking lot."

Ooops. "The Dakota lobby?"

"I think a 'supercilious sack of shit' is going to be a meme. How did therapy go?"

"Good, I think. It looks like Audra's coming home tomorrow."

"That's fantastic. You need anything, let me or Phoebe know."

After Sheldon hangs up, another call comes in from a number I don't recognize. I hesitate, then finally click the green accept button. "Hello?"

"Mr. Anderson?" It's a strange male voice. "This is Dr. Hartlin from the White Plains Hospital. I'm in the ER with Florence Easton, your aunt."

Since my visit, Aunt Flo and I speak almost daily. From Althea, crickets. "What's going on, Doctor?" This can't be good.

"She had a nasty tumble. She's fractured her pelvis, and she has a slight concussion."

I grimace. For a woman her age, it's going to be a lengthy and painful recuperation. I wonder where Althea was when the accident happened.

"Your aunt asked me to call you—I warn you, she's a bit disoriented."

"May I speak with her?"

"Yes, hang on, one moment." I hear noise in the background.

"Brooks!" Aunt Flo booms in my ear.

Well, her voice is strong. That's heartening. "Aunt Flo, what the hell happened?"

"There was a patch of ice on the basement stairs."

What? Okay, she has a concussion, she's mixed up. "Where's Althea? Isn't she with you?"

"She was here and then she wasn't. Althea's been naughty, she hasn't been taking her vitamins."

I play along. "You shouldn't be alone, Aunt Flo. Let me make a few calls, I can be there by dinner time."

"No, I forbid it. I'm fine. I'm not in a room. I'm not even sure they're admitting me. Here, you speak to the doctor." More noise.

The doctor's back. "Mr. Anderson, there's no question that

we're admitting your aunt. She should be in a room later today. We've just given her pain medication. The fracture will require surgery. We'll make her as comfortable as possible."

I ask to speak with Aunt Flo again.

"Yes, who are you?" she mumbles. Whatever they've given her, it's kicked in as fast as heroin.

"Audra's being released tomorrow. Once she's settled in, I'll come as soon as I can. Everything will be fine."

Aunt Flo snores in response.

I rush back to the Dakota. Miss Drake says Mark's been an angel. I've my doubts, judging by the mess in his room. We see Miss Drake off, then go pick up dinner—McDonald's for Mark and Audra, and lamb and beef gyros, extra tzatziki sauce, and feta cheese, with sides of waffle fries for me and Cassie. Audra wolfs down her chicken nuggets—if she eats any more chicken she'll lay an egg—and Mark devours his Quarter Pounder with cheese and bacon, no ketchup, no mayo, no lettuce, no pickles, and no onions.

As the kids watch *Toy Story*, Cassie and I have a moment. "Now about Audra coming home, the doctor's sure it's not too soon?" I ask.

"No, he says there's nothing more that they can do. He wants to see her next week. He says we're blessed that she's made a remarkable recovery. It could've been so much worse." Cassie blankets her fries with so much ketchup you can barely see them. "The hospital bed is being delivered in the morning. And she gets the last of her rabies shots before she's discharged." She takes a gloppy bite of her sandwich. "Any updates on Aunt Flo?" As we waited for our sandwiches, I had texted Cassie and filled her in on what I knew.

"Only that she's resting comfortably in her room. She's a tough old bird but at her age, this could be—" I reach for Cassie's greasy fingers. "I can't lose her. Not when we've just reconnected."

Cassie doesn't pull away. "And still no word from Althea?" She withdraws her hand to grab another fry. "How about Eric?"

"I called his number, it went straight to voicemail." Apparently, Eric was on set in Romania for a low-budget zombie flick.

"How was your session with Dr. Richter?"

"As well as first sessions go. And it turns out she's a woman. She could be Nicole Kidman's doppelganger. She said I could pass for Richard Gere." I make a porcupine face.

Cassie bursts into gales of laughter.

It's good to hear her laugh. It's like a shot of adrenaline. It also gives me hope that we still have a future together.

After Cassie and Mark leave and Audra's finally asleep, I open my laptop. When it comes to writing, I'm not choosy. I can write anywhere: a bathroom, in an airplane, walking down the street or waiting in line at Dunkin' Donuts. My mind's always writing something. It's just a matter of physically writing it down.

But before I start writing, I check my emails and see a message from Althea. It's about fucking time. I'm ticked off that she hasn't called me. I briefly wonder how she got my email address. Aunt Flo doesn't have a computer; she can barely manage her cell phone. I click on Althea's mail: *Brooks, our family is royally fucked up. Tell Eric sorry not sorry, not that he gives a shit. I think you and I could've been friends in another life. Maybe next time. I'll say hi to Berry for you.*

My first reaction is what the fuck? *Say hi to Berry?* And then I remember what Aunt Flo said about Althea not taking her "vitamins." *Shit, shit, shit.* I grab my cell and dial 911. "Operator? Please, I think my cousin's about to do something stupid. Althea —" I struggle to recall her married name. "Althea Croise. Can you please send an officer to do a welfare check at 2189 Quail Run Road in Mt. Vernon?"

The dispatcher puts me on hold. When she returns, she says the local police will go out to the house. Relieved, I thank her profusely. Maybe I'm overreacting and the police will find Althea safe and sound watching Showtime. But until I hear back from the police, I worry. I've barely hung up with 911 when Cassie calls. "Brooks, what hospital is Aunt Flo at? Didn't you say White Plains?"

I did. I get a burst of something sour in my mouth.

"It's all over the news. A woman went berserk at the hospital and tried to kill a patient, then she stabbed a nurse and guard. Another guard shot the woman. I know you said before that you hadn't heard from Althea so—"

Another call comes in; it comes up as the White Plains police. I'm no psychic, but I know what they're going to say even before I tell Cassie I'll have to call her back.

CHAPTER TEN

The hospital insists that Aunt Flo slept through Althea's rampage, but I can't take their word for it. I have to see for myself. I arrange for a private nurse to stay with Audra, then I rush to pick up my Prius from a parking garage near the Dakota. I arrive at the hospital a little past midnight. On the drive up, I get a frantic text from Sheldon: *Jesus Christ, what the fuck's going on?* Dad chimes in, too: *Don't get involved.* I don't understand Dad's attitude, but it's his problem, not mine.

A dozen or so police cruisers ring the front entrance along with several reporters I vaguely recognize. I'm met by a sympathetic hospital staffer who effusively tells me what a big fan she is as she ushers me through a side door to avoid the scrum. We go to the eleventh floor. There, the police forensics unit is busy collecting evidence. I see a long trail of blood on the floor. I don't know where Althea is or if she's even alive. An officer stands outside Aunt Flo's door. I peek in. She's sound asleep, the covers all the way up to her nose. An overnight nurse sits by her bed, engrossed in *Where the Crawdads Sing*. I'm tempted to tell her what I thought of it, but I don't.

I text Cassie to let her know I've arrived and that Aunt Flo's all right. Just as I send it, a middle-aged man in a mismatched jacket and pants shuffles up. I have the feeling he threw on the first clothes he could find in the laundry hamper. There's a gait to his walk, maybe an old football injury. "Mr. Anderson? I'm Captain August Wilson, the Criminal Investigations Commander. It's good that you were able to come so quickly. Can we talk in private?" His tone is pleasant but professional, miles away from Detective Dodge.

We walk down to a waiting room at the end of the hallway. At that hour, it's empty, the overhead TV off. Captain Wilson shuts the door and we both sit down. "Mr. Anderson, let me express condolences on your loss."

This is how I learn that Althea's gone. Based on the news reports I read coming up, I can't say I'm surprised. I guess a part of me still hopes that Althea's email was a horrible joke. The solemn look on Captain Wilson's face tells me it's not.

"When did you last speak with your aunt or your cousin?"

"I spoke to my aunt earlier today when she was in the emergency room. The last time I saw my cousin was when I visited them roughly two or so weeks ago."

"How did Mrs. Croise seem to you then? Pleasant? Friendly?"

"Honestly, she was distant." I squirm under his direct stare. "Captain Wilson, let's just say that I was closer to my aunt than my cousin and leave it at that."

"Were you aware that Mrs. Croise was recently diagnosed as being bipolar?"

"No. My aunt never mentioned it. I became alarmed tonight when Althea sent me a bizarre email. I didn't know her that well, but from what little I saw, she never struck me as a violent person."

"No one is born violent," Captain Wilson says with a deep sigh. "But when you've been on the job as long as I have, you learn the hard way that you never know what a person is truly capable of doing—until they do it."

I ask about the other people who were injured.

"The nurse will be fine, minor defensive stab wounds. The security guard, he's in surgery right now. Young fellow, two kids with a third on the way." He pauses. "Do you know of anything going on between your aunt and her daughter that could've provoked this?"

I thought for a moment. "The house was a sore spot, I know that much. And Althea was having issues after her divorce." I could say, but don't, that Althea had never gotten over her older sister's death. Berry had pushed Althea out of the way seconds before the car plowed into her. In hindsight, I deeply regret not having reached out to Althea sooner. Maybe I could've helped her. Maybe we could've helped each other. Despite Dad's exhortations, I am involved.

Captain Wilson nods. "That makes sense. Your aunt told her realtor she was taking the property off the market. He went there today—I mean, yesterday—hoping to get her to reconsider. He heard someone crying for help and found your aunt at the bottom of the basement stairs. Mrs. Croise drove to her former home in Englewood Cliffs and tried to set it on fire. Luckily, no one was hurt, some minor damage. On her way to your apartment in Manhattan, she got into two fender benders."

Excuse me? I freeze. Althea went to the Dakota?

"According to your doorman, your cousin was loitering and muttering gibberish. He wouldn't let her in and called the police."

Good old Fernando. His Christmas bonus is coming early this year.

"Before the officers arrived, she skedaddled." I haven't heard that word in ages. "She got into another accident, ditched her car, then hijacked a pickup that was double-parked at a bodega."

I'm amazed. Althea is—was—a hundred pounds soaking wet in her high-waisted jeans. Harmless, the last person you'd ever expect to go on a crime spree, yet she'd turned into Bonnie and Clyde without the Clyde.

"Here at the hospital, she bypassed security at the front desk. How we're not sure yet. From there, she went to her mother's room and tried to smother her with a pillow."

The news reports were true. I can only shake my head, astonished.

"The nurse walked in and Mrs. Croise tried to stab her with a knife or scissors. The security guard was alerted by the nurse's screams. Mrs. Croise stabbed him right outside the door. She makes a run for the stairwell and when she refuses to drop her weapon, she's shot several times." He pauses to clear his throat. "Of course, there will be a full investigation, but based on the facts, it looks like a case of justified deadly force."

I'm not an idiot. I understand what Captain Wilson meant. It doesn't make it go down any easier. How the hell am I going to explain this to Aunt Flo? I ache just thinking about it.

"Don't beat yourself too much over it, Mr. Anderson." Captain Wilson's tone is matter of fact. "It's been my experience that when a person wants to kill someone—I mean, *really* kill someone—they find a way. And Mrs. Croise wasn't in her right state of mind. I'm sure she was a loving, devoted daughter. I understand your aunt has a son?"

"Eric, Althea's twin. He'll be out of the country for some time. He's asked me to handle everything." Eric called just before I reached the hospital. Although our connection kept dropping, I heard the shock and bewilderment in his voice.

"I'm not sure when the body can be released. That's up to the coroner." Captain Wilson stands and shifts his weight with a grimace. "Mr. Anderson, I have to ask. It's standard, you know. About identifying your cousin. We can get her dental records. On second thought, given the severity of her injuries, it might be better that way—"

"No. I want to do it," I hear myself say. I wasn't there for Mom or Palmer. I can do this much for Althea.

Captain Wilson doesn't argue with me. We take the elevator

down to the sub-basement and he leads me to a cold, dark room. He switches the light on; he's here often enough that he knows where the switch is. There, on a hard table, is Althea, her body covered by a blood-splattered sheet. I take a deep breath and steel myself. I tell myself it's not Mom and Palmer. Even if I had been in any condition to see them, Dad would've never allowed it. It's not that I'm disparaging or second-guessing the decisions he made. I'm not. Everything he did was out of love and concern. Even so, a big part of me wishes that I had seen them. As horrible and gut-wrenching as it would've been, it would've made it real. After I woke up from what seemed like a long sleep, and even though Dad told me they were gone, I refused to believe it. I couldn't accept that they were dead, and I was alive. It was some great cosmic joke gone wrong. They were going to spring back to life like the monsters and zombies in the horror movies Palmer loved. When I eventually figured out that Mom and Palmer weren't coming back, that it was final, no second acts or encores, I was fucking angry at the world, myself, everyone.

I'm not sure who lifts the sheet. It could be Captain Wilson. It might be me. The first thing that comes to my mind is that this isn't Althea—it's merely a damaged replicant of her, something out of *Blade Runner* (the original, not the execrable remake). The left side of Althea's face is intact. It looks like she's blissfully asleep. But the right side is mush, just bits of skin and blood and bone, exposed like the innards of a squashed raccoon on the side of the road. This is human kill. I'm hard-pressed to remember that this was once even human. I don't know what kind of ammo the guard used, but deadly force doesn't describe it adequately. I'm angry, sad, and depressed. How did Althea end up here? When she and Eric were safely born, the family rejoiced. It was a time for celebration, a bright spot after losing Grandma Emily. Grandpa William told me that babies were the promise of new hopes and dreams. Well, Althea had hopes and dreams, too. Now she was a disfigured, maimed corpse on a slab.

I stare at Althea's face. Suddenly, it's not Althea anymore. It's Mom, lying on the living-room floor of the summer cottage. This thing crumpled on the floor doesn't resemble Mom at all, but I know it's her. This bloody, beaten thing is wearing Mom's pink sweater, the one Palmer and I got her for Christmas. We chose it at the local Woolworth. Dad gave us the money and told us to pick something out. After Mom opened her present, she excitedly put it on right away over her robe. The sweater was big around the shoulders, but Mom didn't care. She said it was perfect. Now I'm back in the living room and the thing on the floor is jerking, her hands flapping as if pulled by invisible wires. I hear Palmer scream. The next thing I know I'm running up the dunes, barely able to breathe, crying hysterically.

I've had this nightmare off and on for years. Dad insists it's just a bad dream. But now, belatedly, I realize it's not. I'm fully awake. It's a true memory. It's real—not fantasy. *I was there. I saw it.* I cling to that fleeting memory, terrified.

"Mr. Anderson, are you all right?" Captain Wilson asks in a faraway voice.

I nod, unable to speak.

Before I go home, I call the hospital and check up on Audra; she hasn't stirred all night. When I get to the apartment, I don't expect Cassie to be awake, but she is. She's curled up on the sofa watching an old Alfred Hitchcock chestnut, *To Catch a Thief*. The plot is both sublime and silly, and the charms of the French Riviera (actually a backlot in Hollywood) are nothing more than a backdrop for the lovely Grace Kelly. I stumble in like a punch-drunk, collapse in Cassie's arms, and sob my heart out. I tell her everything about Althea and what I've remembered about Mom and Palmer. I'm scared shitless, but I'm also glad if that makes any sense. Dr. Richter's right: I *can* remember. The painful memories *are* buried deep in my subconscious, waiting to be unlocked. I just need the right key. It also begs the next question: what else is hidden away?

A few days later, we bury Althea in the family plot next to Grandpa William, Grandma Emily, Uncle Charlie, and Berry. Don, Althea's ex-husband, is there. I had told him about the service as a courtesy and honestly didn't expect him to show. Don is good-natured and grudge-free, and his partner seems equally kind. Don tells me things about Althea that Aunt Flo doesn't need to know: the affairs and the breakdowns. Althea knew when they married that Don was bisexual but insisted it didn't matter. At the end of the day, he wanted kids. She didn't. Now he and his partner are having a baby with a surrogate.

I'm ashamed that Mom and Palmer aren't buried in the family cemetery. This is where they belong. Instead, inexplicably, Dad had them cremated after their funerals. I've no idea where their ashes are. They could be in a storage facility in Queens, for all I know. I gather from Aunt Flo that this is what created the rift—no, make that chasm—between our families, along with Grandpa William dying so suddenly. Dad didn't even go to Grandpa William's funeral.

Aunt Flo's still in the hospital, recuperating from her surgery. The doctors say she should recover completely, but emotionally, she's a wreck. She constantly asks for Althea even though I've told her that Althea's gone. I can't bring myself to tell her that Althea tried to kill her. Fortunately, the guard that Althea injured is doing well. If the wound had been an inch deeper, he would've bled out in seconds. And as Captain Wilson predicted, the guard who shot Althea has been cleared of any wrongdoing.

Aunt Flo's realtor—as persistent as a horsefly on the beach—calls frequently to ask if the house will be for sale anytime soon, as he has potential buyers. My answer is the same each time: hell, no. No one is going to push Aunt Flo out of her house.

At the same time, Uncle Philip's in a hospice on a morphine drip. I instruct Miss Drake to send a large donation for his care. The doctors give him a week, maybe two, Aunt Flo insists that she must visit him, but we both know that's not going to happen.

The police still have no leads on Marshall Reagan—they briefly detained an "acquaintance," but he has an ironclad alibi for the hours in question: he was in jail for breaking a restraining order. But Detective Dipshit is no longer on the case. I get a text from James: *Half of Long Island wants to buy you a drink, the other half wants to kill you. Stay safe.* I have the feeling that I'm still the number one suspect, as absurd as that is.

The results of my semen test are in, but I'm too chickenshit to call Dr. Schultz's office. The only bright spot is Audra being home. We had a party with unicorn balloons and a sparkly ice-cream cake. She's started physical therapy. We make a game of it and tie her leg up in colorful ribbons. Dr. Shannon's mildly encouraging that Audra won't need plastic surgery after all. I hope he's right.

The speech for Dad's gala is done—at least the introduction is. I figure I'll wing the rest. But in a twist I hadn't anticipated, it seems that Miss Drake—who in another life must've been Sherlock Holmes' great-aunt—has located the family who'd rented the last of Grandpa William's cottages that summer. I have a dim recollection of a woman perpetually cradling a baby on her hip while she hung laundry outside. This woman is alive and living upstate, a couple of hour's drive. I add an interview with Olivia Grantham to my growing to-do list.

But today, a week after Althea's funeral, I send Miss Drake home early despite her entreaties that she's fine. Her allergies are in full bloom due to an unseasonably rainy spring. She grudgingly leaves but insists she'll be back first thing in the morning. The woman will not rest. I call a local kosher deli and arrange to have fresh chicken soup delivered to her.

Due to Althea's funeral, I rescheduled my second therapy session with Dr. Richter, but my initial euphoria over remembering something the night Mom and Palmer died has left me in a funk. I'm so goddamn impatient. What if that was all I remembered? Cassie tells me to stop doubting myself and to give it time. I haven't told Dad because I know what his reaction will be: *Brooks, stop being such a fucking idiot. You need to let the past go.* But what if the past won't let go of me?

Before she leaves, Miss Drake reminds me that I'm meeting Dad for lunch at the Yale Club instead of the brownstone. The Yale Club is Dad's home away from home. Dad badgers me to join—I can afford the membership fee—but I beg off. I seriously question the validity of any club that would have me as a member.

The waiter leads me to Dad's table. He's already into his second Manhattan. If he's suffering any ill effects from the dog attack, it's not apparent. "I was about to give up on you. Did you forget we were having lunch here?"

"No. Blame midtown traffic. Miss Drake made sure to tell me." I sat down.

"Good old indispensable Miss Drake. Everyone should have a Miss Drake in their lives." Dad breezily waves at someone. "I took the liberty of ordering for you."

I smile, but inwardly I grimace. Not the goddamn salmon again.

"Do you miss it?" He motions at his drink.

"Not in the slightest. I don't have the taste for it anymore. Not that I haven't tried. One New Year's Eve I tried to drink a glass of champagne and I almost gagged."

Dad chuckles. "Remarkable. My day hasn't started unless I have something strong to drink. When I was younger, I never—but at my age, I can indulge."

If I have to endure another round of grilled salmon, I'm going to make it count. "Dad, do you remember a family named Grantham? They rented one of Grandpa's cottages that summer."

Dad reflects, then shrugs. "No, sorry, the name doesn't mean anything to me. Should it?"

"No, it's not important," I demur. But now that I had Dad's attention, I press on. "How about Bjorn Jurgen?"

Dad recoils as if he's found a bug in his drink. "Oh, God, yes, What a fucking pervert. Ghastly. I only knew him by sight, mind you. I don't think we ever exchanged two words. That was on your mother."

I raise my eyebrows. "Mom?"

"Mmm. She asked me to put a notice on the college bulletin board. About the cottages being available by the week or month. Other than that, I had nothing to do with it." He rubs his hand. "Filthy business. I mean, Althea. Mental instability runs on that side of the family. Not your mother, of course. Shirley could be flighty, and she had her mood swings, but she wasn't crazy. One of her great aunts killed herself. And there was an uncle who ended up in an asylum back in the thirties. Syphilis, if I recall correctly. Now that's a nasty bit of work." He gives me a wink.

The waiter brings our meals: two identical plates of perfectly grilled salmon. I sigh. As Dad digs in with gusto, I feel my cell vibrate. Dad has a thing about cell phones during meals. I check my phone: it's Cassie. "Sorry, Dad, I have to take this." Audra's physical therapist is coming to the apartment, and I asked Cassie to let me know when she arrives. "Hey, baby—"

The words come out in a torrent. "Brooks, they're here and they want to search the house. What the fuck?"

"Cassie, who's there? Who wants to search the house?"

Dad's fork stops in mid-air like a WWI biplane.

"The police, damn it. They asked if they could come in and I said no, not without a search warrant."

Dad wildly gesticulates at me. "Give me the damn phone, Brooks."

Audra's crying in the background. "Mommy, are you going to jail?"

"Give me the fucking phone!" Dad grabs it out of my hands. "Cassie, it's Dad. I want you to listen to me and do exactly as I say." He's in full negotiator, no prisoners mode. "Do not—under any fucking circumstance—allow the police in. I don't care what cockamamie excuse they give you. I mean it. Don't let them in to use the bathroom or get a drink of water or anything else. Have I made myself clear? Good. Brooks and I are on our way with the cavalry. This has gone far enough. Those fucking morons are going to rue the day they messed with me." He hangs up with Cassie, then dials.

"Dad, who the hell are you calling?" I stammer. Everyone in the goddamn room is staring at our table.

Dad's already out of his chair and moving like a lion in the Serengeti. "Who the fuck else? Dalton Crane."

Holy shit. Dad isn't fucking around. I'm nodding acquaintances with Dalton Crane, but he and Dad are great friends. Dalton shows up at Dad's holiday parties with a newer, prettier, and younger version of his last wife. A man on the small side—in his stockinged feet he barely makes the height requirement for the Gravitron ride at a carnival—but as a top criminal defense lawyer, he carries a big stick and an even bigger dick. He started out as an assistant district attorney but crossed over to the dark side. There was no case too grimy, too barbarous, too ruthless, that Dalton wouldn't take—except for Jeffrey Epstein. Even Dalton had scruples. Now allegedly semi-retired, Dalton spends his days playing racquetball and pontificating/playing devil's advocate as a legal analyst on cable news.

"Dalton will meet us there in fifteen." Dad handed me my phone.

I'm almost giddy. The police have no idea what a hornet's nest they've stirred up. Dad's latest driver—a big Zimbabwean fellow with a lead foot—passes every yellow light with seconds to spare. I almost feel sorry for the cops. I said almost. Come at me all you want—I'm wearing big boy pants. But leave Cassie and the kids out of the fray.

At the building foyer, Fernando greets us with a terse smile. "I tried to stop them, Mr. Brooks."

"No worries, Fernando." I slip him two hundred, a token advance on his growing holiday bonus.

When we get off the elevator, we see a gaggle of dark suits around my front door. Dad and I swagger past them. I buzz the door. Cassie opens it a crack. "They wanted to use the bathroom. I told them no."

Dad smirks.

"I'll take care of this, baby." I turn around. "Who's in charge here?" I bark.

A man steps up: youngish, on the balding side. "Mr. Anderson, I'm Agent Fox, I'm the lead agent on a special task force."

"What task force? FBI?" I demand.

"I'm afraid I can't go into any further detail," Agent Fox tersely replies.

Dad elbows past me. "Excuse me. I'm Bernard Anderson, perhaps you've heard of me. Can you please explain why the FBI has jurisdiction in this matter?" Dad's smile was pleasant enough, but don't be fooled. He's a tiger ready to pounce.

"Well, Mr. Bernard Anderson—" Is Agent Fox being snarky?

Bad move. Dad grimaces.

"We'd hoped that your daughter-in-law would agree to an informal search to exclude her husband. But now that you're here, Mr. Anderson, this would go a whole lot easier and faster if you'd voluntarily give us samples. That is, if you have nothing to hide." Agent Fox shoots me this friendly, folksy Andy Griffith grin. He doesn't have the gravitas to pull it off.

"Don't answer him, Brooks." Dalton Crane has arrived. Dressed in sweats, his hair wet and slicked back, he looks like an angry ferret. "This is a fishing expedition. They found DNA and/or latent fingerprint samples at Marshall Reagan's house that they can't identify so they decided to go around my client because no judge in his right mind in this fucking city is going to sign off on a search warrant."

Agent Fox looks like a snowman about to melt into a puddle.

Now partly in the hall, Cassie nudges my arm. "I thought Marshall Reagan was over and done with," she stage-whispers, then louder, "I've told them over and over that you couldn't have been out in Montauk when Reagan died. It's impossible. I told that to the cop who contacted me when we were in Providence. Her name was Martha Leo. And I also told that Detective Dodge. Why won't they believe me?" She glares at Agent Fox.

I stare at Cassie, mystified. She hasn't spoken a word of this. I know from my sources that the police have adjusted their timeline of Reagan's death. According to the coroner, Reagan was dead over a week by the time the landlord came around.

"We're checking her story out," Agent Fox volunteers.

"Please, Mrs. Anderson, do go on," Dalton urges.

"Brooks, the ear infection and croup. Remember?" Cassie prods.

How can I forget? When I picked Mark up from school that day, he was grumpy and complaining that his ears hurt. Otherwise, he seemed fine. By bedtime, he was in agony. We rushed to the ER. As it turned out, he had a double ear infection. The next day, Audra started barking like a seal. That was croup. We barely got any sleep for the next two weeks.

"Brooks, I'm sorry I didn't mention it earlier. It slipped my mind with everything that was going on—" Cassie explains.

"You've got nothing to apologize for, baby," I answer.

"So, it appears that Mr. Anderson has an ironclad alibi for the time in question." Dalton scowls at Agent Fox. "Crime is at historic levels in the city, you can't walk the streets without being mugged or shot, and this is the best you can do with your time and resources?"

A cell phone rings. It's Agent Fox's. He turns his back to us and speaks in a low voice. After a few moments, he puts his phone away. "Sorry to have bothered you, Mrs. Anderson. Your story checks out. Somehow, it fell through the cracks."

"You don't say." Dalton smirks.

Dad angrily mutters under his breath. I'm sure he's thinking of his salmon.

Cassie jams her finger at Agent Fox. "My daughter was petrified that you were taking her mommy away. Is this what they teach you at the academy? I hope you're proud of yourself."

I'm glad her ire is directed at Agent Fox and not me.

"Who is the idiot in charge of this task force?" I demand.

Agent Fox motions at the other cops. "Let's go."

"This isn't the end of this," Dalton bellows.

I wait until Agent Fox and his posse are gone. "I don't buy this, do you? Something's going on, I'm not sure what."

Dalton nods. "This stinks like last week's monkfish."

"Fucking Crookhaven," Dad chimes. Well, technically Montauk isn't in Brookhaven Township—legendary for institutional corruption dating back decades—but it's not the time to argue the finer points.

The elevator opens. It's James, and he's accompanied by another officer I don't recognize. There could be a thousand reasons why James has come here, but from his gaunt, grim demeanor, it's not to ask for a donation to the Orphans' Fund.

James nods tersely at me, then Dalton. "Hello, Mr. Crane. I didn't know you made house calls."

"You're saving me the trouble of a trip down to Police Plaza, Commissioner," Dalton begins. "What went on here is a disgrace. I demand a full investigation."

"You're welcome to file an official complaint, Mr. Crane." James sounds tired. He's led me to believe that he's recovered from his bout with cancer, but I'm not convinced. He turns to me, eyes hooded. "Mr. Anderson, I believe you employ a Miss Lucinda Drake?"

Lucinda? A beat passes before I realize he means Miss Drake. "Yes, Miss Drake's my executive assistant. Has been for years. What's wrong?" Cassie's hand slips into mine.

James' cough is dry and raspy. "There's no easy way to say

this. Miss Drake was found dead in her apartment earlier this morning."

Dad gasps.

Cassie lets out an anguished sob.

Miss Drake? No. I shake my head, unwilling to believe. "You're mistaken. Miss Drake was here. A little under the weather with allergies, but other than that—"

Dalton cuts to the chase. "Commissioner, do you suspect foul play?"

James hesitates, but I know him too well. Of course he suspects foul play. He wouldn't have wasted his time coming to tell me in person.

Marshall Reagan, my ex-wife Nan, and now Miss Drake. Coincidence? Being stuck at the bank during a robbery, that's a coincidence. Wrong place, right time. Otherwise, I don't believe in fucking coincidences.

CHAPTER ELEVEN

P almer was obsessed with horror movies, science fiction shows, creature features, monster flicks, you name it. If it was out of this world, weird, bizarre, unrealistic, peculiar, strange, odd—he loved it. I have a vivid recollection of watching episodes of The Twilight Zone, The Outer Limits, and One Step Beyond with him in the living room at the Big House. The black-and-white television was encased in a big wood cabinet just tall enough that I'd scoot my legs underneath it. Dad hated when I did that, saying that I'd ruin my eyes watching TV that close up. But Mom didn't make a big deal of it.

Every night, Palmer and I would be in our jammies by seven-thirty, eager to watch the Million Dollar Movie shown on NYC's WOR 9. It didn't matter that we'd seen the same movie the night before and the night before that. That was the station's gimmick, playing the same movie on weekday nights and all day on the weekends. Oh, the movies we saw: The Crawling Eye (which scared me so badly Dad threatened to take the TV away), The Hunchback of Notre Dame, King Kong, The Thing, House on Haunted Hill (Vincent Price was a favorite of Mom's), and any movie with Abbott and Costello. I might not have understood everything I watched—in fact, I know I didn't—but I pretended I did. Watching those old movies with Palmer was the highlight of my day. He was five years older than I was and didn't want his little brother hanging around his neck like a horseshoe. So, watching scary flicks together as we ate Jiffy Pop popcorn was a huge deal for me.

Palmer—decades before the hit show Stranger Things—came up with the story of the Ditch Plains monster to our gang a couple of weeks into our vacation. Since our cousins weren't around and we couldn't play with Tor and Sigrid, we had to find new kids to play with.

Arnold (everyone called him Toad, don't ask me why) was a rich city kid staying in a mansion his parents rented for the summer. His parents —Toad was vague on what they did for a living—had dumped him on the hired help while they hopscotched through Europe. Palmer and I met Toad at the beach, and we immediately bonded over our mutual admiration of Abbott and Costello.

There was Ronnie—I'm going to guess maybe a year older than Palmer—a local whose parents owned the modest Blue Heron Motel overlooking Montauk Harbor. He was shy, didn't have much to say, but Palmer said he was a good egg. That was good enough for me.

Rounding out our gang was Gisela aka "Gigi," who lived in Montauk year-round like Ronnie. Her family had deep roots in Long Island; they once owned a lot of land in the area and had grown potatoes when it was possible to make a decent living at it. Now her dad was in the Coast Guard, and they lived on the last bit of land the family hadn't sold.

If Mom was the most beautiful woman in the world, Gigi was a close second. She was thirteen, with long, silky brown hair that shimmered in the sun. Thin and wiry, she was always in shorts, the better to show off her incredibly lean, muscular legs. She never had a harsh word for anyone, a kind and generous soul who'd give you her last penny. She was perfect in every way until it came to her right arm which was a short stump with a flipper for a hand.

Mom sat us down and explained that when Gigi's mom had been expecting her, her dad had been stationed in Germany. The doctor at their base gave Gigi's mom a pill that was supposed to make her sleep better. Well, we know now that pill—thalidomide—caused severe congenital malformations in growing fetuses. I didn't know or care about any of that. All I knew was that Gigi was my friend. I was upset when other kids teased her or when grown-ups looked at her funny. But I was also scared. Mom took sleeping pills sometimes. And Palmer and I took vitamins. Would the same thing happen to us? Mom said of course not, but sometimes, in the middle of the night I'd wake up and check my arm.

Gigi was amazing. Fearless. Nothing fazed her. She had four older brothers and was a true tomboy. She did everything: played baseball, rode bikes, swam. Hell, she even beat me at wrestling. I suppose you could say I had a big, fat, old crush on Gigi. I know Palmer did. Once, we all went into town to get a soda and some brats taunted her. Palmer told them to shut the fuck up. They said make us. He came home with a black eye and a torn shirt, but as I excitedly told Mom, you should've seen the other guys. The truth is, I idolized Palmer. If he had told me to jump off the dock at Montauk Harbor at low tide, I would've done so without a second thought.

After dinner one evening, we kids were goofing around outside. Julian Broadhurst was inside with Mom. Not too far away, Dusty Springfield sang "You Don't Have to Say You Love Me."

"I'm bored," Toad abruptly announced.

Gigi was doing wheelies on her banana bike.

Ronnie was slurping down a cherry Italian ice.

"Did you guys hear those strange noises early this morning?" Palmer asked.

I gave him a look. What strange noises? "I didn't hear anything."

"It was probably raccoons fighting. They make an awful racket." Gigi came to a full stop.

Palmer shook his head. "I know what raccoons sound like when they're fighting. This was different. And I found weird footprints around the house, too."

"Show me," Gigi shot back.

"They're gone now. The rain washed them away." It had briefly rained just after lunch.

"Well, if they weren't raccoons, what do you think it was?" Gigi asked.

"You know what they say about Camp Hero," Palmer answered.

"My Dad says that's a bunch of bunk," Gigi retorted.

"Of course, he's going to say that. He has to, he works for the government. He can't admit that something funny is going on there." Palmer had an answer for everything. He would've made a great politician or a diplomat.

"What do they say about Camp Hero?" I asked.

"Lots of stuff. Like, the military is using it for top-secret experiments. Really weird shit, like mating people with aliens."

Toad laughed.

"No, I mean it. And mind control," Palmer continued. "It's got that strange radar tower transmitting high-frequency electromagnetic impulses. It scrambles your brains like eggs and makes you do crazy shit. I read all about it." When Mom took us into town on errands, we usually stopped at the stationery store. The store had a paperback rack filled with the latest sci-fi conspiracy pulp books. They were cheap—maybe fifty or seventy-five cents—and Palmer cajoled Mom into buying at least one or two each time we went. Palmer was really into these books and had a box full of them under his bed.

I frowned. Migraines? Mom complained of a terrible migraine just that morning.

Gigi looked skeptical. However, Ronnie, Toad, and I hung on every word.

"Guys, I'm telling you, there's a creature running around," Palmer insisted. "It only comes out at night when it's cool and quiet and everyone's asleep."

"If there is a monster, how come the police aren't looking for it?" Gigi asked.

Palmer rolled his eyes. "Because they don't want to cause a panic, silly. Do you think people would want to come out here for the summer if they thought a monster created by mad scientists was on the loose?

Hell, they don't want their kids being kidnapped and tortured and who knows what else."

"Ass probes," Toad volunteered. He'd changed his tune in a hurry.

I stared at Toad, confused. What the hell was an ass probe?

"Palmer's right." As I said before, Ronnie didn't say much, but when he did, we all paid attention. "My Pops says that place is cursed and we should stay away from it. There was a boy who disappeared around the tower. They searched for weeks and never found him."

Palmer's eyes lit up. "See? What did I tell you? I think we ought to go to Camp Hero and check it out."

"At night?" I croaked.

Palmer hit me on the arm. "No, asshole. During the day."

Gigi, Toad, and Ronnie nodded. The next couple of days were supposed to be crummy, weather-wise, so we had plenty of time to plan.

That night, after the lights were out and Palmer and I were in our twin beds, I whispered across the room, worried. "Mommy had a headache."

"Don't worry about Mom. She's fine."

"How do you know that? Do you really think there's a monster?"

Palmer didn't answer for a long time. "There could be."

"I don't believe you." I wanted Palmer to say he made the whole thing up, otherwise I was going to be up all night.

But he didn't. "It doesn't matter what you believe. It's what Mom and Dad believe. Now pipe down and go to sleep." Palmer rolled on his side and soon was asleep.

Not me. I didn't know what Palmer meant by that. And I was terrified.

CHAPTER TWELVE

D alton and I wait in the lobby of Miss Drake's pre-war building on the UES (upper east side). I'm sure it was a quiet area back in the sixties, but now it's a construction war zone. Scaffolding entombs nearly every building on the block. Miss Drake and her late "roommate" had lived there for decades. I never met the roomie. Miss Drake valued her privacy, and I didn't pry.

I'm not sure why Dalton volunteered to accompany James and me. Maybe it was out of morbid curiosity, or he genuinely didn't think I should do this on my own. Dad agreed to take Mark to the Museum of Natural History so Cassie can focus on Audra and her physical therapy. I know the kids are going to take Miss Drake's passing hard. She spoiled them rotten, something I'd heartily encouraged.

Dalton lights a cigarette. "Do you know how I first met your father?"

I didn't, but everyone has a story about how they got to know Bernard Anderson. I was at a book signing in Buffalo once. A woman of Middle Eastern descent came up to me with two little ones in tow. She explained in broken English that Bernard saw her crying at the American Embassy gates in a war-ravaged country, take your pick. He got her and her family on the last Embassy plane out. They don't call him St. Bernard for shits and giggles.

"It was at some conference. Bernard had just returned from being a special envoy for Gerald Ford. Anyway, he gave an impassioned speech about how the world needed more good people. I thought he was speaking directly to me." Dalton let out a rueful sigh. "I was such a chump. It didn't take me long to figure out that changing the world was impossible to do on an assistant district attorney's salary with two ex-wives and a passel of kids. I sold out. It was either that or bankruptcy, and I'm no William Kunstler. I decided that being a criminal defense attorney was my meal ticket. It turns out the guiltier they are, the richer they are, too."

"Are you saying you'd refuse to defend someone who is poor and innocent?" I crack.

"Brooks, all my clients are innocent," Dalton deadpans. "Poor, not so much." He puffs on his cigarette. "I've always meant to ask you this, and please don't take offense. Is it true about you, Truman Capote, and Norman Mailer?"

I know the story. I chuckle. "No, it's pure fiction. The closest I ever got to Norman Mailer was watching him get on the subway at Grand Central." And I was so fucking disappointed. My literary lion looked like any other harried commuter trying to make his connection. I fail to understand why Mailer's work isn't as highly regarded as Capote's, the hell with *In Cold Blood*. Yes, I know Mailer allegedly did horrible things when he was alive, but in some way, I considered us to be kindred souls, even though I'm taller, and some say, more talented. "I did meet Capote, though. It was in the late seventies when Hollywood thought I was the next big whatever. Someone got the bright idea of having the only survivor of a great American true-crime case hob-nob with the writer of a great American true-crime novel. It was a house high up in the Hollywood Hills. Lots of nubile young girls and boys. Lots of liquor and drugs." It was a good thing I was—and still am—a meticulous and voluminous record keeper. Otherwise, the vast majority of those years are just one long drug haze and alcohol bender. I once woke up under the Santa Monica pier with no clue how I'd gotten there.

"And?" Dalton urges.

"Remember, this was when Capote's beautiful swans had abandoned him, sending him into literary and social exile. The Capote I saw was a wasted, wizened old man sitting in a wicker chair. He barely uttered two words to me. If you Google it, you can see some pictures in the archives of Rona Barrett's rag." Rona Barrett had been a big gossip columnist then—not as big as Dorothy Kilgallen, though—but famous enough. In the photos, my eyes are barely focused. I wore a paisley jacket allegedly once owned by Mick Jagger that I'd picked up at a flea market. I paid way too much for it. Capote had on a snappy cravat and a beret that barely covered the top of his head. Bored, I did a couple of lines of coke, left with two girls, and ended up at the Chateau Marmont. That's a whole other book.

James appears. He's ashen-faced and out of breath. I hope his doctors know what they're doing. "You can come now."

I hesitate. "Miss Drake, is she—"

"No, no. She's downtown."

The elevator's out of order, so we take the stairs. James rests after each floor. I ask him if he's all right, but he brushes me off. "Never fucking better," he wheezes.

Miss Drake's apartment is on the sixth floor. Neighbors peek at us as we walk down the hall. Yellow police tape is already crisscrossed on Miss Drake's door.

"Do you know if she had any relatives?" James asks.

"Not in the States. She has a cousin in the Cotswolds, she goes —I mean, she went there—at least once a year. I'm sure the British Embassy can help in that regard."

I'd give Miss Drake a lift occasionally when we were headed in the same direction, but I'd never been inside her apartment. It's neat, prim, and tidy, just like her. Pictures of Queen Elizabeth hang in the foyer. Miss Drake is—was—an ardent monarchist. She never got over Charles and Diana divorcing. And if you really wanted to get Miss Drake riled up, all you had to do was ask her about Wallis Simpson.

My throat tightens. I feel like an intruder. "How was she found?"

"In her bedroom by a delivery guy with chicken soup. The door was wide open. He heard gurgling noises inside. He gave her CPR, but by the time the ambulance got here she was gone."

"Robbery?" Dalton steps on a toy rubber mouse and it squeaks. I didn't know Miss Drake had a cat.

"Could be. It's yet to be ruled out. But it doesn't look like anything was taken—at least, anything of value. Your Miss Drake, she led a sedentary lifestyle?" James asks.

"She was a seventy-five-year-old lesbian with two hip replacements. Yes, she led a sedentary lifestyle," I say.

We pass a semi-open door. Inside, people talk and take pictures. I hurry along. Miss Drake's kitchen is tiny. We all barely squeeze in between the counter and the old fridge. On top of the fridge is a bag of cat food.

"We know Miss Drake was having a disagreement with the landlord," James says.

"A disagreement? More like a battle royale." Miss Drake told me the story one day over tea and a plate of her delicious cranberry scones and now I tell it to James and Dalton. When Miss Drake's partner died, the landlord claimed the apartment no longer fell under rent control and tried to evict Miss Drake. The housing department and the courts ruled otherwise. The landlord tried to buy Miss Drake out, but she refused; this was her home, and she wasn't going anywhere. In retaliation, he cut off her basic utilities and refused to do any repairs. That accounted for the ugly brown water patches and crumbling ceiling in the kitchen. When the courts ordered the landlord to reinstate the utilities and do repairs, he'd do so for a while until the whole vicious cycle started again. As Miss Drake dryly put it, the landlord was waiting for her to either tire of fighting him or drop dead. He got his wish.

"The way real estate has skyrocketed, that's motive for murder," Dalton observes.

"I didn't say it was murder," James insists.

"You didn't say it wasn't," Dalton retorts, always the lawyer. "You know what Ian Fleming said about death: once is happenstance, two is coincidence, and three is enemy action."

"Bond. James Bond," I say in my best British accent.

"Sir Sean Connery," Dalton hoots.

I never met Sir Sean in person, but once upon a time, I'd been hired to do a quick punch-up job to maintain my WGA membership and medical insurance. Sir Sean was attached to the script to attract investors, a common enough occurrence. I badly needed the work. It was—how did Sheldon put it—a fallow time in my illustrious career. I wasn't the new hot thing anymore. I wasn't a thing, period. Some people thought I was dead.

I handed in the rewrite on Friday. On Saturday, everyone loved it. By Monday, the project was dead. As gut-wrenching as it was, it happens frequently. At various stages, Daniel Day-Lewis, Robert De Niro, and Michael Douglas were attached to *Fallen Angels*. You can die of hope in Hollywood. Or cirrhosis of the liver. Pick your poison. I'd learned not to take it personally. And I certainly don't blame Sir Sean for popularizing Aston Martins, Julian Broadhurst notwithstanding. It was a cool car. But not as cool as Sir Sean.

"Come on. Roger Moore wasn't bad," James chimes. "Now George Lazenby—"

Dalton and I groan.

"You know who played Bond that no one ever mentions? David Niven." I'm a fountain of useless trivia.

"Really? What movie?" Dalton asks.

"*Casino Royale*, 1967. Highly underrated."

"Mmmm." Dalton grows serious. "Think about it, Brooks. Marshall Reagan was writing an unauthorized bio about your family, and he winds up dead. Then your second ex-wife—"

"First ex-wife," I correct him. "And Nan overdosed."

"Perhaps," James volunteers.

"And now your assistant, Miss Drake. I rest my case." Dalton shoots me a triumphant look.

I shouldn't be peeved at Dalton, but I am. He only said out loud what I'd been thinking.

James covers his mouth with his hand as he coughs. I don't like the sound of it. "Have you been getting any hate mail? Threats from stalkers or obsessed and crazed fans? Something that stood out of late?"

I grunt. "What successful author hasn't?" I'd had more than my share of nutballs. The mechanic from Ohio who claimed he'd written *Fallen Angels*. The recluse who drove all the way from Winnipeg in an old VW hippie bus and demanded I help him get his masterpiece published because I "owed" him. When I refused, he had porn sent to my house. Or the women—yes, multiple women—who staked out the Dakota insisting that we were married. I can't remember how many restraining orders I'd taken out against these kooks.

"You know, I once had a client who had second thoughts about accepting a plea deal. He tried to change his plea at the last minute, but the judge wasn't having it. A few weeks later, I got an envelope filled with a white substance. It scared the living shit out of my secretary. Hazmat blocked off the entire street. It turned out to be cornstarch. The FBI found my client's saliva on the envelope. Fucking idiot. He would've been out in eight with the plea but now he's looking at another twenty. And he's got to get a new lawyer." Dalton shakes his head.

I laugh, but it's not funny. "To answer your question, Commissioner, I don't know. Miss Drake usually handled that side of it. But I'm sure that if there had been anyone especially troublesome, she would've told me. I mean, Marshall Reagan was one thing." I pause. "Come on. You can't possibly think that Miss Drake's death and Reagan's are related."

"It's not that far-fetched. Think about it. Brooks, you are the common denominator," Dalton says.

I give him an annoyed look; fuck it, Dalton, there's no need to remind me. I now regret that Dalton invited himself along. "Reagan was a slimeball," I counter.

"Yes, but if every slimeball in Manhattan ended up murdered, there wouldn't be enough room in the morgue." James puts up his hand. "Now getting back to Miss Drake, this is my theory. She walked in on something. She wasn't meant to be here. The woman didn't even have time to take off her coat. The closet is right by the front door. Why the hell would she go into her bedroom with her coat on instead of taking it off when she came in? Brooks, does that sound like something Miss Drake would do?"

No, it doesn't. Miss Drake was a neat freak, Mark's room notwithstanding. James is right. The first thing Miss Drake would've done was hang her coat in the closet. She was surprised by someone—or something.

"Did her neighbors report anything out of the ordinary or suspicious?" Dalton asks.

"People noticed a delivery van. It was parked outside the building for the past couple of days and nights. This morning, two guys in khaki uniforms buzzed apartments until they were let in. We've checked with all the tenants who were home at the time. No one got a delivery today or was even expecting one. No repairmen either. And of course, no working security cameras. Hopefully, someone on the block got them."

The more James talks, the more I'm alarmed. What if he's right, that this is some crazed fan of mine on the warpath for some deranged reason? Could Cassie and the kids be in danger? I'm alternately sick and angry but damn it, I'm not taking any chances. I text Sheldon to find out what private security firm my publisher used on my last book tour. Sheldon's in disbelief over Miss Drake.

James coughs into a handkerchief and tries to hide the dots of blood. "Gum disease," he explains.

I don't buy it. And judging from the look on Dalton's face, he doesn't either.

As we leave, Dalton slips me his business card. "You've got my private cell phone number. Call me day or night if something crops up."

I meekly protest that I won't need it.

"Don't be so sure. Why is the commissioner involved in this? Don't you think it's odd?"

No, I don't think it's odd, given our history, but I can't say that to Dalton without compromising James. I stay silent.

Dalton checks his watch. "Well, I must run. I'm on MSNBC at seven and hair and makeup are a bitch. I meant what I said, Brooks. Day or night." He hails a taxi and jumps in.

I decide to walk home. I can use the exercise, but I also need to burn off my anxiety. It feels as though the top of my head's going to explode. As I walk, I check my phone: there's another urgent message from Dr. Schultz. Just what I need on this shitty day. Fuck it, I might as well get it over with. I can't hide from this forever. The nurse puts me on a brief hold. When she returns, she's chirpy like a cashier at a drive-up window. "Mr. Anderson, the test came back positive. That means your sperm is viable."

Viable. It takes a moment for me to digest the word. I burst out laughing. Of course, the procedure failed. Another cosmic joke at my expense. I can imagine Cassie's reaction. "You're telling me the vasectomy was a bust. Do I have that right?"

She giggles. "We ran the test twice, but yes. Dr. Schultz would like you to make an appointment to discuss your options."

Uh, not so fast. I tell her that I'll think about it. I learned my lesson. I'm not doing a damn thing to my dick unless I have Cassie's permission.

There's a voicemail from Uncle Philip's hospice. It's the call I've been anticipating. Uncle Philip passed, quietly and uneventfully, while I'd been at Miss Drake's. Poor Aunt Flo. I hope this won't set her recovery back. She was home now with round-the-clock nurses. Eric had balked, but it was my money, not his. If Eric had his way, the house would be sold and his mother would be in an assisted living facility. I'm determined to keep Aunt Flo home for as long as possible. She doesn't talk about Althea much anymore.

After dinner, while the kids are occupied watching *Luca*, I take Cassie aside and fill her in on James' hypothesis regarding Miss Drake's untimely demise. "You haven't seen anyone strange or weird hanging around?"

"Only you," Cassie says with a smile. It should be a moment of levity, but it's not. "I can't believe Miss Drake's gone. I hope James is wrong and Miss Drake died of natural causes."

I hope so too, for Miss Drake's sake. I tell myself that James has watched too many *Bosch* episodes. "I want to have a memorial service for her. Maybe the British Embassy could help me get the word out to her friends." I stop and take a huge breath. This is probably not the best time to tell her that the vasectomy failed, but it has to be done. "Baby, I've got something to tell you."

"A surprise? I've got one, too. You go first." Cassie gives me this smile. At least someone is smiling.

I clear my throat, nervous as a feral cat hanging from the roof of the Astrodome. "I finally spoke to Dr. Schultz's office. And the word is, well, uh, it looks like the vasectomy—"

Cassie puts her hand over my mouth. "I don't need Dr. Schultz to tell me the results."

There's that goofy smile again. I know this smile. It's the smile Cassie had when she told me she was pregnant with Mark and Audra. Is she for real? "Baby, you can't be serious, are you fucking telling me—"

Cassie nods, her eyes bright.

I'm floored. When did this happen? We haven't had sex in— and then it hit me. *Fucking Chuck E. Cheese.* The kids saw a commercial for Chuck E. Cheese on YouTube and hounded us to take them. So, one Saturday we loaded the kids up in the Prius and went. The place was packed with frazzled parents who seemed stunned at the chaos. But I had to admit, the pizza wasn't half bad. The kids played until they wore themselves out. On the ride home, they'd both fallen asleep in the back seat. It was dark and kind of late. When Cassie suggested pulling into a side street, I thought she was kidding. I weakly protested that I'm too old for this nonsense. I'm on Medicare. I get the Senior Citizen discount. What if someone recognized me? I don't want the world to see my pale bare ass on TMZ. Plus, we don't have any condoms. Cassie ignores me and deftly lowers my seat down as far as it would go without disturbing the kids. Next thing I know, she's straddling my lap and humping like a jackhammer, burying her screams in my shoulders. I held it for as long as I could and exploded. We cleaned the seat as best we could with baby wipes. The kids never stirred. If someone had told me in my twenties that one day I'd fuck my wife in the front seat of a Prius after a noisy afternoon at Chuck E. Cheese, I wouldn't have believed it. But there you go, and I most certainly did.

"I wasn't going to tell you until I had my first doctor's appointment. But it was such a sad day, I thought you needed good news." Cassie gives me a tentative look. "It is good, isn't it?"

"Of course it is," I say, emotional. I love Cassie with every fiber of my being. Besides her and Mom, there's only one other woman in my life whom I loved as deeply and unconditionally. It was a story I'd purposefully left out of *Fallen Angels* for both legal and personal reasons, which will soon become apparent.

It was 1974, right after Nixon resigned in disgrace and Gerald Ford was sworn in. Soon after, our new President asked Dad to be a part of his administration. While Dad globe-trotted, trying to solve one crisis after another, I was sixteen and stuck in our Virginia mansion that was more like a mausoleum. Dad hired a married couple, the Boyles, to maintain the house; cook, clean, the usual stuff. Mrs. Boyle wasn't a very good cook and Mr. Boyle could barely operate a lawnmower. It seemed to me that their main job was to make my life fucking miserable. The Boyles were like that weird couple in Alfred Hitchcock's *The Man Who Knew Too Much* (the odd James Stewart-Doris Day remake). It always felt like the Boyles were watching me, even when I was asleep. The Boyles ate blood sausage, blasted Wagner day and night, and entertained people with bizarre accents. I was convinced the Boyles were Russian spies. Dad said I was being absurd; the Boyles were Irish.

I was going through a hardcore rebellious phase where I hated Dad, hated the world, and hated myself most of all. Looking back, I'm the first to admit that I was insufferable, a number one pain in the ass. At school, I did stupid things like selling pot in the cafeteria and setting off fireworks in the girls' locker room—it was empty, and no one got hurt—but that prank was the last straw, and I was expelled.

At his wits' end, Dad decided to enroll me in an all-male school that I will call the "Ames Academy." The academy promoted itself as a nurturing place for "gifted" children who for whatever reason couldn't thrive and grow in a structured learning environment. In reality, the Ames Academy was an institution of last resort for rich, exasperated parents who had no idea what to do with their troubled kids. And when I say troubled, I mean profoundly mentally and emotionally disturbed.

These kids put my hijinks to shame. One kid threw the family pet into the furnace. Another kid gouged all the eyes out of family portraits. You get where I'm going with this. These sociopaths didn't belong in regular school. Hell, most of them belonged behind bars or in an asylum. This was a toxic brew of budding Columbines, pubescent Proud Boys, and neo-Nazi boot-licking thugs.

I'm the first to admit that I had problems. I was still grieving Mom and Palmer. I was acting out. I had no one to talk to. I was alone. The meds the doctors prescribed didn't alleviate my pain and guilt. In many ways, the meds made it worse. And no matter what school I went to, it was always the same: *"Hey, look, that's Bernard Anderson's kid, you know his mom and brother were murdered,"* accompanied by hushed whispers and knowing glances. Everyone avoided me as though murder was contagious.

So, I began the fall semester at Ames on this beautiful, opulent campus. There were no traditional classrooms. In good weather, we met for "study sessions" on the rolling lawns. When it got colder, we gathered in cabins that dotted the woods like Swiss chalets. Learning was a farce. The teachers weren't much older than their students and many of them had their own issues. Drugs were plentiful. Pot smoke would waft over the cabins. I was the exception in that I had a home to go to. Most of the students were full-time boarders. On the weekends, they'd sneak out to a nearby town, pick up random girls, and bring them back to the dorms to do God knows what. Come Monday, the boys bragged and gloated. I was disgusted. Mom would've been appalled. Well, honestly, if she'd been alive, I wouldn't have been there.

In short, I was extremely depressed and fucked up. Dad was too busy saving the world to save me. I was on the verge of packing my shit and running away when I met "Jennifer Juniper," and yes, if you must know, I named her after that Donovan song. Up to this point, my sexual experience had been pretty much limited to furtive groping in damp basements after a couple of beers or joints. I was tongue-tied around girls my age and said and did idiotic things in a desperate attempt to sound and look cool.

I'm loath to show it to the world, but I have a sentimental side. I still tear up at the end of the cringeworthy *An Affair to Remember* with Cary Grant and Deborah Kerr.

Jennifer stood out. Even at my tender age, I knew she was, well, *different*. Drop-dead gorgeous in a Jane Fonda kind of way, she smelled like honey. Her smile was brighter than a thousand stars in the night sky. She was whip-smart, generous, and sweet. I was smitten the moment I saw her. So were most of the other boys at Ames.

I honestly don't know what she saw in me, but for some reason, she took a liking to me and took me under her wing. I guess it's fair to say that she collected broken things like Dad collected old coins. But there were two problems in this budding, one-sided romance: Jennifer was ten years older and she was married to my Social Studies teacher. "Charles" had done a couple of tours in Vietnam and returned a shattered shell. With his shaggy brown hair and tattered jeans, he touted revolution and was a boisterous member of several anti-war groups. Jennifer and Charles lived in a cottage on campus, and it was an open secret that they slept in separate bedrooms.

It was Jennifer who first introduced me to fine literature like Mark Twain, Henry Thoreau, Nathaniel Hawthorne, Edith Wharton, Tolstoy, Dante, Shakespeare, Charles Dickens, Walt Whitman, Herman Melville, F. Scott Fitzgerald, William Faulkner, Sinclair Lewis, and Edgar Allan Poe. She encouraged me to write and bought me a journal. She saw a kernel of talent in me and nurtured it much like a tiny seedling. She reminded me a lot of Mom, but the feelings I had for Jennifer weren't motherly in the slightest.

It was December. Dad was in some faraway place for

Christmas. Charles was out of town for a big anti-war demonstration. Once Jennifer learned that I was going to be on my own for the holiday, she invited me to spend Christmas Eve with her. She gave me a present, a scarf she'd knitted herself. To cover my embarrassment at not getting her a present, I impulsively kissed her. I'll never forget the look on Jennifer's face. I thought she was going to slap me and tell me to get the hell out and not come back. But one thing led to another and soon we were in a creaky bed doing things that my eight-year-old self would've been convinced were anatomically impossible. I fumbled on top of her until I ejaculated out of fear and exhaustion.

Poor Jennifer. She'd been under the impression that I was older—I was already a strapping six-foot-two and still growing—and most decidedly not a virgin. When she realized that I knew as much about sex as I did about quantum physics, she was gentle and patient. Jennifer taught me everything I know about pleasing a woman sexually. If I'm a good lover, and I like to think that I am, it's because of her.

But I can't sugarcoat it. It was wrong on every level imaginable. Jennifer was an adult, and the wife of one of my teachers. I was a minor and a student. In the eyes of the law, it was criminal. It doesn't matter that we were both willing, it was consensual, it was the seventies, the climate was different. It's still inexcusable. If a teacher ever tried to lay a finger on Mark or Audra—well, there wouldn't be much left of the teacher to bury, let's put it that way. But the main reason why I didn't include Jennifer in *Fallen Angels?* I was petrified that an armchair Agatha Christie would discover Jennifer's real identity and make her life a living hell. I wanted to protect Jennifer. I still do. And yes, I've told Cassie about Jennifer. Well, the parts she needs to know.

Our torrid affair went on for a couple of months. Jennifer was like a drug, better than any pill. Just looking at her got my blood racing. This was more than a bad case of teenage lust or hormones gone wild. I truly loved Jennifer as much as a grieving, rebellious, sixteen-year-old boy could.

It was early April. One lovely spring day between classes, Jennifer told me that she was pregnant. I couldn't have been more excited. I wrote her lengthy letters in which I declared my undying love and devotion to her and our unborn child. Fuck my father. We'd run away to California. It was always sunny there, right? I'd write books. Or maybe screenplays. Oh, the dreams I had for us.

And then before it began, the fantasy was over. Jennifer told me in the cruelest, harshest way possible that we didn't have a future together, that she'd never loved me, and that she was getting an abortion. She never wanted to see or hear from me ever again. I pleaded with her until I was hoarse.

It was a long weekend. That Monday when I returned to school, Jennifer and Charles were gone, their cottage empty. That night, despondent and broken, my life changed for the worse. I did heroin for the first time. I hoped I wouldn't wake up. When I did, the pain was still there, sharp and searing. And for a little while, when I did heroin, the pain receded. The beast was dormant. It seems like a lifetime ago. Hell, a couple of lifetimes ago.

I stare at Cassie, the woman I love beyond all reason. I know how much she wants this baby, so of course, I want it, too. I'm also scared shitless. That's the reality. "I'm thrilled, honey, really I am, but—"

Cassie groans.

"I can't help it. What if the placenta previa happens again?"

"Brooks, I told you. It's rare. The chances of it happening again are like being hit by lightning twice on the same day." She nuzzles into me like the missing last piece of a jigsaw puzzle. "But I don't want anyone to know yet. I mean it. I haven't even told Tammy."

"Okay, baby. You're the boss. You know, maybe this is a sign that we should move out east permanently." We've talked about this off and on, mostly off. Cassie's diffident on the subject. A summer home is one thing, but living in the country full time is another. She loves the city. "There's nothing work-wise that we can't do remotely. And it would be good for the kids. Would you consider it? I mean, seriously?"

"But what about the apartment? Would you sell it?"

"Not a snowball's chance in hell." Even if someone was stupid and rich enough to meet my price—and I had no price—I doubt the co-op board would approve a new tenant. Hell, if I was applying for an apartment now, they wouldn't approve me. They rejected Cher, for fuck's sake.

My cell buzzes. It's James. It's my fervent hope that Miss Drake's autopsy proves she died of anything else but murder. "We don't have to decide now. Let's think about it, okay?" I kiss her and go to my lair. "James, hey. Any news?"

James grunts something that sounds like yes. "It's official. Homicide. The cause of death was cardiac arrest due to a pulmonary embolism."

I'm puzzled. A pulmonary embolism is a blood clot; there's nothing nefarious about a blood clot. When I'm on a long plane ride, I always make sure to stretch my legs.

"The technical term is deep vein thrombosis. The clot usually starts in the leg and travels to the lungs. But it can occur in other parts of the body. During the autopsy, the coroner discovered a needle prick in Miss Drake's shoulder. Her blood work showed a lethal dose of Vitamin K."

"Vitamin K?" My mind races. I think of the *Bugs Bunny* cartoons Palmer and I watched on Saturday mornings at the Big House. Carrots killed Miss Drake?

"Miss Drake's doctor confirmed that she was on blood thinners since her hip replacements. Too much Vitamin K in a person on blood thinners can induce an embolism. It's practically undetectable unless you're specifically looking for it. A recipe for the perfect murder. Which means—"

I curse under my breath. These weren't just robbers—they were hired killers. They knew her medical history. They came prepared to kill Miss Drake—and they did.

That night, for the first time since I'd married Cassie, I dream about Grandpa William's cottage. Mom—what I could recognize of her—cradled a bloodied and battered infant in her arms. A dark shadow stood over her, big and feral judging by its low growls. Palmer jumped on the shadow's back. I screamed as hard as I could, but no one heard me. A warm gush of blood from Palmer's gutted neck poured over me like a rain shower.

I wake up screaming, the sheets soaked with my sweat and urine.

Just a bad dream, Cassie reassures me.

I'm not so sure.

CHAPTER THIRTEEN

*C*amp Hero started as Fort Hero in 1942. With World War II raging, the Feds were more concerned about a Nazi invasion than an alien one. The eastern tip of Montauk was vulnerable. It could be easily accessed or breached by a German U-boat, so the Army, Navy, and Coast Guard did upgrades on the existing air force station. Once the war ended, another war began: the Cold War. And if the conspiracy theorists are to be believed, that's when these alleged German scientists who'd been allowed clandestine entry into the United States began their immoral, unethical, and insidious experiments. Why our government would allow such sick experiments on American citizens, Palmer couldn't really explain. But it didn't matter. He was determined to go to Camp Hero, and he was our Pied Piper.

Palmer told Mom we were going to spend the day at the beach. She made us peanut butter and jelly sandwiches and our thermoses were filled with grape juice. I felt bad deceiving Mom about where we were going, but not bad enough to tattle.

Gigi and Toad were waiting for us further up the block, as we'd prearranged. We hung around for a couple of minutes waiting for Ronnie. His parents were old-school Catholics and Ronnie was an altar boy. In those days, priests were like gods and could do no wrong. I didn't *know it then, but Ronnie was sexually abused by several members of the clergy. They passed him around like an ashtray. When Ronnie finally found the courage to tell his parents, they insisted he was lying and threw him out of the house. Years later, I ran into him as he panhandled near Penn Station. He told me the sordid story over a cup of clear broth, the only thing he could eat. I tried to help him, but he was too far gone. After we last spoke, he died of an overdose.*

When we realized Ronnie wasn't going to show, we set off on our bikes. It was a beautiful day, the air hot and thick, ripe for a late-afternoon thunderstorm. By the time we got to Camp Hero, I was tired and sweaty and having second thoughts about this adventure. The camp wasn't open to the public then as it was still an active military base. That changed in 2002. The Feds handed it over to New York State after the base had been decommissioned.

Palmer guessed there'd be sentries at the camp gates, but there was another way to get in undetected, which all the local kids knew about. Camp Hero consisted of hundreds of acres and there was no way that the entire property could be patrolled twenty-four-seven. It was the perfect hideout for kids to sneak in to drink beer, smoke pot, and get laid. Adults, too, if they knew where to go.

As we entered the camp, I wasn't worried about Mom finding out. We'd get a scolding at best. Mom wasn't big on discipline like Dad was. But I was concerned for Gigi. She was a military brat. If her dad found out, she'd be in big trouble.

Maybe Gigi was able to read my mind due to the radar tower because she suddenly said, "We could be swimming now."

"Well, you can leave anytime you like. Nobody's forcing you," Palmer said.

We followed Palmer down a barely visible dirt path off the main road. We went maybe a mile or so into the woods. Clearly, Palmer was looking for something. He eventually found it: a hole in the fence. We hid our bikes under a bank of trees and covered them with branches.

As we went deeper into the woods, the thing I noticed most was how quiet it was. Occasionally a bird would chirp—I heard some tapping in the distance, undoubtedly a woodpecker—but otherwise, nothing. We passed some concrete bunkers. Some looked in good shape, others were decrepit. And even though we were in the woods, you could still see the radar tower, the 1966 equivalent of today's Siren Head.

It was close to noon, and we hadn't seen any monsters yet. But we did see dead animals: a red fox, a raccoon, and squirrels. But as we walked deeper, I heard a rustling in the underbrush. When we'd stop to catch our breath, the noise would stop, too.

"What do you think killed them, Palmer?" Toad poked a flattened squirrel with a stick.

Palmer studied the carcass. "I dunno. Maybe a wolf or a coyote."

"There are no wolves or coyotes around here," Gigi pointed out.

"You don't know that for sure. These scientists, shit, they can create anything," Palmer shot back. "Maybe the gamma rays got them. Or the monster ate them."

"Or maybe they just died," Gigi flatly said.

"Speaking of eating, I'm hungry." Toad was always hungry. I'd made sure that Mom had packed a couple of extra sandwiches because Toad was always bumming food off us. His housekeeper seemed to be capable of making only three things: hard-boiled eggs, tuna fish on soggy bread, and celery sticks.

We bolted our food down behind a bunker. Toad went off to take a leak. I found another dead animal. This one looked like an opossum to me, but it was so badly decomposed it was hard to tell. I scurried up to alert Palmer of my discovery, but he was otherwise engaged with Gigi. Palmer's hands were on her breasts—they were about the size of drawer knobs, too small even for a training bra—and Gigi's good hand stroked his hair.

I'd never seen Palmer kiss a girl before, except for Mom. It felt weird. And maybe I was a tad jealous. Okay, maybe a lot. But I wasn't going to hang around watching them slobber all over each other. Annoyed, I went back to the dead opossum. Toad came with me. And that's where we stayed until we heard the yelling.

Palmer and Gigi were surrounded by a group of older teens. I'd seen them around town. The boys were crude and loud and the girls wore too much makeup and fake giggled. "Trouble," Palmer would mutter, and we'd cross the street to avoid them.

"Look at the lovebirds. How cute," a girl in a halter top and cut-off shorts jeered.

"How does it feel to make out with a freak?" One of the boys—this one had a crew cut—pushed Palmer.

"Leave us the fuck alone or—" Palmer warned.

"Or what? What are you going to do? Is she going to hit me with her flipper?" another boy, with red hair and freckles, taunted.

"Flipper! Flipper!" the girls chanted.

My heart ached for Gigi, who was near tears. I was sorry we'd ever come to Camp Hero.

"Cut it out!" I screamed.

The third boy—he had this kind of ducktail hairdo and a chain for a belt—grabbed me. "You want to eat dirt, punk?" He tripped me and pushed my face to the ground.

Toad came up behind him and threw the dead opossum at him.

"Fuck!" Ducktail Guy yelled.

Gigi tried to run away but Halter Girl cut her off. "What else is wrong with you? Can't you talk?" Halter Girl sneered.

"Fuck you!" Gigi shrieked.

Ducktail Guy held me down as I tried to squirm free.

Crew Cut Asshole had Palmer in a choke hold.

Toad held the opossum by the tail and swung it like a lasso.

Gigi was pinned against the bunker by the girls.

"I bet she doesn't even have a pussy that works. She probably pees through her ass." Halter Girl poked Gigi in the chest. "Boys are going to have to fuck her in the butt." She pulled at Gigi's shorts. Gigi kicked her right in her girly parts. Furious, Halter Girl pulled Gigi by her hair and smashed her face into the bunker.

Palmer was choking, his face purple.

"You're killing him!" I yelled. Where the hell were the army guys? Couldn't they hear us?

It was then that I saw this, for lack of a better word—thing. It was crouching in the bushes by the bunker. I can't say how big it was or even if it was an animal. It was an indistinct shape with bloodshot eyes, and it growled. I'd never seen or heard anything like it. Not then, not since.

Toad saw it too. Frozen, he dropped the opossum. Pee streamed down his legs.

Freckle Boy grabbed Gigi. "I'd do her, even with no cunt." He threw Gigi, blood streaming down her face, on her stomach and pulled her shorts off. Her underwear was yellow, sprinkled with butterflies. Freckle Boy unzipped his shorts and pulled out a misshapen dick. It looked like something you'd dig out of a vegetable garden.

I threw up chunks of bread and peanut butter.

"Do it!" Ducktail Guy shouted.

An awful screech pierced my ears. It was worse than raccoons fighting. Louder than an air raid siren.

Startled, Freckle Boy dropped Gigi. She crawled away like a centipede.

"What the fuck was that?" Crew Cut Asshole screamed.

The girls didn't wait around to find out. Howling, they all ran off toward Siren Head. Freckle Boy, his shorts around his hairy legs, raced after them.

Crew Cut Asshole let Palmer go and tried to run away, but Palmer grabbed him by the ankle. Crew Cut Asshole fell face first. Palmer grabbed a rock and was about to pound Crew Cut Asshole's head in. I'd never seen Palmer so enraged and out of control. I don't know what I was more afraid of, Palmer or that thing in the bushes.

"Palmer, no," Gigi gasped.

Palmer snapped out of it. He stomped Crew Cut Asshole in the back. "If I ever see your fucking face again, I'll kill you. That goes for your asshole friends, too." I knew he meant it.

Crew Cut Asshole limped away.

Palmer helped Gigi put her shorts back on and carried her back to where our bikes were hidden. Toad and I were right behind. Once we were safely out of there, Palmer cleaned Gigi's face with water from Toad's thermos. "Where does it hurt?"

Gigi opened her mouth.

I felt like I was going to hurl again.

Gigi's front teeth were pushed all the way up into her gums. It looked like strawberry jello. "What am I going to tell my dad?" she moaned.

"Just say you fell off your bike," Toad suggested. "It worked for me when I broke my leg in three places."

We didn't see Gigi for quite some time after that. Later, Mom told us that Gigi had to have emergency surgery to fix her mouth and a broken eye socket. "That was some tumble off her bike," was all Mom said.

"What do you think that thing was?" I whispered to Palmer that night after Mom had tucked us in bed.

"Only one thing it could be. A monster." He sounded happy.

I wasn't. I was petrified. What if that thing had followed us home?

CHAPTER FOURTEEN

I suppose it's fitting that it's a cold, harsh, rainy day for Miss Drake's memorial reception at the Bulldog Tavern in midtown. I forgot to bring an umbrella. Dad got me in touch with Hugh Macomber, the personal assistant of the Acting British General Consul. When I explain that I want to give Miss Drake a tasteful, dignified send-off, Macomber assures me in a voice that sounds so much like Bob Marley's that I expect him to break into "No Woman, No Cry", that it would be Her Majesty's distinct pleasure to handle all the arrangements.

I soon learn that the Consulate's quite familiar with Miss Drake. Her last will and testament are handled by a lawyer affiliated with the Consulate. Miss Drake's estate is left in trust to several godchildren and her remains are to go to her cousin in the Cotswolds who I strongly suspect isn't a cousin at all.

It's been a rough morning already. I got up at sunrise to drive to Mt. Vernon for Uncle Philip's interment. Before I leave the apartment, Cassie's in the bathroom puking her guts out. I ask her if she needs anything, but she motions me away, her head in the toilet. I know morning sickness is normal, but this seems severe. We're still sleeping in separate bedrooms, but at least it's under the same roof. I consider it a small victory.

I'm the only one in attendance for Uncle Philip. Aunt Flo's in no condition and Eric's still overseas. The State Department sent a flower arrangement which is already wilting in the rain. I know I should stop at Althea's grave, but my excuse is I'm running late.

When I arrive at the Bulldog, the entrance is surrounded by reporters, so I slip in through a side door. Macomber told me that the tavern's a favorite watering hole for many British city expats, Miss Drake included. When I step inside, I know why. With its dim lighting, shiny brass bar, and intimate booths, it feels like the sort of pub Winston Churchill might've frequented. I'd been to England once, on a book tour for *Fallen Angels*. I wasn't in the best shape, so my publisher hired a minder who was supposed to keep me out of trouble. Instead, the minder introduced me to his dealer, and I promptly blew a sizable chunk up my nose. I think I was interviewed by David Frost, but I can't swear to it.

The memorial's in a private room on the second floor. I hope the room isn't too large, especially if the turnout is light. It will make me more depressed than I already am. I worry needlessly. The room is so packed I have to elbow my way in. The cynic in me wonders if they've come just for the free food and drink.

I quickly discern that everyone's here for Miss Drake. Huge flower sprays surround a collection of enlarged photos of Miss Drake at various stages of her life: a small child in a white frock, as a teen on a scooter, another as a smiling young woman in a suit at the gates of Buckingham Palace.

I spot Dad, who's attracted to galas and soirees like bees are to pollen. A born ham, if he were invited to a Dairy Queen opening, he'd show up in tails. Dad is in his element as he animatedly addresses a group of shiny bald guys in kilts. In the background, the Hollies are at a "Bus Stop."

"Hey, Brooks." Sheldon rushes up and gives me a bear hug. "What a turnout, eh? Miss Drake would love it."

That she would.

"Is Cassie here?"

I tell Sheldon she's under the weather. I keep my promise to Cassie, even though I dislike fudging Sheldon. I tell myself soon enough he'll know.

Sheldon motions to a man in a black suit who's discreetly positioned a couple of feet behind me. The man blends in if you don't focus on the enormous skull and crossbones tattoo on his neck. "Is that the—"

It is. The man is my bodyguard, or my "sentinel," as the security firm calls him. This outfit isn't cheap, but it's not the time to play Scrooge. I'd pay any price when it comes to Cassie and the kids. If they leave the house for any reason, they have their own sentinels. When I broached Dad about getting one as well—if not for him then for my peace of mind—he brushed me off. "I call him John Wick. He's a former Navy Seal and a martial arts expert. I've no doubt he can fuck someone up good. It won't be for long, just until this nasty business is sorted out," I tell Sheldon. That's my hope, anyway.

Sheldon grabs a pint off a nearby table and takes a long sip. "Brooks, I know this probably isn't the right time to bring this up—"

I know what's coming: Max and the *Three Rivers* sequel. I want to rail at Sheldon, *for fuck's sake, give it a rest, not now, not today.* But I don't. Making impossible deals is in Sheldon's blood.

"I'm thinking of leaving the agency," Sheldon whispers.

Pfffft. I give Sheldon a skunk eye. He periodically brings up the idea of hanging his own shingle, but after a couple of drinks, he talks himself out of it. The economy. The stress. The long hours. He's a senior partner now. It would be like starting over. At his age, he can afford to take it easy—or easier. But Sheldon's a workaholic. He's not going to change. But I also think leaving the agency is more about his pride than anything else. Sheldon won't admit it, but he was miffed when his name wasn't added to the masthead when he became a senior partner. "I made this agency what it is," he railed.

"I'm serious this time. No fucking around. I'm not getting any younger. If I'm going to do it, it has to be now. What do you think? What I mean is, would you stay with me?" There's an edge to Sheldon's voice that I haven't heard before. It doesn't suit him.

"Sheldon, if you're serious, and I mean fucking serious, then you know what my answer is." The question doesn't even need to be asked. Sheldon should know this.

"Yeah, just humor me, it's been a long goddamn day." His eyes dart around like dice on a table. "I have other clients, but with you, it's different. We're brothers. We have a sacred bond. I'd never do anything to hurt you or Cassie. You know that, right?"

I don't like this Sheldon, anxious and unsure. It's not like him. He's supremely confident. He can bullshit his way out of anything. "Take it easy, you worry too goddamn much. I can't say it any plainer than this: if you decide to open your own literary agency, I'm going with you. It's not even open for discussion. Now, are you satisfied?"

Sheldon takes a deep breath. "Good, good. I just had to hear it from your lips. I'm in the process of severing ties with the agency. It's going to take a couple of weeks, maybe months, to unravel everything. But it's going to be great. I know it." He sounds like his old self again and smiles broadly. "By the way, have you heard from Tom Giafrida?"

"No, why. Am I supposed to?" Tom Giafrida is another of Sheldon's clients. A mousy guy with horn-rimmed glasses who looks like the before photo in a muscle man ad, he wrote a Tom Clancy-like thriller while working at Walmart. He sent a cold query to Sheldon, who ended up shepherding a huge multi-house auction for a debut author. It was a feeding frenzy and Sheldon expertly played the houses like a blackjack dealer. Over the course of a weekend, Giafrida went from minimum wage to a six-figure advance. I met Giafrida once at Sheldon's office when I came by to sign some contracts. Giafrida barely acknowledged me. I got a distinct impression that he considered me lowbrow. Oh, well, fuck him and his high horse.

Sheldon waves his hand. "It's nothing, trust me. Minor accounting irregularities. These newbies, they get a bit of money, hire some math geeks, and right away they have to find something to grumble about to justify their paycheck."

A woman—mid-forties I'd say, an attractive champagne blonde, dressed in a slimming military-style jacket and slacks—taps me on the shoulder. The old Brooks would've hit on her hard. "Mr. Anderson? I'm Elaine Brighton, the Acting Consul General for the British Consulate."

"Miss Brighton, nice to meet you." We cordially shake hands. I turn to introduce Sheldon, but he's disappeared into the crowd.

"It's Mrs. Brighton, actually, but please, call me Elaine. Mr. Macomber regrets that he's not here, he was so looking forward to finally meeting you. His youngest daughter is in Kingston and went into labor six weeks early. He's her labor coach, so now he has to do it by FaceTime. His first grandchild, so God knows how long it will take."

"Well, with his mellifluous voice, I'm sure he'll coax the baby out in short order." I nod at the crowd. "And I was afraid no one would come. I didn't realize Miss Drake was so popular."

"Everyone adored Lucinda. She'll be dearly missed." Elaine motions for me to accompany her into an area that's a bit quieter. "Mr. Anderson, I want to tell you about Lucinda, well, as much as I'm authorized to disclose. Even after all these years, much of it is still classified. She was born in Norwich. Her father was a pilot, her mother a nurse. She had an older brother. Her parents and brother were killed in a lorry accident when she was two. Dreadful. She was sent to live with paternal relatives in the Hebrides who didn't treat her well. That's probably where the story would've ended if not for a local schoolmarm that took note of Lucinda's keen intelligence. She graduated at the top of her class. Subsequently, Lucinda moved to London and joined the Foreign Office, where she served her country with honor and distinction on many domestic and foreign operations."

"Do you mean MI6?" It didn't surprise me in the slightest. "Why did she leave?"

"I wish I could say it was of her own volition, but the truth is, it wasn't a good time to have a lifestyle that some in the intelligence community considered a potential liability. She came to America with her partner to make a fresh start. Lucinda had many friends here and they both worked for the Consulate. But when her partner died, Lucinda decided she wanted to try something new, a job as an executive assistant with an up-and-coming novelist. We were quite sorry to see her go and told her if it didn't work out—"

I choked up. The kids were inconsolable when we told them. Mark had taken it especially hard. "Miss Drake was a beloved member of our family." I can't get used to referring to Miss Drake by her first name.

"And how she loved you, Mr. Anderson. You were like a son to her. She always went on about you at functions." Elaine pauses. "But frankly, we were a bit flummoxed when your coroner ruled Lucinda's death as a homicide. Not that we hadn't considered the possibility, however remote, of it being tied to her work at the embassy. It was all so long ago. However, I do grant you that death by injection of vitamins is a tad Putinesque, wouldn't you say?"

I would.

Elaine glances around, almost as if she's looking for someone. "I don't know if I should be telling you this, Mr. Anderson, but our people believe that if it wasn't natural causes, it's far more likely to have something to do with your father. Please don't take offense."

Dad? I'm not offended. I just think it's a ludicrous suggestion. "Why would you say that?"

"Well, they traveled in the same circles, if you get my drift."

This borders on the absurd. Dad had never been—what's the word—a spook. "You can tell your people from me that they're wrong. If my father had known Miss Drake personally or professionally, he would've told me. His memory is excellent. He never forgets a face," I say, emphatic.

Elaine smiles good-naturedly. "I'm sure you're right. This was all before my time, so who am I to say? This is a celebration to honor Miss Drake, not open up a wretched Pandora's box. Now if you'll excuse me, I have to mingle, as you Americans are fond of saying. Good day, Mr. Anderson." She walks off, her bootheels clacking.

Maybe it was a good day for Mrs. Brighton, but what she said about Dad makes a bad day exponentially worse. I sidestep the tempting array of sweet treats on the buffet table; Paul Hollywood from *British Baking* would be envious. I'm not sorry that I have to leave to see Dr. Richter. I'm anxious to tell her what I remember—or hopefully remember—about Mom and Palmer.

As I snake my way through the room, a middle-aged woman in a shacket and high-waisted jeans waylays me. Under her arm is a copy of *Fallen Angels*. "Mr. Anderson—" she begins, her voice low and hesitant.

I'm beyond irritated. This is a memorial service, not a meet-and-greet. First, Mrs. Brighton and her smug accusations, and now this clueless, insensitive clod who wants an autograph. It's not my nature to be churlish with fans, but this woman is pushing it. "I don't have the time, I'm sorry. If you email my publisher, maybe they can send you a bookmark."

Her face turns red. "Oh, you think I want—I don't want your autograph, Mr. Anderson. I just—my name is June—Juniper Faulk. I think you might have known my mother." She says the name in a hushed whisper.

I whirl around, dumbfounded. "What the hell did you say?" I snarl.

The woman takes two steps back, clearly frightened.

John Wick gets between us. "Mr. Anderson—"

I stare at her. *Those eyes.* My past is staring at me. *Goddamn.* "It's fine. Everything's fine." I manage a feeble smile. Inside, I feel as though I've touched a live wire. "Why don't we find someplace quiet and have a cup of coffee." Not a drink, damn it. Maybe some alcoholics can take one drink and stop right there. I'm not one of them.

There's a coffee shop a few doors down from the tavern. I get a black coffee, she gets a double caramel macchiato, the kind of frothy drink Cassie orders and never finishes. We sat in a rear booth, away from prying eyes. Behind us, John Wick's on his cell.

I tell myself that this woman, however well-intentioned, is mistaken. She has to be. Otherwise, it means I have a fifty-year-old daughter. *Fifty!* I can imagine Cassie's reaction. And Dad's. *Fuck.*

I thought I'd experienced profound embarrassment. The time I threw up on Donna Summer's platform shoes. When I broke Stephen Stills' acoustic guitar backstage at the old Fillmore East (we were both in a cocaine stupor). When I ejaculated in the eye of a famous actress in her limo (don't ask). However, this was a thousand times worse. How the hell am I going to explain this?

"I didn't know what to do after Miss Drake died. I'm so sorry, Mr. Anderson," June blurts.

"Why don't we start at the beginning." I sound calmer than I am.

She opens *Fallen Angels* and takes out a slip of paper. "This is a copy of my birth certificate. You can't get a notarized copy anymore. It's all online, you have to order it. But it does have the state seal." She pushes it towards me. "I got Miss Drake's email, I mean, my daughter did."

There's a daughter, too? Jesus Christ. I swallow hard and inspect the certificate. A girl born on December 23, 1975. Her mother's name—*my* Jennifer Juniper—and Charles is listed as the father. I feel slightly nauseous. If this certificate is real—if it's not a forgery or a ruse—it means that Jennifer lied to me about getting an abortion. "You sent this to Miss Drake? When?"

"The day she passed away. The first time I reached out to her, it was about a month or so before that. When I didn't hear from her, I sort of gave up. Then my daughter told me to check my spam folder and there it was. Miss Drake said she needed proof before she could take it any further."

Yes, that sounds like Miss Drake. She wouldn't have mentioned it to me without doing some kind of verification first, God rest her soul.

"My daughter lives in Red Hook. She read about the memorial reception. I'm surprised they let me in." She fiddles with a couple of sugar packets, nervous, or maybe it's the coffee. "I don't come into Manhattan that much. I'm in Pennsylvania. I married my high-school sweetheart right after we graduated. I had kids right away. Baked cookies, did the PTA, all that stuff. I didn't have the ambition or talent to do anything else." Her tone's apologetic. "But the kids turned out all right, so I can't complain too much."

Kids. As in plural. I have grandchildren. My head spins. God, do I feel fucking old. "No need to apologize. Hell, being a full-time mom isn't easy even on the best of days." Cassie loves Mark and Audra to the moon and back, but I'm sure there were days she wished she could trade them in for a snazzy convertible and take off. And, of course, being Brooks Anderson's wife presents other complications. But right now, all I can think is that I'm so fucked.

"I got divorced ten years ago. I didn't want it, but you know how it goes."

That I did.

She tosses her hair back as her mother did. "I put aside the hurt. We managed to stay on good terms because of the kids.

That took time and a lot of therapy." She smiles. It suits her. "I have a boyfriend now who treats me like a queen. It's good." She stops. "I'm so sorry. I have this habit of oversharing."

I chuckle. I've heard the same about me. I have to ask the question, although I suspect I know the answer. "Your mother? Is she—"

"Last spring. Colon cancer." June toys with her oversized hoop earrings. "She was a trooper to the end. She never complained, not once. Not even when she lost her beautiful hair." She tears up.

I stare into my coffee. If it were any blacker, it would be charcoal.

"I guess you're wondering why I didn't contact you sooner?"

It has crossed my mind, yes.

"It was Mom. She didn't tell me about you until she was in the hospice. And then she insisted that I wait a year, that I needed time and perspective."

My tongue is thick. "I have to verify this." I fold the birth certificate and put it in my jacket. *Trust but verify* is one of Dad's mottos.

"Mr. Anderson, she didn't blame you for how things turned out. She never had a bad thing to say about you. She said you were like a sparrow with a broken wing and that you didn't have a choice. All the horrible, hurtful things she said—she didn't mean it. She didn't want you to ruin your life on a fling."

I beg to disagree. Jennifer wasn't a fling. But she was right. I would've done anything to be with her: suffer Dad's wrath, be disinherited and/or ostracized. I was naive. I didn't see the world the way it really was or how the world would've seen us. I saw things the way I wanted them to be, sweet, kind, and non-judgmental. The two worlds—quite simply—were incompatible. But the hurt was real. I have a reputation for being cavalier, for being uncaring and aloof. That's just a facade. I feel things too deeply. Jennifer was an open wound that never completely healed. Now, knowing the truth, maybe it would. It's my hope with Mom and Palmer, too, that remembering that ghastly night, however painful or shocking, would bring me—and damn it, how I hate the word—closure.

June hands me another piece of paper. "She kept them. All of them."

I recognize it. It's one of the many love letters I wrote to Jennifer. I can't bring myself to read past the first paragraph. Any doubts I had about June's paternity were getting smaller by the minute. Naturally, we'll do a DNA test, but my heart knows the results. "Charles raised you?"

"He was sterile because of Agent Orange. Mom broke down and told him. He wasn't angry or resentful. He was a good father, but I always felt something was—off. After he died, Mom confessed that he wasn't my biological father, but she didn't tell me who until the end." She leans forward. "I know it's a lot to absorb, Mr. Anderson. It was for me, too. I've had a year to get used to it. You've only had, what, fifteen minutes."

"Tell me about your children." I almost get ahead of myself and say, my grandchildren.

"Three. They're all doing great. My oldest, Sean, he's in Seattle. He's an engineer with Microsoft. He's got a two-year-old boy and his wife's expecting any day now."

Excuse me? I'm also—potentially—a great-grandfather? *What fucking else?* Oh, Aunt Flo is going to love this. She's always complaining that she wishes our family was bigger. She got her wish in spades. What would Mark and Audra be to my great-grandchildren? Talk about messy family dynamics. Christmas is going to be a bitch.

"Meredith's my middle girl. She's a lawyer and a damn good one. She works for the Commonwealth. She's engaged to a wonderful woman, they just bought a house. And my youngest is Caroline, that's the one in Red Hook. She's a junior assistant at one of the cable networks."

"Not Max," I quip.

"No, another one. Mom loved *Three Rivers*. She loved all your books. Especially—" She thumbs *Fallen Angels*. "Near the end, that's all she talked about. How she knew, even then, that you were going to be a great writer. And she appreciated that you kept her out of it."

As much as I want to stay, I have to go. I give her my cell phone and email; she does the same. "My lawyer will be in touch. We should do a DNA test as soon as possible to clear this up."

"Sure, that's logical. You don't know me," June says with a quick nod. "I could be making the whole thing up, but I'm not. And you're probably wondering, what do I want? I mean, if you are my father."

Dad would say it's about money. That's all they ever want.

"My kids asked me the same thing. Sean was like, Mom, it's a little late in the day for this big Kumbaya reunion. It might be better if you just left it alone. What if he's an—"

"Asshole?" I volunteer.

She gives me an embarrassed giggle. "When you come down to it, I want you to know. Not for me, but Mom. She kept this secret for so long. Maybe she thought by telling me, it made up for it in some way. She's gone, you're older, and he can't hurt her now."

Who can't hurt her? "I'm sorry, who?"

"Your father."

I'm gobsmacked. *What did Dad have to do with Jennifer?*

"Mom said that your father found out about her being pregnant and threatened her. If she didn't break things off and get an abortion, he'd make her life miserable. She'd go to jail. Charles, too. That he knew powerful people and he could—" June abruptly stands. "You know, I've changed my mind. This was a really bad idea. Please, I beg you, don't tell your father about me or my kids." She looks and sounds terrified. If this is an act, it's a good one.

"You've no reason to be afraid," I say. "My father wouldn't hurt anyone. If he did say those things, it was to scare her. And it worked. Please, don't bail just yet. Let's do the DNA, find out one way or the other, and put it to rest once and for all. Isn't that the reasonable thing to do? Are you staying with Caroline?"

"Yes. I'll be there a few more days." June takes a deep breath. "Don't make me regret this, Mr. Anderson." I wish she wouldn't call me that. It makes me feel as old as Methuselah. "It took a lot for me to do this, and I don't want it to blow up in my face." She scurries away, book in hand, like a frightened mouse.

I take a long sip of my now ice-cold coffee. I feel the migraine of all migraines coming on. June's right, this is a lot to process. But I know this: if Dad found out about Jennifer, the ones responsible were those wretched, godawful Boyles, the sneaky fuckers.

My cell phone rings. Of course, it's Dad. "Where the hell are you? I saw you leave with some woman."

"Just a fan looking for an autograph." That's my cover story and I'm sticking to it.

"Vultures. No sense of propriety or decency. Are you coming back, son?"

I explain I have an appointment with Dr. Richter.

"A goddamn waste of time and money. She's just another quack." Dad pauses for a moment. "Are you sure there's not something else? Look, if you're upset about the bodyguard business, don't give it another thought. You have to protect your family the best way you see fit. I'm an old man, no one's going to come after me." He pauses again. "Wasn't that nice of Elaine Brighton to make an appearance? I knew her father. He was in Thatcher's cabinet. A nice enough fellow, but a bit slow on the uptake. Are we still on for lunch tomorrow?"

Inwardly, I groan. Wednesday and his fucking grilled salmon. "Let me check back with you in the morning, okay?" I no sooner hang up with Dad when Dr. Richter's office calls. She has to leave

PJ MCILVAINE

the office early; would I mind rescheduling? Hell, no, not after the day I've had. Old Brooks would go on a bender. New Brooks has to settle for seltzer.

When I get home, Cassie's on the living-room sofa watching a baking show on Netflix. She bloomed in her previous pregnancies. Today, she looks ragged. I feel guilty.

"Tough day, baby?" I kiss her on the forehead.

"I've had better. Now you take over, I'm beat."

I plop down next to her. "The kids?"

"Mark's having a sleepover with Levi. I told Phoebe you'd pick him up tomorrow. Audra's playing in her room. How did it go?"

"Uncle Philip, well—" I shrug. Not much to say about that.

Cassie takes my hand. It feels good. It feels right. "And Miss Drake?"

"That went fine. You should've seen the crowd. I mean, a hell of a lot of people. Dad was there, and Sheldon. And I got the lowdown on Miss Drake. She worked for British intelligence back in the day."

"Really? No joke?"

I loosen my tie and lean back, suddenly bone tired. I've already decided not to tell Cassie about June until we do a DNA test, but that didn't stop me from worrying about it.

"I'm sorry I couldn't get out today. I just didn't have the energy. I got Fernando to pick up your mail from the post office box. You got a bunch of stuff. And a package."

"Thanks, baby." Left unspoken is the reality that I need to hire a new personal assistant sooner than later. I'm not looking forward to it. Miss Drake was truly indispensable. No one can replace her. But that reminds me of something I've been meaning to ask Cassie. "Baby, did Miss Drake help you compile that list of analysts?"

"Miss Drake? No. She didn't help me. Your father emailed it to me."

"Dad?" Why the hell would he do that?

"Mmm. I thought it was a nice gesture, considering he doesn't think much of doctors in general."

That's a fucking understatement. "Did you tell him that Dr. Richter's a woman?"

"No. I never discussed it with him. Why? Is it important? As long as she's capable and helps you—"

I bolt upright, agitated. It feels like a thousand bugs are crawling under my skin. "He gave you a list of names. All-female names. And then one that could be either/or. And you don't find that strange?"

"No, I don't. And what if he did?"

I pace around the room and scratch my arm. "I'll tell you what. Because he was trying to manipulate me. That's what he does—he's a fucking genius negotiator, how do you think he got Iran and Pakistan to the table? He's a master at spinning things in a calculated way so you think you came up with this fantastic fucking idea first, but it was him pulling the strings like a puppeteer. He knew I'd pick a man. And he calculated that when I found out he was a she, I'd stay with her because not to would make me look like a sexist pig. He played the odds, and he was right."

Cassie shakes her head in disbelief. "Brooks, you're not making any sense."

"I didn't tell him that Dr. Richter was a woman!" I scream as I gasp for air, the bugs strangling me. I fall to the floor. Mentally, I know I'm having a panic attack. After Mom and Palmer, I'd curl up into a ball and zone out. But this attack was different. It was worse. This wasn't me; it was a hysterical, writhing kid strapped to a table. There was something hard between my teeth. My hair was on fire and my head exploded into a thousand colors.

"Brooks, take a deep breath, it's going to be okay." Cassie's beside me. She rubs my back, her voice a balm. "It's just anxiety, let it go. You're with me. I won't let anything bad happen to you."

I focus on her voice and her touch. The bugs slither back under the rocks they came from.

"Is Daddy sick?" Audra hovers over us. Such a brave little peanut and I'm a puddle of nerves.

"Daddy's fine. He's just sad," Cassie gently says.

"Sad about Miss Drake? Me too, Daddy. We can be sad together." Audra places her hand on my arm, her nails done in Pepto-Bismol pink.

Slowly, I get my bearings back. I ride the anxiety like a surfer until it recedes. "Audra, sweetie, can you show Daddy how well you can draw a unicorn?" I ask once I'm able to speak.

Audra toddles off with a slight limp.

I hold Cassie's hand against my cheek. "Something bad happened to me, baby."

She tousles my hair. "I know, honey. It's been a rough patch. Audra, your aunt, and uncle, the baby, Miss Drake—"

"No, no. It's something else. Something from—" I try to gather my thoughts but it's like scrambled eggs. "I can't shake the feeling that whatever it is, it's got something to do with Dad. And it's really fucking bad."

Cassie gives me a deer-in-the-headlights stare. She's bewildered and I don't blame her. How can I expect her to understand when I don't understand it myself?

"You have a complicated relationship. You both have strong personalities, it's natural you're going to butt heads. Your father refused to acknowledge me for the longest time, but he seems to have thawed out. And you can't deny that lately he's been nothing short of amazing."

"Don't you think I know that?" I stammer, feeling dirty and disloyal. I lost count of how many scrapes he'd bailed me out of as a kid. Yes, there were times when we didn't speak, but now we could have an intelligent, even pleasant conversation. Look, Palmer was Dad's favorite; he's never gotten over losing him. Although Dad would never admit it, I'm sure he wishes it had been me instead of Palmer. And strangely enough, I don't begrudge him, because I've thought the same thing. Guilt pushed me to the brink. I've used up my nine lives. I don't have any more lives to spare or in reserve. And Cassie's right, as usual. Dad saved Audra's life.

Cassie cups my chin. "You should talk to Dr. Richter about this. And you need to schedule a check-up, you're way overdue. You're getting older and you need to take care of yourself. You're up at all hours, you barely sleep—you can't do it on willpower alone."

The old Brooks could. I was a fucking supernova. The new Brooks is a creaky relic from a bygone era.

"If this keeps up, you might have to take something. They're always coming up with some new drug. Maybe you need a mood stabilizer."

Yes, an array of new wonder drugs with a long list of side effects that make you sicker than the condition they're supposed to cure. Mood stabilizer, my sorry white ass. But it's the kick I need. I get up, determined to show Cassie, and myself, that this panic attack is just a one-off. "Baby, no fucking way. I'm not going through that shit again. Are you hungry? Because I am." I haven't eaten all day, and suddenly I could devour a horse.

Cassie laughs. "Is this your half-assed way of changing the subject? It's in the oven, one of your favorites, baked ziti, and garlic bread from the place down the street. I had it delivered. Why don't we have an early dinner, get Audra down for the night, and watch a really bad movie." She pads into the kitchen.

I follow her, hungry for something other than baked ziti. But I'm not going to push it. I'm like a junkyard dog, I'll take whatever scraps I can.

"Do you think I give a shit that Dr. Richter's a woman? For fuck's sake, Brooks, if I made a Broadway production out of all the women you see, I'd be—"

"Jealous?" I tease. I like Cassie being jealous and possessive.

She hits me on the arm. "An idiot. Like the woman you saw today. Who cares? I can't worry every goddamn time you—"

Who the hell is Cassie talking about? Elaine Brighton? "Baby, back up, you're going too fast. What woman?"

Cassie takes the ziti and bread out of the oven and sets them on the counter. "You and some random woman in a coffee shop. One of my friends was passing by, saw you, took a picture on her cell, and sent it to me. The woman isn't even your type, you like them younger and with bigger boobs."

Cassie's being flippant, but I'm fucking furious. "What the hell kind of friend is this? Are you spying on me now? I want to see this goddamn photo."

"Brooks, come on, you're getting all bent out of shape for nothing."

"I'm not fucking around, Cassie. Let me see it. Now, damn it!" I'm so angry I can barely see straight.

Cassie reluctantly gives me her phone. I found the picture. "You tell your friend to delete it. Right now. And she better not have sent it anywhere." That's all I need, for June and me to be splashed on *Page Six.*

Cassie does what I ask. Then, in tears, she throws her phone at me and clocks me good. She has a good arm. "I don't know why I bother. You're such a fucking asshole."

I'm immediately contrite. "I'm sorry. It's just that—"

"Are you fucking her?"

"No, of course not." I realize I have to pivot to plan B: the truth. I pull out a chair. "Sit down."

"I don't want to fucking sit. I'm not a child. You don't get to tell me what to do, especially when you're fucking other women." Cassie gives me a death stare.

"I'm not, I swear. The woman in the coffee shop. I don't know how—there's a high probability that she's my daughter." From the look on Cassie's face, I'm afraid she's going to throw something else at me, and it won't be a cell phone. I duck, just in case.

"Your daughter? Is that the best you can come up with? You fucking—" She stops when she realizes I'm serious. She slowly sits down like a deflated birthday balloon.

I tell Cassie about Jennifer—rather, the stuff I left out before. I show her the birth certificate.

Cassie doesn't say a word. This is worse than throwing things at me or screaming. I can't tell if she's confused, upset, angry, or something else entirely. And I'm afraid to find out.

"How do you expect me to feel? This happened before I was born."

Ouch. Kick me in the groin, why don't you.

She throws up her hands. "So, you're telling me I'm a grandma."

"And a great-grandma," I tease her, now that I know she's not going to grind me up for sausage. "The hottest pregnant great-grandma I know."

It's like a terrible romantic comedy. We both laugh at the absurdity of it. At least, we can still laugh together, if nothing else. "I'll call Lloyd Parsons in the morning." Parsons is the lawyer who handled my other paternity cases that disintegrated once the DNA results came back negative.

"And we don't say anything to your father."

"Not until we know for sure. If it's positive, and I think it will be, we'll tell him after the gala." That's also when we're going to tell Dad about Cassie's pregnancy, when she's well past the danger zone. Talk about a one-two punch.

Cassie kisses me and it's not just some maternal peck. "What the hell am I going to do with you? Being your wife is so fucking hard." She sounds alternately proud and despondent.

Inside, I cringe. "Hey, I warned you, repeatedly." I had, but Cassie probably thought I was exaggerating. I wasn't. "And being your husband is no Sunday picnic in the park," I joke. Who the hell am I kidding? Compared to Nan and Marilyn, Cassie's a goddamn angel.

She arches her eyes. "Oh, I remember. You said life with you was like a rollercoaster. That it wouldn't be dull or boring. But honestly, I could go for dull and boring right about now."

I see her point. I've had enough excitement for one day. Old Brooks thrived on chaos and tumult. New Brooks is a curmudgeon.

I tell John Wick he's done for the night. I call Aunt Flo and commiserate about Uncle Philip. We get Audra to bed early and watch a really sucky movie—*Jaws 3D*. Cassie's in bed by eleven, but I'm still too fidgety. I plan to work on the book until I'm distracted by the pile of letters on my desk. I'll let you in on a trade secret: writers are great procrastinators; we get easily sidetracked by shiny things just out of reach.

I dive into the pile. As I suspect, there's a ton of junk mail, solicitations, and slick political flyers that go straight to the garbage. There's fan mail by people who know how to use Google. I put those aside; if they've taken the time to find me, I can find the time to reply. Then there's the package Cassie mentioned: a medium-sized cardboard box. I pick it up. Not heavy, but not light either. My name's handwritten in a barely legible scrawl that I don't recognize. There's no return address. I smile as I imagine Miss Drake inspecting it. I wonder if she knew how to defuse a bomb with a bobby pin.

I glance at the postmark and get a bad feeling. The package is from Montauk. I haven't been to Montauk since, well, that horrific summer. I don't know anyone in Montauk. Let me amend that, not anyone who'd send a parcel to my business post office box instead of my home address. The package was mailed a week or so before Marshall Reagan had a date with a blunt instrument. Oddly, the package was sent by media mail and not first class. Media mail is cheaper but takes longer to arrive. *Hmmm.* Was the sender a tightwad—or was it deliberate?

I whirl my chair around and stare out into the dark skyline. I methodically chew on what I know about Reagan's murder from my sources and what's been published. Reagan's rental was ransacked, his killer or killers were looking for something. Something they were reasonably positive Reagan had in his possession. What did Reagan have that someone would kill for? It can't be anything monetary; Reagan declared bankruptcy more times than Trump. So, if we're to believe Julian Broadhurst's "daughter," the only thing Reagan had of any value was his book about the murders. What was the word Reagan used? *Incendiary?*

I don't like where this road is going. If Reagan suspected that he was on a hit list, why the hell would he send anything to me? Our hatred was mutual and deep. If anything, Reagan had more reason to hate me than I did him. I prevented Reagan from banking a huge payday. He had every reason to want me dead.

I shift uneasily in my chair and let my thoughts go to places I don't want to go. If the box had been sent by first-class mail, Miss Drake would've picked it up much sooner. What if she'd been under surveillance and they'd been waiting for her to pick it up? *Shit.* Are the contents of this box the reason why she was killed?

I don't care that this box may contain evidence in a high-profile murder investigation. And I don't give a damn that in opening it, I might compromise evidence or that the authorities could construe it as a criminal act. But then again, maybe I was letting my imagination run away with me. Maybe the box contained a complimentary supply of breath mints. Or a gag gift.

Fuck it. There's only one way to find out. I tear the box open. It doesn't contain breath mints. Inside is a thick stack of documents, along with a letter addressed to me. It's short and to the point: *You need this more than I do. MR.*

It took me until dawn to sort out the box's contents: Reagan's book research. As much as I hate to admit it, I'm impressed. He was a sleazebag, but a thorough one. Somehow, he'd gotten his grimy hands on a slew of confidential, internal, investigative reports from multiple arenas: hospital records, witness accounts, etc. Some of this material duplicates what I already have. Some are new. And there's material I didn't even know existed. It's a goddamn treasure trove, and I had that fucktard, Reagan, to thank. But why me? And what did he expect me to do that he couldn't?

In my initial perusal of the documents, three things jumped out at me. There's a name on a notecard in what I presume is Reagan's handwriting: *Dr. Herman Bethel.* The only Bethel I know of is the town where Woodstock, the seminal music festival, was held. *Strange.* Who is this Dr. Bethel? I'll have to research this further. Damn, I could use Miss Drake's exemplary investigative skills.

The second file is from Sheriff Cooper, the erstwhile first officer at the crime scene. This is the file that the local police department has maintained was missing all these years. I've no idea how Reagan obtained it, but knowing his methods, it couldn't have been legal. Cooper's report contains copies of the love letters that Mom allegedly sent Julian Broadhurst, letters that the sheriff claimed he found in the front seat of Julian's Aston Martin. I know Mom wrote the letters; I recognize her handwriting. But to call them love letters is an insult to romance. These letters are revoltingly profane, graphic, torrid letters, and given my history, that's a lot. There's little that can shock me anymore. These letters did. Even more damning, the letters make it painfully clear that Julian Broadhurst hadn't been a spurned lover at all—that it was Mom who'd been shamelessly and relentlessly pursuing *him*. I'm crushed. How could Mom, a proper married woman, act this way? My first impulse is to destroy the letters, but the journalist in me won't allow it. When I began this, it was to find out the truth, no matter where it led, and no matter how painful. I can't reconcile these awful letters with the mother I knew and loved. But even if—if—Mom had an affair with Julian, she didn't deserve to die over it. Or Palmer.

The third thing I don't expect is a file on Dad. Much of it is stock material detailing Dad's meteoric rise in diplomacy after his family tragedy and his long, lauded career on the world stage. But buried in the newspaper clippings and computer printouts is an obituary for Benjamin and Miriam Anderson of Milton, Massachusetts, my paternal grandparents. According to the obit, my grandparents died in a house fire. The cause of the blaze was deemed "inconclusive." Dad has never said a word of this. In fact, he's intimated that my grandparents died of natural causes. Well, I suppose only a sadist would call death by smoke inhalation a natural way to go.

I grab a wastepaper basket and throw up what's left of the fucking baked ziti.

CHAPTER FIFTEEN

We were halfway through our summer vacation in Montauk—the middle of July—the sticky dog days where you got tired of being at the beach all day and having burgers on the grill.

We were all getting on each other's last nerve. Mom was irritable and tired. She used to be the first one out of bed; now, most of the time, she was in her pajamas all day. And it seemed like she was picking on me for every little thing: not making my bed, not putting away my toys, and forgetting to flush the toilet. I couldn't do anything right.

Palmer was a grouch bucket, too. I thought we'd bonded over our misadventure at Camp Hero—secrets have a way of doing that—but he treated me as though I were invisible. He'd take off early and return barely in time for dinner. It annoyed the hell out of me, but Mom didn't seem to care. Summer had turned into a bummer. I was lonely and I missed Berry something fierce.

Something was going on in Ditch Plains, and it wasn't just me being a mopey brat. Rumors and whispers were growing like crabgrass. Ronnie and Toad would fill me in when we'd get ice cream in town. Gigi was still recuperating from her mouth surgery.

Ronnie licked an ice-cream sandwich. "I heard some farmers are reporting baby chicks being born with two heads. And finding weird symbols painted on their coops and barns."

"No way," I blurted.

"My landscaper said there's been a ton of dead animals in people's yards, really gross, their insides torn out." Toad slurped on a cherry popsicle. "And I overheard my housekeeper say that the police arrested a naked lady dancing on the beach by a bonfire after midnight. It was some kind of satanic ritual."

I lapped up every word as I dug a wooden spoon into my blue Italian ice.

At dinner that night, when I breathlessly reported to Mom and Palmer what the kids had said, Mom's response was succinct. "It's a load of hooey."

"What's hooey?" I asked.

"Crap," Palmer snorted.

"Palmer, we don't use that word in this house," Mom remonstrated. She never cursed. Dad might occasionally say damn or hell when he was trying to fix something around the house. As things stood, we hadn't heard from Dad in weeks. Mom insisted that he was busy with his summer courses, but that excuse was wearing thin. And it sure didn't stop Julian Broadhurst and his Aston Martin from coming around.

"Would you rather I say caca? Or bullshit?" Palmer pushed his plate away and bolted from the kitchen table. Seconds later, he slammed his bedroom door so hard my glass of milk shook.

Mom sighed. "Don't pay attention to him, Brooks. Your brother's going through a phase, his hormones are all over the place."

I didn't know what hormones were, but it sounded as appealing as a mouthful of dirt. But I was worried about Palmer, and I decided then and there to follow him the next morning and see what mischief he was up to.

I pretended I was still sleeping when Palmer got up and dressed. He packed lunch, a couple of thermoses, stuffed them in his backpack, and took off on his bike. I'd asked Mom to make my lunch the night before because I told her that Ronnie and I were going fishing all day. It was a lie, but she didn't question me. I caught up with Palmer a couple of blocks over on Old Montauk Highway. I kept a discreet distance behind. After a while, he made an abrupt turn onto a dirt road not too far from Ditch Plains. I didn't know this area well. It was mostly scrub brush dotted by the occasional cabin or cottage. Us kids had no reason to go this way. The homes here weren't as nice or as well kept as Grandpa William's. But Palmer seemed to know his way around. He went down a mile or so and parked his bike under some bushes. I did the same.

It was a rickety old cottage on the cliffs with million-dollar views, a developer's dream or nightmare. A broken picket fence ringed the front yard, if you could call the clumps of dirt and sand a yard. A dragonfly windchime hung on the front porch. I didn't have to look at the decrepit mailbox to know who lived here: Julian Broadhurst's Aston Martin was parked in the shitty side yard. Why was Palmer skulking around here?

Not long after, Julian, dressed in a cut-off T-shirt and pants, came out of the house. He didn't seem to be in a hurry. After puttering around, he hopped in the Aston Martin and drove off. Palmer scooted back to his bike, jumped on, and followed Julian. I followed them both. I didn't know what I was doing or why. It felt like a stale Three Stooges routine. Any minute, I expected Moe to slap me upside the head.

When Julian finally turned into a short circular driveway, I was relieved as my legs were just about to peter out. I'd never been to this side of Montauk. The houses here weren't renovated summer cottages like Grandpa William's. No, these were mansions on lush grounds, large garages, and in-ground swimming pools. In the background, an orchestra of lawnmowers and leaf blowers played.

Not only was I tired, but I was also bored. This was no fun. For a moment, I worried that Palmer had figured out that I'd tailed him like a junior James Bond. But Palmer, hiding behind a grove of manicured hedges, was too preoccupied watching the house.

I'd lost track of Julian, and then I spotted him on the front porch. He was in white overalls, splotched with dried paint, and perched on a ladder. I soon realized that this house wasn't in pristine condition like the other estates we'd passed. There were brown patches on the grass, and crabgrass had taken up permanent residence. The porch steps sagged, the railings were broken in places, and the paint on the house was peeling. Is this why Julian was here, to paint the house? Mom had made it sound like Julian was a hot-shot Manhattan artist. Somehow, I don't think Peter Max would've approved.

A man, dressed in a suit and tie and holding a coffee cup stepped onto the porch. I knew who he was right away: Mr. Papadopoulos, but everyone affectionately called him Papa. He owned the Silver Dollar Diner on Montauk Highway. Papa, who must've been pushing seventy, was a gregarious Greek who'd once owned a chain of prosperous diners all over the island. Now he was down to only one. Papa was a topic of great and heated discussion in Montauk. Some wags declared that the precipitous slide in Papa's fortunes corresponded to when he married his second wife—his much younger second wife—after his first wife of forty years passed away. The second wife had been a waitress at one of Papa's diners. Everyone knew that his adult children were unhappy with the second Mrs. Papa, whom they considered a gold digger. I asked Mom what that meant and all she said with a tight grimace was "nothing good."

Anyway, when Dad used to come out, it was a big deal for us to go to the Silver Dollar on Sunday mornings for their all-you-can-eat brunch buffet. At $4.95 for adults—kids under twelve free—it was one of the best-kept secrets on the South Fork. The food was incredible, and the portions were gargantuan. I could barely make a dent in my thick stack of Silver Dollar pancakes. And Palmer and I loved the mini-jukeboxes at each booth, three songs for a quarter. Sadly, the Silver Dollar burnt to the ground during the spring of Jimmy Carter's inauguration. Arson was suspected but never proven. Supposedly, there was a huge insurance payout. It would've broken Papa's heart, had he still been alive. A couple of months before the fire, he slipped on a patch of ice in his driveway, twisted his neck, and died instantly. An accident, some said. Others said differently. After years of litigation, the county bought the land parcel from Papa's estate at twice its estimated value and made it a parking lot for the highway department. Once the funds cleared, the second Mrs. Papa promptly married her eldest stepson and they absconded—I mean, relocated—to Canada.

Julian was painting all right, maybe the walls or the ceiling. Papa put down his coffee cup to point something out to Julian, who seemed to take it in his stride. Satisfied, Papa got into his car, a white Cadillac convertible parked next to the Aston Martin, and drove away.

Julian returned to his work. But not for long. A woman came out of the house—the second Mrs. Papa. I'd seen her in town coming out of the liquor store. She drove a Cadillac convertible too, except hers was pink. And she always had her dog with her, a miniature French poodle who resembled a gussied-up feather duster.

The second Mrs. Papa, her hips swaying, came up to Julian, who was back on the ladder. She was in a flimsy nightgown—a negligée, but I didn't know the word then—that was so sheer you could see her panties and furry pink mules that matched her car. The feather duster bounded after her, yapping. From the way the second Mrs. Papa rubbed Julian's thigh, I didn't get the impression that she was going to help him paint.

After an unseemly amount of rubbing, the second Mrs. Papa went into the house while the feather duster—God, how I hated that fucking mutt—stayed on the porch, sniffing. The second Mrs. Papa must've turned on a radio and pushed the volume up because suddenly "See You in September" by The Happenings blasted. After a few minutes, Julian tossed his paintbrush into a nearby bucket and went inside. I was perplexed. It wasn't even eleven o'clock yet, a bit early for a lunch break. Did I say I was so goddamn naive?

Suddenly, Palmer raced across the front lawn, holding his backpack. I almost chased after him. He jumped the wrought-iron fence that surrounded Papa's driveway. I nearly screamed, "What the hell do you think you're doing?" But I froze.

Palmer went to the Aston Martin and lifted the hood. It made a clang. The feather duster tore across the porch, barking and growling. Palmer threw something at the side of the house, maybe a branch or a twig. I couldn't see Palmer that well—the car hood obscured my view—

but the damn feather duster wasn't barking anymore. I don't know what scared me more—the feather duster not barking or Palmer.

Palmer was back at the Aston Martin. He opened his backpack and took something out of it, I'm not sure what. He poured it into the engine. When he was done, he bent down on the right side of the car and scratched something on the door. From my vantage point, I couldn't make out what it was. Finished, Palmer bounded back across the street. Maybe this had taken all of twenty minutes at most, but it felt like a millennium.

I thought I'd done a good job of hiding myself, but I was wrong. Palmer grabbed me and boxed my ears so hard I heard church bells. "What the fuck are you doing here, you little twerp? Spying on me? I swear, I'm gonna kick your ass so hard you won't be able to shit for a week."

Sobbing, I put my hands over my face.

"Shut up, you fucking baby." He gave me a good kick. I went sprawling face first in the dirt. "Does Mom know?"

I shook my head, still crying. I was used to Palmer rough-housing with me. Sometimes we'd wrestle when a commercial came on while we watched TV. Mom would tell us to knock it off before someone got hurt. We were just fooling around. Palmer would never hurt me, unintentionally or on purpose. But this wasn't the same. Palmer was different and I was fucking terrified of him.

"The dog," I choked out. "What did you do to the dog?"

"I didn't do anything to the fucking dog. Now stop following me around, you asshole. And don't you dare say anything to Mom, you hear me? I know where you sleep." He got on his bike and pedaled away.

Of course, I couldn't tell Mom. If I did, I'd get in trouble, too. And although I didn't understand why Palmer had done what he did—or what Julian had done, for that matter—I couldn't rat Palmer out. He was my brother and I loved him even when he was acting like a big fat turd. Nothing—or no one—could shatter or break that bond.

The next time Julian Broadhurst came to our house, he didn't drive the Aston Martin. He had an old, rusty, Grandpa bike. When Mom *asked Julian what happened to his car, he blamed the idiot at the gas station for putting in the wrong grade of gas and seizing the engine. Julian ended up raising such a stink that the owner of the gas station repaired the car for free and fired the gas attendant. But Julian neglected to tell Mom what someone had scratched on the side of his car:* Pervert.

CHAPTER SIXTEEN

After my increasingly frantic phone calls and texts to Dalton Crane, he agrees to see me first thing at his law office. Given his reputation, I imagine he's in a glossy high rise in the heart of midtown. No. Dalton's office is in a funky storefront in Greenwich Village. He's a one-man outfit; his ego's too big to be a partner in a white-shoe law firm. A buxom blonde secretary ushers me into Dalton's office. If her décolletage were any lower, they could be appetizers at the Yale Club. From the way Dalton leers at her, I surmise that she's the next Mrs. Crane, the seventh or the eighth, I've lost track.

Dalton's on the phone as he gestures to me to sit down. While he's occupied, I survey the impressive array of photographs on the wall: Dalton preening with various state and local dignitaries like the mayor and governor, national figures like Clinton, Obama, and Biden, and a myriad of celebrities such as George Clooney. I smile. Clooney had been my first choice to play the male lead in *Three Rivers,* but he turned the part down faster than it took to brew a cup of Nespresso. I often wonder how he felt when the series swept the Emmy Awards.

"Don't give me that bullshit, Leroy," Dalton says as he winks at me. "This case should've never been brought to the grand jury. The lead detective is a serial liar, your investigators hid exculpatory evidence, and now your assistant DA conveniently forks over sixteen boxes of documents on the eve of the trial." He pauses for a moment. "That's not my fucking problem. You take this to trial, the gloves are off. And yeah, that's a threat." He slams the phone down, infuriated. "Bunch of assholes. Since Cy Vance retired, the DA's office has been nothing short of a fucking nightmare. I should run for it, but it's more fun kicking their butts than kissing them." He sounds happy at the thought. "Brooks, would you mind telling me what's so goddamn important that you called me at one-fifteen in the morning?"

I'm prepared. I take out my checkbook. Yes, call me Rip Van Winkle, but I still have a good old-fashioned checking and savings account. I believe in cash, not bitcoin. The "nut"—as I call it—the big money from my writing, is carefully invested by an impeccable blue-ribbon firm. No fucking startups for me, although if I'd invested in Amazon, Facebook, and Google when I had the chance, I'd be a billionaire like Jeff Fucking Bezos. "Not another word until I officially retain you as my attorney. I know how this goes."

"Well." Dalton cocks his head, intrigued. "Usually, potential clients tell me what the issue is, I frown heavily, tell them they screwed up, and that I'm the only lawyer who can help them. Then I throw out a random number, they initially gag, and then we meet somewhere in the middle where they don't declare bankruptcy." He tells me the number.

Without blinking, I double the amount and hand him the check. I've already told my money guys to shuffle accounts to cover it. This is no time to skimp. Dalton's the best at what he does, no fucking 800-lawyers for me. "This seals it, correct? Everything I tell you from this moment on is considered privileged and confidential. You can't divulge what I say to anyone, not the police, and not even my father."

Dalton looks like a wounded buffalo. "Brooks, I take my oaths seriously, at least my attorney one. As for your father, it's your name on the bill of retainer, not his." He opens his desk drawer, retrieves a strongbox, unlocks it, puts the check inside, and locks it again. "Just so you know, I also accept Zelle, PayPal, and Venmo." He barks into an intercom. "Aphro, I'll need a bill of retainer for Mr. Brooks Anderson before he leaves."

"Aphro?"

"Short for Aphrodite. And don't get any ideas. She's married."

I snort. Since when did that ever stop Dalton Crane?

Dalton leans back in his chair. "Now what the fuck is this all about?"

I sigh. "Dalton, I think I screwed up."

He waves his hand as if he were holding a butcher knife. "Brooks, believe me, there are many levels of fuckery and I'm skilled in all of them. You can't tell me anything that I haven't already heard."

I clear my throat and tell him about the box from Marshall Reagan.

Dalton pounds his fist on the desk. "I knew I hadn't heard the last of that ratfucker. All his research. You're sure?"

"It looks like it to me."

"Postmarked before his death? Nothing on the box that indicated it was from Reagan?"

I nod.

Dalton clasps his hands together. It almost looks like he's praying. "And you picked it up from the post office."

I know Dalton has a purpose to all these questions, but it feels as if I'm being cross-examined by the great Charles Laughton in *Witness for the Prosecution*. All Dalton needs is a wig. "No."

"Oh?" His voice rises. "Your wife?"

"No, not Cassie." I fidget under Dalton's intense gaze. "It was picked up by someone who I don't want to get involved in this mess any more than I have to."

He gives me a sour look. "It's a little too late for that. I'm not asking you anything that the police won't."

I know. "All right. It was my doorman, Fernando. Cassie wasn't feeling well so she asked him if he wouldn't mind doing it."

Dalton rubs his chin. "Mmm. You know what the police will say. That you asked someone else to pick it up because you were expecting it."

"That doesn't make sense," I hoot. "Why would I kill Reagan after he mails me this goodie box?"

"Not you. The guys you hired. Maybe they were fucking morons who just wanted to scare the living shit out of that asshole and they took it too far. Of course, it's illogical and nonsensical. But you're a writer, you specialize in the illogical and nonsensical. A good prosecutor could make the case that you set it all up as a distraction. I'm sorry, Brooks, but the police will want to talk to Fernando to confirm your story."

"No, he can't have the police sniffing around," I retort. This is getting way too fucking complicated.

"Why not? Fernando, he's not a serial killer, is he?"

"His immigration papers are fake. He could be deported."

"And how do you know all this about your, uh, doorman?"

"Because I helped him get the papers." Fernando was my drug dealer back in the day. Low level, no kingpin. He was fair and he never ripped me off. We lost track of each other and then in the late nineties, he sought me out and asked if I could get him a job, any job, he wasn't picky. By now, we're both clean and sober. The doorman at the Dakota had just retired. I pulled some strings. Sounds great, right? The only hitch is that Fernando had to prove that he's in the country legally. He had an immigration attorney who claimed to have an in at the State Department, but it would run Fernando fifteen thousand. I'm extremely dubious—this attorney sounds shady as fuck—but I fronted the money anyway. Fernando got his papers and the job. He's a model citizen.

Married, four kids, six grandchildren. Not even a goddamn parking ticket. And he's done countless favors for me. I can't take the chance of fucking things up for Fernando. I tell Dalton as much.

"A man of valor. How rare." Dalton sounds slightly sarcastic, but I let it pass. "Okay, let's put that aside for the moment. Reagan's papers. Does it contain anything embarrassing or criminal or inflammatory about your family?"

"If you mean something that I'd kill over, no."

Dalton gives me a piercing look.

"Potentially embarrassing, yes. But again, nothing worth a man's life."

"Well, *someone* thought it was," he correctly observes. "Just what the hell is in this damn box?"

"For one thing, it raises the possibility that the police were hasty when they closed the investigation and also in their eventual conclusions."

"Meaning?"

"The possibility that Julian Broadhurst is innocent." Well, the cat's out of the fucking bag now. "That's the direction Reagan was leaning in. Another culprit and an entirely different motive."

"I see. And you suspect the documents are the motive behind Miss Drake's death."

"Dalton, the woman didn't inject herself and she sure as hell wasn't pumped with a toxic dose of Vitamin K for her scones recipe. These thugs, whoever they are, thought she had them or knew where they were. But—"

"I knew there had to be a *but* in there somewhere," Dalton deadpans.

"At one time, Miss Drake worked for British intelligence. I got that straight from the Consulate."

"Oof." He rubs his forehead. "Hypothetically speaking, have you made copies of Reagan's documents?"

Indeed, I have.

"Are the originals and copies in a safe place? I'll need one set."

The originals are in my safety deposit box at the main branch of Chase Manhattan. One set is tucked away in my writing lair. Another set of copies is in the reliable hands of John Wick, who waits outside for my instructions.

"Who else knows?"

"Only you. Not my wife or my father. I didn't want to put them in a position where they might have to testify against me if it went that far." The last thing Cassie needs is more stress. And the last time Dad testified under oath was before Congress. He wouldn't be pleased to be dragged into this.

Dalton shrugs. "Your wife has marital privilege. Unless you waive that, she can't be compelled to give testimony against you, even if she wanted to. It's the law. So, you can tell her whatever you want. However, Bernard's another matter. I strongly urge you to keep him out of this. Father-and-son relationships are complicated enough. I speak from experience. Do you understand?"

I do.

Dalton strokes his chin. "The fact that you called me immediately when you opened the box and realized its contents makes a strong case that you had no criminal intent. In your actions, you were transparent and forthcoming."

Fucking A, I almost say.

"I can handle the Suffolk County District Attorney. I know this clown personally; I have a house in Sag Harbor. He's up for re-election next year and he's not looking to make waves. But the Suffolk police, hell, that's another story. You're their number one target and they want to nail your ass. Until this is settled, I wouldn't cross the county line. On the bright side—"

I nearly laugh. There's a bright side?

"The Manhattan DA's dick is going to be harder than Priapus' when he learns about this box. Face it, it's a jurisdictional *WrestleMania*. But the best thing you have in your corner is me.

I'm a goddamn grizzly. I'll fight tooth and nail any attempt to charge you over this." Dalton grins and sure enough, he does look kind of bearish. "Brooks, I'm not going to sugar-coat it. No doubt some aspects of this will have to be artfully finessed, especially if the contents of Reagan's research are leaked to the media. Bernard would hate that."

On that, we're in total agreement. If Mom's obscene letters to Julian Broadhurst are splashed on Roger Friedman's *Showbiz411*, Dad will have a fucking coronary. "What do I do now?"

"Give me a copy and go about your business. I'll set things in motion and see what shakes out."

"In other words, play it—" My cell phone vibrates. "Sorry, Dalton, just one moment." It's a text from Lloyd Parsons confirming he's set up a DNA test with June. I'm relieved. Now that I've gotten used to the idea, I want June to be my daughter, strange as that may sound. Charles did the right thing. Now it was my turn to step up, however late in the day. I mean, there are worse things in life at sixty-five going on sixty-six than discovering you have a daughter, grandchildren, and great-grandchildren. *Right?*

Dr. Richter manages to see me before lunch. Today's she's changed up her look entirely: a Boho Stevie Nicks-ish midi-dress with long flowing bell sleeves and fashionable suede ankle boots. Elegant and expensive. No off-the-rack for Dr. Richter.

"Well, I must say, you weren't kidding when you said you were a writer. I didn't know you were *that* Brooks Anderson. I've read some of your books. I'm sad to say that I didn't think your last one was any good." Dr. Richter gives me an apologetic shrug.

"You're not alone," I say good-naturedly as I sit down. A reviewer for the *Washington Post* called it four hundred and sixty pages of fried clichés, unbelievable plot twists, and bleak, unsympathetic characters you wouldn't invite to Thanksgiving dinner. Nevertheless, it's been on the bestseller lists for over one hundred and thirty-five weeks. Not that I'm counting, mind you.

She removes her glasses. "So how are we doing today, Mr. Anderson."

"Well, honestly, the past couple of days have been challenging. I think I've made some progress, but I'll let you be the judge of that."

"And the other matter?"

It takes me a moment to realize she means the vasectomy. "That's been resolved." Cassie's feeling a bit better, and she's taken to wearing my oversized shirts to hide her baby bump from the kids. I think it's adorable.

Dr. Richter tilts her head. "I take it you've remembered something."

"I'll let you be the judge of that." I tell her what I've remembered about Mom and Palmer. I wait for her reaction which is hard to gauge, as she has a perfect poker face.

"That's it?" Dr. Richter finally says.

Talk about pricking my balloon. Empathy isn't Dr. Richter's strong suit. I feel like I've failed an audition. For fuck's sake, I'm paying her eight hundred dollars out of pocket for these sessions. How much did her outfit cost anyway? Maybe Dad's right after all. Another shyster. "I know it's not much, but I feel I'm on the verge of a breakthrough." That's what I want and need to believe. Badly.

"How can you be sure that what you recalled is in fact reality?" Dr. Richter asks.

I wince. I've asked myself that question a million times. "Am I one hundred percent sure? No, just as I'm not one hundred percent sure that I won't walk out of this building and a brick won't land on my head. However, I have a reasonable expectation based on logic and probability that's not going to happen. Call it a gut feeling. I was *there*. I wasn't alone. I don't know who—or what—it was. But whatever happened, it scarred and scared me so much that I've been running from it ever since." I abruptly stand, irked. "Look, if I'm wasting your time—"

"Why so defensive, Mr. Anderson? Have I struck a nerve?"

I sit down again.

"I'm not here to be a yes woman and nod my head like a bobblehead doll. You have to do the work. I can't do it for you. If you want to remember what happened, it also means rejecting any preconceived ideas you have regarding it. You need for Julian Broadhurst to be the monster in this scenario. What if he isn't? Are you prepared for that possibility?"

"I am," I emphatically answer. "My mind isn't a steel trap. I've only just become aware that my mother's relationship with her alleged killer might've been more than what I thought." I throw up in my mouth a little.

Dr. Richter scribbles something down in her notebook. "How does that make you feel?"

I grip the armrests of the chair. What the hell does she expect me to say? That I was thrilled that Mom was fucking Julian while Palmer and I were out for the day or while we slept steps away?

"I'm angry. I'm furious. I feel misled, betrayed, confused, sad, and filled with regret. She was a good, decent person. A fine mother. And even if she did have an affair with that douche, she didn't deserve to die, and neither did her unborn baby or my brother." I'm usually guarded so I surprise myself with that emotional outburst.

"I'm sure this is difficult for you," she murmurs.

Difficult? It's fucking torture.

Dr. Richter closes her notebook. "I think that concludes our session for today."

But I'm not done. "Dr. Richter, I have a question for you. I know this is a long shot, but does the name Herman Bethel mean anything to you? I believe he was a doctor or a psychiatrist, I'm not sure which."

Talk about hitting a nerve. Dr. Richter opens her desk drawer and jams her notebook in it. "Mr. Anderson, you think they're not the same? You believe psychiatrists are merely witch doctors in Brooks Brothers suits?"

"That's not what I mean," I hasten to add. "And it wasn't my intent to offend you."

She gives me a frosty glare. "Psychiatrists are trained, medical professionals. We didn't graduate from Voodoo University—at least I didn't. I take great pride in helping people. I have a waiting list a mile long. I can afford to pick and choose my patients. Now if you'll excuse me, I have to make sure I shrunk that head enough." She rushes out of her office, her sleeves trailing behind her like wings.

I make my exit, perplexed. Although I hadn't articulated what I meant particularly well, I'm at a loss as to why Dr. Richter's reaction had been so vehement.

John Wick is in the lobby. I take out my cell, which I'd shut off as per Dr. Richter's "rules" and switch it back on. Immediately I see a slew of texts from Phoebe and Cassie. *Shit.* I'm supposed to pick up Mark from his sleepover at Sheldon's before noon and I'm late. I shoot a text to Cassie that I'm on my way to get Mark, then call Phoebe to assure her that I haven't forgotten my firstborn.

Phoebe answers halfway through the first ring. "Brooks, thank God. Please tell me Sheldon's with you." She sounds as if she has something stuck in her throat.

"No. The last time I saw him was yesterday at the reception for Miss Drake." Was that only yesterday? Jesus. Now that I think about it, Sheldon never answered my late-night texts.

"He didn't come home last night, Brooks. And would you believe that a slew of investigators from the Attorney General just knocked on my door with a search warrant."

I do a double take. *What the hell?*

"They're taking his computers and all his files. Brooks, I don't know what's happening."

Now I remember what Sheldon said about financial

irregularities at the agency. Was he trying to tell me in an obtuse way that he was in deep shit? *Impossible.* Sheldon's the most ethical and honest man I know next to Dad. When Sheldon finally sold *Fallen Angels,* he refused to take a commission because it was a royalty-only deal. Sheldon adores his wife and kids. He's an avid churchgoer, he co-sponsors a camp in the Poconos for disadvantaged children. In other words, he's a straight arrow. I can't imagine him doing anything even slightly improper or inappropriate. "I'm on my way. Whatever this is, I promise we'll work it out."

I call Sheldon's cell. It goes straight to voicemail: "Hey, this is Sheldon Adler, I'm either negotiating a million-dollar deal or I'm picking up doggy doo." Sheldon has two obese pugs named Winston and Churchill who aren't properly housebroken. "Please leave your name and number and I'll get back to you. Or I may not."

"Sheldon, where the fuck are you? Stop dicking around. Phoebe's worried sick and she's not the only one. Please, buddy. Call me as soon as you get this," I roar.

John Wick and I walk over to the car the security firm has rented, a gas-guzzling Toyota 4Runner, double-parked on a side street. Cassie would kill me. The security firm uses a different car every day. A parking ticket slides under the windshield wiper. John Wick tears it up. Not my car, not my headache.

As we drive to Sheldon's, I get a text from Dad: *Are you all right?*

I text back: Yes, of course, why wouldn't I be?

Dad replies: *There was a hit and run not far from the Dakota, a middle-aged man. I know you like to run before the kids get up. I got spooked.*

Traffic's a bitch. When we finally get to Sheldon's, the investigators have already cleared out. I check on Mark, Levi, and Bella. They're all hunkered down in the playroom watching

Jumanji, the Robin Williams version and the best one of the franchise, in my humble opinion.

Phoebe paces in the living room, alternating between denial, shock, and hysterics. This is where we had our christening party for Audra. Sheldon had insisted on paying for everything. He always went overboard. "Do you have a lawyer, Phoebe?"

"Why? Do you think I need one?" She stares at me, her eyes red and puffy. "I don't care what Sheldon's done or what they think he's done, Brooks. I want him home. He's not some criminal. He might be hurt somewhere or scared out of his mind." She collapses on the sofa and sobs uncontrollably.

The doorbell rings. I answer it.

It's Dalton Crane in a spiffy three-piece suit. Pancake makeup smudges the collar of his white shirt. *What the hell is he doing here?*

"I was just about to go on Fox with Alan Dershowitz when I got a tip." Dalton motions for me to step outside.

My stomach seizes. I know why Dalton's tracked me down. The police are going to arrest me over Marshall Reagan's documents. Even in death, the asshole won't leave me alone. "What do I do now, Dalton?"

"You don't have to do anything."

"I mean, I don't want to be arrested at my apartment. Can I quietly turn myself in? Can we avoid a perp walk?" The media scrum will be insane. I don't want Cassie or the kids to be subjected to it. Let the press have their piece of meat. I can handle it. "We have to alert Dad. I don't want him to be caught off-guard."

"No, no." Dalton grabs my arm. "Brooks, it's not about you. It's your agent, Sheldon Adler. A hit and run. It happened—"

Behind the door, Phoebe screams. If her scream was a knife, it would pierce steel.

I finish Dalton's sentence. "Near the Dakota. Is he—"

"Barely. From what I've heard, it doesn't look good. I'm so sorry."

Sheldon lingers for a week, stuck in a twilight zone between life and death. His broken bones aren't the issue. It's irreversible brain trauma and there's zero activity from the scans, but Sheldon's heart hasn't gotten the memo. Phoebe and I take turns at his bedside, hoping for a miracle that never arrives. It's only when Sheldon's organs fail that Phoebe reluctantly decides to take him off life support. Sheldon's heart finally gives up and he quietly slips away on Palmer's birthday. It feels like fate because Sheldon's my brother as much as Palmer was. I hold Sheldon's hand and cry like a goddamn baby.

It takes the authorities less than twenty-four hours to arrest the fucking idiot Sheldon paid with the vintage Patek Philippe watch I'd given him to celebrate *Three Rivers'* unexpected Emmy wins. The fucking idiot pawned the watch, appraised at over six hundred thousand dollars, for a paltry one hundred and seventy-five bucks, which the fucking idiot then gambled away at Mohegan Sun.

That's only the start of the great unraveling. Sheldon lost his shirt due to the shenanigans of a third cousin twice removed who had about as much business being a money manager as me competing at the Summer Olympics as a gymnast. At first, Sheldon covered his losses by borrowing from Paul to pay Peter. When that well dried up, he dipped into his clients' accounts (I'm the sole exception) and misappropriated their advances and royalties. Initially, they were piddling amounts that could be explained away as accounting errors.

But then the pandemic hit. Publishing slowed to a crawl. Instead of cutting his losses and fessing up, Sheldon embezzled increasingly larger amounts. I'm sure he was convinced he'd recoup once life and business got back to normal. Sheldon's plan might've worked if Tom Giafrida's wife hadn't hired a forensic accountant to go through her soon-to-be ex-husband's finances. That audit uncovered a huge discrepancy between what Giafrida was owed by the agency and what he netted. When Giafrida complained to the senior partners at Crown-Hawkins, they ordered their own audit and discovered a shortfall of over—*gasp* —ten million.

The agency gave Sheldon an ultimatum: quietly reimburse the agency and resign. When Tom Giafrida got wind of this, he alerted the Attorney General. Sheldon learned he was under investigation the day of Miss Drake's memorial service. Sometime later, Sheldon went to the Garment District—he's clearly visible on the security cameras from a nearby store— and cajoled a fucking idiot with a monster truck to run him down so Phoebe could collect his life insurance. Of all the stupid, hare-brained schemes. Sheldon might as well have gotten a gun and shot himself in the foot. But Sheldon wasn't thinking clearly or rationally, he was in flight mode. When I'd been in the thrall of heroin, I knew that desperation all too well. The fear of being discovered, the shame, the longing, the ecstasy of getting high, and then the inevitable free-falling. It's like jumping out of an airplane without a parachute. Ten times out of ten you land safely, and then the next time you break every bone in your goddamn body.

Sheldon was presumably at peace, but he'd left behind a goddamn colossal mess. His dopey cousin ended up buying a one-way ticket to Brunei—no extradition treaty. He left behind a pregnant wife, two pregnant mistresses, a slew of angry investors, a leased BMW he totaled on the way to the airport, and a checking account with a grand sum of sixteen cents. The Feds were still estimating the loss at the cousin's firm, but it was well north of seventy-five million dollars.

Sheldon's funeral is a sad, small, somber affair. There are more cameras than mourners. Sheldon's parents and his only sibling died long ago. There's no one from Crown-Hawkins, not even a goddamn potted plant. But Aunt Flo still has the presence of mind to send a beautiful flower arrangement.

Dalton Crane refers Phoebe to a former lawyer for the

Securities and Exchange Commission. The lawyer is brutal in his assessment. Everything would have to be sold: their brownstone (which Sheldon had mortgaged without Phoebe's knowledge), the vacation home in Aruba, cars, stocks, the whole enchilada. Of course, the insurance company refused to pay out on Sheldon's large policy because of the suicide exclusion clause. Phoebe has some money set aside, but it won't be enough. I tell Phoebe that I will help her but she won't hear of it. Lorne Michaels himself assures Phoebe that her job is secure, but she insists on leaving for Minnesota immediately after Sheldon's funeral. At heart, she's just a small-town girl who'd fallen head over heels with a big city guy and the cut is just too deep.

After Sheldon's funeral, we go to a restaurant so the kids can order fancy milkshakes festooned with cookies and candy. Dalton and I sit at the bar. I nurse a black raspberry seltzer as he downs Don Julio Anejo Tequila shots like Perrier.

"We really ought to go out drinking," Dalton says between shots.

Old Brooks would've drunk him under the table. New Brooks is up half the night pissing cloudy water. "I don't drink anymore," I say.

"All the more reason you should hang out with me." Dalton signals to the bartender with the pierced nose to keep the shots coming. Dalton raises his glass. "There's only one good thing about this goddamn mess." He pauses like King Lear, his words slurred. "That motherfucking Marshall Reagan has nothing to do with it."

I can drink to that, and I do.

"Brooks, you ever feel like you've been hit by a two-by-four?"

"Every goddamn day," I answer.

He gulps down another shot.

"Bad news?" I ask.

"The worst." He looks as miserable as I feel.

"Another divorce?"

"I wish. I'm going to be a father again." He downs two shots at once.

I decide that Dalton's not in the best frame of mind to offer my sincere congratulations. "Your secretary?"

"Worse. My wife. And it's mine, unfortunately. I don't get it, Brooks. We had a deal. No kids. For ten years I've been married to this woman, a corporate headhunter. I've been faithful, more or less. Now she decides she needs a baby because forty is the new twenty and she'll regret not having one when she's sixty. I'm so fucking screwed." Dalton wipes his forehead with a napkin. "Eight kids. I'm going to be seventy-three in October. Do you know the reason I can't retire? These fucking brats. Bunch of greedy little shits. Always got their hands out, begging for more. You know my mother tried to kill me after I was born." He motions again at the bartender with the pierced nose.

Talk about changing the subject. I did not know.

"Hmm. When she failed, she killed herself. My father found her, the poor bastard." Dalton drums his fingers against his glass. I've heard of Dalton's father, mostly from Dad. Judge Elliott Crane has been on every Supreme Court shortlist since the George H.W. Bush administration. Always a bridesmaid, Dad had said.

And I thought I had it bad. "That's awful." I mean it. But I don't like the way Dalton's two-fisting it. Funerals are macabre enough. "Dalton, don't you think you should ease up—" I feel something cold on my pants. A waitress accidentally spills a tray of drinks on me. Now I'm going to stink like a goddamn gin mill.

"Mister, I'm super sorry. I'm all thumbs today." The waitress hands me a towel.

I shrug. I mean, what else? It's been that kind of day.

Before I leave, I call an Uber for Dalton. He says it's not necessary, but we both know it is. Cassie and the kids are already back at the apartment. When I get home, Cassie gives me a stink eye.

"The waitress spilled a drink on me," I explain.

"Smells more like a whole bottle."

"I'm not drinking," I assure her.

"Dalton sure was."

"I'm not Dalton," I shot back.

The day after Sheldon's funeral, I drive Phoebe, her kids, and their dogs to LaGuardia. I don't think the kids entirely understand what's going on because Levi takes me aside and asks me when their Daddy's going to join them. I tell Levi soon. Phoebe promises that she'll keep in touch for the boy's sake. I'm not sure she will.

When I return to my car—John Wick's parked next to me—I get a Google alert on my cell. *Eureka!* The police have made an arrest in the Marshall Reagan case. Apparently, the suspect, Solomon Burke, a felon with a long rap sheet, was in some kind of relationship with Reagan. He was nabbed at a motel in Wyoming after checking in with Reagan's American Express card. Burke's story is that Reagan invited him to Montauk for a round of tiddly-dicks, but when he got there, Reagan was already dead. Burke readily admitted to swiping Reagan's credit card to settle a debt he claimed Reagan owed him. To no one's great surprise, the authorities don't buy Burke's story. Soon, Dalton calls me, gleeful. Any interest the cops had in me for Reagan's death has now fizzled like a wet fart. And no one, except for yours truly, gives a shit about the documents Reagan sent me before he was killed.

But there's no news, either good or bad, regarding Miss Drake's case. The woman has no known enemies, she was beloved by all. The trail of the strange delivery men is colder than polar bear poop in the Arctic. And after pressure from the British Embassy, the coroner backtracks on his initial conclusions about Miss Drake's cause of death. Now it's all "inconclusive." James insists the case is still ongoing and active, but grudgingly admits that the investigation's at a standstill (i.e. dead-end) unless something new develops.

A few days after the arrest of Solomon Burke, the Suffolk District Attorney holds a press conference extolling the fine investigative work of the Suffolk police. The case seemingly solved, I cut a final check to the security company and regretfully send John Wick on his next assignment.

I'm still waiting for the DNA results. Despite Lloyd Parsons' strict admonitions that June and I shouldn't have any communication until the tests come back, we've been texting and emailing frequently. To me, it's a foregone conclusion. I still haven't yet reached out to her children. Once we have the official results, I will. I'm sure it will be awkward and challenging.

After repeated nudges from Dad, I bought a new tux for his UN gala, which I'm looking forward to about as much as a colon resection.

Today, Dad badgers me into meeting him at the Yale Club despite the fact it's not Wednesday. I grudgingly agree when all I really want to do is hide away in my lair and write. Writing to me is like breathing. I must write every day, but with everything going on, just finding time to brush my teeth once a day is a feat. I'm behind on the book. I don't have Sheldon to kick my ass when I fall into a rut or cheer me on when I'm in the zone, which is becoming more and more infrequent. Losing Sheldon is like losing my arm.

However, this time I'm smart. I get there early, beat Dad to his usual table, and order my lunch: the most expensive burger on the menu—Wagyu beef—and all the fixings: bacon, marinated mushrooms, aged Cheddar cheese along with a large side of extra crispy onion straws doused in a spicy remoulade sauce. Damn the cholesterol. If I so much as see grilled salmon, I'll grow gills.

Dad, freshly showered and impeccably dressed, saunters through the dining room, stopping to greet his many pals with a *bon mot*. As I watch, I'm forced to admit that Dad still has it, charisma or whatever you call it. Not that he always did. When I was little, I remember him being taciturn and stern. Dad rarely cracked a smile. And he never played football or baseball with me and Palmer like other Dads. Mom always had an excuse: Dad was busy, he had papers to grade, he had a lot on his mind, etc. And Mom had drilled it into us that we were never to disturb Dad when he was in his study. A jetliner could crash into the house, but that room was off-limits to us. No, Dad developed this easy self-confidence and affability after Mom was gone. Men admired him, women loved him.

Over the years, Dad has had quite a few girlfriends. He was discreet and never shoved his paramours in my face, but I knew. He never introduced me to any of his dalliances or made them a part of our lives save one: Netta, a wonderful woman who worked at the State Department as a translator. She never judged me even when I'd show up for dinner stoned out of my gourd. She was kind and supportive when Dad was harsh and unforgiving. I assumed they'd get married eventually. Then one day, Netta was gone. Dad never mentioned her again.

Dad sits down, his martini at the ready. "Have you been waiting long, son?" He sounds mildly perturbed.

"No. Your grilled salmon is on the way." I must sound as dour as I feel.

Dad took a short sip of his drink. "Well, I have news that might cheer you up."

I doubt it, but I'm all ears.

"There's going to be a formal announcement at the gala: the official formation of The Bernard S. Anderson Initiative."

Dad's been kicking this idea around like a bald tire for years. I didn't see the difference between this "initiative"—other than it bore his name—over countless other nonprofits and organizations that already existed. But Dad insisted his group was going to be different: a think tank that did more than just dream up grand ideas but would actually implement them, the hell with politics, red tape, culture wars, gender, race, and financial inequality.

"It's finally going to happen, Brooks. We have a Board of Governors, we have the land, and the architectural plans which are simply marvelous. Now, all we need is donors and I'm sure that will be no problem." Knowing Dad and his schmooze network, getting donations should be easy. Don't get me wrong; Dad has his favorite charities and he's a generous benefactor. But he's always been adamant that this initiative isn't some kind of frivolous passion project, although in a way that's exactly what it is. The bottom line is that Dad wants other people's money to fund his utopian fantasy. Only then, so went his thinking, would people take it seriously. He has more to offer than Bill Gates or George Soros—at least, Dad believes so.

"Yes, it sounds great in theory," I half-heartedly muster.

Dad frowns. "You know, it wouldn't hurt you to indulge me and show a modicum of excitement. I've had to humor you plenty over the years."

What the fuck was that supposed to mean? I'm about to make an angry retort when our meals arrive. Dad grimaces as he realizes what I've ordered for myself. "Is that good for you, Brooks?"

"Probably not, but once in a while it won't hurt."

"Your wife might have other ideas."

"My wife isn't here." I dig in, determined to enjoy every freaking morsel.

Dad does the same. "Speaking of Cassie, how is she? And the kids?"

"Cassie's feeling a bit better. A bug of some kind. Audra's making remarkable progress. Mark's still moping over Levi."

"He'll get over it. Mark's quite a boy. I need to spend more time with him, now that he's on the cusp of being interesting."

I cringe. "Dad, please."

"It's the truth. It was the same with you and Palmer. I couldn't have a decent conversation with you until you were five or six and even then—"

Yes, Dad told us that often enough. After the first time, it ceased to be amusing. "Whatever." I take another bite of my burger. A pocket of hot grease burns my tongue.

Dad finishes his drink and motions at our waiter for another. "Don't you miss it, son?"

"Miss what?"

He points at his empty glass. "That. I mean, after all this time, would one drink hurt? It might do you some good. You're awfully tense. Are you and Cassie still sleeping in separate bedrooms?"

Why the hell did I tell him that? I ignore his remark. "Dad, being an alcoholic isn't something you can turn off and on like a tap." I like to boast that I've been clean and sober for twenty-five years. It has a nice ring to it. It's a nice blurb on the back of a book cover or as a quote in an interview. The truth, however, is slightly different. When Cassie told me she was pregnant with Mark, I told her I was thrilled and promised to go with her to her next doctor's appointment. Instead, I took off on an epic bender. Maybe it was my last desperate gasp of freedom. Maybe it was my way of bucking against being broken domestically. My fear of fatherhood. Or—more likely—I was being a total asshole.

Miss Drake finally tracked me down to a wedding in Locust Valley. Somehow, I'd been mistaken for a member of the band. I threw up on the mother of the bride. And yes, there is video. Anyway, once I sobered up, I begged Cassie for a second chance. She didn't make it easy. I had to work my butt off to regain her trust. Eventually, she took me back on two conditions: that it would never happen again, and we'd get married before the baby was born. I happily and enthusiastically agreed. We didn't even have a prenuptial. I have no fucking doubt in my mind that if I ever relapsed, Cassie would kick me to the curb without looking back. The woman has a spine of steel. She'd do what her mother should've done; if she had, her parents might still be alive.

Cassie's father was a high-functioning drunk, a beat reporter for a daily in Cleveland. He aspired to be Jimmy Breslin, but he had neither the talent nor the ambition. Her mother had long given up trying to rein him in. Just before Cassie moved to New York, her parents died in a car accident. Her father crashed their car after one too many beers at a local dive. The car exploded. Cassie isn't going through that hell again. So, no, I'm not tempted in the slightest to start drinking again. Old Brooks would already be three sheets to the wind. New Brooks, fuck no.

"Have you thought about what you're going to do? About getting a new agent. I can talk to Ben Underwood if you like. He doesn't usually handle your genre, but I'm sure he'd make an exception for you." Ben Underwood is Dad's literary agent, an old-timer. Dad's book on the art of negotiation is standard fare in many colleges and universities. He's also under contract to write his "memoirs" but he doesn't seem to be in a hurry to write it.

I sigh. I know Dad means well, but it's the wrong time. Once the full extent of Sheldon's perfidy became public knowledge, Crown-Hawkins dissolved. The agency had an insurance policy which covered all the clients that Sheldon had misappropriated from—no one would lose a single goddamn penny—but there was no insurance for the agency's tattered reputation. There were grumblings from other clients; why hadn't Sheldon dipped into my account? Despite my protestations of being in the dark, no one believed me. Tom Giafrida kept the fire going by inferring to anyone with a camera that I'd done something shady. Despite all this, I'd gotten calls about potential representation from several agents, but I'm simply not interested. My publisher is still firmly behind me and that's all I care about at the moment. "I don't need an agent right now. I'll revisit it later." A fresh wave of anguish sweeps over me. Oh, Sheldon, why did you have to fuck everything up?

"Do you think that's a good idea? You know what they say, strike while the iron is hot. I don't know what you saw in that fucking hack to begin with. Adler was a leech, a show-off, and a blowhard. And paying someone to run him down. I mean, how gauche."

Sheldon's barely cold in the grave. I'm dumbfounded. I put my burger down, no longer hungry.

Dad is nonplussed. "Oh, don't give me that look. It's the truth. Everyone knows it except you. And I told him as much."

Is that the liquor talking? "You told who what?"

Dad smears his salmon with tartar sauce. A drop of it falls on his tie, but he doesn't notice. "Sheldon, who else? He came to see me about a week or so before he—" He wipes his mouth with his napkin. "Would you believe the fool had the goddamn temerity to ask me for a bridge loan? That once he finalized some contracts, he'd pay it back with interest."

A stream of bile rises like lava in the back of my throat. I can only imagine the agony, the torment, the absolute desperation Sheldon must've felt to run to Dad to beg for money, of all the fucking people in the world.

"I told him in no uncertain terms that I wasn't his piggy bank. That he shit in his damn bed and it was up to him to clean his fucking mess. As long as he hadn't stolen from you, it was none of my affair. As for his other clients, well, frankly, that's what they get for trusting the creep."

For a moment, I tell myself that Dad's playing some kind of sick, twisted, practical joke until I remember that he has no sense of humor. Dad's weapons of choice are sarcasm and irony. He can slice people into ribbons with a clever phrase or a witty comeback without drawing a drop of blood. "What the fuck, Dad? Why didn't you tell me?" I fume.

Dad waves to the waiter that he's done. The waiter swoops in and removes the offending plate. "Why? Brooks, isn't it fucking obvious? Because I knew you'd do something foolish and ill-advised if I did."

I'm so angry I tremble. "Damn straight I would have." I

would've moved heaven and earth, entire constellations, mountains, continents, rivers, to help Sheldon. I would've done the same for Palmer and Mom. Of all the arrogant bastards—

Dad chuckles and gives me a wry smile. "Oh, Brooks, so goddamn naive and idealist. You still don't get it. You can't save everyone. You have to pick and choose your battles, and Sheldon wasn't worth the effort. Some people are simply collateral damage."

Incensed, I throw my napkin on my plate. It's better than throwing a glass of lime seltzer at Dad's head. "Is that so? But I thought you could. Isn't that the point of your goddamn initiative? Or is that how you get your jollies, by playing judge and jury, deciding who lives and who dies? Fuck you and your collateral damage. Sheldon wasn't just my agent and friend. He was my brother." I'm on my feet, shouting. Every eyeball in the place is fixed on me.

"No, Brooks. Palmer was your brother. Look what happened to him." Dad's face is shiny and plump like a ripe tomato on the vine. And then he gives me a look—I know this look. Once when I was a kid, I'd done something to displease him. Something minor, something not worth remembering. Dad didn't have to say a word. He just gave me this look, the one he's giving me now. As a kid, I was so scared I peed in my pants. I feel that way now, minus the peeing.

"Son, you're agitated. Please sit down and get hold of yourself. You're embarrassing me and you're making a damn fool out of yourself."

Instead, I storm away, the hell with Dad and his smug superiority. He can shove it along with his Sockeye salmon. "What the fuck are you looking at?" I mumble to one of Dad's colleagues, a high-ranking mucky-muck, as I leave.

Outside, I swallow in the fresh air. My chest is caught in a vise, my lungs ready to burst. I'm so angry I can barely walk. I find a bench and try to collect my thoughts. *What the fuck had just happened?*

Sheldon was a good man who'd done a bad, horrible, terrible thing. There's no glossing over that. He abrogated his fiduciary responsibility to his clients. He put his family in a financial morass. And the whole suicide-by-stranger idea was beyond stupid. Dad refusing to help Sheldon is one thing. I can accept that, begrudgingly, although Dad could well afford it. But Dad should've told *me*. It was my decision to make, and he'd taken it from me without blinking. Sheldon's clients, Phoebe and the kids, the people who would be hurt the most by Sheldon's actions—that didn't enter into Dad's thought process. As he put it, they were collateral damage. They didn't matter. They were expendable. No wonder Dad had done so well in the world of politics. Had he always been this cut-throat and cruel or had I just never noticed until now?

I remember what June said about Dad threatening her mother. I believed they were idle, empty words, but now I wasn't so sure. The man I just had lunch with isn't the father I know. That man is cold and ruthless. That man could be in a steel cage and stare into the dark, bottomless eyes of a great white shark— and I'd no doubt the shark would end up in a bowl of shark fin soup.

Somehow, I calm down. I check my cell. Cassie's just left a message for me to pick Mark up from school; Audra's physical therapy is running late. I write Cassie back and assure her I'll get Mark. I hail a taxi. If we don't hit traffic, I should get there just as the kids are dismissed.

The Burroughs School is the most expensive day school in Manhattan. Initially, I wasn't inclined to send Mark there. There's a perfectly fine public elementary school within walking distance of our apartment, but Sheldon talked me into it because Levi's already enrolled. I finally relented. Dad, who is friendly with some Yale alumni who are members of the Burroughs

School board, made sure that Mark and Levi were in the same class.

I arrive at the school minutes after the kids have been dismissed. Parents and students mill around by the front steps. The male students, swarming like wasps, are dressed in their distinctive lemon-colored blazers and khakis. I see Mark's teacher; Mark should be with her, waiting for either me or Cassie, as is our routine. He knows better than to wander off. Anxious, I push past a group of kids. And then I spot my son. Mark is at the street corner and a man—a stranger in a beige trench coat, his back to me—holds Mark's hand. *Shit.*

I take off like American Pharoah in the Kentucky Derby—I won ten thousand on the nag—petrified that this lunatic is going to throw Mark into a van and take off. Visions of poor Etan Patz on a milk carton thunder in my head. Why the fuck had I terminated the bodyguards? I scream for Mark, but I'm not sure he can hear me above the noise and traffic.

Mark instantly turns around and his face lights up. "Daddy!" He races to me, his heavy backpack making him waddle like a listing battleship.

Relieved, I sweep him into my arms. I've been accused of being absent, of not being in the moment. Of living in my head, oblivious. Old Brooks: guilty, guilty, guilty. New Brooks has never been more here with my boy safe in my arms. "Buddy, are you okay?"

Mark wags his finger at me. "You're late, Daddy."

"No, baby, I'm just in time." I hold Mark firmly and bound up to the trench-coat man, his back still to me as he flirts with some woman. "Hey, you!" I shout. "What the hell do you think you're doing?"

The man whirls around. It's Tom Giafrida, and I could fucking kill him.

CHAPTER SEVENTEEN

Grandpa William showed up one Friday morning in early August. He, Mom, and Palmer had only scant weeks to live.

Grandpa William parked his fire-engine-red DeSoto with the chrome grille where Julian Broadhurst usually parked his Aston Martin. The DeSoto was bigger than a boat, had no air conditioning or power steering, and ate gas like Halloween candy. I loved that car to pieces and dreamed of it being mine one day. After Grandpa William died, I don't know what happened to it.

Mom acted like she was happy to see her father, but she barely hugged him. Grandpa William didn't look well at all. He was a big man with an even bigger heart, but overnight he'd turned into an old, shriveled version of his former self. He'd lost at least a hundred pounds, maybe more. I knew Grandma Emily's losing battle with cancer had been hard on him. And he was still working, he hadn't taken a day off in years. At Grandma Emily's funeral, Mom urged him to retire and take it easy. Money wasn't an issue; his pension was considerable, and his house was paid for. Mom urged him to buy the sailboat he always wanted and sail around the world. But Grandpa William just shook his head sadly and murmured that it wouldn't be any fun without his love bug—Grandma. They'd fallen in love in the third grade; I don't think either of them ever looked at anyone else from that day forward.

After Grandpa William settled in the spare bedroom, he took a long nap. When he woke up, he insisted on taking us all out to an early dinner at a fancy restaurant in Southampton. Palmer ordered London broil. I wanted to try the stuffed shrimp with crabmeat. Mom told me I had to order from the kiddie menu, but Grandpa William winked at me and said I could order whatever I wanted since he was paying for it. After Mom kicked me under the table, I reluctantly ordered a kiddie cheeseburger, fries, and a strawberry ice-cream soda. Palmer was sullen and kept staring out the window. Since the escapade with the Aston Martin, Palmer had barely spoken to me. Mom seemed a bit off as well. She pecked at her flounder and didn't even finish her dessert. I filled in all the awkward silences with tales of the notorious Ditch Plains monster. Grandpa William rolled his eyes and harrumphed frequently but went along with it.

When we were done, we took a walk down Main Street. Most of the stores were closed by that time. Southampton was chic then as it is now, but it was still affordable. Once the sun set and it was uncomfortably chilly, Grandpa William took us for a ride on Dune Road. I was tired and stuffed from dinner and dozed on and off. I was barely aware of Grandpa William and Mom having some kind of argument. Palmer was asleep, too—at least I think he was. The only thing I remembered was Grandpa William telling Mom to think twice before doing something hasty that she'd come to regret. "He's not perfect, but no one is. He's a good man." Mom quickly changed the subject to the weather.

The next morning, Grandpa William roused Palmer and me early to go fishing in his sweet spot: the jetty off Ditch Plains beach. Palmer wasn't into it, moaning and groaning the whole way there. Grandpa William finally told him to knock it off. I don't think we caught a single fish that day, not even a nibble. I didn't care. I was happy just sitting next to Grandpa William and listening to his endless supply of stories.

It was a bit overcast and blustery; we pretty much had the beach to ourselves. Palmer had brought his boogie board with him, so after we ate

Mom's picnic lunch and digested a bit, he went in the water. I decided to stay with Grandpa William. As we waited for something to bite, he asked me if I was having a good summer. Of course, I lied and said yes. I've gone over that conversation a thousand times in my head. I wish I had told him the truth: that Dad had abandoned us, about Julian Broadhurst sniffing around Mom, us kids going to Camp Hero, Palmer vandalizing the Aston Martin. I should've begged Grandpa to take me home with him. I felt safe with him. But I didn't say any of that. Grandpa William tousled my hair and that was that.

By four or so, Grandpa William called it a day. The Aston Martin, fully repaired, was parked behind the DeSoto. Julian Broadhurst sat next to Mom on the front porch. Mom explained that Julian had dropped by to return a book she'd lent him. She spoke a bit too fast, and her voice was a bit too high.

Julian got up and extended his hand to Grandpa William. "It's a pleasure to meet you, sir."

Grandpa William was ordinarily courteous and well-mannered. I'd never heard him utter an angry or thoughtless word. I'd never even heard him curse. I think he would've been polite to the devil himself. But there was a long pause before Grandpa William shook Julian's hand. Palmer glowered at Julian. Thankfully, Julian got the message and didn't linger.

That night for dinner, we had chicken parmesan and spaghetti, one of Grandpa William's favorite dishes. He joked that it had more cheese than chicken. My piece of chicken was burnt on one side, but I didn't say anything. I cut around the burnt part.

Grandpa William fiddled with the television antennae, so we got enough reception to watch The Ed Sullivan Show *all the way through before it crapped out. The next morning, we saw Grandpa William off. He handed me a dollar and told me to be a good boy for Mom. He hugged Mom and for a moment, I thought he was going to cry. Palmer was on the porch, silent with hooded eyes. And then Grandpa William got in his DeSoto and drove away.*

If only I'd had the courage to tell Grandpa William what was going on. He might have been able to stop Julian Broadhurst. Mom and Palmer might still be alive.

If only.

CHAPTER EIGHTEEN

Tom Giafrida looks as shocked and surprised to see me as I do him. "Hey, Brooks." A mop-top in a yellow blazer like Mark's scampers up to him.

"Don't hey me, you asshole. Where the fuck were you going with my son?" I demand.

Mark covers his ears. "Daddy, you said a bad word."

My blood boils. There are going to be plenty more bad words.

Tom blanches. "Mark is your son? I saw him step off the curb and I pulled him back."

Entirely plausible, but I'm too wound up. "Look, you have a problem with me, say it to my face. That's what a man with balls does. They don't go on fucking Instagram or fucking TikTok or run to fucking Roger Friedman. You leave my kid out of it, you piece of shit. Stay the hell away from him or I swear I'll rip your fucking spleen out with my teeth."

A crowd has gathered. I hear a mix of gasps and laughter. A lot of kids beside Mark are covering their ears. Some adults, too. A lot of cell-phone activity. *Oh, my fucking Lord.* Don't people have better things to do? I briskly walk away and pull Mark alongside me.

Giafrida follows, his son in tow. The son of a bitch doesn't know when to leave well enough alone. "Brooks, there's been some kind of misunderstanding—"

I wheel around. "Listen to me, you overgrown weed. There's no misunderstanding on my part. You've slandered me all over this goddamn town, you sniveling shithead. Do you think I'm going to let you stab me in the back like you did Sheldon? You fucking ingrate. Sheldon made you a millionaire and you do him dirty like that? And your book sucks, by the way. I'm warning you for the last time, if you don't knock it off, I'm going to slap a cease-and-desist on your pathetic ass. Now get the hell out of my face before I fucking knock it to Staten Island." I turn and face a gaggle of shocked helicopter moms. "You got all that, bitches? Good. Talk about it at your next Oprah Book Club meeting. Until then, fuck off." I bolt away with Mark firmly in hand. I walk so fast his feet barely touch the ground.

"Daddy, you're going too fast," he complains. He's right.

I take a long breath and slow down. I pick him up again. His beautiful chestnut-brown eyes brim with tears. "Daddy didn't mean to frighten you. I'm sorry, little man."

"Am I in trouble?" His voice trembles.

"No, sweetie." I sigh. "But Daddy is."

The Burroughs Mom network has done its job. The minute we're home, Cassie confronts me, cell in hand. "Brooks, what the fuck am I going to do with you? You scared the living shit out of everyone. Why can't you pick up our kid from kindergarten without making a fucking scene that gets you trending on Twitter?"

"Mommy, you said a bad word," Mark points out.

"Don't be a smarty pants. Go to your room," Cassie orders.

Mark scampers off.

"It wasn't my fault," I begin.

"It's never your fault," she shoots back.

"If the term wasn't almost over, I'd pull him out of that lousy school."

"It's not a lousy school. Your father said you were in a bad mood at your freaking lunch." Cassie storms into the living room.

I scoot after her. "Oh, you already talked to him? Did he tell you what he said?"

"I don't care what he said. I care that you told the president of the parent's association to fuck off."

"I didn't know it was her. My venom was directed at Tom Giafrida, the fucking pipsqueak. In that trench coat, I thought he was a pervert kidnapping our son. Under the circumstances, I think I showed considerable restraint."

"Threatening to rip Tom's spleen out was restrained? He's not the bad guy here. His son is in Mark's class. I know you're angry and upset, but you can't take it out on the—"

"Sheldon went to him, baby." My voice cracks. I tell her exactly what Dad did. "He never said a word to me, Cassie. Not a goddamn word. Sheldon was out of his fucking mind, he's got an excuse—but Dad?" I collapse in a heap on the sofa.

Cassie's next to me in an instant. "Bernard really did that?"

I nod.

"Then that was an exceedingly shitty thing to do. I'm sorry, honey. I really am."

I lay my head on her shoulders. She strokes my chin. It tickles, but I don't ask her to stop.

"I know you're hurting. We all are. But you can't lash out like that."

She's right, of course. I've screwed up yet again. I promise to do better but I always find new ways to fuck things up. It's a real talent. Cassie doesn't need this, especially in her condition. And yes, I know pregnancy isn't an illness, but it's my responsibility to keep her peaceful and stress-free, and all I've done is add to it.

"I'm sorry, baby," I mumble, ashamed. "Can Mark go back to school?"

"Of course he can. I don't know about you." Cassie gets up. "Can we talk about this more later? I promised the kids I'd take them to the park before dinner. And you have a visitor. He's upstairs. The IT guy from the security company." She goes to the coat closet, puts on a long sweater, and nimbly tucks her hair inside a knitted cap. She could've passed for a high-school senior—an extremely sexy, pregnant, high-school senior. I love her so.

Cassie grabs her cell. "Come on, kids. Mommy needs to blow off some steam."

Fuck. I'd completely forgotten. My mind is turning to mush without Miss Drake. I bound up the stairs. The security company is insistent that we should have our apartment and computers checked out by one of their professionals. At first blush, I thought it was kind of silly. Who the hell would want to bug me? But after further reflection, I relented.

I don't know why I get it into my head that the IT geek is going to be like Noomi Rapace in *The Girl with the Dragon Tattoo* trilogy. Ms. Rapace was fearless in it, a real badass with her piercings and spiked hair. No one else can play Lisbeth Salander. It's like Humphrey Bogart as Rick Blaine or Harrison Ford as Han Solo. You can't picture anyone else in the role.

But the guy hunched on my sofa in my lair is more like Gene Hackman in *The Conversation.* This man is around the same age as me, give or take a few; he's got a thin comb-over, sunken eyes, clad in a button-down collar, and linen pants. The only things that stand out are the green frogs on his socks. He stands up and sticks out his hand at an awkward angle. I think he means to shake hands, but instead, he shoves a business card at me. "I'm Collier Moynes, private surveillance professional. The agency sent me." He sounds like a retired CIA operative. "What can I do for you, Mr. Anderson?"

"I'm not quite sure, to be honest." We both sit down. "I don't think anyone is spying on me. At least, I hope not."

Moynes smiles. Thirty years ago, with a full head of hair, some women would've found him attractive. "You'd be surprised, Mr. Anderson. In today's world, we're all being watched by somebody. You just aren't aware of it. A cheating spouse. A disgruntled boss. The porn guy. Parking your car under CCTV. Everyone has something to hide. Even me." He lets out a little laugh. It's not reassuring. "But really, Mr. Anderson, my purpose, and it's one I take seriously, is to give my clients peace of mind. We all deserve a measure of privacy. Consenting adults and all that. I don't care what you do in your bedroom or your backyard, and neither should the government or anyone else. Maybe I'm just an old-fashioned kind of guy, but I believe that there are things that aren't meant to be seen or shared on Instagram." He leans forward. "I understand you're skeptical, but let me assure you that I'm not some run-of-the-mill investigator. It might come as a surprise to you, but I used to work for the government."

No, that doesn't come as a surprise. Moynes might as well have had "Spook" stamped on his forehead.

"I've been involved in many high-profile, sensitive cases. Julian Assange. Edward Snowden. Jennifer Lopez. I'm discreet, trustworthy, and reliable. I've been doing this for a long time. I'm happy to sign a non-disclosure agreement."

"Well, if you're good enough for Jenny from the Block," I crack.

Moynes reaches into his suit pocket and removes a ballpoint pen. "Here, let me show you how easy it is to be recorded without your knowledge." He hits a button: my "Well, if you're good enough for Jenny from the Block" replays. "Clear as a bell, eh? It's a handy gizmo, a sixteen-hour, voice-activated recording pen. You can plug it into any computer and save the recording to your hard drive, the cloud, whatever." He hands it to me. "Keep it with my compliments. I give them out like Easter candy. You can buy them on Amazon for less than a hundred."

Shades of James Bond. I put the pen on my desk. "So, tell me, Mr. Moynes, how would this work? You'd check my computers for any bugs, viruses, or hacks? I already have a good virus program—"

"Programs can be easily bypassed. We're talking about all electronic devices: tablets, cell phones, the whole nine yards."

I frown. "I thought cell phones couldn't be bugged."

"That's a common misconception. Random SMS messages, using public wifi—cybercriminals are coming up with new ways and scams to compromise and steal your private information and you wouldn't be aware of it. In our field, it's standard to do a full electronic surveillance sweep, identify any threats if found, remove them, and suggest appropriate countermeasures. I take it this is for your home office. It shouldn't take more than a day, depending on what's found. As for your vehicles, I'd check for GPS tracking devices. And again, all in confidence. If you get my drift, your wife will never have to know." He gives me a knowing leer.

"I don't think that's going to be necessary," I reply. "But since you're here, perhaps you could help me with this." I motion at Miss Drake's desk across the room, the Mac hard drive glowing as if it were Chernobyl. "I need to access the desktop. I thought I'd written down the correct password but—"

Moynes' eyes light up like a kid on Christmas morning opening his first present. He heads to Miss Drake's computer; it will always be Miss Drake's computer. As he works on that, I check my cell. There's a barrage of texts from Dad about the incident at Burroughs that would make a steelworker blush: *Couldn't those fuckers see you were protecting your child?* That's one of the milder ones. And from Dalton Crane: *Don't be surprised if you're hit with a restraining order.*

"Mr. Anderson?"

I see that Miss Drake's computer is up and running.

"You'll be the only one using this computer, right? I removed the master password. If you like, you can input a new one. But for now, you're fine."

I reach into my pocket to give him a tip.

"No, my pleasure, from one writer to another. I wrote a memoir about my espionage work. When I couldn't get Langley to sign off, I self-published it. It hasn't done too badly on Amazon. Look it up."

I show Moynes out. "If I want to proceed on the other matter, I'll give you a call." I offer my hand again. He must have a thing about being touched because once again he avoids me.

"I'm also available for movie consultations. I worked on the *Mission: Impossible* franchise. And *Bridge of Spies.*" He gives me a friendly nod as he enters the elevator.

I'm not sure I want Collier Moynes nosing into my life, but at least he'd gotten me into the computer. The email inbox is full of unread messages; a lot of people hadn't gotten the memo of Miss Drake's passing. I'm a popular guy. Everyone wants a piece of me. There are emails from reporters asking about my run-in with Tom Giafrida. Emails marked "urgent" and "priority response" from the producers on *Three Rivers.* Emails from underlings of Jeff Fucking Bezos, Elon Musk, and others. Emails from my long-patient editor at Harper Collins inquiring about the status of the book which doesn't have a name yet. They gave me all that money for "a title to be decided." Also, emails between Miss Drake and June, just as June said.

It belatedly dawns on me that the care and feeding of Brooks Anderson isn't a one-person job, it requires a fucking army. I have the constitution of a water buffalo, but even so, I have a shitload of work to do if I'm going to meet my publisher's deadline. Keep in mind that in publishing, which can often seem like the Bataan Death March, there are deadlines and then there are *deadlines.* But tonight, if only for a few precious hours, I want to switch my brain into a holding pattern.

When Cassie and the kids come home, I tell her that she has the night off. I feed the kids and pay rapt attention to their stories of crazy squirrels in the park. I give them their baths. They both fall asleep watching *Trolls World Tour*.

After I finish taking a leisurely hot shower to wash off the stink of Tom Giafrida, Cassie's in our custom king-sized bed, editing a hard copy of a client's manuscript with a trusty yellow marker. The fact that she's in our bed doesn't go unnoticed by me. She's in one of my vintage Willie Nile tees accrued from my salad days hustling for any kind of writing work: porn, reviews, term papers. I wasn't choosy. Somewhere in this universe, a man can boast that I got him an A-plus on his thesis on Hermann Hesse.

Cassie's so engrossed in her work that she's unaware that I'm staring at her from the bathroom door. At moments like these, more moments than I care to admit, I'm acutely aware of our differences, age, and otherwise. The year Cassie was born, I'd already burned through two wives and countless lovers. I was still addicted to heroin. At first glance, Cassie and I are an odd pair, like mismatched socks. She's five foot three. I have to crouch going through some doorways. She's a natural blonde. I'm now completely gray. Her skin is like alabaster; when she goes for blood work the nurses always have trouble finding a good vein. I can stay in the sun for hours and not get burned. When you get right down to it, Cassie isn't my "type" at all. I tend to navigate towards voluptuous women, women with meat on their bones. Cassie's on the thin side. Her breasts barely fill a B cup. But when she's pregnant, her boobs swell. Even this early, they're filling out. She'd breastfed Mark despite having inverted nipples. Scout's honor, I'd never heard of such a thing. But we got a breastfeeding doula and Cassie made it happen. When Audra was born and so tiny, she could only be fed through a tube, Cassie religiously pumped her breasts for when Audra would be able to latch on. Other women would've given up. Not Cassie. Did I say she has a spine of steel? Fuck that, it's titanium.

When Cassie and I first met, I was in one of my mad monk fugues. For all of my bad-boy reputation, I've gone through periods of restraint and yes, celibacy. I hadn't had a real girlfriend in months. I'd pretty much given up on having a mature relationship. I'd grown this Rasputin beard and resembled a disheveled grizzly. I was edging toward sixty fucking years old and feeling every bit of it. The last thing on my mind was love or anything remotely close to it.

But an anniversary edition of *Fallen Angels* was coming out, and Sheldon persuaded me to do a publicity tour. After going back and forth for weeks, I agreed to meet a freelance reporter for a short interview, forty-five minutes tops, at Dunkin' Donuts, of all places. Cassie was already waiting at a table. She was dressed in a demure blazer and skirt outfit, her hair in a messy half-up, half-down do with garish purple feather dangle earrings. The earrings captivated me. Then I heard her voice. I was done.

Fifteen minutes into the interview, as Cassie asked me intelligent and thoughtful questions, I wondered what she was like in bed. (She was nothing like that). My desire for her was complete and overwhelming. I'd never experienced anything like it, not with Jennifer or anyone else. I chastised myself. Cassie was at least thirty years younger than me, if not more. I told myself it was impossible. The tabloids would have a field day. And Dad; she's after your money, she has a shitload of student loans. (She did). I didn't want the interview to end.

Two hours later, after we'd drunk enough coffee to fill Hoover Dam, Cassie grabbed her pocketbook to leave. I asked her out for drinks. She politely refused; she had a boyfriend. (She didn't). Of course, this was like waving a red flag in front of a bull. Hiding my disappointment, I gallantly hailed her a taxi. As she climbed in, her skirt hiked over her thigh, I caught a glimpse of her underwear: Hello Kitty briefs. That was the last straw.

By morning, thanks to Miss Drake, I knew where Cassie lived. Her favorite band. (Fleetwood Mac). And that she loved peonies. I repeatedly asked Cassie out to dinner and again, she declined. I scoured her social media posts and discovered that she was going to Paris for a month to visit a friend from college. I immediately booked a suite at the Ritz Paris and left on a midnight flight before Cassie arrived. The only person I told was Sheldon, who, to his eternal credit, didn't try to talk me out of it. I greeted Cassie with an armful of white and pink peonies and fresh croissants at her friend's apartment in Neuilly. Cassie was dumbfounded. (Not really). Her friend thought it was hilarious and called me a crazy American. It was a magical time. It was Paris in springtime, and no one gave a rat's ass about our age difference. Cassie and I had our first kiss by the Eiffel Tower under a night sky full of stars. The night before we're due to leave, we make love for the first time and I discover, to my great surprise, that Cassie's a virgin. (I should've ended it right there). Once we are back in Manhattan, Cassie promptly moved in with me, and that was that. (And yes, I paid off all her student loans). Dad was aghast. Was I back on drugs? (Hell, no). When Cassie and I married at City Hall, officiated by then-Mayor de Blasio (don't get me started on him), Dad refused to attend. Sheldon and Phoebe were the only witnesses.

I know people snicker behind our backs. At the park, people think I'm Mark and Audra's grandfather. Let them gawk, I don't give a flying fuck. I love my wife and kids. I pay my taxes, I donate to charity, I vote. On paper, Cassie and I don't work, but it does—until I do or say something that screws it up. Frequently.

I step into the bedroom wearing the gag gift the "kids" gave me for my last birthday: silk emoji boxers. It's a cornucopia of ridiculous emojis: smiley faces, sad faces, puke faces, and curly mounds of smiling brown poop. For the longest time, poop was

Mark's favorite word, which he unabashedly shouted at to anyone within hearing distance. We finally got him to understand that the "p" word should only be said at home. I wiggle my butt for her benefit. "Come on, you know you love it."

"You're an idiot." Cassie doesn't look up from the page she's editing.

I suck her big toe. Cassie's toes are perfect to nibble on.

"Do you want to talk about your father?"

Hell, no. I'd sooner drill screws into my head. I want to forget the whole fucking mess. Old Brooks would've been stoned out of his mind long before this. New Brooks finds solace in bare feet. "Have I told you today that you're an amazing wife and mother and that I love you with all my heart?"

Cassie stifles a grunt. "I'm still mad about the vasectomy."

"Are you going to hold that between my legs for the rest of my life?" I slowly work my way up. Cassie doesn't swat me away. I take that as a sign to keep going.

"How did your IT guy work out?" She exchanges the yellow highlighter for a red one. Red ink is bad. Cassie's going to rip this poor writer a new asshole. She's not the kind of editor to hire if all you're expecting is puffery. She's fucking brutal. She hates *Fallen Angels*. She didn't finish *Broken Bridges*. She thought *Three Rivers* was pretentious claptrap. Thus far, there's nothing I've written that she's approved of except for Amazon wish lists. And even then, I forget something.

I'm up to her thighs. Cassie's soft skin smells of cucumber and melon. "Sort of a strange dude. But at least he got me into Miss— I mean the computer."

"That's good, isn't it?" She slashes wildly with her red pen.

"He wants to do a sweep. Check out all the computers, cars."

Cassie's pen stops in mid-air. "For what?"

"Bugs, viruses, hackers, that kind of thing."

Cassie shrugs. "It sounds like a waste of time. I mean, you're not seriously thinking of doing it, are you?" There's an edge to her voice. The book she's editing must be a real dog. I tell her all the time that she should be writing her own books; God knows, she's got enough material.

"Not really. But, yeah, you're probably right." I'm now into Cassie's sweet spot. Still no resistance. Emboldened, I slip her panties off. I'm hard as a rock until I see spots of dried blood in her briefs. My dick goes limp. "Cassie."

"Brooks, don't freak out."

It's a little late for that.

"I already spoke to the doctor. Some women spot throughout their entire pregnancy. It's not a big deal. Nothing to be alarmed about."

I'm underwater without an oxygen tank. Cassie seems calm. I'm not. "For real?"

She kisses the tip of my nose. "Aside from the morning sickness, I'm fine. I'm going to the doctor next week."

"You mean *we're* going." I hug her so tightly, I feel her ribcage. The placenta previa with Audra had taken a toll on me. I'd come way too close to losing both Cassie and Audra. It had taken Cassie months to recover. We tempted fate yet again with Audra's dog bite, but you can tempt fate only so many times. "Will they do a sonogram? Do you think they'll be able to tell if it's a boy or a girl?" We'd known beforehand with Mark and Audra, but we didn't make a huge hoopla about it. No explosive gender reveals for us.

"Maybe. If the baby cooperates. But this time I want it to be a surprise." The book forgotten, Cassie snuggles against me and her tongue darts in and out of my mouth like a hummingbird.

But the moment's gone. I'm not going to take any risks. "Why don't I give you a back rub." I massage her shoulders just the way she likes it: slow, steady, and firm. "It's not the ideal time, but it looks like I may go upstate for a day or two for an interview. I'm still working out the details. I was thinking after we see the doctor, how about we go out to Water Mill for a long weekend with the kids. The contractor says the house is just about finished." I can't wait to show Cassie and the kids all my little surprises.

"That sounds like a plan." She purrs like a cat. "You *are* happy about the baby, aren't you?"

"Of course I am. How many other seniors can brag that they're going to be a dad and a great granddad in the same year?" I joke. "The stork is working overtime."

"Speaking of special deliveries, you got a package from FedEx while you were in the shower. Fernando brought it up."

I stop mid-massage. "At this time of night? Did you notice who it was from?"

"Just that it's from an attorney. It's not a restraining order if that's what you're worried about."

I leap out of bed so fast I nearly pull a hamstring. It has to be the DNA results. "Where is it?"

"On the coffee table."

I get the envelope and hop back to Cassie. She playfully grabs it out of my hand and rips it open. "The moment you've all been waiting for," she says in her best Maury voice. "Brooks Anderson —" She scans the documents.

I wait. Cassie's playing this to the hilt. "Well?"

"You are not the father."

"And?"

She gives me a sad little smile. "Brooks, I'm sorry."

I see that Cassie's serious. I still don't believe her. I don't want to believe her. But it's there in black and white from three different labs: June and I aren't a DNA match. It's not even close, there isn't a ghost of a chance. I should be elated, right? I'm shattered. Hell, I'd been so sure. June had been so sure. She was Jennifer Juniper's daughter—but she wasn't *my* daughter. I fold the papers and stick them back in the envelope.

Cassie puts her arms around me. "Honey, I know you're upset, but maybe it's for the best. We don't need any more complications, and this would be gigantic. Your father would have a fit. You know he would."

I can't deny that. Everything Cassie says is true. I'm still gutted. "What are you saying, exactly? That Jennifer lied?"

"No, not at all. She was mistaken. If it wasn't you and it's physically impossible for her husband to be the father, it's got to be someone else. What other explanation is there?"

I grabbed my cell phone. "Or maybe the results are wrong."

"From three different labs?"

I get Lloyd Parsons' answering machine; I leave a terse message. After I hang up, I start pacing, my nerves jumping.

"Why do you want it to be true so badly?" Cassie asks.

It's a reasonable question. I just don't have an answer—or an answer that will satisfy Cassie. "And why do you not want it to be?"

"You're disappointed, but don't take it out on me."

I shake my head. "You don't get it."

"You're wrong. I do get it. You were enamored with the idea of having a kid come out of thin air because of this —*entanglement*. It appealed to your vanity and your ego which is bigger than the Milky Way. You had a fantasy built up in your head of this big, messy family as if our family isn't messy enough. I warned you not to get emotionally attached to the idea that June might be your daughter."

She had, but damn it, it's not the time to remind me. "Listen, if all you're going to do is give me a fucking attitude, I'll sleep in the spare bedroom."

"You sleep there every goddamn night, so why should tonight be any different, you asshole," she snaps. A minute ago, I had her purring. Now I'm an asshole again.

Enraged, I slam the door behind me. I'm not sure who I'm more fucking annoyed with, the lab, Cassie, or me. I can only imagine poor June's reaction. I sure as hell hope that Parsons hasn't sent her the results yet, that he'd have the common sense to know I'd need to speak with him first.

So much for my night. I trudge up to the lair and check my cell. Well, at least I wasn't trending on Twitter anymore. I need to focus on the book; it's not going to write itself. I idly finger Marshall Reagan's documents. I still can't figure out who Herman Bethel is; all my internet searches have come up dry. There must be something I've overlooked, but I'm damned if I know what. What would Miss Drake do? Determined, I pick the papers up and settle in. Hell, it beat night terrors and sleepwalking.

It's close to three o'clock in the morning. I've drunk so much seltzer my pee fizzes. I'm bleary-eyed when I open the file Sheriff Cooper compiled on Julian Broadhurst. The sheriff hadn't spent much time on it. From his vantage point, he'd no reason to. It was open and shut. He had a culprit and a motive. It was just a matter of tying up loose ends so he could close the case. I skim it half-heartedly until I get to the last pages.

Somehow, Cooper's handwritten interviews and notes with Dad shortly after the murders are in Julian's file. I knew Dad had been interviewed, but I'd been told the notes had been accidentally shredded after Cooper retired from the force. But here they are, hiding in plain sight. If Cooper were still alive, he'd have some explaining to do. How in the hell had Reagan acquired them? And was inserting them in Julian Broadhurst's file deliberate on Reagan's part? A horrible cosmic joke? An innocent mistake? The more I reflect, I'm convinced Reagan did this on purpose. He was a jerk, but he was too smart to make such a bonehead error.

As I read the pages, the hammer inside my head pounds. This isn't merely an interview. It's Dad's version of the summer of 1966. *And it's a pack of goddamn lies.*

He called two to three times a week.

He visited us several times.

Everything was fine between him and Mom.

He had no idea that Mom was pregnant.

By the time he got to the house that night, Mom and Palmer were already dead.

A thousand electrodes explode in my head. The pain's so intense I can barely see. Why the fuck would Dad lie so demonstrably? These weren't just little white lies; they were a volcanic eruption of lies, a tsunami of falsehoods, a blizzard of untruths. I'm crushed. It feels like the first time Palmer and I watched *The Wizard of Oz* and our faces fell when instead of a great and all-powerful wizard behind the curtain, it's a flustered carnival barker with a fake moustache. I'd always considered Dad to be an honest man, a man I've always looked up to and respected. And yes, despite our many differences and estrangements, I saw Dad as a source of strength and inspiration. Even after what Dad did to Sheldon—which was unforgivable—I still want to believe. I can't anymore. The bandage is ripped off, the wound exposed. I can think of only one solid reason why Dad lied so shamelessly, without reservation or hesitation, to Sheriff Cooper. And it's the most hideous lie of all.

Dad was there much, much earlier. He's the shadowy figure that haunts my nightmares. This is no false memory. I know this now to the depths of my soul. Even so, a tiny voice whispers, *well, so what if he was?* Even if Dad's timeline is off—well, off a lot—that didn't mean anything nefarious. Maybe Dad had arrived right after the rampage. Maybe he was shell-shocked and paralyzed, as I was. I can accept that, except for one fucking thing. *Why lie about it?* And why maintain this pulp fiction that we were one big happy family that summer when we most certainly weren't?

There are many things I don't know, but I know this: I wish to hell that Marshall Reagan had never sent me this fucking box. I feel something that I haven't felt in years, something I truly believed was dead and buried: the old Brooks' compulsion to take something to blot it all out. It roars back to life, this gnawing hunger. New Brooks is rocked. I will myself to ignore it, but the jagged knife digging into my brain plus the throbbing in my veins is a recipe for catastrophe.

I rush into the kids' bathroom—which is the farthest room from the master bedroom—and crouch on the cold floor. I claw at my head. I'm so goddamn tired of this shit. The cure is worse than the disease. This is cancer buried so deep it's going to kill me to get it all out. Oh, if Sheldon and Miss Drake could see me now: sixty-five fucking years old in goofy emoji boxers writhing like a toddler. I should be over this. I thought I *was* over it. I can't change the past. Remembering what happened to Mom and Palmer isn't going to bring them back, but it was fucking tearing me apart.

"Daddy?" Mark, his eyes half-open and clad in Baby Yoda pajamas, is in the doorway.

Mortified, I pick him up. I see my reflection in the bathroom mirror and it's someone I haven't seen in decades. I wish I could say that I didn't recognize myself, but I did. What's the line in that old Simon and Garfunkel chestnut? Something about darkness being an old friend. Except this is the sound of screaming. I like to pretend—or play—at being tamed. Domesticated. A wild tiger who'd finally met his match. Now I realize I've been lulled into a false sense of complacency, an untruth I live with every damn day. If Dad has lied, then so have I. Old Brooks was always there, lurking beneath the ocean surface like a shark waiting for the exact moment to strike or a rattlesnake hiding in the desert sand for an unsuspecting victim. My beast is a silent predator, dormant, and most of all, patient. It'll torment me when I'm vulnerable. I know this even though I can't say it aloud. It's why I have Naloxone strategically placed in the house and my car. I've even stashed it at the house in Water Mill. I don't ever expect to use it, because if I do it'll be the end of my life with Cassie. It's like car insurance. You pay the premiums and complain about it until you run through a stop sign higher than the International Space Station and broadside a school bus full of kids.

I can't admit it to anyone—not even Cassie—but I fucking loved being a junkie until I didn't. Alcohol was a vice, an addiction, an accessible balm, but it wasn't like shooting up. I've snorted enough cocaine up my nose to fill a couple of tractor-trailers—it's a wonder I still have an intact nose—but it's nothing compared to heroin. When I was a junkie, there were days when I would've walked through broken glass on my bare knees to get a fix. I'm not proud of it, but there was a time when I reveled in my bad-boy reputation. There is the infamous cover of me on *Rolling Stone*, you know it, it's the one by Richard Avedon. It's a collector's piece now. I have the original signed and framed. It used to hang over the fireplace mantel, but Cassie hated it, so it now hangs in my lair. I understand why she detests it so much. It's a hideous photo, snapped in the blinding blitz of *Fallen Angels.* I was bare-chested, barely tipping one hundred pounds, my hair dyed jet black, my skin white and pasty. A junkie's pallor. Corpses had more color. I was a walking skeleton. If you look close enough, you can see the needle tracks on my arms. It scared some people. Others wrote me off as a poseur, a fake, or an example of performance art. The beast was on full display then, lapping it up.

I didn't need a therapist to tell me why I was a junkie. But no amount of drugs or drink could erase the fact that I hadn't done anything to help Mom and Palmer. Why hadn't I screamed? Ran for the neighbors? Thrown a rock through the window? It's a lapse in judgment that I can never atone for. I love Cassie and the kids, and I try to act normal, but I'm not. Maybe my brain was normal once upon a time, but it was rewired from that horrendous night on. Maybe the reality is that I can't be what Cassie and the kids need me to be at any given time, a reality that's finally settling in. I berate Dad for his lies, but who the hell am I to judge? The apple doesn't fall far from the tree. I hate clichés, yet I'm a walking one.

But at that moment, as I hold Mark, my sweet, innocent son, I will myself back to being his daddy and not some pale, pathetic imitation. "What's the matter, big guy? A bad dream?" I try to sound jovial, but inside I shake like a palm tree in a hurricane.

He sleepily nods.

"Yeah, me too." I bring him back to his room and tuck him in. "How about I stay with you? Would you like that? We can dream together, but good dreams only."

I lay down next to him and my legs hang over his twin bed. He snuggles up against me. His skin smells like watermelon, thanks to his kiddie body wash. I put my arm around him. As long as I have Mark close, the beast will sleep—for now.

"Poop," Mark mumbles as he closes his eyes.

CHAPTER NINETEEN

The last day of Mom and Palmer's life started innocently enough. It was a beautiful late August morning. A cool ocean breeze cut through the humidity. Mom told us over waffles that we were going back to the Big House in a week or so to get ready for the new school year. Mom seemed especially anxious to get home. I was, too. But since Grandpa William's visit, Mom had seemed better overall; more attentive and energetic, and not so lethargic.

After breakfast, I went outside to play. As I did wheelies, Mom was in the house cleaning and vacuuming. The hum of her routine was comforting. Palmer had taken off shortly after breakfast; he said something about collecting seashells, but I'm not sure I believed him.

After the Camp Hero incident, the gang had kind of drifted apart. Toad's parents returned home early from their European vacation and had him on a tight leash. Ronnie was busy helping his parents out at their motel. Gigi's family had gone to Maine to visit her grandparents, but when I rode around the neighborhood earlier, I saw their car in their driveway. They must have come home the night before. I wondered if her parents had forbidden her to hang with us. I would have.

Around noon, I went up to the beach at Ditch Plains. I was still full from breakfast, so all I took with me was water and green grapes for a snack. The beach was dotted with sunbathers and swimmers taking in the last rays of summer before fall arrived and Montauk shut down for the winter.

I threw my stuff and blanket on the sand and dove into the water. It was so warm that it was like taking a bath. It was almost too warm. After a couple of laps, I dried off and hiked up into the dunes. The tall grass swayed to the beat of a dozen different tunes: The Beatles, The Beach Boys, The Four Seasons, and Petula Clark, another of Mom's favorites.

Further up, I saw a couple lying on a blanket in the sand. It was only when I got a bit closer that I realized it was Palmer and Gigi. I hid behind a bush and watched as Palmer held her and stroked her hair. He was smiling; I hadn't seen him smile like that for a long time. When they started kissing, I crept away.

I got home before Palmer and took a shower first because he'd use up all the hot water. Mom hadn't been to the market in a couple of days, so all we had for dinner was hot dogs, baked beans, and semi-stale buns. We ate outside on the rear patio, sitting on the redwood set Grandpa William had built. Palmer joined us when we were nearly finished. I thought it was weird that he had a dress shirt on—we lived in T-shirts—until I saw these raspberry blotches dotting his neck.

Mom grinned as she handed him a paper plate. "Palmer, did you fall into a patch of poison ivy?"

Palmer blushed.

After dinner, we stayed outside looking for satellites until it started to rain. At eight, Ed Sullivan came on. I remember falling asleep during the Topo Gigio routine. At some point, Mom moved me to my bed because the next thing I vividly remember is Palmer shaking me awake. I know I ran to the dunes or at least I started to run there. The rest is a blur. Hours later, Sheriff Cooper found me in the dunes.

I've replayed that day a million times in my head. For a few brief hours, we were all happy. A family. And at the end of it all, that's how I want to remember them. How I must remember them if I'm going to keep their memory alive.

CHAPTER TWENTY

I nurse my cup of black coffee outside the center conference room at the Jacob Javits Center. It's still early, not too many people around, but I expect that to change. I'm here because Dad's on a panel at a symposium. He extended a personal invitation for me to attend via his mailing list. As a rule, I'm not big on these things. I'm not a political creature like Dad. I'm registered as an Independent, but I vote Democratic. Usually, I beg off when Dad invites me to these functions, but not today. The beast wants fresh meat, not grilled salmon.

Cassie's just rousing when I fix the kids' breakfast and ask them to be good for Mommy until I come home. Before I leave, I throw Mark's bed sheets and pillowcases in the washer to get rid of my sweat stink from the night before.

Dad is on the first panel of the morning. This conference is sponsored by an outfit called Global Solutions for a New World. The Board of Directors is a virtual who's who of influencers, world leaders, shakers, billionaires, and politicians. I know the foundation is legit. Hell, Melinda Gates is the keynote dinner speaker. At twenty-five thousand dollars a pop for tickets (dinner not included), I hope these serious people get more than rubber chicken and frozen cheesecake topped with fake whipped cream.

Dad's a regular fixture at these events and is showing no signs of slowing down. And they say my ego is humongous? In the past year alone, Dad's traveled to Dubai, London, Beirut, Saudi Arabia, Paris, Berlin, and Canberra, and that's not including Zoom meetings and other video conferences. Dad thrives on this; the plane rides, the lush hotel suites with complimentary breakfast pastries, and Japanese Shiatsu massages. To me, it's like being on a book tour. The first couple of weeks are tolerable but it soon becomes a grind. I'm irritated, churlish, and can't wait to sleep in my own bed again.

I wait quietly for Dad to finish. I don't ask for special favors. One of the roving Global Ambassadors dressed in a garish white-and-blue costume that looks like something out of a Jerry Lewis comedy, recognizes me. He asks if I'd prefer to wait in the VIP lounge, but I decline.

I check my cell again. Still no response to my messages and voicemails from Parsons. And nothing from June, either. I have the sinking feeling that Parsons has already sent her the results of the DNA test and she's blocked me.

"Well, look who decided to come out of his coffin," a familiar voice rings out.

I twirl around. It's Marilyn, a torpedo in heat, and she's headed straight at me. Sweet Jesus, I need this like a case of the clap.

Marilyn flings herself into my arms and poses like a cheap hooker. I know there's a photographer somewhere. Marilyn probably hired one herself. Back in Dad's day, a woman like her would've been labeled a "man-eater." In today's progressive climate, she's just a good old-fashioned star fucker. After our divorce, she latched on to D-list celebrities and one-hit wonders, you know, the singers you see in those late-night best-of album commercials. Marilyn reinvented herself every couple of years.

Now she was positioning herself as some kind of avant-garde fashion guru/hustler. Although I begrudged Nan for bilking me, at least she hadn't made a career of belittling me with one hand while taking my money with the other. Unlike fine wine, Marilyn hasn't aged well. A wax dummy has more expression. If she gets one more Botox injection, her face will shatter. I don't know why seeing Marilyn gets me so worked up. That's a lie. It's because she's a reminder of the man I used to be. The man I'm afraid I still am.

I step away from Marilyn. I really want to ask her how many dicks she sucked to get an invite, but since reporters lurk, I refrain. I give her a frosty glare. "Did you get your fangs sharpened just for today?"

Marilyn's laugh is brittle. She has a glass with something orange in it. I'd bet the house in Water Mill it's not juice. "You need to get out more often, darling. I'm looking for investors for my new company."

"Bitches R Us?" I quip. "Oh, look, isn't that Richard Branson?"

Marilyn takes off like a bottle rocket.

Dalton Crane bolts up and laughs like a kid who's just placed a whoopie cushion in the principal's chair.

I laugh even louder, the weight on my chest receding. "Fuck it, man. What are you doing here?"

"I'm supposed to be on a panel about criminal justice reform. Imagine that." He sounds amused that anyone would consider him an expert. "But the truth is, I came for the gift-bag swag and free food." He held up a plate of bite-sized pastries. "You heard the latest about Solomon Burke?"

I haven't.

"The judge denied his bail. I don't get it. Aside from the credit card, they have nothing. No fingerprints, no DNA, no murder weapon. And Burke's lawyer is doing jack shit."

"If you believe the guy's being railroaded, take the case and be done with it," I shoot back. "It sounds like you want to."

Dalton shivers as if I've handed him an electric eel. "Hell, no. My pro bono days are long behind me, brother. I have mouths to feed." He pauses to stuff a cream puff in his mouth. "Are you here for Bernard? Moral support?"

Mercifully, a Global Ambassador beckons. "Mr. Anderson?"

"Catch you later," I say to Dalton.

I follow the Global Ambassador down a corridor to a bank of private suites. She opens the door to one. It's semi-filled with dignitaries and other convention-goers. Dad is turning on the charm to a group of enthralled listeners. "I told GW that Iraq was going to be the bane of his existence." He spots me and broadly smiles. "If you'll excuse me." He dutifully trots up. "Brooks, you should've told me you were coming. I would've given you a ride."

"I wasn't sure I was coming until the last minute. I need to speak to you in private. Please, Dad." Is that urgency or desperation in my voice? It's increasingly difficult to know the difference.

"Sure, son. I have time." Dad ushers me into a more secluded area. We both sit down at the same time on a faux leather sofa. He turns to me, expectant. "What's this all about, Brooks? You don't look quite yourself. Bad night?"

"It's about the book, I'd like to clear up some details for my research. Bear with me even if it feels like I'm dense or repetitive." I feel like a grad student proposing a thesis subject to an exalted professor.

Dad puts his hand on my knee. "If it's important to you, then it's important to me. I'm here for you, son. I always will be."

I swallow hard. "Dad, when we left for the cottage that summer, did you know Mom was pregnant?"

Dad grits his teeth before he answers. "Don't you think it's a wee bit early in the morning to dredge all that up? Yes, of course, I knew. I was thrilled. But there were practical considerations. Another child on my salary alone wouldn't have been easy. In those days, they didn't have maternity leave as they do now. But I told your mother I'd pick up some extra tutoring or classes, that we'd work it out. But she wasn't sure."

"Sure about what?"

"The pregnancy. She needed time to decide."

I bite my tongue. "You mean get an abortion."

"It wasn't legal in New York, not then. But there were some doctors who'd do it if you knew where to go. I wasn't happy about it, but it was her decision and I'd support her. Especially after the baby she lost." He lowers his head and breathes sharply. "That was my fault. I should've fixed that broken step in the basement. You were so little, you probably don't recall it, but your mother had a tough time. Your Grandmother Emily stayed with us for a spell."

I remember that time quite vividly. Mom wailing in her room. I thought I'd done something bad. I made her get-well cards and slid them under her door. I wonder what happened to those cards.

"Now we'd call it postpartum depression. I never thought you or Palmer were in any danger. And she got better. She went back to work, resumed her life. But this time, she became obsessed with the idea that there was something wrong with the fetus. The doctors said the chances of that happening again were minuscule. But your mother was fixated on it. The only thing I said to her was that if she was going to terminate the pregnancy, she had to do it soon."

I sit there and say nothing, mostly because I've no intention of interrupting Dad. This is the first time, indeed, the only time, that he's been—what's the word—loquacious about Mom. Mentally, I know where Dad's going with this, but emotionally, it's difficult for me to reconcile. Mom always wanted a little girl. She never made a secret of it. I don't care what Dad says. I can't fathom Mom getting a backstreet abortion unless it was a dire circumstance. And he lied to Sheriff Cooper, but I keep that in my pocket for now.

Dad gesticulates with his hands as if he's washing them with boiling water, except there is no water. "Brooks, your mother was a hurricane in heels. Are you aware that I was engaged to another woman when we first met? Maybe that was part of the attraction for her, that I was with someone else. Something to be conquered. A trophy." He sounded melancholy; I'm not sure if he is talking to me or himself. "I was out of my league with Shirley. I couldn't say no to her. No man could when she set her mind on something. And for some strange reason, she wanted me. I was flattered. I don't know, it might have burned out if she hadn't gotten pregnant with Palmer. Come on, Brooks, don't look so shocked. Do the math. The ink on our marriage license was barely dry when Palmer was born. Illegitimate children weren't a thing back then. It was a stigma I wouldn't have subjected my son to. It's not how I was raised." His grin is thin and strained. "Shirley was a carnal woman of great passion. That's a genteel way of putting it. The letters she used to write me. Oh my God. They should've come with a fire extinguisher." He pats my knee again. "You seem to have this romanticized notion of what our marriage was like. It was like any other marriage between young people who barely knew each other. We had our highs and our lows. I'm sure there were days when we didn't like each other or when we wanted to throw in the towel. But we were both strongly committed to each other and to you boys."

"Then why did you abandon us?" I blurt.

Dad gives me an odd look. "Where the fuck did you get that crazy idea?"

I reach into my jacket, take out a copy of his interview with Sheriff Cooper, and silently hand it to him. "Do you remember this?"

"Vaguely. I mean, it was so long ago." He hands it back to me. "So?"

"Is it accurate?"

Dad creases his caterpillar eyebrows; they have a life of their own. I almost think they can crawl off his face. "As far as I can remember."

I stuff the paper back in my jacket. "You never came out. Not once. You didn't call. You just vanished."

Dad looks bewildered. "But that's not true, Brooks. You just don't remember. I came out several times. We went to the beach, I took you to the movies, we went out several times for brunch and dinner. I called regularly. Every time I spoke to you, you said you were having the summer of your life. And Palmer, he frequently called me collect from a payphone in town." He shoots me a look of quiet concern. "Your brother was quite concerned about you."

I'm dumbstruck. I have no idea what the fuck Dad's talking about.

"Mmm. That you were leaving the house at all hours of the night and hanging out with those awful Jurgen kids. He told me all about this monster you were trying to create. A bid for attention, I suppose. Mom was worried as well. She wanted you to see a child therapist when you got home." He took a deep breath. "The truth is, Mom had issues and she was afraid she'd passed them on to you. In those days, women like her were called high maintenance. Later, manic-depressive. Now, the diagnosis would most probably be bipolar, like your poor cousin Althea."

I can barely speak. Where did Dad get this garbage from? He has it all wrong. Palmer is the one who was leaving the house surreptitiously, not me. And Mom wasn't crazy. Far from it. She was level-headed and grounded. "Dad, you have this ass backward. I'd remember if you came out, that's not something I'd forget. That summer, Palmer was all over the place. Yes, granted, Mom had her bad days, but she wasn't—"

"Insane? No one said she was. You say I have it wrong? May I point out that you're not the most reliable narrator in this story." Dad stares at me with a mixture of pity and patience. "Brooks, you have no idea how bad it was. When the sheriff found you in the dunes, you were catatonic. I only wish I'd found you first, I would have—when you came around in the hospital, you didn't speak. Physically, you were fine, no wounds, not a scratch save for mosquito bites. But you'd suffered a severe mental and emotional trauma. The doctors were certain in time it would pass. Instead, you got worse. It was like you'd reverted into this unrecognizable, feral creature. You'd tear at your clothes. You hurled your feces on the wall. You refused to talk or walk. You'd bang your head against the wall for hours on end. I was beside myself. The doctors were baffled. They wanted to lock you up in an asylum. They said you were a danger to yourself and others. I refused to sign the commitment papers. I tried and did everything in my power to bring you back. No treatment was too expensive or outlandish. The house in Flushing, I sold it to pay your hospital bills. Finally, I found Dr. Bethel. He was the one who gave you relief from your torment. He brought you back to be who you are today."

My mouth is like parchment paper. The words come, haltingly. "What exactly are you saying?"

"Only what you think you remember and what actually happened are two different things. Dr. Bethel warned me this might happen. It's a trick the mind plays when things are simply too painful to accept. The mind, or in this case, your memory, creates an alternate reality, one that's more palatable. And any gaps in those hazy memories must be filled. Nature abhors a vacuum. Someone has to be the bad guy, Brooks. The monster. Or in this instance, the guilt you feel because you lived, and they died. It was too much of a burden for a little boy. I see that now."

"Well, that fucking sucks." So, the breakthroughs I had—or thought I had—were merely figments of my imagination? *I was my own unreliable narrator?* I'm miserable and angry. I pin everything on remembering so I can get past this pile of shit, and now I can't even count on that. Was this some kind of cruel, cosmic joke? I try to get my bearings. "You were there, Dad. That night, I know it. I didn't imagine that."

In an instant, Dad's demeanor changes. Before, he was understanding and patient—two words I wouldn't ordinarily associate with him—and now he's irritated and annoyed. "You wanted this talk. So, let's just stop dancing around the elephant in the fucking room. Let's say, for argument's sake, that Julian had it out with Palmer or some iteration of that, Mom tried to break it up and things spiraled out of control. Could that have happened?"

I nod. Palmer was a hothead and he hated Julian. That wouldn't be a stretch at all.

"All right. Now can you imagine any scenario where Mom would hurt Palmer or you, for that matter, in any way?"

I stare at Dad, stunned. Is this a trick question? "No fucking way!" I cry. Just thinking about it makes my stomach twist into a pretzel knot.

"We both agree on that. So, once you eliminate that, Brooks, there's no other answer. It's Julian Broadhurst. It can be no one else, logically." He stretches his arms. "I have an idea. Why don't you and Cassie get a babysitter and come to the brownstone for dinner this weekend? I'm having people over for a little soirée, nothing fancy. I can promise you good food and conversation. Dalton's coming. He tells me you've become great pals." To his credit, he doesn't sound the least bit jealous.

"This weekend? No, sorry, I have to take a rain check. I'll be out of town for a couple of days on business." I haven't told Cassie yet, but I'll be back in time for her doctor's appointment.

Dad checks his watch. "If your plans change, you're always welcome. I have to get ready for my panel. If you have the time, stick around, we could grab lunch later." He pats me on the back. "I hope our little chat has helped. My advice is to let the past stay dead and buried with Marshall Reagan." He shambles off.

A Global Ambassador passes by with a tray of ombré-colored

drinks festooned with ridiculous paper umbrellas. It's the kind of drink you'd find at a Hawaiian luau, not a quasi-political-social-cultural confab in Manhattan. Without thinking, I reach out to grab a drink, and then I see Mark's face. Startled, I stop myself and jam my hand in my pocket. Frustrated, the beast growls deep inside me. I win this battle but I'm cognizant that I'm teetering on a razor's edge. Next time—and I know there will be one—I might not be lucky. Old Brooks could blame youth and immaturity when I blundered. New Brooks doesn't have those excuses or illusions anymore.

CHAPTER TWENTY-ONE

I bolt out of the Jacob Javits Center. The morning had started bright and sunny, but now clouds have rolled in, draping the city with a thick gray haze that matches my mood. My mind's still trying to take in what Dad just told me. I admit some of it rang true. That I'd been in a bad way after Mom and Palmer died wasn't news, but like the murders, I'd blocked it all out. And yes, Mom hadn't been quite herself that summer. Was that why Grandpa William came to see us that weekend? Was it to talk her out of an abortion? Grandpa William was a devout Catholic. He wouldn't have approved of Mom getting an abortion, no matter the circumstance.

But all that other fucking bullshit—no. Sure, on the surface, the way Dad spun it sounded reasonable, but I have a hard time believing it. Still, the only way Dad would've known about the monster is because Palmer told him. But putting aside all that, I'm forced to agree with Dad. Julian Broadhurst killed Mom and Palmer. There is no other plausible explanation. I remind myself that Marshall Reagan's only goal was to come up with a different alternative for the murders to get a lucrative book contract. I'm not Marshall Reagan.

And yet—*and yet*—I can't shake the nagging feeling that I'm missing something, a crucial ingredient, like when a baker forgets to put sugar or baking powder in a cake. As hard as I try, it doesn't come to me. Perhaps I'm trying too hard. I finally decide to let my subconscious do the heavy lifting. Hopefully, the answer will reveal itself when I least expect it.

By the time I arrive at the Dakota, the fine mist has turned into a biting rain. Fernando's by the entrance, umbrella in hand. "Mr. Brooks, how—"

And then out of the blue, a whir of red storms up and punches me square in the jaw. If it had been a right hook, I'd have been down for the count. I fall back, flustered. People around me gasp.

"You motherfucker!" the whir of red screams.

Fernando runs up, wielding the umbrella like a bayonet. "Mr. Brooks, are you all right? Should I call the police?"

I nurse my jaw as the whir of red comes into focus. It's a young woman in a crimson jacket. "Yes, call the goddamn police, so I can have this son of a bitch arrested for being an asshole. How could you do that to her? Just when she was beginning to believe you."

I know who this is. It's Caroline, June's daughter, my granddaughter in another reality where the DNA tests came back positive.

"Mr. Brooks—" Fernando shields me with the umbrella.

I wave him off. "No, no. I'm fine." I gamely smile at her. She has Jennifer's piercing gaze. "I know you're upset. I am, too."

"Upset?" She looks like she's ready to sock me again. "You couldn't tell her to her face, so you had your fucking lawyer send her a cease-and-desist? Really?"

Lord, what a fucking temper. If she were any angrier, her ears would be smokestacks. But I've no idea what the hell she's babbling about. "Who sent your mother a cease-and-desist?"

"Your lawyer, who the fuck else? That if Mom ever tried to

contact you or spoke about you publicly, you'd sue her for harassment, defamation, libel, and character assassination."

That goddamn Parsons. I'm going to kill the bastard. "You have to believe me, he sent that without my approval."

"I don't believe a fucking word out of your goddam mouth. My brother warned her that she was playing with fire by getting in touch with you. That you and your father would squash us like bugs. I'm the one who told her not to listen to him. I encouraged her. Do you know how hard it was for her to come to you? Dad crapped on her, now you. She hasn't stopped crying since she got that stupid letter." Her voice chokes. "I was such a fucking fool."

"No, Caroline, listen to me—" I put my hand out, but she bats me away.

"You stay the fuck away from us!" Caroline barrels down the sidewalk. To emphasize her point, she holds up her middle finger.

Fernando gave me an embarrassed shrug. "Women."

At this point, I figure the day can't get any worse. Of course, I'm wrong. From the elevator, I hear the kids screaming. Mark and Audra are in the living room fighting over the remote. "If you guys can't watch TV nicely, then no one does." I grab the remote and put it on a shelf out of their reach.

"It's her fault. I'm sick of *Vivo.*" Mark pushes Audra. She falls on her butt and bursts into tears.

"Excuse me, young man? You don't ever push your sister like that. To your room. Now. Time-out."

Mark groans. "Nobody likes me!" He stomps to his room.

Cassie waddles in, still in her pajamas. "It's been like this all morning."

I pick Audra up and comfort her. "You're fine, sweetie. Can you play quietly while I talk to Mommy a little bit?"

Audra nods. I get her settled down on the sofa with several of her singing storybooks. That should keep her busy, for oh, ten minutes if I'm lucky.

I follow Cassie into the kitchen. "Guess what just happened downstairs?"

"Am I going to see it on Facebook?"

"Most likely. I ran into Caroline. Or I should I say, her fist."

"Caroline? Who's—" And then it comes to her. "Oh."

"Can you believe that son-of-a-bitch lawyer sent June a cease-and-desist letter? And without telling me. Fucking—"

"The poor woman. That's a horrible way to find out." Cassie gives me a side-eye: you should've told her yourself, asshole. "You left early. Did Mark have an accident during the night? I found all his sheets in the washer."

I freeze. I'm sure Mark has already forgotten. It would've been the easiest thing in the world to tell Cassie what was going on. That I was afraid I'm on the verge of relapsing. Fearful that I'm losing my grip on reality. Scared shitless that I'm going to lose her and the kids. It's a balancing act and the scales are tipping in the other direction. As much as I know in my heart what I should do, the other side is winning. We are just starting to find our way back to each other after the vasectomy debacle. Audra's doing so much better. And now we're having another baby. How many times can I fuck up and expect her to be supportive? So, I do what I usually do when I'm cornered. "Yeah, it was no biggie. He went right back to sleep. Look, my interview came through and I have to go upstate."

"Now?" Cassie doesn't look thrilled.

"I promise it won't be more than two or three days, I'll be back for the doctor. But I need to use your car." I grab an apple from the fruit bowl on the counter. Cassie's always saying I need to add more fruit to my diet.

"Why? Is something wrong with yours?"

"It's the IT geek, Moynes. I've arranged for him to check my car out while I'm away and then when I come back, he'll do your car, the computers, and cell phones." I'd already texted Fernando to have Cassie's car brought over from the parking garage.

"I thought you weren't going to bother with that shit."

"No, I said I was going to think about it."

Mark rushes in. "Can we go to the park today?"

"You're in time-out, buddy," I bark.

Cassie ignores me. "We'll see. Maybe if it clears up later and you clean your room."

Mark scampers out.

I glare at Cassie. "Why are you getting all flustered?"

"I'm not." Flustered, she grabs a wet dishrag and furiously wipes the counter. "Do you have to go? Why can't you do it by phone or email?"

This isn't like Cassie. She usually doesn't interrogate me. "Is this about me going away or is it about me using your car? What's the problem? Am I going to find used condoms in the back seat?"

Cassie throws the dishrag at me. "That's not funny, Brooks." She bites her lower lip. "Promise me you won't be angry."

I chuckle. "What, you got a dent? That's why we have insurance, we'll get it fixed."

She leans against the counter. "Promise."

"I promise. Scout's honor and all that."

She takes a deep, apprehensive breath. "It's not my car, Brooks. It's yours. If this guy looks it over, he's going to find a thingie."

I frown. "What kind of thingie?"

She blushes. "The GPS kind."

"A GPS—" I open my mouth, then close it. Fuck me with a wooden spoon. I didn't just hear Cassie say she's bugged my car. "Let me get this straight. Without my knowledge, you had a tracking device installed in my car. Is that the gist of it?"

Miserable, Cassie nods.

Incensed, I hurl my apple against the wall. I am not Norman Mailer.

"Remember when I was pregnant with Mark, and you

disappeared? Miss Drake said there was a way to keep tabs on you. Brooks, I was so worried."

Miss Drake. Naturally. She'd been a spy in a tweed suit and all that intelligence shit was second nature. I wonder if she'd known Ian Fleming. Or Kim Philby. I'd never know now, would I? "Worried it would happen again? Because you didn't trust me all this goddamn time. Do you have any idea how this makes me feel? And please, don't tell me you did it for my own good. This is on you, Cassie. In the years we've been married, not once did I—" I stop myself short. Who the hell am I to berate her? I'm just a pompous, pretentious asshole. I wait a moment and collect myself before my anger snaps like a rubber band. "Okay, okay. If the car's ever stolen, it will be easy to find." I hug her. Hell, if she can get past the vasectomy, I can get past this.

Smelling like vanilla and brown sugar, Cassie melts into me. "I love you so much, Brooks. More than you could ever know. If something ever happened to you—"

"Nothing's going to happen to me, baby. I'm the man with a rod of steel. I'm indestructible. Hell, you and Keith Richards will outlive me." I kiss away her tears. "That's all it is, right? Just the car? Nothing else?" I'm ready to forgive and forget.

Cassie hesitated. "Well—"

I break away from her, the burning in my head an inferno. "You mean *everything*? My emails? Texts? My cell?"

The torrent of tears down Cassie's face is my answer.

I'm so infuriated I can barely see. I fly into the master bedroom, grab a weekender from the closet, and madly stuff my clothes in it.

Cassie pads in. "Honey, let me explain—"

"Don't give me that honey shit. There's nothing to explain. I understand everything." I go into the bathroom to get some toiletries, then change my mind. Fuck deodorant. I'll pick up what I need when I get there. It's not the boonies.

I go into my lair and pack everything I have on the book—

all the material Miss Drake collected along with Marshall Reagan's documents—into a plastic tub. I remember to take my laptop. I drop everything at the front door, then return to the bedroom. Cassie, quiet and pale, sits on the bed, tissues in hand.

I throw some useless crap into my suitcase. "Do you think the minute I leave the house I go buy drugs? Or I hit the liquor store? Pick up women for random fucks?"

She grimaces. "Of course not."

"Then what? Is this how little you think of me? Of our marriage? Because I don't get it." I gather some of my ties from the closet although why I do I've no idea. The last time I wore a tie was to Sheldon's funeral. "Your father was an abusive drunk, he'd slap your mother around. But have I ever done anything like that to you?"

She shakes her head.

"Have I ever done anything that would warrant you sticking a tracking device up my ass?" The vasectomy aside, the answer is no, and we both know it. "Did you put a camera in the bathroom too? Our bedroom? Am I going to see us fucking doggy style on TikTok?"

Cassie, a bit green around the gills, covers her mouth. I should stop, but I don't, I'm just too fucking boiling.

"The car, I could rationalize that. Hell, maybe even say it's a good idea. But the rest of it?" I'm wound up like a pitcher in the ninth inning of the World Series. "Have I ever gone through your emails or texts? Not once. And I know all your goddamn passwords. You've gone on business trips. I never said a peep. You go out every fucking year with your college roommates. Did I ever for one fucking minute think that you were going to get hammered and suck some bastard's dick in the Hamptons while I'm home with the kids? It never even crossed my fucking mind. Because I trusted you. And I was under the illusion—or delusion —that you trusted me."

Cassie squirms under my stare. "I do trust you. But I was scared. And it's not like I read your texts and emails every day."

Un-fucking-believable. "So that makes it acceptable? Jesus Fucking Christ, Cassie. Is that the best you can do?" I jam the suitcase shut and haul it to the door. I text Fernando that there's a change of plans, I want my car and not Cassie's. I send a message to Moynes that we have to reschedule the car inspection. "Cassie, I'll call you when I get there." My voice is flat and perfunctory as if I were addressing an assistant and not my wife. "Maybe my going away is a good thing. We both need some space to think about what we want and where we go from here."

Cassie tugs at my shirt. "Please, Brooks. You can't leave it like this. I don't even know where you're going."

"Well, that's what your fucking GPS is for, isn't it?" The pain in my head is like a thousand jackhammers. Talk about *déjà vu.* This is a replay of when I begged Cassie not to leave after she found out about the vasectomy, except now she's the one pleading. I see she's anguished. So am I. But I have to get away before I say or do something I can't take back.

Mark races up and throws his arms around my legs. "Daddy, I'm sorry. I promise I'll be good to Audra. Don't go."

My heart craters. "Kiddo, listen to me." I kneel and look him straight in the eye. "Your Daddy loves you very much. This is about me doing my job, just like you going to school and doing what Mommy says. I won't be away long, I promise. When I come back, we'll do lots of fun things. I want you to make a list for me. Can you do that for me, buddy?"

Mark bravely smiles and nods.

In the living room, Audra's fallen asleep clutching a songbook about princesses. I kiss her lightly on the forehead. She doesn't move.

I pick up my shit and leave. I know Cassie's standing in the hallway waiting for me to turn around. I don't.

Out front, my car's waiting. Before I hit the road, I stop at the nearest Apple store and go on a shopping spree: two laptops, desktop, tablet, cell phone with a new number, and an assortment of expensive and probably unnecessary add-ons. Since I'm OCD about backing all my data to the cloud, I have the salesman erase all the data on my devices. I tell him he can junk the old devices, donate them, whatever. I'm starting fresh.

But before the old phone's erased, I see that my dust up with Caroline is blowing up on social media. Someone uploaded a video of it on Instagram. From Dad: *What the fuck was that all about?* Dalton chimes in: *MMA fighter in training?* And finally, James, who's been silent of late: *New developments on Miss D. Talk later.*

Also, Lloyd Parsons wakes up. He calls and gives me some half-assed story that sending cease-and-desist letters is standard. He sent them before on my behalf and I never complained. And he doesn't understand why I'm so upset about the DNA results as he's under the distinct impression that I want the results to be negative. *What the fuck is that supposed to mean?* I'm not in the mood for his mealy-mouth excuses and rip him a new one. "You're fired. Send me my fucking file. I paid enough for it." Parsons is lucky I'm not reporting his ass to the State Bar.

I briefly toy with stopping at a garage and having them remove the GPS device, but fuck it, I'm already behind schedule. I'll deal with that crap later. Belatedly, I get on the road. The last time I'd traveled upstate was for Woodstock '99 on behalf of *The New Yorker*. The concert was staged on a decommissioned army base, shades of Camp Hero minus dead creatures. I was a couple of years into my recovery and figured this would be a good test. I got a bad vibe about the event the minute I got there, never mind the overflowing toilets and overpriced water. I soon realized that I was too old for this shit. I left long before the mosh pit turned into a gang rape pit.

I'm going to Castorland, a tiny village in Lewis County that I'd never heard of; population less than 400 per the last census, median home value 111,000 dollars. Please don't judge me. When you've only lived in New York City and Long Island, you tend to have a skewed view of the state. Living downstate, you think upstate is just the same only with more trees and deer. It's not. New York State is big and diverse. The further I go, I cross an invisible line economically and culturally. Ramshackle houses and rusted hunks of metal are as much a part of the landscape as scrappy grass and decaying pines. Faded and frayed Trump 2020 flags droop like wilted tulips. When I stop to fill up, everyone's behind the wheel of a tricked-out pickup. They all chuckle at my Prius.

At least the long drive gives me a chance to think. Exactly who the hell is Dr. Herman Bethel and what had he done to me? Since I wasn't about to ask for Cassie's help, this might be a job for Collier Moynes. As for Cassie, I'm lost at sea without a compass. I hate the idea of being watched and micromanaged. I'm a man, not a Corgi on a short leash. If Cassie had come to me a couple of months after all this tracking and admitted it—but to do it for years? She had to have seen the profane messages Marilyn sent me to hook up for sex and drugs. I'd rebuffed Marilyn every fucking time. But who was I to play the victim? I hadn't fessed up to the vasectomy. Sheldon's voice is in my head: *Two wrongs don't make it right, Brooks. You love Cassie. End of the fucking story.*

It's dark when I pull into the Watertown Hotel; fifty bucks a night, free wifi, and a complimentary breakfast buffet. It's not the Plaza, but hell, I've crashed in worse dumps. Without distractions, I can make real headway on the book. But as I check in, I can't help but notice the liquor store with the garish neon sign directly across the street.

Dinner is a couple of granola bars and cookies I bought at the gas station. I call Aunt Flo—she's already asleep—and give her caretaker my new number. I FaceTime Cassie and the kids. Mark and Audra have just gotten out of the bath, their hair still sopping wet. Cassie's overly exuberant and fills in all the empty, thorny pauses with blather. I don't say much. I promise Mark I'll call in the morning before he goes to school. Cassie makes a point of saying "Love you" before we hang up. I don't reply because I'm still a petulant asshole. Afterward, I regret it because she's trying. I'm not.

My room faces the street and has a great view of the liquor store, which is doing brisk business. Maybe liquor isn't the only thing they're selling. What's the recreational drug of choice in these parts? Pot? Oxy? Coke? Meth? The beast is starting to rouse. I scratch my arm until it's raw.

I'm tempted to go out for a stroll, but luckily, my cell rings. It's James. "What's with the new number?" He sounds good—okay, maybe not so good—but better than the last couple of times when he's sounded like he's swallowed razor blades.

I settle down in a lumpy chair. "No biggie. The old one fell in the can," I lie. "Now what about Miss Drake."

"Well, it looks like our British friends weren't being exactly truthful. She was still doing work for them off the books. Recent work, too. I got that straight from a birdie in DC."

Shit. "What kind of work?"

"The kind you don't want *The New York Times* writing about. She was sitting on something, Brooks. I'm sure of it. That would explain why the consulate strong-armed the coroner into changing his conclusions on the autopsy. Why bother to do that if they weren't afraid of something coming out?"

"And Elaine Brighton tried to throw me off the scent by giving me a bone." I chew on this. "Any ideas on what it could've been?"

"I'm working on a few theories. Nothing I can speak about yet." He pauses and takes a sip of something. "You sound beat. Bad day?"

"Something like it. Long drive. I'm upstate."

James chuckles. "That explains it."

I return to the window. The liquor store will be closing soon. "Give me a good reason not to leave my room tonight."

"Oh. One of those days." He sighs deeply. "I could tell you the rigamarole about having a great wife and family. Why the fuck would you want to screw that up? You think your shit stinks any worse than mine? Do you know what today is? It's Leo's birthday."

I'm immediately contrite. "I'm so sorry, man." How could I have forgotten that? Miss Drake wouldn't have. She knew birthdays, anniversaries, holidays, national pizza day, all the important dates. She ensured I made the appropriate gesture or response. And Miss Drake wouldn't have gotten me a room that faced a liquor store.

Leo was James' adopted son. James' sister, Allison, was Leo's biological mother. Allison was a lovely, talented girl who sang in the church choir. She became a devoted parishioner of the Church of Smack courtesy of her loser boyfriend. When Leo was born, he suffered from severe withdrawal and nearly died. James and Susie—his wife—were childless and devout Catholics. They brought Leo home. Allison was in no shape to take care of a sick infant, let alone herself. For years, Allison was in and out of rehab until her body finally gave out.

Leo grew up to be a fine athlete. There wasn't a sport he couldn't play and play well. The kid never gave James or Susie a moment of trouble. A born leader, everyone said. Prom Night, Leo and his girlfriend were voted King and Queen. Afterward, his group wanted to go to the Hamptons to party at a house a parent had rented. Leo agreed to be the designated driver. It rained, the road slick, and poor visibility. The kids never had a chance when a semi plowed into them and sent Leo's car airborne on the Long Island Expressway. Five families were destroyed in an instant. So many people came to Leo's funeral they put a projector in the parking lot for the overflow.

James' faith never wavered, but God wasn't through testing

him. Six months after they buried Leo, the cancer that forced Susie to have a hysterectomy right after their marriage returned with a vengeance. Six weeks to the day of her diagnosis, she died. As inconsolable as James was, he didn't fall into the abyss, although he easily could have. A year later, he married Janice, the overnight nurse who cared for Susie in her final days. Janice was a widow with six kids under twelve. James' friends thought he'd lost his mind and tried their best to talk him out of it. I was the only one who didn't. He asked me to be his best man because, as he said, I understood. And I did.

So today of all days, who am I to fucking whine and moan? Compared to what James has been through, Cassie tracking me like a big-game hunter is nothing.

"Listen to me, Brooks. You go out there now, chances are you're coming back in a box. Last week, there was a bad batch of heroin that killed eight poor fuckers. It's not like the old days when you could get high with a reasonable expectation that you'd be alive the next day, even with the crap the dealers put into it: baking soda, starch, caffeine. And when you had your vacation in the ghetto, no one was going to fuck with a big white dude with money. The last thing they needed was for a rich white kid from the burbs to die because of their bad shit."

I never thought of it quite like that, but James is right. My white skin had been my armor, my privilege, my access badge to a pharmaceutical wonderland. I could afford the good stuff and I was discerning enough to know the good stuff from the bad. Besides, I wasn't your typical stoner. There were extended periods when I didn't use or used sparingly. I sold my soul for Black Tar, never my body. I was also a generous junkie; I never hoarded, I always shared, and I never ripped anyone off.

"It's different now. Supply decreased and the dealers got too goddamn greedy. Now they've graduated to adding Fentanyl, Benzocaine, amphetamine, and boric acid. Hell, we're even seeing heroin and cocaine laced with Ketamine and Levamisole. I shit you not, it's a fucking epidemic. You're a good man, you have a good life. Think of what it would do to Cassie and the kids. I've buried too many already. I swear, I'd fucking kill you first." James' tone is emphatic.

I close the curtain. I'm not going anywhere tonight. "How are the kids?"

"Oh, between soccer, lacrosse, gymnastics, and softball, I'm more like a chauffeur than anything else." We share a knowing chuckle. "Brooks, I'll keep you posted about Miss Drake. Come back in one piece, okay?"

"You bet," I say, and I mean it. But addicts always mean what they say at the time, don't they?

Enough fucking around. I fire up the new laptop and arm myself with abundant amounts of pitch-black coffee. I crash around two but am up again at six, writing. I take a break to check my emails. There's a breaking news alert from *The New York Times*: *British Consulate General Dead in Apparent Manhattan Hit and Run*. Stunned, I read the story. The previous evening, Elaine Brighton left her tony apartment for a quick jog around the neighborhood, her usual routine after dinner. When she didn't return home when she was supposed to, her husband got worried. He found her a few blocks over, her body crushed like a Halloween pumpkin. A security camera from a nearby building captured Elaine's final moments: jogging with headphones as a speeding black SUV jumps the curb and mows her down before careening away. The police eventually recovered the vehicle, which was originally reported stolen from Virginia, abandoned in New Jersey. By all appearances, it looks like a tragic accident; Elaine was in the wrong place at the wrong time. Just another bad luck story, nothing to see here.

I'm not convinced.

Neither is James, who texts me a few minutes later: *Brooks, exactly what did Elaine Brighton tell you about Miss Drake?*

CHAPTER TWENTY-TWO

I was sick for a long time after Mom and Palmer died. Well, that's what they called it, but it wasn't a cold or a virus. I just know that every time I opened my eyes, they knocked me out again. I missed two years of school. My memories of that time are hazy. I was stuck in a labyrinth—shades of Jack Nicholson in The Shining—and no matter how hard I tried, I couldn't find my way out. I suppose that was how my brain's defense mechanism worked. The memories were so painful that my body completely shut down.

When I finally became aware of my surroundings, not only Mom and Palmer were gone, but so was Grandpa William. We never returned to the Big House or to the summer homes in Ditch Plains. I never saw Berry or any of my cousins. It was as if Mom's side of the family had been erased.

Due to Dad's career, we hopscotched all over the place. I'd no sooner get used to a new home and school than we'd have to pack up again. Dad was so busy, there were times I didn't see him for months. I got it into my head that he stayed away because he was angry at me—angry that I'd lived and not Palmer. To get his attention, I did increasingly stupid things—cut myself, shoplifted, smoked and sold pot, mouthed off to teachers. A teacher once berated me in front of the entire class for being "intellectually lazy." Everyone laughed, but she was right. It wasn't that I couldn't do the assignments. I did the bare minimum but nothing more. Not only was I lazy, but I was also dead inside. No dreams, no ambitions, just aimless. After the fiasco with Jennifer Juniper, my love affair with drugs began in earnest. I bounced from one private school to the other. I'd stop using for a while and then I'd relapse. One day up, one day down. I was a human yo-yo.

Dad was patient but even he grew weary of my antics. When I was nineteen, we were back on Long Island. We were living in Glen Cove, an easy commute for Dad who was now working at the United Nations. We made a deal: if I got clean and sober, he'd pay for college. The deal lasted all of one month. He'd bought me a car for school—a Renault, of all things—and I totaled it. Instead of going to class, I sold my textbooks and spent it all on drugs.

Dad didn't have to say a word—all he had to do was raise his eyebrows in quiet disapproval—and I'd go off on another bender. If it wasn't drugs, it was alcohol, it didn't matter which. One day, I came home at dawn and found my shit on the front lawn. My key wouldn't work. Dad had changed the locks.

It was only when Fallen Angels became a bestseller that the ice between us began to thaw. To be honest, I don't think Dad has even read it. Even now, after all this time, Dad still has the uncanny ability to make me feel worthless and insignificant—a bug on the windshield or an ant under his shoe. I try to live up to his impossible standards and fail. At some point, I gave up.

I tell myself his opinion doesn't matter.

I tell myself that I'm used to his indifference.

That I don't need his approval.

But who am I kidding?

Not me. And certainly not him.

CHAPTER TWENTY-THREE

The Grantham home, a two-story farmhouse typical of the area, stands at the top of a long, winding driveway dotted with trees and bushes. From my research, I know that it was once a thriving dairy farm of over two hundred acres. Now it's down to eighty acres, and as I park my car on the side grass, the only animals around are a sleepy hound-dog on the front porch and a bunch of chickens pecking around the yard. I hear a tractor engine in the distance. Even though I can't say it to Cassie, she's right. I could've easily done this interview by phone or email. But I need to do this in person, not only for Mom and Palmer, but for me. I badly want to hear from someone else who had been there that summer—if you will, an impartial observer—that Julian Broadhurst was a Dr. Jekyll and Mr. Hyde even if it was only second-hand.

Olivia Grantham is a spry, no-nonsense woman with short, spiky, steel-gray hair. She greets me in the driveway and walks me over to a renovated barn behind the main house. We go into the kitchen. I smell something freshly baked. "It's my apple fritter quick-bread, just took it out of the oven. Would you like some coffee or tea, Mr. Anderson?"

I have the impression that my visit is some kind of a big deal. Olivia is dressed in a smart lavender suit with a gem-encrusted hummingbird pin on the lapel, hardly the kind of outfit you'd wear to pick eggs from the chicken coop.

"It's Brooks, please. Tea with lemon sounds great. But you shouldn't have gone to so much trouble." I sit down on a hard-backed wooden chair sporting rooster cushions. The entire kitchen is a shrine to roosters: mugs, figurines, plaques, plates, even the curtains. Any minute, I expect a rooster to pop its head in and crow.

"Oh, it's no trouble at all. And I'm fine with just Olivia." She sets a rooster teacup in front of me. She doesn't sit down.

"You have a nice set-up here."

"Thank you. I like having my own space. It's close enough to help out, but far enough to be out of the way. When the grandkids were small, I stayed in the main house mostly, but this was my retreat when I needed peace and quiet. The property has been in my husband's family for generations. We're mutts, a mix of French, English, and Swedish. My granddaughter and her partner live in the main house now. They want to turn it into an organic farm."

"So, you're not from around here?"

"No, my family's in Binghamton. Alex and I met at college. He was two years older, an art major. Very polite, cultured, dressed like a fashion model. He was a real dreamboat. After we graduated and got married, we moved to Manhattan. Alex got an entry-level position at Random House."

"Olivia, would you mind if I recorded you? I'm not good at transcribing my handwriting." I put a microcassette tape recorder on the table.

Her cheeks turned bright pink. "I don't mind at all. I'm flattered that you'd think what I'm telling you is that important."

"You're doing fine," I reassure her. "So how did you find out about my grandfather's summer cottage?"

"As I remember it, Alex came home one night and said that a co-worker had a house for rent in Montauk dirt cheap, two hundred and fifty dollars for the entire summer. We jumped at it even though I had no idea where Montauk was. Alex showed it to me on a map. Jackie was eighteen months old at the time—we named her after the First Lady—and I was pregnant with Tiffany. Our apartment was so stuffy we'd sleep out on the fire escape at night. So, as you can imagine, the idea of spending the whole summer at the beach sounded like Heaven on a plate."

I hear rustling behind me.

A man emerges from a rear room—an elderly fellow with a neatly clipped beard. He too is in a suit. "I'm off to do a couple of errands while you're busy, Olivia. I'll be back shortly." He grins at me, nods, then leaves by the rear door.

"That's Aaron Holt," she offers as if she owes me an explanation. "Aaron owns the next spread over. He's a retired city engineer, just a fancy word for the garbage man, but his pension is nothing to sneeze at. It's hard to make ends meet on social security alone and the kids have all this student loan debt." She goes to the counter, slices thick slabs of apple bread, then brings them to the table on a rooster platter. "I saw your mother at the office Christmas parties. Shirley was such a beautiful woman and so vivacious. She had everyone eating out of her hand. I don't mean that in a bad way," she rushes to add. "The first weekend we moved in, she made a point of dropping by to make sure I was okay after Alex went back to the city. She didn't have to do that. I was just a stay-at-home wife, nothing special. But she was genuinely interested in me, and we became good friends. Maybe that's because we were two lonely pregnant broads stuck out in the boonies." Her smile is rueful.

"Did my mother talk about her pregnancy? How did she feel about it?"

She scrunches her face like a dishrag. "I'm not sure what you mean."

"Well, was she happy? Upset? Ambivalent?" I can't bring myself to ask her if Mom wanted an abortion.

"She was happy. Very much so. She wanted a baby girl in the worst way. She even had a name picked out: Amelia."

I lean back in my chair and suck wind. "So in your opinion, she wasn't scared or worried?"

"About the baby? I knew she'd lost one. She didn't go into too much detail about it. But I can tell you she wanted this baby. A bit apprehensive, yes, but so was I. I had two miscarriages before Tiffany. But it's not like we obsessed about it. I had Jackie to look after, and she had you boys and her work. Alex came out nearly every weekend. It was good. At least, that was my impression." She slathers whipped butter on her bread. "From what your mother said, I got the sense that your father wasn't pleased about having another child. Shirley didn't say it outright, she was too polite for that, but sometimes when I was over, he'd call her, and they'd argue."

My heart leaps into my throat like a car with no brakes. "Did my mother say she was unhappy in the marriage?"

Olivia takes a sip of her tea. "Well—not in so many words. That would be speculation on my part, and I was told I had to be careful."

"Who told you to be careful?"

"My kids. Well, really Jackie. She lives in New Mexico now, but when I told her that your Miss Drake had contacted me, she thought it was a bad idea. It was so many years ago, why poke a hornet's nest?"

I nod and hope she continues to disregard her daughter.

"In those days, I was a real doormat: never question your husband, obey implicitly, put food on the table, keep quiet, know your place. It's different now and I'm glad. I didn't like what happened. I mean, afterward. It was ludicrous. But Alex insisted I had to stay out of it, that it wasn't our business. I didn't understand why he said that at the time, so I went along. The dutiful wife." She clucks her tongue. "But then, when that other writer called—"

"Marshall Reagan?"

She slowly nods.

"What wasn't your business, Mrs. Grantham?"

"All that drivel about Julian Broadhurst. That's why you're here, isn't it?"

This is an unexpected bonus. "You actually knew Julian Broadhurst?"

"Everyone knew Julian, if you get my drift. After he finished a job, he'd come over and tell your mother and me all about it. We'd all have a good laugh over a couple of glasses of wine."

"You mean a paint job? He was an artist, right?"

She snorts. "If that's what you called it. Julian was as much an artist as I was an opera singer. He had a talent all right, but it didn't have anything to do with painting."

I take a deep breath and wade in. "I guess you don't believe that my mother and Julian were having an affair."

"Of course not. It's absurd. I said it then and I say it now." She is emphatic. And genuine.

"Even though there were love letters."

Olivia makes a corkscrew face. "I don't know anything about any love letters. Shirley was a good woman and a great mother. She loved you and your brother very much. She didn't entertain any men, including Julian. I know that much."

"But how can you be sure?" I persist.

Olivia shoots me a confused look. "You really don't know, do you? You see, that's exactly what I mean. You repeat a lie long enough and it becomes the truth. Julian Broadhurst wasn't interested in women—*any* woman—unless he was paid. Do I have to draw you a picture?"

Julian was gay? Nothing much shocks me anymore, but this does. "And you know this because—"

"Because Alex, my husband—he was gay, too."

It feels as though a mule has kicked me in the stomach. There was no grand, passionate, love affair gone wrong with Mom? Julian wasn't a jilted lover? It was all a lie?

"That weekend, we were supposed to be here. But Alex hadn't come out for a couple of weekends, so I decided to surprise him. We took the train in, Jackie and me. When we got to the apartment, I heard noises coming from our bedroom." She bit her lip. "It was Alex and another man. I didn't know what to do. I was in shock. I finally went home to Binghamton and the next day I went into premature labor. We almost lost Tiffany." She pauses, her face a tight grimace. "I want to say it was a surprise, but if I'm being honest, there were signs. In college, he'd vanish for a couple of days. I thought it was another woman. I postponed the wedding twice. After we got married, he seemed to settle down. I assumed the affair was over."

She stirs her now stone-cold cup of tea. "I couldn't tell my parents what had really happened. Alex was distraught. He said it was a horrible mistake and it wouldn't happen again. Like a fool, I believed him. He couldn't change who he was any more than he could change the color of his eyes. We finally divorced when the kids were in high school. When he got sick, we told everyone it was leukemia, but it was really AIDS. I nursed him in his final months. Jackie still won't accept it, won't accept that her sister is gay, either. We don't celebrate holidays as a family anymore."

Olivia stares at me, hands clenched. "The difference between Julian and Alex is that Julian didn't hide it. He wasn't ashamed of it, and back then, let me tell you, you didn't advertise it. You didn't flaunt it. Julian didn't care. He was a beautiful, kind, gentle soul, and he's been made out to be a monster. Nothing could be further from the truth."

"Then why didn't you say that at the time?" I ask.

"I told you—Alex forbade me. He said it wasn't our place, we didn't know what happened, and we needed to stay out of it. It was only later that I realized that Alex was afraid, just like all the others."

"The others?"

"The people Julian had relationships with when he was out east. They were all terrified of what an investigation would reveal. Julian had been with some powerful people. How do you think he was able to afford that fancy sports car? So, the police didn't ask too many questions—didn't ask any questions at all, frankly. People were more than ready to close the book and forget all about that summer. Alex, too."

The hammer in the back of my head is getting ready to pound. "Do you think Julian and your husband were lovers?"

"I've asked myself that. It's possible. When Alex passed, I found pictures of him with men. He didn't even have the decency to destroy them."

I've had years of practice with deceit. I know without a doubt that Olivia Grantham is telling the truth as she saw it, and as painful as it is to hear, it must've been equally painful for her to admit it. "What do you think happened the night my mother died?"

"I think Julian walked into something. He told us earlier in the week that he was going away for the weekend. That's what gave me the idea to visit Alex. All I can think is that Julian's plans changed at the last minute. Julian wasn't a violent man. Once, Jackie screamed her head off because there was a spider in her bedroom. Alex would've killed it without a second thought. But Julian gently cupped it in his hand, took it outside, and set it free. Does that sound like a killer to you?" She shakes her head, resolute. "I don't think so."

I thank Olivia Grantham profusely for her time. She packs slices of her apple bread for me for the road. Mr. Holt returns as I get to my car. I drive for a bit, but I soon pull off the main road, my hands shaking. How did I not see this? So much for being a crack journalist. All that fucking malarkey about Julian being a protégé of Peter Max. I hadn't found one iota of evidence proving that. Why had Mom developed this strange affinity for him? What on earth did they have in common?

With my mind reeling in a thousand directions, I absent-mindedly check my cell, which I'd put on mute while I'd been at Olivia's. There's a "priority urgent" email from Hunter Talley, one of the producers on *Three Rivers*. Talley is a nice guy who isn't going to be one for long if he stays in the business; nice guys like Talley get chopped up like carrots and onions for a beef stew. Well, his urgent missive is that the Max honchos want to set up a meeting. (In other words, nothing that can't wait).

Sure, I diffidently write back. I don't have Sheldon to act as a go-between anymore. There's a short text from Cassie; she's taking the kids to a birthday party after school and the buzz is *The Mandolorian* is going to make an appearance between hopping galaxies.

I pick up some lunch—a greasy burger and fries, which I end up throwing away after one bite—and return to the motel. It's not until I'm in my room that I realize I accidentally turned off the ringer to my cell phone. There's a voicemail from a 212 number I don't recognize. I assume it's a scam call—it doesn't take long for robocallers to find you—and I almost delete it before I decide to listen to it. It's a man's voice that sounds vaguely familiar: "Mr. Anderson, this is Dr. Sanders, I'm your wife's obstetrician. She's here at my office with your children. There's been a complication with her pregnancy. Can you please meet us at New York-Presbyterian as soon as possible?"

Frantic, I'm out of that motel faster than a Learjet. I can't get hold of Cassie; either she's switched her phone off or it's ran out of juice. I barely remember the drive back to the city; I'm on autopilot. It's a miracle I don't cause a major pile-up on the New York Thruway. All I can think of is Cassie and our unborn child. I swear fealty to every deity in the universe to keep them safe. I berate myself for leaving the way I did. Have I caused this? If so, my marriage is over, and so is my life. I don't want a life without Cassie. I do not call Dad.

But someone has alerted Dad because he's in the hospital waiting room with Mark and Audra. Mark is on his tablet and Audra's curled up, asleep.

"It's about fucking time," Dad grumbles. "I have a life, you know. I was supposed—"

Incredulous, I hold up my hand: not fucking now. "Do you know what happened?"

"I was hoping you knew. They won't tell me a goddamn thing. HIPAA and all that crap."

It feels like hours before Dr. Sanders appears. I remember him the moment I see him: a lanky, transplanted Texan with a handlebar mustache, a younger Sam Elliott. "Mr. Anderson," he says, his eyes downcast.

I steel myself. "Where's my wife? I want to see my wife." I don't recognize my voice.

Dr. Sanders takes me aside. "Cassie's still groggy and disoriented from the operation. She's in recovery, it'll be a few hours before we can transfer her to a room."

Operation? Good Lord. Another placenta previa? "You're sure? She's going to be okay? What about the baby?"

The doctor's mustache droops. "Mr. Anderson, the pregnancy wasn't viable. It was ectopic, the embryo was growing in her right fallopian tube. I'm sorry."

Not viable? My knees wobble but I will myself not to fall. "Is this because of what happened with Audra, the placenta previa?"

"No, not at all, this is a completely different situation. Unfortunately, a tubal pregnancy isn't something we can predict. Cassie did the right thing coming in when she did. If she hadn't, we might potentially be having another conversation." He must see my face because he puts his arm around my shoulder. "Your wife is young and strong, she'll bounce back. I know how much she wanted this baby. But—"

Here it comes. I'm so fucking anxious I bite the inside of my mouth.

"We had to remove the fallopian tube. It was too damaged. I know Cassie's not going to be happy about that. However, the good news is that her left tube is intact."

It takes a moment for me to realize what he means. "Cassie can still conceive?"

"If that's what you guys want. I've had patients with one fallopian tube who have successful pregnancies. Later on, if there's an issue, Cassie can see a fertility specialist. It's not hopeless by any stretch." He gives me a reassuring grin. (I'm far from reassured). "Cassie should be home in a week or so if there aren't any complications. Bed rest, no straining, no heavy lifting. I know it's hard when you have small kids. I have three of my own. But Cassie's body needs time to adjust, and so does she. And no sex for at least six to twelve weeks."

Sex is the last thing on my mind.

In recovery, Cassie's in a small cubicle, an IV in her arm. At first glance, she seems to be dozing, but when I come in, she stirs. Her hair's a mess, her eyes are sunken; she looks like a broken doll. To me, she's the most beautiful thing in the world. She reaches for me, and I grab her hand like a life preserver. "The kids," she murmurs.

I kiss her forehead and stroke her hair. "They're fine."

"The baby."

I shake my head.

Cassie begins to sob. "So, it really happened. It wasn't a dream." She tries to sit up and winces. "I want to go home." Spent, she falls back against the pillow.

"Honey, no, not tonight. You just came out of surgery."

She closes her eyes and turns away from me. "I'm sorry."

I swallow hard. What the fuck does she have to be sorry about? I'm the one who should be down on my goddamn knees. "Shhh, none of that. The doctor says you're going to be fine.

When you're back on your feet, we're going to take the kids and go anywhere you want."

This only makes Cassie sob harder.

A nurse flutters in. "Mr. Anderson—"

I'm miserable. I'm upsetting Cassie, the last thing I want to do. I don't have Miss Drake to fall back on. I don't want to go. I want to stay with Cassie. I'd have slept on the bare floor, but the kids need me. They can't stay in the waiting room all night. "Sweetie, I promise, we'll be back in the morning first thing." I gently knead her shoulders until she drifts off.

In the waiting room, Audra's awake and playing with one of her unicorn toys.

Dad is on his cell.

Mark looks up from his tablet. "Is Mommy coming home?"

"Not tonight, son. Soon." I put on my best Daddy face. "Time to go home, kids. We've bothered Grandpa enough for one day."

Dad shoots me a questioning look: *Well?*

"Can I see Mommy?" Mark asks.

"Mommy's asleep right now. We'll see her tomorrow when she's feeling better. Have you had anything to eat?"

Mark and Audra shake their heads.

"I got them some cookies," Dad says.

"I missed the party," Mark whines. "Mommy was going to take me."

I hug Mark. "I'm sorry, buddy, but there will be other parties. Maybe we can get Baby Yoda to come for a visit."

Mark's face lights up. "Tonight?"

"Not tonight. Come on, get your backpacks." I turn to Dad and say in a low voice, "Cassie had an ectopic pregnancy. It was rough, but she should be okay."

Dad looks surprised. "Wait, I'm confused. Didn't you have a vasectomy?"

It's not the time to remind me of that debacle. "It would appear that Mother Nature had other plans."

Dad grimaces. "It's just as well. More likely it wasn't yours, Brooks. I warned you. Women like her can't keep their goddamn legs closed."

I stare at him, horrified, unable to believe what he's just said. Is he out of his fucking mind? Judging from his haughty expression, he doesn't seem to think he said anything wrong. *The son of a bitch, how dare he?* Now I'm livid. Honestly, if this bullshit had been said by someone else—trust me, I've been in bar-room brawls for less. Instead, I scoop the kids up and hurry away. As I do, something stirs in my mind like the fading embers of a fire. I'm in the doorway of Grandpa William's summer cottage as the television roars in the background. Dad is in the living room, his face twisting with feral rage. "You didn't think I was going to let you take him," he bellows. Then the fragment disappears like vapor.

"Come on, Brooks, give me a fucking break, it's been a long day," Dad shouts.

No disagreement there. It had been a long, fucking, horrendous day.

It's almost midnight when I finally get the kids settled down. Mark's still whining about missing the party, but once I tell him that he can miss school, he's pacified. I promise Audra that I'll make Mickey Mouse pancakes for breakfast just like Mommy does. That and two rounds of reading unicorn picture books do the trick.

The kids have kept me from dwelling on everything, but now that the house is a tomb, I'm a ticking time bomb. I go on a frenzy. I clean the kitchen, load the dishwasher, and pick up toys in a futile attempt to switch my brain off. It doesn't work. It takes a moment like this—a life-defining moment—to give me much-needed clarity and perspective. I see everything with scalpel-like precision. First, I'm such a fucking idiot. My pigheadedness got in the way of my better judgment. And because of it, Cassie was forced to endure this alone when she needed me the most. Once again, I'd let her down. How can I expect her to forgive me when I can't forgive myself?

My cell pings non-stop. I'm inundated with inquiries from the media horde. Miss Drake would've handled it in a heartbeat. I finally issue a statement to the Associated Press: this is a private matter and kindly leave us the fuck alone. I'm positive that someone is going to start a whisper campaign—if they haven't already—about how my "affair" caused my poor wife to lose our baby.

I call the night nurse at the hospital at least a dozen times for updates. Cassie's now in a private suite far from the maternity ward. The nurse assures me that Cassie's doing as well as could be expected; with all the meds they've given her, Cassie should be out well into the morning.

Even so, when my cell phone buzzes, I answer without checking who it is. It's Hunter Talley, probably the last person, besides Dad, that I want to speak to. "Hey, Brooks, I wanted to quickly touch base before the Max meeting tomorrow." He sounds unnaturally perky.

Excuse me? What meeting? "Hunter, this isn't a good time. It's not a fucking good time at all." The hammer in my head is a hacksaw. I've scratched my arm so much it's chopped meat.

"I know it's late on the East Coast, but this won't take long." He plunges on, cheerfully oblivious. "Look, let's lay our cards on the table. I think there's been a misunderstanding—"

I'm in an I-don't-give-five-fucks mood and I don't care who knows it. "There's no misunderstanding on my part. I know what the contract says." I'm brutally aware that I'm walking a tightrope without a net. I don't want to take it out on Talley, who hasn't done anything—other than being a network shill—to deserve it. But, well, he called me, it's not the other way around. Doesn't he get Google alerts?

"Well, Brooks, our lawyers, and I mean *all* the lawyers, have gone over the contract and they're all quite confident that they're on solid ground on the right of first refusal." He sounds like a fifth grader giving a book report.

I'm sure he was instructed to say this, but the fact that he says it without knowing the goddamn facts irks me no end. "They're wrong. I know every line in the contract because I wrote it, along with my agent—my agent at the time." Sheldon would've mopped the floor with these assholes. "Because not only do I have the right of first refusal, but I also retained the right to approve any project based on my characters in perpetuity, including and not limited to sequels, prequels, you name it." I'd learned a few tricks. "This was a limited series with an expiration date. Everyone knew it when we signed the contract. Don't insult me with your canned bullshit when we all know you don't have a dick to stand on."

There is silence. I hear someone mutter in the background. It sounds suspiciously like "We're fucked."

"Hunter, don't tell me that you have me on the goddamn speakerphone?" I roar.

"No, of course not," he says uneasily. "The suits are going to take it to court. They have deep pockets and they're determined."

I laugh. Was this lame attempt supposed to scare me into meek submission? "I hope they do. What, you think I'm talking out of my ass? The best entertainment lawyer in the country reviewed the deal. It's ironclad. Ask the suits that were there: Otto, Martin, Ivor, and the Italian guy—Francesco, like the pasta sauce."

"I can't, uh, they're not with the network anymore."

"Not my fucking problem, kiddo."

Talley takes a deep breath. "Brooks, I'm imploring you to not be that guy."

I lean against the window and stare out at the city that never sleeps. "What guy would that be?"

"The guy that's going to end up on the front page of *Variety* for being a butthole. The sequel's happening whether you like it or not. You don't want to write it, you've moved on, fine, so step aside and let someone else do it. You're going to get paid either way. Name your price and let's end this idiotic charade before someone gets hurt."

At last, we finally get to the heart of it. These bozos think if they throw enough green at me that I'll fold like a paper airplane. "I'm going to say this slowly so the cheap seats can hear. We have a binding contract. I was paid, I delivered the material, I fulfilled the terms. The fact that some moron wants to rewrite the contract is of absolutely fucking zero concern to me. So yes, let's end this fucking charade because my integrity doesn't come with a price tag. Now if you want a new project, that's a conversation I'm happy to have at a more appropriate time. But so far as *Three Rivers* goes, it's a non-starter, non-negotiable, non-fucking-everything. Understood?" I click off. And they say I'm fucking difficult?

Now that I've given up on sleep for the night, I hunker down in my lair, determined to make sense of everything I had on Mom and Palmer's murders. Julian Broadhurst being gay was a huge gaping hole in the case that the police had been far too quick to close. However, that didn't explain Mom's love letters. Could she have fallen in love with Julian and when he rebuffed her, they had a violent fight, and he killed her and then Palmer in self-defense? As distasteful as it was, I had to be fair and admit it was a possibility—and it still left Julian the culprit. I should be pleased—but I'm not. That left what I remembered about Dad, or thought I remembered, anyway. Was it possible that Dad had that conversation with Mom at the Big House and not at the cottage and I'd gotten the timeline and place mixed up?

Since I'm missing Cassie terribly, I do what I do best when I'm wired up: I fucking procrastinate. I make long lists of all the pros and cons, theories, documents, research, etc. That kills a couple of hours. It's sunrise before I finally crash on the living-room sofa. I'd rather burn myself out than sleepwalk or have another round of night terrors. But my brain is too fired up. More texts from Dad. Delete, delete, delete. I check my emails; more threatening crap from Hunter Talley. Delete. Other messages from reporters. Straight to trash.

There's an email from Collier Moynes. I'm surprised he responded so soon. Just before I saw Olivia Grantham, I texted Moynes to see if he could dig up anything on the elusive Dr. Herman Bethel. *There's a reason why you couldn't find anything,* Moynes cryptically writes. *Does Camp Hero mean anything to you?*

I freeze. I almost delete the email. Wasn't I dealing with enough shit? Once I thaw out, I click on the links that Moynes provided. According to these documents (much of them redacted), Dr. Herman Bethel was in reality Dr. Harold Betel. The family had changed their name when they fled Germany after World War II. There were allegations—never proven—that Betel senior had been a disciple of Josef Mengele, the notorious Angel of Death at Auschwitz, the Nazi concentration camp. During the Cold War, the son became a psychiatrist and worked for the U.S. government at Camp Hero in the early sixties—the period we'd vacationed in Montauk. By the winter of 1967, Dr. Bethel had decamped to Virginia to open a clinic for profoundly disturbed children. After a young patient died in his care and other parents complained about the clinic's controversial techniques— psychosurgery, transcranial magnetic stimulation, magic mushrooms, electroconvulsive therapy—the state medical board stepped in and revoked the clinic's license. Dr. Bethel's trail after that is somewhat murky, but his death notice mentioned a daughter.

I stop reading, the pain in my head a sharp ache. Electroconvulsive therapy is another word for shock treatment. This is what Dad subjected me to, a helpless, vulnerable child in deep, paralyzing grief. Now that the dungeon's been unlocked, terrible memories seep through me. The uncaring attendants who all ignored my entreaties as they strapped me down to a cold, hard table like an animal. The sting of the electrodes plugged into my skin. How the room trembled when the jolts began. And, worst of all, my screams. Afterward, the disorientation, the brain fog, stuck in limbo not knowing what was real and what wasn't. Dad was supposed to be the one person —aside from Mom—that I could count on to protect me from monsters. What if I'd gotten it all horribly wrong? *What if Dad was the monster?*

CHAPTER TWENTY-FOUR

"Are you sure you don't mind if I go out for a bit? I won't be too long." I put on my jacket.

"Where are you going again?" Cassie is in the living room, supposedly working on her laptop. It's been three weeks since she was discharged from the hospital. The private duty nurse I hired quit after barely a day. I couldn't blame the woman. Cassie's a terrible patient. She refuses to stay in bed, rejects her pain meds, insists she's fine when she's clearly not, and rebuffs my many attempts to discuss what had happened. Cassie's mood shifts like the weather. One minute she's sunny, the next stormy. Dr. Sanders had warned me that it would be like this—Cassie's healing physically, mentally, and emotionally—but it didn't make it any easier to bear. Cassie's put on a brave face in front of Mark and Audra, but they sense something's wrong. Over pepperoni pizza and slushies, I explain that Mommy isn't feeling well, and she'll get better, but in the meantime, we all need to be patient and understanding. Do I say this for them or me? I'm not sure. All I know is that when Cassie locks herself in our bedroom and cries, it's a stake in my heart. I tell myself it's going to take time, but deep down, I'm afraid the stopwatch is ticking. Cassie's slipping away from me and soon the space between us will be too great. How in the hell am I supposed to help her when I'm dealing with my own bag of shit?

But as the saying goes, life goes on, and the world doesn't wait. While Cassie was still in the hospital, I made some executive decisions. I hired a housekeeper/nanny and struck gold with Mrs. Germaine, a New Orleans transplant, a convivial lady with an infectious laugh, and impeccable references. The fact that she makes the best beignets I'd ever tasted outside of Bourbon Street plays a huge part in her getting the job. Cassie grumbled about it at first, but she quickly realized it wasn't a war she was going to win. Now she and Mrs. G are trading recipes and fangirling over Noel Fielding's hair.

And while I'm still not yet ready to look for a new literary agent, thanks to Dalton I have a new entertainment lawyer since my previous one retired; this attorney is a young and hungry barracuda who understands the power of "no" and isn't afraid to say it. If the Max suits make good on their threats to sue me, at least I have a team in place. I forward the numerous business proposals I've received since Sheldon's passing to the new entertainment lawyer. I know the drill: unless there's a contract with an extravagant number of zeros, it's all smoke and mirrors.

"Baby, remember, I have an appointment with Dr. Richter." Which is mostly true. I bend down to kiss Cassie goodbye. She turns her head and my kiss lands in the air. It stings like a hot poker. "How did you sleep last night?"

"Lousy."

That makes two of us. The mattress in the spare room is harder than cement.

"Where are the kids?"

"Mrs. G is dropping Mark off at school. Audra's still asleep. If you need me—"

"For what? I'm sick and tired of lying here like a lump and staring at the walls. I want to go out for a drive."

I feel like a stern parent, the one who always puts a damper on things. "No way, baby. You heard what the doctor said. Bed rest. No car racing, no parachute jumps, no rocket trips to the moon—"

Cassie gives me the finger. I'm thrilled.

I get to the elevator as the doors open. "On your way out, son?" It's Dad. He reeks of very expensive aftershave in his bespoke suit.

Trapped like a badger, I step into the elevator. The doors close with a sickening thud.

"Are you having phone troubles? You haven't returned my messages or calls. How's Cassie? Did you get my flowers? How are the children? I can take Mark off your hands for a couple of days, my schedule is free."

I got his flowers. I tossed them in the goddamn trash.

"Jesus fucking Christ. Are you still annoyed about that girl, the one who slapped you silly?"

The internet trolls wasted no time in outing Caroline. Some of my so-called fans showed up at her doorstep. But with no comment from either of us, the story died a quick death. I sent June an email asking for another DNA test at a lab of her choosing, but so far, she hasn't replied. I'm not surprised, but I still hope.

"Brooks, come on, this is ridiculous. How long are you going to give me the silent treatment?" Dad harrumphs. "Look, I'm willing to concede that perhaps I crossed a line at the hospital."

This is Dad's idea of an apology. I give him a stark look: *Really?*

"I can't lie, son. I don't pretend to understand what you see in her. I mean, I get what she sees in you." Dad doesn't know when to quit. Maybe this works at the negotiation table with world leaders, but with me, it's a tiresome, relentless grind. I'm sick of it. "But it's not my life. If you're happy with her—" He shoots me a half-hearted shrug.

I've had my fill of his pretentious shit. I press the stop button on the elevator, and it slams to a halt. "If you want to talk, by all means, let's fucking talk. But don't you dare say another word about my wife. Tell me about Dr. Bethel. You remember, the doctor who fried my brains like it was a science experiment. I was only eight fucking years old." I'm so angry I shake. Lava spews in my veins.

"Brooks." He puts his hand on my shoulder.

I roughly push him away.

"Son, listen to me. I don't know where you got this—"

"Do you deny it?"

"Dr. Bethel did what no other doctor could do. If his methods were unorthodox, well, that's for others to say, not me."

This is what we call, in parlance, a non-denial denial. Exhausted, I push the ground-floor button. "Did you know that he was in Montauk the same time we were that summer? That's quite a coincidence, wouldn't you say?"

Dad impatiently rolls his eyes. "Are you going to start with this cockamamie conspiracy nonsense? Mind control? Bending spoons? What's next, seeing ghosts? You're not in a good place, Brooks. Is that goddamn therapist making it worse?"

"Were you aware that Julian Broadhurst was a homosexual?"

"What?" Dad looks befuddled. "That's fucking bullshit. Is this crap you're making up for your book? Or are you getting this from that ghoul Marshall Reagan? I'm telling you this for the last time, you're going down a rabbit hole. You need to focus on the here and now, not the dead and gone. Get your fucking head out of your ass. The gala's only three weeks away."

The elevator doors open. I storm off, his words ringing in my ears. Dad's life has room for only one person: himself. Everyone else is immaterial. I'm acutely aware that I'm merely a bystander, a rubbernecker, a mute witness to the great achievements of the all-knowing, all-powerful St. Bernard. And I'm so fucking over it. Now more than ever, I'm determined to find out the truth, if that was even possible at this point. Someone has to know something. And it might just be that the person I'm on my way to meet can shed some light.

Of all the people who'd reached out to me to offer their condolences about Cassie, my dad's old flame, Netta, would've been far down the list. She asked if we could meet; I readily agreed.

It's a small, out-of-the-way eatery in Chelsea, the kind of place you'd go only if you knew it was there. I think I'm early, but Netta's already tucked away behind a decorated screen. Her smile is as warm and inviting as the delicious aromas that waft in from the kitchen. She looks exactly as I remember save for a few strands of gray that peek out from beneath a scarf.

I squeeze myself into the small banquette.

"Would you like something? The owner is a good friend. I come here every time I'm in New York, which isn't that often." Netta takes a sip of something hot.

"You look well," I say.

"I'm surprised you remember me at all. It's been so many years." She takes another sip. "I'm sure you must be wondering why I contacted you. But first, I must ask, how is your wife coping?"

"I can't lie, it's been difficult." I find myself tearing up.

"You both wanted this child."

"Very much."

Netta reaches for my hand. "I've thought about you often, Brooks. I was exceedingly fond of you."

"And I of you." Which is the truth. When Dad was brusque and unkind, I could count on Netta to be sympathetic and comforting. She wasn't Mom, but it seemed to me that she and Dad were good for each other.

"You were in so much pain. You had this tough-as-nails veneer, but I knew. I often told Bernard that he was too harsh with you, but he made it clear that it wasn't my business.

However, when I learned what happened to your wife, I knew I couldn't stay silent any longer."

Cassie? What does she have to do with this? I lean forward, expectant.

Netta speaks softly and carefully chooses her words. "It was 1980. When my parents passed, I moved to Manhattan, eager for a challenge. Through friends, I began work at the United Nations. I was—how would you say it—a policy wonk. That's how I met Bernard. He came to discuss some initiatives with my boss. I was attracted to Bernard immediately. He was unlike any man I'd ever known: a burning intelligence, cultured, sophisticated. A man who treated me as an equal and not a subservient appendage. We traveled extensively, for a time we even lived together. But I was under no illusions. I knew there were other women. But he was discreet. I told myself that as long as he came home to me, the other women were insignificant." She toys with the gold bangles on her arms. "I'd just celebrated turning forty when I realized I was pregnant. There was no doubt Bernard was the father."

I raise my eyebrows. I've little doubt that Dad wouldn't have been pleased.

"I know what you're thinking. That Bernard would be furious about my pregnancy. But he surprised me by being supportive and attentive. He accompanied me to the doctor, he filled my prescriptions, he made sure I ate well and rested. The other women simply faded away. It was a wonderful time, probably the most wonderful time of my life. I began to entertain the notion that we had a future together." She pauses, her eyes brimming. "When I was six months pregnant, I went into premature labor. The child lived only a few hours. The deformities were so severe the doctors couldn't tell me what sex it was."

"I'm so sorry, Netta," I murmur.

"I was devastated. Bernard seemed equally distraught. A few days later, I was discharged. I waited for him to pick me up. I waited for hours. I grew fearful that he'd had an accident or had fallen suddenly ill. Eventually, I took a taxi to our house." Her face hardened. "All my belongings were on the curb by the trash cans, and strangers were pawing through it like wolves. Bernard was home. I saw the light in his study. I pounded on the door. He never answered. I never heard from him again."

Am I surprised? Shocked? *Not at all.* The great humanitarian —as the world knows Dad—is capable of deliberate and unnecessary cruelty when it suits his need or purpose. I can admit it now; I couldn't have six months ago. Dad had done it to me, to Sheldon, and who knew how many more like Netta who'd been caught in his web. In Dad's world, we were game tokens that could be disposed of as easily and as readily as last week's garbage.

"I was shattered. But after much thought and deliberation, I concluded that our relationship had run its course. The loss of our child had merely accelerated the inevitable. I picked up the pieces of what was left of my life. I had my work, I had friends. But instead of getting better, I got steadily worse. The doctors had no explanation. Unfortunately, by the time I realized what had happened, it was too late. I had emergency surgery, which saved my life but left me sterile."

I broke out in a cold sweat, acid bubbling in the back of my throat. I suddenly have a really bad feeling—a really bad fucking feeling—of where this is going.

Her nails dug into my hand. "It was my prescription, Brooks."

I strain to hear her as the buzz-saw roars through my head.

"Bernard made a ritual of it. Every morning, every evening, he insisted on watching me take my prenatal vitamins. I thought it was touching, so I humored him."

Despite the hurricane howling in my head, I know what she's going to say before she says a single syllable.

"The vitamins weren't vitamins at all. They were a black-market version of Thalidomide."

I can't breathe. The room spins as if I'm caught on a runaway carnival ride. I grip the sides of the table to keep my balance. "Netta, no. You're wrong. I know my father's faults better than anyone. He can be thoughtless, insensitive, even brutal, but—" I can't say the word: *murderer.* Because once I do, it takes on a life of its own.

Netta stares at me, her eyes bright. "Brooks, do you think I want to be right? I told myself there had to be another explanation. But the laboratory confirmed it. I still couldn't accept it. I refused to believe that someone I loved and trusted could be that heartless, so inhumane—so profoundly evil." She lowers her eyes. "Bernard's a powerful man, Brooks. More powerful than you realize. And men like him have even more powerful friends, and their interests are entwined and aligned. During my years with Bernard, I turned a blind eye to many things." She takes another sip of her drink, but it's empty. "I lived in fear for years. I moved from place to place, crippled by paranoia and anxiety. I nearly lost my mind. I think for a time, I did."

"And now?"

She lifts her head defiantly, fire in her eyes. "Thanks to a dear colleague at the State Department, Netta Shivraz died in a plane crash. I was reborn as Abedini Zohrabi. I live in Seattle. I operate a homeless shelter. I'm known as the Persian Cat Lady. I never married. My life is rich and full. I thought I'd put the past behind me. But when I read about your wife, it all came flooding back to me. I knew I couldn't stay silent. I was terrified that Bernard had done something to your wife."

"No, no. Cassie had an ectopic pregnancy, just one of those—" I'm sick to my core. I tell myself that Netta is mistaken—but what if she's not? "I can't imagine what you went through. That you felt compelled to go to such extreme lengths. I believe you. But at the same time, you're asking me to believe that Dad's a—"

"I said what I came to say. Nothing more. What you do with it is up to you. Brooks, you've always lived in fear; as a young man, and still, I sense. It's far easier to tell yourself that you *want* to remember what happened so long ago than *to do* it. Because the reality is that you're frightened of remembering what it is you've tried so hard to forget."

Netta's right. *I'm fucking petrified.* I'm like a kid who has stumbled upon a loaded gun in his parents' bedroom. On a cellular level, I know picking the gun up and waving it around like a drunk cowboy is wrong and foolish. But the compulsion is too strong, and I'm not of an age to fully comprehend the dire consequences of my actions. I certainly don't mean for the gun to go off accidentally and gravely wound my baby sister. But it does, and I have to live with the consequences.

All my life, I desperately wanted to believe that Dad was a good, noble, honorable, decent man incapable of doing bad things—any bad act. I've clung to this illusion like a drowning passenger hanging onto a piece of wreckage from the *Titanic*. Because, deep down in my gut, even though I can't say it out loud, I know that if Dad had slipped Netta a poison pill to terminate her pregnancy, the probability that he'd done other, exceedingly horrible things is high. It's a place my mind isn't yet prepared to go and maybe never would be.

Before we say goodbye, Netta offers one bit of advice. "Brooks, don't make the mistake I and countless others have made in underestimating Bernard. He's cunning, calculating, wily, shrewd, devious—Machiavellian. There's nothing that he won't do or say in his own self-interest. He's a cobra, waiting in the weeds to strike at the most opportune moment—when his opponent is at their most weak and vulnerable. You be the cobra, Brooks. Wait for the right moment. And trust no one—not even yourself."

Do I have it in me to be a cobra? When it comes to dealing with network assholes, I can be demanding, arbitrary, argumentative—but it was never with evil or nefarious intent.

Sheldon and I had the bad guy/good guy routine down to a science. But in the rarefied atmosphere in which Dad exists, where selling your soul and scruples is commonplace, and being ruthless and cut-throat are virtues—I'm a clueless newbie. I still want to give Dad the benefit of the doubt—any doubt I can muster, frankly. But it's getting harder, harder than I want to admit.

However, one thing I'm sure of is that aside from Cassie, I don't know who I can trust—I mean, drop-dead, end-of-the-line —trust. Miss Drake and Sheldon are gone. I sure as hell can't confide in Dalton. As much as I like him, he and Dad are too close for comfort. I can guess what James will say: *Where's the fucking proof? Exactly what are you accusing your father of?* As the saying goes, you only get one shot at the king. And Bernard Anderson wasn't just a king—he was a fucking emperor.

But right now, I have another snake to deal with—a lesser variety than the mighty cobra, but a snake nevertheless. And this time around, she's not going to distract me with her psychobabble.

"Well, Mr. Anderson." Pseudo Nicole Kidman eyes me from behind her trendy owl-rimmed glasses in full scolding schoolmarm mode. "I appreciate that emergencies come up, but twice you've canceled at the last minute. This is unacceptable. I have patients, committed patients who put in the time and effort, and I can't waste my precious—"

"Well, if I remember correctly, you said you could afford to pick and choose your clients. Yet you led me to believe that you had no idea who I was at our first appointment. Can you clarify that to me?"

She shoots me an imperial, haughty look. "You misunderstood me, Mr. Anderson. I said I had a long waiting list. You seem agitated, I daresay, even testy."

"Quite the contrary, I'm perfectly calm. And I'm waiting for an answer other than you trying to change the subject." I meet her look with one of my own.

Dr. Richter removes her glasses and throws them on her desk. "Okay, yes. I knew who you were. I said otherwise to make you feel more comfortable in our session. That was a mistake on my part. I should've been candid with you. I guess even therapists get starstruck."

"So why did you bring Julian Broadhurst up?"

"I don't know. Perhaps I thought it might jar your memory."

I don't fucking buy it. Bull-feathers.

"Mr. Anderson, I do believe you're going off on a tangent. You're upset about something."

How astute of her. I want to say, *you're goddamn right I'm upset, you fucking bitch with your plastic smile and your silicone boobs.* Instead, I smile like a choirboy. "How about this? Do you think electroshock treatment is an appropriate therapy for young children?"

Her face goes blank. "I can't answer that."

"Can't or won't? It's either a yes or a no. I mean, you shouldn't have to think about it. At least, I didn't."

Dr. Richter puts her glasses back on. "I don't appreciate being put on the spot. As for treatments, it would depend entirely on the circumstances. Babies, small children, of course not. As for a juvenile, it might be a proper course of treatment if the patient was properly diagnosed and deemed to be a danger to himself or others. Why are you asking me this, Mr. Anderson? Has something happened? Have you been experiencing irrational thoughts such as suicide or self-harm?"

"Irrational thoughts?" I'm incredulous. "That's quite a leap. I asked you, and politely, I might add, a simple question. Why would you respond by asking me about suicide?" I wipe my sweaty palms against my jacket.

"Given your history of drug and alcohol abuse, I think it's an extremely reasonable question. Are you depressed? Upset?" She scribbles in her notebook.

I could kick myself. It only now occurs to me that Dr. Richer could be working in cahoots with Dad. Is she reporting back to him about our sessions? Is that why Dad put her on the list of therapists he'd sent to Cassie? I abruptly stand. "I think we're done. Please give my precious slot to someone else. Have your secretary send me a final bill."

The doctor seems taken aback. "Mr. Anderson, I don't think that would be in your best interests. Today notwithstanding, we're making tangible progress. You could be on the verge of a breakthrough. Tell me, have you had any more flashbacks?" She tries to sound earnest and compassionate, but there's an edge to her voice. Fear? Concern? Or something else? Perhaps she doesn't think I'm serious. I am. I walk out of her office as she calls after me.

I rush outside like a diver with the bends. I gasp for air, my chest a vise. All I want is to go home to Cassie and the kids before another panic attack grips me. I take a few steps to the corner and try to hail a taxi. People pass by me, oblivious to my distress. Then someone brushes up against me; I feel a sting on my neck. I remember thinking, *did I just get stung by a goddamn bee in fucking New York City?*

After that, everything goes black.

CHAPTER TWENTY-FIVE

Woozy and disoriented in the mother of all brain fog, I open my eyes. The early morning sun filters through the curtains. My body aches as if I've been hit by a backhoe and run over by a tractor-trailer. My mouth is dry and the back of my throat is on fire. I clear my mind long enough to realize that I'm hooked up to all kinds of machines that burp, beep, blink, hum, and whir at will. *What the fuck?*

"No sudden movements, Mr. Anderson. Let me get your doctor." The female voice is filtered and hazy. I catch a glimpse of white as she darts away.

No sudden movements? *Fuck that shit.* I abruptly sit up as my veins throb. I feel a tug. Something has come undone from my arm or my penis—or maybe both. I nearly pass out, but I force myself to come back from the gray. I focus and take stock of my surroundings. I'm in a hospital, that much is clear.

What the hell happened? I sort through the possibilities. A heart attack? Mugging? Hit by a car? Stroke? Fell into a manhole? Abducted by aliens? The Bermuda Triangle?

"Mr. Anderson, nice to meet you now that you're awake. I've been a big fan for years." A man in a white lab coat saunters up.

He offers me his chubby hand, his fingers thick like sausage links. "I'm Dr. Nealon."

I stretch my legs. Something pops. "I have to call my wife. She'll be worried sick. I have to let her know where I am. Which is where, exactly?"

The nurse from before returns and tries to ease me back onto the bed. I brush her off like a cockroach.

"Mr. Anderson, you're at Mt. Sinai. Your wife was here earlier. Your father is here. Would you like to see him?" Dr. Nealon makes a move to reattach the IV.

I pull my arm away. "No need for that, I'm not staying." I lurch out of bed. The room whirls a bit, but nothing I can't handle. I'm a fucking vampire.

"Doctor—" the nurse says.

"It's fine, I'll handle it."

The nurse scurries off.

"Mr. Anderson, what you're experiencing is perfectly normal. The grogginess, the disorientation—"

Fuck these hospital gowns. How can you have an intelligent conversation while your bare cheeks hang in the breeze? "Where are my clothes?" I've already concluded that Dr. Nealon's a dipshit.

"Do you know why you're here, Mr. Anderson? Or even how long you've been in the hospital?" Dr. Nealon sounds like he's talking to a petulant toddler: *If you eat your fucking broccoli, you'll get a treat, my boy.*

The hell with my butt. I rummage around for my pants or my cell. I'm not fussy, whichever comes first. "To be honest, I don't have a fucking clue." I suddenly realize that my voice is raspy. I sound like I've swallowed glass.

"A week."

"A week, what?" What the hell is this fool jabbering about?

"Maybe I should get your father to explain—"

"I don't want my fucking father!" I roar.

The door opens. It's Dalton Crane. "Doctor, can I please speak to my client alone?"

Client? *Oooh, this sounds foreboding.* The last thing I remember is hailing a fucking taxi and now I need a lawyer. How did I get from there to here?

Dr. Nealon throws up his hands like a waiter who has given up trying to collect the dinner check. He slams the door behind him so hard a machine sputters like *Wall-E.* I think this is against hospital policy.

"Brooks, what in the hell do you think you're doing?" Dalton sounds tired.

I pull another thing out of my arm and shuffle over to the closet. "I'm going home to my wife, what do you think?" I'm not at one hundred percent yet, but I'm getting there. My knees quiver like a virgin at the drive-in. I plop myself down on a nearby chair and look for my shoes. "That idiot doctor said something about me being here for a week. What the fuck did that mean?"

"Brooks, you really don't know? Yes, you've been in the hospital for a week."

A week? A whole fucking week? Still not convinced, I stroke my chin. Fuck, I had stubble all right. "Was I hit by a bus or something? Because that's what it feels like."

"What do you remember?"

There's something in Dalton's tone that sets off alarms. "Are you asking me as my lawyer or my friend?"

"Both."

"The last thing I remember is leaving my therapist's office. Nicole—I mean, Dr. Richter. I wasn't happy with the way our sessions were going and I told her I wouldn't be coming anymore. And that was it." Where is Dalton going with this?

"And Dr. Richter was alive when you left?"

I twist my face. "No, she was on her desk doing a—"

"Brooks, can you be goddamn serious for once in your fucking life," Dalton snaps.

"All right. Dr. Richter was alive and breathing. She wasn't thrilled about me leaving but otherwise—" I can't find my shoes. Fuck my shoes.

"Nothing else?"

"I hailed a taxi."

"Yeah, but did you get in it?"

My stomach knots. "I don't know." I suddenly feel dread; I mean, hard, cold, debilitating dread. Where is Cassie? I want my wife.

"Brooks, think hard. You don't remember anything?"

I shake my head, confused.

"You vanished. I mean, fucking vaporized into thin air. No one knew where you were. Cassie and Bernard were frantic. I'm calling every goddamn hospital and morgue in a four-state radius. Finally, after three days, the police found you in an abandoned warehouse in Staten Island, wasted out of your goddamn mind. There was enough ketamine, fentanyl, and heroin in you to kill ten men. Your heart stopped twice in the ambulance."

I manage a weak, painful chuckle as my lungs wheeze like bellows. "Good one, Dalton. Did I jump off the Empire State Building, too? Or stop a speeding train?" Then I realize he's serious. "Come on, man, that's fucking *insane*."

"There are pictures. And video. It's all over the fucking internet. It's not pretty." He gives me this pitiful look.

An army of sledgehammers pounds my head. "I don't care if they have pictures of me fucking the Four Horses of the Apocalypse at the Met Gala. It's a goddamn set-up."

"A set-up by who? Damn it, Brooks, I want to help you, but I can't if I don't know what the hell happened. If you're going for an insanity defense—"

"Insanity for what? What the fuck did I do?"

"Dr. Richter's dead, Brooks. And it looks like you were the last person to see her."

Faux Nicole Kidman's dead? Well, she was a lousy therapist, but even so, I didn't wish her ill. Not ill enough to kill her. "You mean I was the last person to see her alive—other than her killer."

"And you just went out on a drug-fueled bender immediately afterward for shits and giggles." He shoots me a pained grimace. "It's bad, Brooks. It's fucking bad."

"Nothing is that bad. Once I explain to Cassie—" She'll understand. She must.

"Cassie's gone."

What does he mean, *gone*? There's gone and there's gone.

"I spoke to her just before she left. She took the kids and the housekeeper to your aunt's place. She had to. She was under siege at the Dakota and God knows it wouldn't be any better in Water Mill. I'm going to be honest with you, Brooks. I don't think she's coming back. I know that look. When you've been divorced as many times as I have—"

No, no. I know Cassie. If she was fucking done with me, she'd tell me to my face. Cassie's not the type to shy away from a fight. I'm sure she's fucking livid with me, but once she hears the facts, she'll come around. But Cassie had done the right thing. The farther away she and the kids are from this, the better. I am eerily calm. I know what I must do. "Now if you don't mind, I'm getting the hell out of here unless the police are waiting in the hallway to arrest me."

"No, but they're going to want to talk to you, and soon. I can't fob them off forever. You need to come up with a better alibi than the amnesia card. But there's something else. The weapon that killed your mother and brother; it was never found, correct?"

I find my shirt and pants in the closet. They smell like shit, but I have no choice. Still no shoes. And no sign of my cell phone or my wallet. Cassie would've had the presence of mind to cancel my credit and debit cards. Fortunately, I keep a couple of thousand—okay, more—for emergencies in the lair. It's more than enough. "Why are you asking me that? No, it wasn't. There was speculation that it was some type of hammer. Do they know how Dr. Richter was killed?"

"Blunt force trauma from a painter's hammer. It was lying underneath her. I've been reliably informed that the preliminary tests show that the hammer has traces of blood other than Dr. Richter's. Older blood. Do you understand what I'm getting at?"

I think I do, but I'm pumped with so many drugs I barely register a reaction. I'm too busy trying to find my shoes. The hell with it. I find a pair of fucking flip-flops that a former patient left behind. Cassie has dozens of flip-flops. I can't stand the fucking things. I don't like anything between my toes. It's a texture thing.

Dr. Nealon bursts in. "Mr. Anderson, I'm telling you in the strongest possible terms that leaving at this point of your recovery is most unwise." He looks to Dalton to back him up.

"I'm on your side, doctor, but absent a court order, you can't force Mr. Anderson to stay," Dalton answers.

The doctor's face puckers as if he's sucking a goat's tit. "Well. If that's the case, I can't be held responsible for what happens if you—"

"If I leave and have a fucking heart attack on the sidewalk? Don't worry, I won't sue." I push past him. The fucking flip-flops are already annoying the hell out of me. I want to throw them out the window.

Dalton catches up with me by the elevator. "What am I supposed to say to Bernard?"

I'm in agony. I want to trust Dalton. That he's sincere and on my side. But what if he's not? "Tell him I'll come to the brownstone for a fireside chat later tonight. He'll know what I mean." The elevator doors open, and I step inside. The doors close on Dalton's bewildered face.

The media hyenas are out in full force at the Dakota. I don't see Fernando; maybe he has the night off. I enter the building through a back delivery entrance. After I shower, dress, and throw those fucking flip-flops away, I write letters to Mark and Audra. I write as if it's the last chance I have to tell them what's in my heart because it probably is. I tell them how much I love them and they're the best things, aside from Mommy, that's ever happened to me. I ask them to be good, to look out for one another, and to keep the squabbling to a minimum. I tell them we will all be together soon. I don't know if that part is true. But fuck it, if the beast is going down, it's going down as Babe Ruth.

Dad is in his study, as I knew he would be. Even though it's somewhat balmy, he has the gas fireplace at full blast. "Jesus, where have you been? I'm not a night owl like you." He pours something amber-colored into two glasses. "I've been saving this for an extra-special occasion. Twenty-five-year-old bourbon, set me back nearly thirty thousand." He hands me a glass, almost giddy.

I recoil in disgust and throw the glass into the fire. It explodes into a mini fireball, crackling and hissing.

Dad sighs. "Really, Brooks, you're such a fucking drama queen. And so utterly goddamn predictable." He sits down in his favorite chair. "You have only yourself to blame for this regrettable situation. All you had to do was stop with the fucking questions. But you just couldn't leave it alone. You were like that as a kid, always picking at scabs."

I stare at him with a mix of incredulity and fury. "Miss Drake? Elaine Brighton? Dr. Richter? Marshall Reagan? I sure as fuck didn't kill them."

"I beg your pardon. You sent Miss Drake home early. I liked her, she was a damn good spy. She fooled everyone, even the Russians."

"Were you one, too?" I ask.

His smile is tight. "We go by many names."

I have many names, too, none of them decent.

"As for Elaine Brighton, she took pity on you. That was her mistake. And once you discovered the Richter woman was Dr. Bethel's daughter—oh, on that one, you did me a favor. Would you believe the bitch was trying to blackmail me?" He smirks in between sips. "But I'll be fair. This is all Marshall Reagan's fault. We had a deal and at the last possible moment, the bastard developed a conscience." He plunks his glass down on a small table. "Would you please sit the fuck down? You're making me nervous. You look like you're ready to keel over."

He's not wrong. I feel old and worn out and battered. Maybe it's because I'm coming off all the drugs. My body's taken a beating, but my mind is razor-sharp. For the first time in my life, I see Dad for what he is: a fucking sociopath in a jacquard smoking jacket.

"How much do you remember, Brooks?"

"Enough," I say. Which is the truth.

"Well, that's most—unfortunate. But you know what they say: c'est la vie. What tommyrot." He raises his glass.

"Why?" I ask, my voice on fire. "Why drug me? I could've died."

"Why?" He seems genuinely amazed. "That should be obvious, Brooks. It was to discredit you. Not my first choice, but —" He casually shrugs. "When Dr. Bethel died, I thought I'd covered all my tracks. But it turns out that he taped your therapy sessions, tapes of you saying I—well, use your fucking imagination." He pours himself another drink. "Are you sure you don't want some? For what I paid for it, it's a shame to drink alone."

No one would've blamed me for taking a drink. Instead, I grit my teeth. This son of a bitch isn't going to get the better of me. Not tonight. Not tomorrow. Not ever.

He lights a cigar. "Well, you asked for this meeting, Brooks. What exactly do you want?"

"The truth," I say.

"The truth? Are you sure about that? Because I'm not." Dad raises his eyebrows. They look as if they're about to take flight.

"Why don't we start at the beginning? Your parents. Were they horrible? Abusive? Is that why you killed them?"

"Brooks, you've been reading too many pulp novels. Your grandparents were kind, honorable, and dull. Your grandfather was happy behind his counter selling buttons and bows to bored housewives, and your grandmother never had an original thought in her life. They expected me to carry on the family tradition. But I had bigger dreams and ambitions. But once they were gone, I saw it as an—*opportunity.*" He says this without a trace of grief or remorse.

"And Mom? Was she an opportunity too?" I can barely say a word.

Dad fidgets in his chair. "I loved your mother as much as I could love any woman. Not many men can say that about their wives. You certainly can't say the same. When Shirley got pregnant, I did the right thing. When I held Palmer for the first time—" His eyes mist. "It was a revelation. I loved him more than anything. I wanted it to work with your mother. So, we moved to the suburbs, fucking *Leave It to Beaver*, meat loaf, peas, and pearls. I told Shirley no more babies, but she was insistent. She didn't want Palmer to be an only child. But you were nothing like Palmer. You were greedy, grasping, howling non-stop, demanding from morning until night, a fucking nightmare. I hated coming home because of you. That's a horrendous thing for a father to admit—not to love their flesh and blood."

I can't stomach any more of his cornucopia of bullshit. "You never loved anyone but yourself."

His face creases with anger. "Now see, this is where you get me fucking annoyed. You claim to want the truth, but you only want your version of it. Your mother and I, we both made mistakes, we weren't cardboard cutouts. She went back to work and things got better—until she announced she was pregnant. I was furious. And then she tripped on the broken step in the basement."

"Tripped, fell, or pushed?" I interrupt.

Dad takes another sip of his drink, and his face flushes. "Does it matter? The baby wouldn't have survived regardless. The only good thing to come out of it was that there was no more talk of more children. We limped along, fell into a domestic rut. Shirley got it into her head that I was cheating. She'd show up at my office out of the blue and accuse me of cheating in front of my students. It was juvenile and embarrassing."

The liquor fuels Dad's diatribe, but I've no doubt that he was unfaithful. I let him ramble. Why stop a man when he's digging his own grave?

"Just before you all left for Montauk, Mom learned she was pregnant. So much for the goddamn pill. I demanded she have an abortion. We argued about it all summer. I finally told her if you want this child so badly, fine, you can have your divorce—but I'm taking Palmer. All I wanted was my son. But that wasn't good enough for her, the fucking bitch."

I arch my back. "Is that why you killed her?"

"You silly boy," Dad says with a wry chuckle. As if this is in any way, shape, or form humorous. "I'm a peaceful man. Violence must always be a last resort, used only when all other possibilities are exhausted." Now he's in fucking professor lecture mode. "Things were at a stalemate until Palmer told me about this British guy with a fancy foreign car hanging around the cottage. Can you believe that your brother was jealous of that fop?"

I most certainly can. I was there. I saw it. And I'm sure Dad egged Palmer's hatred.

"I didn't come that night with bad intentions. I wanted to reconcile."

"Did you figure out that a divorce wouldn't look good on your résumé? Too expensive? Or is it that your mistress dumped you?"

From the sour expression on Dad's face, it must be the latter.

"I wanted us to be reasonable. But your mother had other ideas. She was into all this feminist claptrap about how she'd been suppressed and abused by men all her life and how having children had kept her from reaching her full potential. The more she ranted, the crazier she got. She grabbed a hammer from the kitchen and made all kinds of wild threats. I left, thinking she'd cool down. When I returned, they were all dead. Who killed who —I have no idea. And that's the truth."

I give Dad a level stare. "You don't expect me to believe that bull, do you?"

Dad laughs and calmly puffs on his cigar. "Come on—it's a good yarn. It's entirely plausible. It's human nature to whitewash events. Area 51, JFK—"

"I know what I saw," I insist. "Don't blame Mom or anyone else. You killed them. Not Julian. Not the boogeyman. You."

He shot me a side-eye. "You know all this for a certainty through your drug haze? Hypothetically speaking, let's say you're right. In the heat of the moment, I had to make a split-second decision. It was a fucking war. If you don't fire first, you die. If you hesitate for one second, you die. There's no time for second-guessing. Do you think Truman lost sleep over launching the fucking A-bomb? Do you realize how many lives he saved? Sometimes you must do a bad thing to achieve a good thing. And I've done a lot of good things, Brooks. Does one bad act negate a lifetime of achievement?"

More than one bad act—I think of Netta, but I can't bring her into this. "Palmer was your pride and joy. How could you have ever—" My voice chokes.

"Palmer was highly regrettable. But for fuck's sake, Brooks, it wasn't supposed to be him." He stares at me, his face full of anger. The mask is finally off.

This is the truth I've waited for all my life. My first reaction isn't anger, but a tidal wave of relief.

"I thought Palmer would understand. That I had no choice, it was either them or us. She was going to take him from me. It would be our secret. No one would have to know. Then I saw you outside the window. Palmer lunged at me. The little shit tried to kill me, his own father." He sounds bewildered. "I had to defend myself. I took no pleasure in it. When the life went out of him, it was like killing the best part of myself." He shoots me this sad, sorrowful look as if I'm supposed to feel sorry for him.

I feel only revulsion and disgust. The lauded Bernard Anderson, on whom the United Nations is about to bestow their highest humanitarian award, is undeniably batshit crazy.

"I searched that fucking beach for hours. If it hadn't been for that goddamn sheriff showing up when he did—"

I would've died, too. I choke down years of guilt and bile. "You put the love letters in Julian's car. You moved his body."

He chuckles in acknowledgment. "It gave the authorities all the motive they needed. That dumb-fuck cop was so eager to close the case. We don't want to scare the tourists with a serial killer on the loose." He slurs his words. "In the hospital, I never left your side—well, except for when I went to see your grandfather after Shirley's funeral."

I close my eyes. God, not that.

"I thought it was the decent thing to do. He'd been kind to us. He lent us the money for the down payment on the house in Flushing. I wouldn't have breathed a word if I'd had any idea his heart would give out. And that awful Jurgen family. The pervert son was prowling around that night and saw me get rid of my bloody clothes. Naturally, the idiot blabbed to his father who thought I was made of money. The car was so mangled that the police never bothered to check the brakes." He shoots me a look of paternal concern. "You don't look so hot, Brooks. I warned you. You're not ready to handle the truth."

Dad's wrong. Yes, I'm shattered, but I wanted the truth, no matter where it led. I just didn't know it would lead to *him*.

"I was convinced the minute you woke up you'd squeal like a

pig. Instead, the shock was so profound you were a zombie. Of course, I had to keep it that way. For your own good."

I nearly throw up in my mouth. "So, all the drugs they gave me, the shock treatments—it was to *prevent* me from remembering? You fucking son of a bitch." My own father had sent me down the long, black road of addiction.

"Get off your fucking pedestal, Brooks. You saw it like me—as an opportunity. You've done well for yourself mining your pathetic life for every goddamn penny, the murders included. Without that, you'd still be a hack jerking yourself off writing porn."

I'm beyond nauseated. Next, I suppose he expects me to thank him for killing Mom and Palmer. It's fucking grotesque.

"The life you have is the one you robbed from your brother—not to mention me. How could I ever think of remarrying after such a heinous tragedy? I've had to maintain this pathetic charade of playing a grieving widower doing his utmost to support his poor, mentally disturbed, drug-addled son. And it worked until by some goddamn miracle you got clean and sober. You cobbled a career together. We began to have a normal relationship."

"It was never normal," I grunt.

"Okay, then amicable. Until you had to go and knock up Cassie." He looks disgusted. "You seemed happy, dare I say, maybe even stable, which was always my greatest fear. Your memories might come back. When you had Mark, everything changed. Don't you see? God gave me a second chance. Mark's so much like Palmer. Inquisitive. Intelligent. I could do a lot with that boy."

My blood runs cold. A second chance to do what? To screw Mark up? No fucking way.

"I'm in my golden years. I should be able to sit back and enjoy the fruits of my labor for a life well-lived. Instead, Marshall Reagan crawled out from under a rock. You decided to counter his book with one of your own. I did my utmost to dissuade you, because you nosing around might trigger your memory. I had to find a way to show you that you couldn't trust those memories. That I was a loving, doting father who'd protected you. And, to reinforce the idea that me hurting anyone—much less my own flesh and blood—was inconceivable. I swear to you, Audra wasn't supposed to be injured. How was I to know the damn dog would go nuts?"

The old Brooks would've grabbed a fireplace poker and beat him to a fucking bloody pulp. The new Brooks restrains himself. This is progress.

"It was an experimental serum one of our allies cooked up to heighten aggression in combat situations. Unfortunately, it was shelved after clinical trials."

"Unfortunately?" I bellow.

"It was a fucking goldendoodle. You thanked me, remember? Even Cassie thought I was a gladiator."

I'm speechless, trapped in my own fucking horror novel. Audra's mangled leg is not hypothetical. This isn't just insanity. It's the essence of evil and malevolence. That is Dad's ace in the hole; the innate goodness of people refusing to believe that someone they admired and respected could be so fundamentally demented. "You've gone to excruciating lengths to cover all this up," I finally say.

"What I've done—what I've been forced to do—it's not about me. It's about *them*."

"Them?" Now I'm lost in the weeds.

"Allies and enemies shift like sands in the Sahara. One day we're at war, the next day we're breaking bread at the same table. It's about perception and legacy. I'm the great Bernard Anderson. I've saved lives, stopped wars, maintained fragile allegiances that would've snapped like a twig. Should all my good deeds be tainted and negated by an incident that nobody—aside from you —gives a fuck about?"

Incident. That's all it is to him. I don't bother to hide my disdain.

"That's always been your Achilles' heel. You focus on the small, unimportant details. How do you think I got to be where I am? It was by playing a long game. No one wants my dirty laundry aired for fear of what else might be exposed. I've been meticulous, better than goddamn Daniel Ellsberg. I can burn governments to the ground with one fucking click."

Clearly, Dad believes this shit, or is this megalomania a manifestation of his mental illness? "I'd argue that it would just be easier to get rid of you permanently. Or me, for that matter."

"Maybe if you were Brooks Whogivesashit living in downtown Bumfuck, Idaho. But you're not. As for me, what makes you think they haven't tried? They long ago determined that it was simpler—and less complicated—to pay me off. How do you think I amassed my fortune? It wasn't by selling Girl Scout cookies at Costco. Make no mistake, I'm alive because I'm still useful. My name and reputation carry weight and cachet. The day that ceases to be the case will be my last." He sits on his chair like a haughty potentate on a throne. "My legacy can't be tainted."

I jab my thumb at him. "You had my lawyer manufacture those fake DNA results."

"Fucking right I did. Do I want the world to know you were molested as a child? The bitch was lucky I didn't have her arrested. And her daughter was only looking for a big payday. Good riddance to them." He rises, unsteady, the drink taking over. "Now that we have all that unpleasantness out of the way, there's no reason to go nuclear."

"Are you out of your fucking mind?" I sputter. "You're a murderer. Audra could've died. You had me kidnapped, drugged, and God knows what else. Cassie's left me. And now you're trying to make me out to be a killer. I'd say that's going nuclear."

Dad holds up his hand. "I can fix it. For example, with Dr.

Richter. Evidence is contaminated or lost all the time due to sloppy police procedures. Of course, for this to work, you'll need to go to rehab for an extended period. When you're released, a redemption tour. The media will eat it up."

"And what about Cassie?"

Dad shrugs. "Accidents happen. Ask Miss Drake." He dodders toward me. "I have donors galore for the foundation. The gala's in less than a week. Don't force me to turn it into your memorial service. We're more alike than you think. We're survivors. I know you. You don't want to end up as maggot food like Althea."

His words strangle me. "I'm nothing like you," I finally spit out.

"It's a blow to discover your hero has feet of clay. I understand. It happens to everyone. It happened to me with Robert McNamara." He sounds vaguely disgruntled.

"You were never my hero," I say, emphatic. "People have a right to know the truth."

Dad blows a puff of smoke in my face. "The truth is what I say it is, and you're in no position to bargain. Hasn't a week in the hospital in a drug stupor taught you anything? No one gives a fuck about you. Your wife has washed her hands of you. Your police friend—that James fellow, I know all about him—has one foot in the grave. He's not going to jeopardize his pension for an addled addict. You can forget about your former dealer, Fernando. He's been on my payroll for years. And Dalton will follow the evidence which will point to you: Mom, Palmer, Julian—"

I can barely breathe. "That's fucking ludicrous. I was eight years old. A child."

"*An eight-year-old disturbed child with violent tendencies.* But don't believe me. It's all on the tapes. And tapes can be doctored. Face it, Brooks. I've been doing this far longer than you. I know all the angles. I know you've been recording me from the moment you arrived. Do you take me for a simpleton?"

"I don't know what you're talking about," I stammer.

"Brooks, don't embarrass yourself further than you already have." He motions at me. "Give me the fucking phone."

After a moment, I retrieve my cell from my pocket.

Dad snatches it out of my hand. "So fucking predictable." He deletes the recording, then tosses my cell in the fire. "I hoped we could come to an accommodation, but you leave me no choice." He takes out his cell and dials. "This is Bernard Anderson of 1560 Vanguard Place. My son broke in, he signed himself out of the hospital against doctor's orders. He's high, acting erratic, and making all kinds of wild threats and insane accusations. He's armed and—"

The last thing I see as I rush away is Dad's arrogant smile.

CHAPTER TWENTY-SIX

I f Dad thinks I'm so fucking predictable—well, so is he. I counted on his last-minute curveball. As I scurry away from his building, a hard, biting rain greets me, much like the rain that long-ago night in Montauk. In the background, police sirens blare at warp speed. I walk fast and keep my head down. A bull's-eye is strapped on my chest. I can't afford any careless mistakes or fuckups. If my plan works, it'll all be over soon. In any event, Cassie will know the truth; she's the only one who matters. If it goes sideways—well, it'll be a hell of a headline, even if I'm not alive to see it.

As I hurry to the prearranged meeting place, I worry that Collier Moynes is going to stiff me—or worse, that he's a mole for Dad. But thankfully, no. Moynes is inside an immaculately restored 1967 Ford Fairlane parked in a dark alley close to a Starbucks that has reliable internet.

"Did you not understand the word inconspicuous?" I gripe as I hop in.

"It was the best I could do on short notice. Clean plates and insurance, twelve thousand miles on the original engine, and it's never been on the highway. My brother Kieran left it to me."

Any other time I would've loved to shoot the breeze, but I'm in no mood for chitchat. I reach into my jacket pocket and hand Moynes the military-grade two-way audio-video recording pen available at Amazon for under two hundred bucks, thank you Jeff Fucking Bezos. Moynes plugs the pen into a cord and attaches that to the USB port of his laptop. A few short clicks and Dad appears on the screen: "Jesus, where have you been? I'm not a night owl like you."

"Didn't I tell you? The best Prime purchase I ever made." Moynes does his thing and then slides the laptop over to me. "The file is converted and encrypted, just like you asked."

I send the file and decryption code to Cassie, James, Dalton, and June. I know I can count on Cassie, no matter what happens to me. She will protect the kids. I hope June's curiosity will overcome her anger. James and Dalton are the wildcards in this deranged deck. Once I finish sending the emails, Moynes hands the car keys to me.

"You know, I can't make any guarantees about the car. Are you okay with this?" It's not really what I'm asking, and we both know it.

"Kieran went to Canada instead of Vietnam. He died before the Carter pardon, so yeah, I think he'd be fine with it." He takes out a pack of Winstons, lights two cigarettes, and hands me one. Even though I haven't smoked in years, I'm grateful.

"The State Department recruited me fresh out of college. Eventually, I became a freelance contractor off the books, the kind of ops where if you get caught you—well, you make sure you don't get caught. That's when I met Netta. She was so bright and full of ideas that didn't translate well in the real world. I mean, the geopolitical world," Moynes relates.

"Did you know my father, too?"

He exhales a huge puff of smoke. "Bernard was a first-class asshole; arrogant, smug, and superior. He fit right in. He thought he could do no wrong until an operation he approved went wrong. A massive clusterfuck. Good guys died, our guys, and innocent civilians, too. I had proof of Bernard's malfeasance—it wasn't the first time, either. There was going to be a Senate investigation." He takes another drag. "I was sacked on the eve of my testimony. Like you, a set-up by Bernard. I lost everything; my wife, my kids, the dog, the snow blower. An old pal took pity on me and gave me a job doing security work. I changed my name and my face. All the while, I kept tabs on Bernard. I'm patient because I know he's going to overplay his hand one day." He gives me a concerned look. "You don't have to do this alone."

He's wrong. "I'm done living in fear. I'm not looking over my shoulder for the rest of my life. Fuck that. Besides, I'm not alone." I pat the pen in my coat lapel.

Moynes opens the glove compartment. "You're going to need more than that." He takes out a small pistol.

"No," I demur.

"Don't be that asshole. It's a Ruger SR40c. It'll do the job in a pinch." He gives me a quick demonstration on how to use it.

I reluctantly put the gun back in the glove compartment.

Moynes gets out of the car. "Am I going to see you again?"

I shrug. Who the hell knew?

He unexpectedly leans in and gives me a hard hug. So much for him being a germaphobe.

Water Mill is out of the question; it's the first place the cops would look. I reconcile myself to the idea that we won't be moving there anytime soon, if at all. All that money down the fucking drain. But Cassie can recoup it and then some. I drive well under the speed limit and stay off the main roads. When I reach Montauk, the rain has fizzled out. Thanks to the crummy weather and the late hour, there's no traffic. I drive around Main Street to where we used to hang out, but all the old haunts are gone, the grocery store, the stationery store, the corner market, and the bike shop. I go past where Grandpa William's cottages once stood. Now it's just a monstrous, walled-off compound filled with artificial light. I wonder if the current owners know what happened here. Well, at least they didn't make a movie about it à la *Amityville Horror*. Small blessings.

I park the Fairlane off-road and head up to the beach. The sky is covered with clouds, the moon peeks through like a voyeur in a peep show. Dogs yelp in the distance. Everything looks the same and I'm relieved that the dirt path Palmer and I used to climb up to the dunes is still there. We always considered it our private property. It's ironic how I avoided the beach all these years. I always had an excuse. But not tonight. I'm eight years old again and hiding from the monster.

The wind whips against me when I reach the scrub grass, the ocean roar resounding in my ears. I should've cribbed that pack of cigarettes from Moynes. Staring at the stars that blanket the sky, I think of my mother. She wouldn't have liked much of what passes for pop music these days, but I'm certain she would've loved Coldplay. That horrible night comes back to me like a grainy black-and-white silent movie: Mom lifeless on the floor, Dad slicing Palmer's throat, the fountain of blood, the shock and terror on Palmer's face, and Julian Broadhurst driving up in his Aston Martin as I escaped.

Now that I can acknowledge it and not jab myself with a needle, I realize that a part of me always knew what Dad had done, but I'd been unable or unwilling, to reconcile the truth with the honorable St. Bernard. I wanted to believe in the illusion—or rather, delusion. He was still my father. His blood was my blood. I feel rage and relief and yes, pity. All this carnage for what? A goddamn legacy? A fucking think tank?

I'm not sure how long I've stood there, but the rain mixes with my tears. Then I remembered what Miss Drake said to me the day I married Cassie. Miss Drake caught me fumbling with my tie. I guess she assumed I was nervous about taking my vows, which wasn't the case at all. I was anxious about everything else. Miss Drake expertly tied my tie and said, almost to herself, "You only get one chance in life to do the right thing." At the time, I thought she was referring to Cassie's pregnancy. Now, it's not so clear.

The sun rises and I feel an overwhelming sense of serenity. Behind me in the tall grass, I hear something rustle. I'm sure it's Cassie. She read my mind and knew exactly where to find me. I whirl around, excited and pleased. I say her name.

It's not Cassie.

Before I can react, there are two bright flashes of light in the darkness. The first shot hits my left kneecap, the second my right. I crumple to the ground. My blood pours into the sand. The pain is excruciating but bizarrely enough, all I can think is that I won't be playing catch with Mark in Central Park anytime soon.

"Your old man was right. You're one stupid motherfucker." Detective Dodge towers over me. The bastard holsters his service revolver, then puts gloves on. He gets another gun from his jacket and fires a couple of rounds in the air. After that, he stomps my forearm with his shoe and places the gun he just fired in my hand. When he's sure my prints are on it, he kicks that gun aside. "The report will state I got an anonymous tip about your whereabouts. I asked you repeatedly to drop your gun. You refused and fired first. It was either you or me. A clean kill, by the book." He sounds pleased. I suspect it's not the first time he's done this.

I'm so cold my teeth chatter. My legs are dead weights. I'm a turtle on its back, helpless, unable to move. And I'm so fucking tired. If I close my eyes, my next stop is a coffin.

Detective Dodge removes his gloves, then fires his service revolver into my left shoulder. *Fucking asshole.* "I'm going to tell your old man that you pissed and shit in your pants as you begged for your life." He towers over me and grins like a circus clown.

I wish I could say that in those fleeting moments, my life

passed before me. Or that I came to some marvelous epiphany about life. That the universe revealed its secrets to me. That my life had meant something profound and meaningful that a future Ernest Hemingway or Tom Wolfe would write about me for posterity. Alas, there's none of that. Instead, I break out laughing as I recall ghoul-faced Ed Sullivan and that insipid Topo Gigio.

"What the hell are you laughing at?" Detective Dodge barks.

"You," I groan with my last ounce of energy as I fire the Ruger I hid in my coat pocket straight at Detective Dodge's forehead. In disbelief, he teeters for a second, then slumps on top of me. I taste blood or is it something else? Moynes was right, after all. I'm not going to be that asshole.

Mercifully, I black out. When I finally come to, Cassie cradles my head in her lap while James wraps tourniquets around my knees. Dalton is on his cell phone fulminating about a fucking helicopter. I tell myself through a fog of pain that I must be hallucinating or I'm back on drugs. This can't be real. *But it is.*

In the copter, Cassie strokes my hair. "It's over, Brooks. It's fucking over," she whispers sweet and low so only I can hear. "You're not getting rid of me that easily, you asshole." Lucky me.

I want to say something, but I can't. I need every ounce of my waning strength to stay alive. For Cassie. For Mark and Audra. And, also to finish the goddamn book. Where the fuck is Sheldon? All I can do is hold Cassie's hand tight and hang on for another bumpy ride.

CHAPTER TWENTY-SEVEN

Eighteen Months Later

T hey say time heals all wounds.
      Screw that shit.
   Whoever came up with that pearl of wisdom never experienced their kneecaps being shattered into a zillion shards. At least the shot to my shoulder was clean and went right through without hitting an artery. After two knee replacements and a month of rehab, I now have enough steel in my body to trip metal detectors. I won't be running sixty-yard touchdowns or climbing Mt. Kilimanjaro, not that they were on my fuck-it list. I wake up in pain and go to bed with it. That's the new normal. The doctors say with time the pain should lessen, but honestly, I don't give a shit. The pain is a badge of honor, and every step I take is a gigantic fuck-you to Dad.
   Due to my surgery, I missed Dad's gala. What a fucking shame. As it turned out, so did he. While I was in surgery, a maintenance worker discovered Dad's broken body early one morning after he took a swan dive from a rooftop in Co-op City in the Bronx, where David

Berkowitz, the infamous Son of Sam, once lived. The complex is home to nearly forty-five thousand people. No one saw or heard a thing. How Dad got there, no one knows; the last twenty-four hours of his life remain a mystery. No one is shocked when Dad's death was ruled "accidental."

Dad's colleagues lobbied for a grand funeral, preferably in Washington, D.C. As the sole executor of Dad's estate/will, I quickly nipped that shit in the bud. Weeks later, when I was able to hobble around on crutches, we held a small service for Mark and Audra's benefit. No matter what Dad had done, he was still their grandfather. The funeral home asked if I wanted his cremains. I did not.

For all of Dad's supposed powerful friends, he had a hell of a lot more enemies. Once he was gone, the vultures anxiously circled. Dalton and I made it abundantly clear that I've no desire to expose classified secrets or topple governments. It helps that the CIA Director is reportedly a huge fan of Three Rivers. I know what I said about people having a right to know the truth, but there is truth, and there is truth. Cassie isn't happy, but after a lot of convincing, she goes along with the plan. Dad's secrets are the only leverage we have and I'm not about to have that go up in smoke. So, after months of prolonged, secret negotiations, the Feds and I signed a confidential agreement regarding the legacy of Bernard S. Anderson. The story—what you're reading now —will be kept under court seal for one hundred and twenty-five years after my last blood descendant passes. In other words, a really fucking long time. That's the price I gladly pay for my family's safety and security. Even so, there's a hell of a lot of clean-up to do.

The FBI announced that I'd been the innocent victim of a failed extortion attempt. All the videos and pictures of me doing drugs were fabricated. The media lapped it up.

After an exhaustive investigation, the Attorney General of New York closed Sheldon's file, since Crown-Hawkins and all clients affected by Sheldon's alleged misappropriation had been reimbursed. Since it was belatedly determined that Sheldon was a victim as well, Phoebe got their brownstone back, which was a good thing since she didn't last six months in Minnesota. In an odd twist I couldn't have predicted, Phoebe is now dating Tom Giafrida. I'm not sure how I feel about that. As for Sheldon's crook of a cousin, he met with an unfortunate accident in Brunei.

The big loser is the Suffolk County District Attorney. The police union wanted my head. The DA threatened to charge me until Dalton showed him the video of Detective Dodge shooting me first, unprovoked. To settle the matter, I plead "no contest" to possessing an unlicensed firearm and get six month's suspended probation. Subsequently, the DA lost his re-election in a landslide. Dalton celebrated with a bottle of 1841 Veuve Clicquot. I stuck to orange vanilla seltzer.

Aunt Flo is frail but content in Grandpa William's house. She visits Althea's grave weekly. She still has no idea how her father, sister, nephew, and daughter really died. I intend to keep it that way.

Cassie had a falling-out with Tammy after Rob ran for the state senate and used the video of the dog attack in his campaign. He lost, largely due to PETA. I like to think that my generous and anonymous donation to his opponent turned the tide.

While I was in rehab, I received a blank postcard from Hawaii. With the money I subsequently wired to a foreign bank account, I'm sure Collier Moynes can buy any fucking car he wants, not to mention an island or two. If not for him, Cassie would be a widow. When he hugged me in the Fairlane, he slipped a tracking dot in my sleeve and sent the coordinates to Cassie.

Fernando gave notice at the Dakota. I never saw him again.

In a twist right out of a romantic comedy, Gigi and Toad married, had a child, broke up, reunited, and had two more children. They live in a castle with a thriving vineyard in the south of France thanks to a private equity investor.

Sufficiently outraged by another potential miscarriage of justice, Dalton signed on as Solomon Burke's defense attorney. The trial abruptly ended in a mistrial when Dalton proved that Detective Dodge had tampered with crucial evidence. Burke walked out of the courtroom a free man with over a million dollars in his GoFundMe campaign. In *his glory, Dalton dismissed gossip about him running for Manhattan DA as poppycock. I'm hedging my bets.*

Miss Drake, Dr. Richter, Elaine Brighton—their cases remain "unsolved."

Agent Fox, or rather, former Agent Fox, is presently awaiting trial on Rikers Island. Dalton declined to represent him.

After the Burke debacle, Detective Clemente resigned from the force. With the help of a silent partner, she currently operates a Caribbean food truck. Her Jamaican oxtail stew is to die for.

Six months into his retirement, James, the bravest man I have ever known, passed away from the bone cancer his physicians say was linked to his service at the 9/11 pile. After some high-level prodding, the 9/11 victims' compensation board posthumously approved his claim. His family will be well taken care of. Rest easy, buddy.

I'm stunned, but not entirely surprised, that Dad wasn't bluffing about his fortune. He was absurdly, ridiculously, embarrassingly rich —dare I say, almost as rich as Jeff Fucking Bezos. Who said evil doesn't pay? It was money I didn't want or need, but no one else wanted it, either. Fortunately, Cassie and I were in total agreement that no one man—or family—should have that much money. It's a burden and curse. But I had to hand it to that shrewd, sneaky old bastard. He placed the bulk of his money in a Byzantine labyrinth of trusts and offshore accounts that's virtually impossible to unravel. What I can freely access is the monthly interest and quarterly dividends—a healthy chunk of change that's more than the yearly budget of many nations. I can never make up for what Dad did, but I try. I'm now the patron saint of anonymous donations, hard luck cases, and lost causes.

Cassie says I've mellowed out; I'm not so high-strung and nervous. I don't know if I'd go that far, but now that I need to lose money legally, I've become a Hollywood player. I launched a production company and put Eric in charge of it. He still can't write for shit, but he does have an amazing eye for talent. Next month we're going into production—finally—on the film adaptation of

Fallen Angels *with Leonardo DiCaprio playing me. And we've somehow cajoled the great Robert Redford out of retirement to play Bernard.*

After dueling lawsuits, Max and I reach a settlement, thanks to my new bulldog of a literary agent—my granddaughter Caroline. Sheldon would've fucking loved her. The entire gang is back for an encore—Nicole Kidman, Mark Ruffalo, and yes, even goddamn Richard Dreyfuss—but per our contract, we're careful not to call it a sequel or a prequel. I simply call it "the thing."

My publisher graciously extended the deadline for my book about Mom and Palmer. With that monkey off my back, Cassie and I decided we needed a change of scenery and rented a three-story glass house in Malibu. I'm no longer afraid of the beach. Inspired, I banged the book out in under six weeks. It certainly wasn't the book I'd originally set out to write, but it was the book I needed to write. Cassie says if you don't count all the curse words, it's the best thing I've ever written. I'm not as effusive—I'm my own worst critic—but the public and critics generally agree with her. An "unputdownable, unforgettable, free-wheeling memoir-thriller hybrid of fact and fiction in the grand tradition of Norman Mailer and Truman Capote" is how the lead critic of The New York Times *described it. But a reviewer for* USA Today *was brutal in her assessment: "five hundred and sixty-five pages of unparalleled self-indulgent drivel from a literary lamb that skirts the issue of who done it to instead focus on a miasma of half-baked grudges and loony conspiracy theories." Of all the reviews I've gotten on this book, this is the only one I have framed and hanging in my new writing lair.*

Based on my book, Priscilla Garrett sued Suffolk County for malicious prosecution. In a twist only I predicted, her case was dismissed when a DNA test of a paternal relative of Julian Broadhurst showed beyond any doubt that it was impossible for Julian to be her biological father.

I'm utterly dismayed that an animated version of Rocco the Stinky Raccoon is a huge hit on Cartoon Network. Naturally, my publisher now expects a slew of new Rocco books involving all kinds of scatological activities. So far, I've resisted.

For obvious reasons, the house in Water Mill was sold for a handsome profit. We looked at so many houses my feet got blisters. A compound in Chappaqua was a strong contender, as the thought of being Bill Clinton's neighbor tickled my fancy. However, after many midnight discussions, we went in a different direction: a sprawling, semi-restored 1876 farmhouse on two hundred pristine acres in Sullivan County. I can easily trek to the Dakota when and if the need arises. Mark loves his new school, and Audra—who has made a complete and remarkable recovery—is delighted with her new pet, a unicorn (goat) named Matilda. To my neighbors, I'm just an old, grumpy, son of a bitch with money to burn who drives a restored, fire-engine red DeSoto.

Mrs. Germaine—her first name is Hermione—is now my personal assistant. She's thorough and efficient. Cassie and the kids adore her, but there's only one Miss Drake.

From my office window—where I am at this very moment—I can see Cassie, swelling with twins due around Thanksgiving, as she directs the landscapers who are planting her new peony garden. We are also installing a pool and a playhouse for the kids. The pool is so big it requires its own ZIP code. If all goes well, the entire clan will be here for the holidays, and we will meet my grandchildren and great-grandchildren for the first time. It's enormously messy and complicated and nerve-wracking. Cassie and I have never been happier.

After the twins are born, I'm going to take a step back. It's Cassie's time to shine. She sold her debut book (using her maiden name) titled The Third Wife, *an upmarket thriller about a troubled psychologist/parent (who may or may not look like Sandra Bullock) ensnared in a web of revenge and kinky sex when the principal of the prestigious Manhattan academy her son attends is murdered during a school field trip to the Bronx Zoo. It's not based on true events.*

As for me, personally, there are good days and better days. Yesterday morning, I woke up outside on the patio in my birthday suit at four in the morning. The beast rouses every once in a while, but he's weak and growing weaker. I don't worry about him anymore. I have too many other things to worry about.

I often dream about Mom and Palmer. The dream is always the same. We're in the backyard of the Big House, the sun shining in the sky like a bright, shiny marble. I whine about Palmer hitting me too hard. Mom, sitting on a lawn chair as she reads a manuscript, yells at Palmer to knock it off. Later, Mom buys us ice cream from the Bungalow Bar truck. We fall to sleep listening to the Rolling Stones.

It's a good fucking day. I'll take it.

THE END

ACKNOWLEDGMENTS

To all the guitar gods and literary heroes who have inspired and uplifted me both near and far on my writing odyssey. There are simply far too many to name, from Crosby, Stills, Nash & Young (a special shout out to Graham Nash for being kind and generous) to Harper Lee. It's not about the ride, but where you end up.

To my beloved family who supported and believed in me through thick and thin and all the highs and lows (and there were many lows): my husband William, my daughters Adrienne (Will), Heather (Tim), Stephanie (Jimmy), and my grandchildren Mikey, Kevin, Audrey, and Sam.

Last, but certainly not least, my eternal gratitude to my fellow travelers and trapeze artists who encouraged me on this particular writing journey, especially when I had no idea what I was doing. They know who they are (I'm specifically not looking at you, Phil Krampf).

A NOTE FROM THE PUBLISHER

Thank you for reading this book. If you enjoyed it please do consider leaving a review on Amazon to help others find it too.

We hate typos. All of our books have been rigorously edited and proofread, but sometimes mistakes do slip through. If you have spotted a typo, please do let us know and we can get it amended within hours.

info@bloodhoundbooks.com

Made in the USA
Middletown, DE
21 August 2023

37087509R00179